The holiday season has always been filled with love and good will. In this special collection, three of Arabesque's most popular authors share their stories of passion, love and above all, the true meaning of the holiday season. Sit back and enjoy three short stories guaranteed to give you SOMETHING TO CELEBRATE.

BOOK YOUR PLACE ON OUR WEBSITE AND MAKE THE ARABESQUE ROMANCE CONNECTION!

We've created a customized website just for our very special Arabesque readers, where you can get the inside scoop on everything that's going on with Arabesque romance novels.

When you come online, you'll have the exciting opportunity to:

- View covers of upcoming books

- Learn about our future publishing schedule (listed by publication month and author)

- Find out when your favorite authors will be visiting a city near you

- Search for and order backlist books

- Check out author bios and background information

- Send e-mail to your favorite authors

- Join us in weekly chats with authors, readers and other guests

- Get writing guidelines

- AND MUCH MORE!

Visit our website at
http://www.arabesquebooks.com

Something To Celebrate

FELICIA MASON
MARGIE WALKER
BRENDA JACKSON

BET Publications, LLC
www.msbet.com

BET BOOKS are published by

BET Publications, LLC
c/o BET BOOKS
One BET Plaza
1900 W Place NE
Washington, D.C. 20018-1211

First Trade Paperback Printing: November, 1999
First Paperback Printing: October, 2000
10 9 8 7 6 5 4 3 2 1

Printed in the United States of America

Contents

The First Noel

BY

FELICIA MASON

Dear Reader:

The magic of Christmas is a gift. It's not a present like the ones found under trees or exchanged during the celebration of Kwanzaa. The gift of Christmas is something that resides in the hearts of every man, woman, boy, and girl who recognizes and accepts that Christmas isn't about jingle bells, snow-covered lanes, candy canes, and Santa Claus. Yes, those things can make Christmas bright; but the true gift is the one found in Luke 2:1–21.

As Kia rediscovers in "The First Noel," Christmas is a place in your heart.

Thank you for reading Kia and Franklin's story. I hope you enjoy it and the other two stories in this holiday anthology. As we all approach and observe the holiday season, I hope that you will have something to celebrate.

Merry Christmas,
Felicia Mason

For more information about Felicia Mason and her novels, please see www.geocities.com/Paris/Gallery/9250/

Prologue

December 12
11:58 P.M.

A ngry flames licked up the bedroom walls, the heat so hot it singed her skin. Kia stared at the fire consuming the curtains. She'd saved money from baby-sitting jobs and got them on sale at Sears. Now they were burning up. Everything was burning up.

Mesmerized, Kia watched the fire dance from panel to panel. It jumped to the broad beam that supported the roof.

"Kia! Kia! Where are you? Where's the baby?" Her sister's voice came from a distance, but it was enough to spur Kia into action.

Joshua! She snatched the crying toddler from his makeshift playpen. Protecting his head with her hand, Kia dashed toward the door. A panel of wood crashed down, burning embers cascaded around her.

Kia screamed.

Joshua's frightened tears turned into a wail.

She stomped at a piece of smoldering wood near her feet.

Clutching the child to her, she tried to quiet him so she could think.

"Shh, precious. It's okay, it's okay. Auntie's here. Auntie's here."

Kia glanced around. There had to be a way out. The only other option was the dormer window, but it was tiny and they were on the third floor. Even if she managed to get herself and Joshua to the window, she couldn't jump. It was too far.

"Kia!"

"Up here. We're in the attic."

"Mommy!" Joshua cried. The child pulled toward his mother's voice.

Kia clutched him closer. "Stay with Auntie, precious. We'll get out of here. I promise."

Trapped in the attic room, Kia watched the flames close in.

Off in the distance, Kia could hear the fire engines. Help was coming. But it was coming too late.

Chapter One

Seven years later

"Come on, Josh. You're gonna be late!"

The eight-year-old dragged into the foyer, his coat trailing behind him on the floor. "Do we have to?"

"Yes. We do. Where are your mittens?"

"It's not that cold out. Besides, mittens are for kids."

Kia Simmons cocked her neck at her nephew. "And, you, I suppose, aren't a kid?"

Joshua shrugged. "You know what I mean."

Kia tried not to smile. Joshua had been excited about First Baptist Church's Christmas pageant, until he found out he was a shoe-in for the role of Joseph. Joseph had to be nice to Mary. Kia knew that Joshua's crush on Shelby Knight, the little girl portraying Mary, would leave her little man tongue-tied and flustered.

It was time for that talk with him, probably past time. But Kia hadn't figured out how to broach the topic.

Without thinking, she brushed her hand over his fade haircut and caressed Joshua's cheek. He was growing up so fast.

"Ma, not the hair, okay."

Kia laughed. "Come on, Mr. *GQ*. I'm going to warm up the car. Zip your coat and put your gloves on. Don't forget your hat, either."

By the time Kia pulled her Camry into the church's parking lot, snow was falling. "I hope the roads won't be too bad when we get out of here."

"There's Mike, Ma. Can I go ahead?"

"All right, just don't forget . . ."

"To zip up my coat. I know. I know."

In a blur of bulky winter clothing, Josh was out of the car and crunching through the snow to see his Sunday school friend.

Kia smiled. Before she knew it, he'd be headed to college. Maybe she could convince him to go to Pitt or Duquesne, schools nearby.

A moment later she laughed. "First, you've got to get the boy out of elementary school."

Bundling up, Kia pocketed her keys and reached onto the backseat for the book she'd read while the children practiced. She made sure Josh got his dose of religion. Kia had long ago abandoned her own spiritual upbringing. Her job now was to make sure Josh was exposed to the basics. He could make up his own mind about church and faith when he got older.

For tonight, Kia's plan was to find a seat somewhere in the back of the church's multipurpose room and start the murder mystery novel she'd been itching to read.

Once inside, she shrugged out of her wraps and made a beeline to the back of the room where tables and chairs had been pushed out of the way.

"Oh, Sister Simmons. So glad to see you. I saw Joshua a few moments ago. Brother Tyler will get all the kids rounded up in a couple of minutes. Come give us a hand."

Kia bit her lip and quickly looked for an out. Mavis Washington was the sort who'd put you to work if you weren't careful. Kia had been dodging the woman's efforts to get her into the young adult missionary group for more than a year. Without telling the busybody outright that she didn't do the church thing, Kia could only hope for a disappearing act.

"I'll be right back, Sister Washington," Kia said. "I'm going to run to the ladies' room."

With haste, she got out of the woman's line of sight. Kia had absolutely no intention of spending the evening in the rest room. Maybe she could find an unlocked, and out-of-the-way, Sunday school classroom.

Ducking down the hall that led to the classrooms, Kia heard the Sunday school superintendent ringing a bell. That, she knew, was the children's signal to gather around. Brother Tyler ran a tight ship. Josh and all the other children knew that, so she didn't worry about his welfare while at the church. First Baptist was about the only place where Kia didn't fret over Joshua's safety and well-being.

Kia tried the door at the first classroom. Locked.

She frowned and went across the hall to the next. The door-knob turned. Kia felt against the wall for a light switch. When light flooded the room, Kia saw walls decorated with bold posters of Bible heroes. A big picture of a manger scene was taped to the chalkboard. The riot of colors all over the place reminded her of a classroom at the school where she worked as a teacher's aide. All of the red and blue chairs at the round tables were Lilliputian size. The primary-grade children obviously met in this room.

"That won't do."

Turning off the light, Kia closed the door and headed to the next classroom. Just as she was about to turn the handle, she heard the children's voices ringing out as they sang "Silent Night."

"No fair hiding."

Kia started. She looked up, then up some more. He was the size of a lumberjack—not that she'd ever actually *seen* a lumberjack. His plaid shirt looked like soft flannel. The jeans and work books added to the effect. Everything about this man was just plain big. Not fat, but solid, dependable. Like a rock.

"You scared me."

"Sorry about that," he said, but he looked more amused than sorry.

Kia had never seen him around First Baptist and assumed he was a new member.

"If you're trying to find a place to hide from Sister Washington, a few other parents are in the room two doors down."

Kia immediately took offense.

"What makes you think I'm hiding? I'm not. I was just . . ."

He grinned. "Yes?"

She gave up and laughed. "Okay, so I was looking for a quiet place to read."

He glanced at the book in her hand. "Hmm, that looks like interesting church reading."

The twinge of guilt Kia had already been feeling about taking a novel into church intensified. But a murder mystery was a better option than her first choice, a hot romance. Surely God wouldn't mind if she spent an hour or so reading a mystery in his house.

"Well, it's either this or, uh, never mind . . ." Kia's voice trailed off as a tantalizing image of this man as the hero in her own personal romance came to mind.

She shook her head. If she wasn't careful, the Lord was gonna send a lightning bolt straight to her head.

"I'm Franklin Williams," he introduced himself as he stuck out a large hand in greeting.

Kia swallowed and tried to get her errant thoughts out of the gutter. "Hi. I'm Kia Simmons. You must be new here."

"I was just thinking that about you."

Her smile widened. "You were? I mean, no. I'm not new. I just don't attend the morning services. Usually just Sunday school."

"Well," he said, "Looks like I need to start coming to Sunday school."

Franklin smiled. So did Kia.

Suddenly, she couldn't think of anything else to say.

When he bent down to pick up a toolbox, that's when she noticed his hands. They were large and well shaped.

"Nice to meet you, Kia Simmons. Maybe I'll be seeing you around sometime."

Kia's flirtatious smile held lots of promise. "Maybe so."

Hefting his toolbox in one hand, Franklin slipped a hammer through a loop in his jeans. "Time to get to work," he said.

Kia enjoyed his backside view as he headed toward the multipurpose room. She wanted to claim that the warm fluttering feeling in her stomach was simply the heat warming the large church building, but she knew that couldn't be the case.

Her sister had always said you could find a good man at church. For the first time in Lord only knew how long, Kia found herself interested in a man.

"Maybe Kim was right, after all."

Franklin listened to the instructions on how the pageant director wanted the set built. Unfortunately, his mind kept straying to the woman he'd just met in the hall. All the adults working with the children were in here. That would mean she was one of the parents. But which child was hers?

While he knew many of the kids, he didn't know them all. He glanced over Sister Redfield's head trying to figure out which cute little girl or active little boy was Kia Simmons's child.

"Will that work out all right?"

"Beg pardon. What was that again, Sister Redfield?"

The woman patted his arm. "I'm being a worrywart again, aren't I? After all these years, you know how to build the set."

"Yes, ma'am. I do. Just show me where you want it."

Franklin let the pageant's stage director lead him to the spot where the manger scene would be. With half an ear, he listened to the things she wanted done differently this year.

When he smiled, Sister Redfield took that as encouragement to launch into an even more detailed description of her ideas about this year's set. It had been a long time since he'd flirted with a woman. Kia Simmons looked so guilty standing in that doorway he couldn't help but rib her about it. She had a pretty smile and her skin looked as soft as her hands had been.

While Sister Redfield chattered on, Franklin wondered if there was a Mr. Simmons in Kia Simmons's life.

Chapter Two

Peeking over the edge of a door decorated with tinsel and angels, Kia spied the likely hideout room. She knocked on the open door before entering.

"Hi. Is this the waiting room?" she asked.

A man and a woman chuckled. "Yeah," the older man said. "If you're waiting until Sister Mavis forgets she wanted you to do something."

"This would be the place then. Hi, Shirley," Kia greeted her friend as she walked in. "I was just looking for a quiet place to read," she added as she held the novel up, confirming her intent.

"Come on in. I'm here grading papers. The last bunch before Christmas break. Glory hallelujah!"

"You know you miss those kids when they're gone," the man said.

"Uh huh. Well, right now, they're working my last nerve. I told them Friday if they didn't straighten up and fly right, there'd be no Christmas party."

"And they believed you?" the man said.

"Sure. They think I have an in with Santa Claus," Shirley said. "Kia, have you met Willie Smith? He has the twins."

The man stood up and Shirley completed the introductions while the two shook hands. After a few moments of small talk, Kia settled into a chair at the conference room-style table. Willie leaned back in his seat and propped his legs up on a second chair to resume his nap. Shirley went back to her papers, and Kia opened her book.

The story started with a bang, and under any other circumstance would have kept her riveted. But after reading the fifth page three times, Kia gave up the pretense. Her thoughts kept straying to the man she'd met in the hallway. Franklin Williams.

It was a strong name for a sturdy man. Kia had to admit, she'd always been partial to husky men. She liked them solid, like a wall of protection.

"Hmmp. Who are you kidding?" she thought. *"It's been so long that you don't even know what a preference is anymore."*

Her last serious relationship had been . . . Kia frowned. How long *had* it been? She calculated for a moment. Not since before the fire.

Has that much time really passed?

For the answer, all she had to do was think about Joshua.

Kia sighed. She probably wasn't even Franklin's type. And although he had flirted a bit, he was probably married. Some church men were like that, just naturally friendly.

Forcing her thoughts away from a path leading nowhere, Kia again turned her attention to her novel. A few minutes later, she marked her place with a dollar bill and told Shirley she'd be back.

Kia made her way to the ladies' rest room. She pushed the door open and smiled. The comfortably feminine lounge area always amused her. A faintly sweet scent came from baskets of potpourri. With its soft lighting, pink floral sofa, and easy chairs, the room seemed far more inviting than the sanctuary. It looked more like a parlor than a rest room.

"I wonder how many people hide out in here on Sunday mornings?" she mused as she made her way to the stalls.

Kia had barely secured the door on her end stall when she heard people burst into the lounge area.

"Girl, I tell you, that brother is fine."

"Let me see that lipstick. I need to touch up these lips. Make 'em more kissable. You think he'll ask me out?"

"He better not. He's going to ask *me* out."

Kia smiled. She couldn't help being party to the conversation. Girl talk was the same all over the place. She was going to have a time on her hands shielding Joshua from fast girls like the ones in the lounge.

"Hmmph, you have a man. What you need with another one?" said the one with the husky voice.

Kia waited for the answer.

"Hey, the more the merrier, I always say."

"You heard Pastor Jamison preaching about greed."

A sudden clatter let Kia know that one of the girls had either dumped her purse or her makeup bag.

"That's right." The girl's next words were a bit muffled. Kia strained to hear. A moment later, a kissing sound came from the lounge area.

Lipstick, Kia surmised to herself.

"And you heard him talking about the lust of the flesh."

The two women chuckled in a knowing way. Kia suddenly wondered if they were a bit older than she'd originally estimated.

"Let me smell your perfume," the husky-voiced one said.

"This is Shalimar. But I'm wearing Chanel No. 5."

"I think I'm going to trap him with a bit of cleavage."

"Girl, you better quit. You in a church, not a club. My hair look okay?"

"It's the bomb, girl."

The two giggled together.

Kia could only assume that they primped in front of the mirror.

"You gotta go?"

"Nope."

"Me, either. Let's go make ourselves seen."

Kia heard some rustling and then a snap. A few moments later, she heard nothing but silence. The two had obviously gathered their cosmetics and departed.

Kia left the stall, washed her hands, and touched up her own lipstick. The lingering scent of Chanel floated through the lounge. She envied the freedom of the two young women. If teenagers, they were probably sixteen or seventeen, years younger than Kia's mature twenty-five. Not that she'd change anything about her life—except maybe she'd add a little male companionship. Kia realized and recognized that she'd had responsibility thrust on her at an early age. Consequently, she'd missed out on a lot of the frivolity of youth. That was a fact of life.

Besides, she thought, how could you really miss something you've never had? Her thoughts quickly turned to Franklin Williams, the man she'd met in the hallway.

"Now, he is one *fine* brother," she said, mimicking the girls she'd overheard.

Back in the hideout classroom, Kia settled in a chair and reached for her book.

The door flew open. "Oh, there you all are," Mavis enthused. "I've been looking all over the place for you."

Willie Smith groaned. "That's why we were in here," he said under his breath. Shirley hit him with the pen she was using to grade papers.

"Sister Simmons and Sister Thompkins, Brother Tyler needs your help with the children in the fellowship hall. You schoolteachers know how to get them in order."

"Well, I'm not really a teacher," Kia protested under her breath.

Glancing at Kia with a guilty smirk, Shirley gathered up her papers.

"And Willie Smith!" Mavis said, clapping her hands in

front of her ample bosom. "Why, I didn't know you were here until Brother Williams told me. I thought you'd dropped off the children and left. Brother Williams was just asking if you'd come help him unload supplies from his truck. Oh, it's such a blessing to have so many parents interested in our young people's pageant every year."

With that, Mavis sailed out the door, confident her charges would follow.

"We'd be more interested if we had someone a little less enthusiastic," Shirley said, clasping her hands together in imitation of Mavis.

"Next time I'm staying in my car," Willie muttered.

"It's cold outside, Willie," Shirley pointed out.

"Better cold than at the mercy of Mavis."

"It can't be *that* bad," Kia said.

"You ever see a tornado close up?" Willie rumbled.

"No. Just on television and in the movies."

"Hollywood comes out here and follows Mavis for a week to see what real destruction is all about."

The two women laughed. "Shame on you, Brother Willie," Shirley said.

He grunted. "It's the truth and you know it."

Laughter and conversations bubbled in every corner of the multipurpose room. More than once, an adult voice could be heard over the hubbub, saying, "Listen, children," or "Shhh."

A woman Kia didn't recognize worked with the youngest children, the four- and five-year-olds, in one area. The six-year-olds were making so much noise in their corner that Kia couldn't tell if they were loud because they were supposed to be learning carols or if they were just being regular six-year-olds.

She searched the large room for Joshua. It didn't take long to find him. He sat quietly in a small circle of children, seemingly oblivious to the squeals, play, and conversation all around. The little girl sitting next to him looked just as uncomfortable. Kia had to smile. She waved at him, then chuckled at his grimace.

Shirley joined her, looking out over the organized chaos of the pageant's first rehearsal.

"Is it always like this?" Kia asked.

Shirley laughed. "Every year. Remember, though, this is just the first night. In a week, you'll see things coming together. By the nineteenth, the night of the pageant, you won't believe how it all just flows. Mavis can be bossy, but she knows how to put on a show. Where's Josh?"

"Over there," Kia said, pointing him out.

"You've done a good job with him, Kia. You should be proud."

"He's a good kid," she said. "I'm proud of *him*."

Shirley was one of the few people at First Baptist to whom Kia felt really close. That was because their friendship had developed at work. Shirley knew how much Kia doted on Joshua.

"Have you met Franklin Williams?" Shirley casually asked.

Too casual in Kia's estimation. She eyed her friend. "Yes, a little while ago."

Shirley glanced at her and smiled. "He's a master woodworker. Cute, isn't he?"

Kia hesitated, not willing just yet to take the bait.

"If you like big teddy bears," she eventually mumbled.

"Um hmm," Shirley said with a knowing smirk. "Just so you know, he donates his time and talent to the church whenever something is needed. And he always builds the sets for our plays and pageants."

"That's nice," Kia said.

Shirley cleared her throat and leaned in a bit toward Kia. "He loves kids. He's single, too. I think you two would look great together."

"Shirley, I've told you before, you don't need to go around trying to fix me up with your friends. I'm fine."

"Yeah, fine like Sleeping Beauty. You need a handsome prince to come kiss you awake."

With that bit of advice hanging, Shirley motioned Kia in Franklin's direction, then sauntered away.

Kia just shook her head.

Looking around to find the best place to use her limited pageant skills, Kia's gaze found Franklin's. He smiled, and she took that as an invitation to join him.

"Hello again," he said when she arrived next to his temporary saw horse.

"You ratted on us."

"Just looking out for my own interests," Franklin said.

"What does that mean?"

Before he could answer, Mavis Washington swooped in with a clipboard and orders.

"Sister Simmons, right over here, please. If you'll direct the children to their spots. Everything is marked on the floor. Here's the guide. I'll be with the teenagers in classroom number 8."

With no opportunity to object, Kia found herself hustled away and suddenly surrounded by little people asking questions. Above their heads, she caught Franklin looking in her direction. She shrugged her shoulders. When he smiled at her, Kia felt a distinct fluttering somewhere in the region of her heart.

"First my stomach, now my chest," she surmised to herself. "Maybe it's the flu."

The rest of the rehearsal time flew by quickly. Before long, the Sunday school superintendent rang his bell announcing dismissal. Within five minutes, the multipurpose room was full.

"Where in the world did all of these people come from?" Kia asked.

"All over the complex," a deep voice answered.

Kia turned and saw Franklin. Her heart did a surprising little somersault. Definitely not the flu, she decided.

"The young adult choir had rehearsal tonight and all of the

teenagers were down the hall getting their parts for the Christmas program.''

She'd noticed the teenagers, a diverse group of young people, and wondered which two were the ones from the rest room. "I thought there were a lot of cars in the parking lot," she said. "How long have you been a member here?"

"All my life."

Brother Tyler's closing remarks cut short the rest of Kia and Franklin's conversation. They joined the others, who were forming a snaking circle around the room.

"I want to thank you all for coming out tonight, and especially the parents who are helping," Brother Tyler said. "We couldn't do this without your support. All the children should have their parts now. I'd like to ask the parents to make sure they rehearse during the week."

Joshua ran up to Kia's side. "Here's my stuff, Mom."

She took the papers and nodded, motioning with a finger to her lips for him to be quiet.

"As you leave," Brother Tyler continued, "please be sure to pick up a copy of the schedule. We'll have rehearsals here at the church Wednesday and Friday and then again Monday, Wednesday, and Friday next week. The children will be fitted for their costumes this Friday. The ladies from the women's sewing circle will be here to get everybody's measurements. Now, does anybody have any questions?"

Mavis Washington stepped forward with her clipboard. "Don't forget the Friday-night fellowship, Brother Tyler."

"What's that?" Kia whispered to Franklin.

"A church get-together. We haven't had them in years, but Sister Mavis thought this would be a nice time to start them up again. It's BYOD."

"BYOD?" Kia asked.

But before Franklin could lean down and answer her, Brother Tyler was talking again.

"That's right, I almost forgot. This Friday, after the pageant rehearsal, we'll be having a fellowship service. For those of you who don't remember those, we sing and play games."

"And eat!" someone hollered out.

The adults in the room chuckled, and a discussion started about Sister Emmalyne's rolls and Sister Brisbane's sweet potato pie.

Brother Tyler rang his bell again, this time to quiet the grown-ups. After a moment, the conversations ceased. "Everybody, bring a dish to share and we'll all have a nice time in the Lord. Any other questions?" he asked.

When no one had any, he asked the people to join hands for closing prayer.

Kia noticed Josh trying to decide if he should move or just take little Shelby Knight's hand. The decision was made for him as the circle closed. He glanced up at Kia, then took Shelby's hand to his left and his mother's hand to his right. Kia smiled as she bowed her head.

A second later, her right hand was enveloped in a warm, large but gentle grip. Kia's eyes flew open and she glanced right. Franklin's smile was almost shy as he bowed his head when Brother Tyler started praying.

Kia prayed, too. But her prayer was that she not faint in the next five minutes. Their hands fit together like they were made for each other. She could feel the calluses on his hands and she wondered what her own felt like to him. She hadn't had a manicure in ages.

By the time she relaxed, Brother Tyler was saying "Amen." Kia hadn't heard a word of the prayer.

Franklin squeezed her hand before letting go. Kia wanted to believe it meant something. But when she looked up at him, his steady gaze and honest eyes didn't hold any hidden communication, at least not any she could detect.

"It was a pleasure meeting you, Sister Simmons."

"You, too," she said. "And call me Kia. Sister Simmons sounds so old."

"Can I start the car?" Joshua asked.

"No, young man, you can't. Did you speak?"

"Hi," Joshua said to Franklin.

"Hello, my name's Williams. Franklin Williams," he said as he stuck out a hand to the boy.

Joshua looked at the big man, then shook his hand, man to man. "My name is Joshua Simmons and this is my mom."

"Pleased to meet you, Joshua. And you, too, Mom," he added to Kia. "What role are you playing in the pageant?"

"Joseph," Joshua mumbled with a marked lack of enthusiasm. "I have to be Mary's husband."

"That's a very important role," Franklin said.

"It is?"

"Sure. Joseph was Jesus' earthly father."

Joshua considered that for a moment. "Yeah, I guess so. But I have to," he paused and glanced at Kia.

She hesitated for a moment, then took the cue. As much as she wanted to fulfill every need in his life, she knew Joshua lacked male role models. A man who, according to Shirley, donated his time to help the church and loved kids couldn't be all that bad. Could he?

Kia decided to trust her instincts. "I'm going to get my coat and a copy of the rehearsal schedule. Then I'll warm up the car. Don't forget . . ."

"To zip up my coat," Joshua finished.

"That's right," she said. "Nice meeting you, Mr. Williams."

With another look at the child she'd raised as her son, Kia left the two. She felt something close to a pang of jealousy when Joshua immediately turned back to Franklin and started talking. From the corner of her eye, she saw Shirley approach.

"You don't have to worry about him with Franklin," Shirley said.

"What makes you think I was worrying?" Kia said as she slipped on her coat.

Shirley raised an eyebrow at her, and Kia sighed.

"He just took to the man in a matter of seconds and I was dismissed so they could discuss men stuff."

"And what's so wrong with that?" Shirley asked. "Josh has a good head on his shoulders. And there are some things a man just can't talk to his mother about."

Kia tugged a bright-blue cap on her head, then put on matching gloves. "First of all, Josh is eight years old. That's hardly a man. And second . . ."

Shirley placed a hand on Kia's arm. "And second, you have to let him grow up. Would you rather he look up to some street-corner thug or drug dealer?"

"No," Kia mumbled.

Taking a deep breath, she quelled the retort that begged to slip off her tongue: She provided everything that Joshua needed. Josh was her responsibility. She couldn't let anything happen to him. Kimberly would never forgive her if anything happened to the boy. But Shirley was right, and she knew it.

"Let it go, Kia," Shirley said. "You can't protect him from all the monsters in the world. You can, however, make sure he has a solid foundation and knows right from wrong. You're doing that, but you have to give him some wings to fly, too."

Kia swallowed back the unexpected tears that threatened to flow. "Thanks for being my friend."

"Anytime, kiddo."

The two women hugged, then Shirley shooed Kia out the door.

"What did you two talk about?" Kia asked Josh as she maneuvered the Camry along the street. Plenty of salt had been put down, but the snow continued to fall pretty heavily. Slick spots were hidden from view.

"Guy stuff," Josh answered. "Mr. Franklin said only the best and most mature eight-year-olds get to play Joseph in the play."

Kia glanced at Josh for a moment before turning her attention back to the snowy road.

"Then you should feel honored," she said.

Josh nodded and looked out his window.

"Hey, Ma. If it keeps snowing like this, we might not have school tomorrow."

"Don't count on it. This is Pennsylvania, remember. Snow doesn't slow things down."

"Mr. Franklin said he's looking forward to the Friday Fellowship. I am, too."

"That a fact."

"Can we bring something special?"

Kia wasn't sure what Josh had in mind as special, but payday was another week away. Whatever they took to the dinner, it would have to be in the kitchen already.

As Josh chattered on, Kia wondered what she could make that might please Franklin Williams.

Chapter Three

Wednesday night, Kia had an appointment. With a reminder to be on good behavior and a promise to pick him up promptly at eight o'clock, she dropped Josh off at the church.

He was unusually quiet at home that evening. Every one of her attempts to get him to talk fell flat.

She watched him lay out his clothes for school. He paid such care to each choice and piece that Kia knew something was up.

"Special day tomorrow?"

"Huh?" Josh turned, obviously surprised to see her at his door.

Kia entered the bedroom and leaned on his dresser.

"You look like you're preparing for something special," she said, taking a look at the pants and shirt he considered.

A pile of apparently already discarded options was on the floor. Kia scooped them up and headed to Josh's closet to hang them up.

"Try this," she said, tossing him a vest. "Combined with the shirt you have there, she should be really impressed."

"Mooomm."

Kia replaced the last shirt on a hanger, then sat on Josh's twin bed. "Yes?" she innocently said.

"I'm not dressing up for a girl."

Wisely, Kia didn't say anything as she watched him stare at the clothes on his bed.

"I'm just thinking about my image, you know," he said.

"Your image?"

"Yeah. How I project."

Apparently satisfied with the vest and the outfit, Josh moved the clothes off the bed and draped them over his desk chair. He checked his book bag, then snapped the flaps together.

"Hey, Mom?"

"Yes, precious?" Kia waited for his usual protest to the "baby" endearment. When it didn't come, she smiled.

"What does it mean to sacrifice?"

Kia's eyes opened a bit. She knew she could give him lots of examples, including sacrifices she'd made along the way. But she had a feeling Josh was talking about something else.

"Why do you ask?"

Meandering from the desk to his dresser, Josh opened the second drawer and pulled out underwear and a T-shirt. After tossing them in a chair shaped like a basketball backboard and hoop, he faced Kia.

"Tonight, Mr. Tyler was telling us about why we celebrate Christmas. He said baby Jesus grew up and sacrificed a lot for us."

Hardly a theologian, Kia nodded. She could only hope her less than stellar and awfully dusty knowledge about this sort of thing wouldn't let her down. She'd stopped believing in miracles and whatnot a long time ago.

"So that got me to thinking," Josh continued. "If he sacrificed his life and I'm playing his earthly father in the pageant, shouldn't I make a sacrifice, too?"

Kia nodded. "That sounds like a good idea. What did you

have in mind? Maybe giving up a couple of toys or games and giving them to needy kids?''

His mouth dropped open and his eyes grew wide.

Kia chuckled. ''I guess that's not what you had in mind, huh?''

''Uh, no. I was thinking I could just sacrifice and, you know, act like Shelby's OK to be around. Know what I mean?''

Biting back her smile, Kia nodded. So that's what the clothes . . . and the secret conversation with Franklin Williams were all about.

''Tell you what,'' she said. ''Since you and Shelby are playing important roles, why don't you think about getting a Christmas present for her.''

Josh's face lit up. ''Really? I can?''

Kia nodded.

''How much do I get to spend?''

''That's up to you. How much do you want to sacrifice of your own money to buy something for her?''

''My money?'' Josh asked.

''Sure. You get an allowance. Surely you'll be able to buy Shelby a present from that money.'' When he didn't look too excited about making *that* big a sacrifice, Kia offered another suggestion. ''You're quite the artist. Why don't you make something for her?''

Josh's frown amused Kia, but she did her best to hide the smile she knew her little man wouldn't appreciate. She got up and headed toward the door.

''Mom, it takes money to please a woman.''

Kia paused at the doorway. ''Who told you that?'' That was the last thing she needed him to grow up thinking. Sure, money made a difference, but it didn't make a person.

Josh shrugged.

Kia tried again but couldn't get an answer out of him. ''Is that what your friends at school say?''

He just shrugged again.

''It doesn't take money to show your love, Josh.''

"Yeah, I know. But it helps."

She couldn't disagree with him on that point. For a moment, she wondered if Josh knew or suspected just how precarious their financial situation was. On the next payday, Kia had to pay the rent, the car insurance, buy enough food to get through the end of the month, *and* eke out something to pay on the bike she had on layaway for Joshua. *She* definitely knew the meaning of sacrifice.

Right now, it didn't at all look as if the ends were going to meet.

"Well, I'm sure you'll think of something," she said, then wondered if she said it to convince herself rather than her young charge. "Christmas is still two weeks away. Lights out in thirty minutes. I'll be back to tuck you in."

Long after Josh lay in bed softly snoring, Kia stared at the ceiling from her own bed. She'd been flying blind raising her nephew. Kimberly hadn't left an instruction manual on how to care for her son.

"Raise him the way we were raised, little sister," Kim had said. "Make sure he loves God, respects his elders, and grows up a gentleman."

Kia remembered the words as if they were spoken just yesterday. She wiped the sudden tears from her eyes and turned over on her stomach, a plump pillow braced under her arms.

She stared in the darkness toward the photograph that had been taken right before Kim died.

"I'm trying to do right by him and by you, big sister," she whispered. "Sometimes I just don't think I have it in me."

As usual, no answer came to her soft-spoken worries. In the beginning, shortly after she'd convinced the Social Services people that she could take care of a toddler even though she was only a few months shy of eighteen, Kia relied on Kimberly's voice to guide her. It always seemed to come when she found herself uncertain about what to do or say.

But the guidance stopped coming more than a year ago. At first, frightened, Kia panicked. Then she realized that she'd been relying on all the wisdom her sister had imparted during their years together. For all intents and purposes, Kim was the only mother Kia ever had. The two sisters always looked out for each other, Kim leading the way.

"A boy is different, though," Kia said, her voice now muffled by the pillow. "Sons are to be cherished, molded into strong black warriors."

Laying her head on the pillow, Kia closed her eyes and tried to imagine what her sister would do with an eight-year-old. She waited, and waited. Nothing came, though. Not the answers she sought, not even sleep, which would have been a sweet escape from the worries she harbored.

Several hours later, a restless sleep did come. The thought, however, that stayed with Kia as she tossed and turned through the night was that while *she* knew nothing about properly training a warrior, Franklin Williams would.

Friday arrived quickly. Kia decided that trying to impress anyone, including a tall, dark carpenter, probably wasn't one of her better ideas. She ended up making a chicken pot pie, one of Josh's favorite meals, as a hearty offering for the church's Friday fellowship on a blustery winter day.

Several vehicles arrived at the same time in the First Baptist parking lot. Greetings were shouted out as heavily bundled people scurried to the warmth of the fellowship hall.

"Whoo-wee, I tell you, I'm not used to these Pennsylvania winters," a woman said.

"Ruth Childers, you've lived here all your life," someone answered.

"That don't mean I'm used to or even like wintertime," Sister Childers said on a laugh as she deposited her big pot on a table, then shook out of her coat, gloves, scarf, and hat. "Let me wash my hands and get my apron, then we'll see what we have here. Emmalyne dropped off 'bout six dozen rolls earlier today, so I know we got some bread."

As Ruth Childers and a few women hurried to open up the kitchen, several men made quick work of setting up tables and chairs for the potluck dinner. They left plenty of room for the young people to practice. As fast as a table was put right, two teams of women came through rolling out white table coverings and situating pinecones as centerpieces.

After hanging up his coat and Kia's, Josh ran off with his friends. At loose ends, Kia stood in the middle of the floor looking and feeling out of place. Everyone seemed to have a job to do. Taking note of what everyone was wearing, Kia gave a silent sigh of relief. At least she'd dressed properly and appropriately, or "decent and in order" as she'd heard someone say years ago. At the last minute, she'd changed out of the jeans she'd planned to wear and opted for a pair of corduroy slacks and a cream sweater. No one except some of the younger children wore jeans.

Josh, of course, looked as though he'd just left a photo shoot for *GQ* Jr. Kia smiled. At least with his new crush, she didn't have to fight with him about taking baths or wearing clean underwear.

"What book are you reading tonight?"

Kia turned and found Franklin Williams standing right there. The sudden and now-familiar warmth infused her, and she felt a smile fill her face.

"I thought I'd do a little work tonight," she said.

"Well, that's the least you could do given that shameful behavior Monday night."

His smile let Kia know that the teasing came with good spirits.

"This fellowship is BYOD you told me. So, where's your dish, Mr. Williams?"

He leaned down, close to her ear. Kia got a subtle hint of an aftershave or cologne that made her suddenly want him even closer.

"Call me Frank," he said. "And I make a mean spoon bread."

"I'm impressed."

Franklin grinned. "I'm a single man, Sister Simmons. And I like to eat."

Kia took a breath. She may not have had a lot of practice in the dating arena, but that sure sounded like an opening. Dare she flirt?

Yes.

She opened her mouth to say something saucy like "I'll remember that."

"Hi, Brother Williams."

The words Kia had been about to utter died on her lips as she watched a very buxom woman sidle up to Franklin. A moment later the woman's heavily applied perfume reached Kia's nose, and apparently Franklin's, too.

He turned away a moment before letting loose a big sneeze.

"Bless you," Kia automatically said.

"Excuse me."

"Oh, that's all right," the young woman said. "Are you coming down with the flu? It's going around, you know."

"Uh, no," Franklin said while waving the air in front of him. He tried to stifle another sneeze. "Charmaine, what in the world are you wearing?"

The girl looked at her clothes. "Just some leggings. You like them?"

Kia had had enough. Franklin obviously had a prior relationship with her.

"Excuse me," she said as a general farewell to both of them.

"Kia, hold up." He reached out and grabbed Kia's hand before she could escape. "I'm talking about that bottle of cologne you dumped on before you came in here."

Charmaine pouted.

Kia paused.

A closer look at the girl indicated she wasn't as old as her voluptuous figure indicated.

"You always treat me like a baby."

"That's because you're fifteen. Did you speak to Ms. Simmons?"

Charmaine rolled her eyes and stuck a hand out to Kia. "Hi."

Uncertain, Kia glanced between Franklin and the girl. "Hello. I'm Kia Simmons."

"Charmaine's my name. Is Joshua your son?"

"Yes. Well, I mean . . . You know him?"

"He's a cutie. My little sister likes him."

Right then and there Kia decided maybe she needed to monitor Josh's activities in church as well. If the little sister was as fresh as this one, Josh would be in way over his head—sort of like the way she felt with Franklin.

"Aren't you supposed to be in choir rehearsal or something?" Franklin asked.

"I can take a hint," the teen replied as her gaze dipped to the hand Franklin held in his. The girl sized up Kia, then sent a sly smirk Kia's way.

With another not quite innocent look at Franklin, Charmaine sauntered away.

Even though she had ten years on the girl, Kia felt as if her own body belonged to a teenager. She knew she didn't have the classic looks of a Halle Berry or a Tyra Banks, and that was just fine. But when standing next to a teenager built like Jackée, Kia felt pretty certain she looked more like a flat-chested Olive Oyl.

"I'd better go," she said as she tugged on the hand Franklin still held in his.

"Will you have dinner with me tonight? I'd be happy to share my meal with you."

Kia glanced at their joined hands. Franklin didn't seem in any hurry to let her go. Truth be told, Kia liked the feeling of being enveloped in his arms, particularly since holding his hand was about as far as anything would go between them.

"We're, uh, we're eating here. At the church I mean."

"I know. Sit with me."

His smile made Kia forget what it was she'd been thinking. *Breathe, girl.*

Kia took a breath. "I, uh . . . Joshua . . ."

"Is welcome, too."

"Oh." The small word sounded more like a whispered sigh.

"Is that yes?"

Kia managed a nod. Franklin squeezed her hand.

"It's a date then."

A moment later, he was gone. Kia stood there in a daze, wondering what had just happened.

"You work it, girl. I saw you and Frank Williams earlier. He's just your type."

"I don't have a type, Shirley. I've never even had a . . ." Kia fell silent and glanced around to see if anyone had overheard her near confession. But too many conversations were taking place all around them for anyone to be concerned with theirs.

"Um hmm. And that's the problem. I keep telling you, you're going to wake up one day and Josh is going to be gone and you'll be sitting around wondering what happened to your life."

"My life is just perfect, thank you very much."

Kia spied Josh with a group of boys and girls and waved for him to join her. His immediate frown let her know that eating dinner with her wasn't what he'd planned.

"He'll be fine," Shirley said. "You're the one who needs some socialization skills."

"I have a son to raise. I don't have time to socialize."

Shirley shook her head. "We'll just see about that."

Josh ran up just as Shirley got up and took off. "Yes, ma'am?"

"It's time for dinner. That deacon's going to pray."

"That's the pastor, Mom. His name is Reverend Jamison."

Kia took another look at the man who was calling for everyone's attention. "Oh, well, whatever."

"Can I eat with Mike and Grady? Please?"

"Well . . ." Kia began.

"We'll be right over there," he said pointing to a table that had been claimed by two boys and three girls. Kia noted that little Shelby Wright sat among them.

"Okay," she reluctantly agreed. "Just make sure . . ."

Josh was across the fellowship hall before she could change her mind or finish her sentence.

". . . to eat some vegetables."

Moments later, the room fell silent while the pastor blessed the meal. Then, table by table, the church members went through the buffet lines filled with the casseroles and other dishes brought by each family.

"Is this seat taken?"

Kia looked up. "Yes. I think you reserved a spot here."

Franklin smiled as he pulled out the chair next to Kia.

"I could eat a horse," he said. "I had a busy day and missed lunch."

"Sorry, no horsemeat allowed in my kitchen. But it looks like you'll have plenty to choose from," she said with a nod toward the buffet tables.

"So, what *did* you bring to share?"

"Come on folks, don't dawdle. If Reverend Jamison gets up there before you do, there won't be anything left."

The people at the table next to Kia and Franklin's laughed as the church's husky youth minister put an arm around the shoulder of the senior pastor.

"Now, you all know, I've been trying to cut back," the reverend said. "You gotta tell the missus to stop cooking like she does."

Franklin held Kia's chair as she rose. "You'll like everyone here. We're just one big family," he said.

"Frank, how's the set coming along?" the gray-haired Reverend Jamison asked.

"I made a lot of progress tonight. We'll pick up the hay in time for next Wednesday's practice. No need tracking all that in here too early."

The two tables of church members made their way to the buffet line. Kia looked around to check on Josh. He and his friends were busy talking while they waited to be called up.

"I see you have some help this year," Reverend Jamison told Franklin. "I don't think we've met," the minister said to Kia.

Franklin made the introductions. "Reverend Avery Jamison, this is Sister Kia Simmons. Her son is portraying Joseph in the pageant this year. And Reverend Thomas here is our youth minister. He leads the children's church services."

After the how-do-you-do's, the youth minister excused himself, and Reverend Jamison made no secret of sizing up the couple. He nodded. "It's about time, Franklin."

"Now, Pastor," Franklin said.

Kia watched the exchange with interest. *Time for what?* she wondered. Then she got a hint and felt heat rush up her cheeks.

"Oh, Reverend Jamison!" Mavis Washington hustled over and put an arm through the pastor's. "We need your help in the office."

"Duty calls," Reverend Jamison said.

"You want me to make you a plate, Pastor?" asked one of the kitchen women monitoring the food supply.

"Yes, thank you kindly, Sister Smith. And, uh, make sure I get a double helping of that ham and some of Sister Emmalyne's rolls."

"What about that pressure of yours, Pastor," someone in the line called out.

The minister chuckled. "I tell you, you all are worse on me than the missus."

"Pastor, this really is important," Mavis Washington interjected a moment before she hustled him off to her emergency.

When Kia and Franklin finally made it to the serving dishes, Franklin looked around. "All right, which one?"

Smiling, Kia pointed out the deep dish pot pie she'd brought. Franklin took a double helping.

"You're not going to save any for anyone else?"

He glanced at her as he moved on to a green bean casserole. "I like to savor the good stuff."

Not at all able to think of an appropriate comeback, Kia dipped a serving spoon into what may have been potato salad.

Back at their seats, Kia stared at her plate trying to figure out where all the food came from. She'd apparently taken a little of this and a bit of that; which would have been fine if she could have identified half of it. That looked like mashed sweet potatoes. Kia stuck her fork in.

"I was washing the sawdust off my hands and clothes and missed grace," Franklin said. "Would you say it with me?"

"Oh, uh, sure." She lowered the fork to her plate and bowed her head.

Franklin took her hand in his, and her eyes popped open.

"Father God, thank You for the food we're about to eat. Bless the hands that prepared it for the nourishment of our bodies. And thank You, Lord, for the beginning of a new friendship. Amen."

With that, he dug in like a man who hadn't eaten in days. Kia sat there. Was she the new friend?

After taking a long gulp from his glass of fruit punch and wiping his mouth with a paper napkin, Franklin turned toward her. "So, tell me about yourself."

Chapter Four

"**Y**ou took the question I was about to ask you," she said. "What do you want to know?"

"Everything."

Kia chuckled. "Well, that won't take long. I've lived here with Joshua about two years. I'm a teacher's assistant at Tubman Elementary. And Josh is playing Joseph in the Christmas pageant."

Lifting her fork to her mouth, Kia used eating as an excuse for not revealing more. "What about you?" she asked.

"Now, wait a minute. You left out all the important stuff."

"Like what?" she mumbled between bites.

"Like where you learned to throw down on some chicken pot pie." He lifted her free hand. "You sure you're not married?"

Smiling now, she nodded. "I think I'd be the first to know. And thank you. That's one of Joshua's favorites, so I figured I couldn't go wrong."

They both looked toward the table where the children were arriving with their plates. Josh put his plate down, leaned toward Shelby and said something. A moment later, he straightened and headed back to the buffet line.

"What's he doing?"

Franklin smiled. "My guess is, trying to please the little lady."

Kia leaned up to get a better view, then started to rise. "Maybe I should . . ."

Franklin stayed her with a hand over hers. "He's okay. He just went to get extra napkins, see."

A little embarrassed, Kia sat down again and picked at her food. "I guess you think I'm smothering him."

With a gentle finger, he lifted her chin. Kia's breathing stopped. She met his gaze with wide eyes.

"I'm not thinking anything like that."

Right then, Kia knew she wanted him to kiss her. She savored that thought for a moment, then tuned in to what he was saying.

"From what I've seen of Joshua, I already know you're a terrific mom. He's a good kid, well behaved. It's easy to tell which ones have some home training and which ones run wild."

She blinked and smiled a tiny smile.

"Take Charmaine, for instance," he said. "That girl has been grown since she was ten. Her mother works doubles in Pittsburgh. That forty-minute commute each way really eats into the time she's able to be at home with her kids. There's an older brother, but he's in jail, and the little one, well, at least a responsible neighbor looks out for her."

"But she comes to church," Kia pointed out.

Franklin pointed around the crowded fellowship hall. "That's because the boys are here."

"So are the men," Kia said, thinking about the way the girl had eyed Franklin.

"Yeah, well, she's also a first-class flirt. But most of them are at that age. I bet you were, too."

She shook her head and carefully studied the food on her plate. "No, not really."

The admission came out sounding almost resentful, something that surprised Kia. She'd been tried and tested, but she could honestly say she'd never resented anything about her life. Until maybe right this moment. She regretted not having more experience at flirting.

Suddenly uneasy with the direction of her thoughts, Kia frantically tried to think of something to ask him. Her mind, however, refused to cooperate. So she focused on her food.

"Kia, what's wrong?" Franklin asked before taking another forkful of pot pie.

Wondering if her uncertainty showed that easily, Kia asked, "What makes you think something's wrong?"

He shrugged. "You just seem suddenly quiet. I didn't mean to make you uncomfortable."

She shook her head, pasted a smile on her face, and cut a small piece of ham. "You didn't. I'm fine. Tell me about you."

Franklin studied her, then let the moment pass.

"My life's an open book. What would you like to know?"

"Everything," she said, repeating his earlier request of her.

Franklin smiled and then told her about learning to whittle at his grandfather's knee. "My first big woodworking project was a bookcase for my bedroom."

"How'd it turn out?"

He chuckled. "A mess. I was barely ten, but learned quickly. These days I concentrate on furniture and smaller items, things that can be shown or sold in galleries."

"I'd like to see some of it," Kia said, hoping she wasn't being too forward.

"It's a date then," Franklin said.

A date? Kia stared at him, mouth open and eyes wide. "You want to go on a date. With me?"

Franklin lifted her hand and pressed a quick kiss to it. "I'd love to. Thanks for asking."

He winked at her, then grinned. After taking a deep drink from his punch glass, Franklin excused himself for a moment.

Before Kia had time to recover from the surprise kiss, he was up and gone.

Kia sat there stunned. What had just happened? Did they suddenly have a date planned?

Shirley plopped into the seat across from Kia. "So, how's it going? You two seem to have hit if off. He's perfect for you, you know."

With eyes still a bit unfocused, Kia looked at her friend. "I think I need a babysitter."

"Excellent!" Shirley's outburst drew a couple of curious glances.

"Shh," Kia pleaded.

Shirley waved a hand. "Don't worry about these folks. I'm so glad this is working out. He's a strong man, and not just physically, either. He's strong in the Lord."

Kia sighed. "Then why is he interested in me?"

That, Kia realized, was what had her so confused. Franklin was a church man. She, on the other hand, could find Genesis, the Book of Psalms, and Revelations in the Bible. Other than remembering the Lord's Prayer, that was the extent of her religiousness.

She couldn't even claim to be the most attractive woman in the church. She didn't know how to flirt or really communicate with adults. Her entire work and home life revolved around children.

"Maybe he sees what I see in you," Shirley said.

"What's that?"

"Potential. And what's this about needing a babysitter?"

Kia's smile, tentative, hopeful and happy, told the story. "It seems I have a date."

Franklin watched the boy, not at all surprised that Joshua followed him into the men's room. He'd seen the young man watching him from across the fellowship hall.

"What's going on, buddy?"

Joshua shrugged as he leaned against a white porcelain sink.

Franklin paused at a urinal and did his business, all the while looking at Josh through the mirror. He patiently waited for the boy to voice his concerns.

When Josh didn't make a move, Franklin mused aloud. "Sometimes," he said, "a man needs to have a heart-to-heart talk with another man. Someone who's been there and maybe could share some ideas. Somebody to bounce things off, you know?"

Joshua nodded, but didn't say anything. Franklin zipped his pants and went to the sink next to Josh to wash his hands. He took his time at it, sensing Josh seemed to have a weighty matter on his mind.

When Franklin reached for a paper towel, Josh finally spoke up. "Brother Williams, I, uh, need to talk to you about something."

"Shoot," Franklin said as he tossed the balled-up paper towel in a trash bin. "What's up?"

Joshua looked at his feet, then, taking a deep breath, he stood up straight and tall and looked up at Franklin.

"I saw you talking to my mom and I want you to know it's all right with me. You have to be nice to her, though, if you take her out. And no kissing on the first date."

To keep from smiling, Franklin bit the inside of his mouth. Then he folded his arms and stared down at the boy. "What makes you think I'm interested in your mom that way?"

Mimicking the older man, Josh folded his own arms. "I saw the way you were looking at her."

Franklin nodded and pursed his lips. "Sort of like the way you were looking at Shelby Knight?"

Josh lost some of his bravado at that. But to Franklin's delight, the boy rallied quickly.

"It's different with grown-ups."

"I see." Franklin considered things for a moment, then decided to negotiate. "No kissing on the first date, huh?"

"That's right. Kissing leads to babies. And we don't have room in our apartment for a baby. There's just enough room for me and Mom. She's not really my mom, though. She's my aunt. My real mom died a long time ago."

That was news to Franklin. He concealed his surprise by asking another question. "Is holding hands okay?"

Joshua thought about it for a moment, then nodded his consent.

"Any other rules?" Franklin asked.

"You have to treat her nice. Mom doesn't know about going out. She always stays home with me."

Another bit of intelligence Franklin found particularly useful. That meant there was no other man in Kia's life.

"And you have to buy her a Christmas present," Josh added.

Franklin did laugh at that. "Did you have something particular in mind?"

Joshua shook his head no. "I'm going to do something nice for Shelby. I don't know what, though," he said with a frown. "I don't have a lot of money."

"Hmm, maybe I can help you with that."

"I'm not allowed to take money from strangers."

"Oh, so now I'm a stranger?" Franklin asked, while giving Josh bonus points for being a levelheaded kid.

The boy shook his head. "You know what I mean."

"Actually, I do. And I wasn't considering giving or loaning you any money. I had something else in mind."

"What?"

"I can teach you how to make something for Shelby. It'll be extra special because the gift came from your hands and your heart."

Josh pondered that for a moment or two, then his face lit up. "That's a sacrifice, isn't it?"

"Well, it could be. You'll have to sacrifice some time that you might otherwise spend with your friends to make your gift."

"Shelby has a lot of that girl stuff that she puts in her hair. And she has a lot of purses, too. Could I make something for that?"

Franklin nodded. "You could make a jewelry or keepsake

box, or maybe something similar to a keyholder that her ribbons and purses could hang from.''

Franklin watched as Joshua considered the possibilities. When a smile lit the boy's soft brown face, Franklin gave a sigh of relief. He hadn't truly realized just how much he'd been hoping for a connection with Joshua. But he also knew he had a responsibility to every young male in the church.

Apparently satisfied with the conversation, Josh headed to a urinal, then washed his own hands.

"One more thing, Joshua."

The boy glanced back at the man as he set up his paper towel for a free throw.

"He shoots," Franklin said, following the toss. Josh's balled-up tissue landed squarely in the trash bin. "And he scores."

"What's the other thing?"

"No kissing Shelby. It's a little early for that. You have to respect our women and girls. That means being courteous and treating them the way you'd want your mother or your sister to be treated."

Josh shuffled his feet. "Well, a couple of the guys were talking about how they, you know, how they get girls to do things."

This isn't exactly where Franklin thought the conversation was headed, but there was no going back now. It was better for a young man to get the facts than to get that raggedy street knowledge that led to so many problems.

Franklin stooped down so he was at eye level with Joshua. "What your friends and acquaintances do has nothing to do with how you act," he said, pointing to the boy's chest. "You have to listen to your head, not the other parts of your body. Sometimes it's difficult, but walking in the way of the Lord isn't always easy."

"What's God got to do with it?"

"Everything," Franklin said as he stood up. "The Lord sees you even in the places you think no one's watching. He's there to forgive you when you mess up, to guide you when you need direction, to give you support when you think you're all alone. You know, Joshua, it takes a man of courage to walk the path no one else walks.''

As the two headed to the door, Josh looked up. ''I have courage.''

''I know you do. Now let's get back to the fellowship hall before we miss all the desserts.''

Later that night, Franklin wondered if he'd overstepped the bounds. He was, after all, essentially just another man at the church. He didn't have any claim to Joshua Simmons or any of the other children.

In his workshop, he cut the wood he'd need to make the garden planters for one of his customers. The pieces would go on the couple's backyard deck as soon as spring arrived.

''Another five months from now,'' Franklin muttered.

Western Pennsylvania's winters lasted a while, but Franklin could work on the projects he didn't have to think about while his mind wandered.

He'd made a date with Kia Simmons for Saturday night. Franklin grinned. He couldn't wait. He also knew he needed to tell her about Josh.

In her own bedroom, Kia paced the floor. Josh had fallen asleep long ago, but as the clock ticked later and later, Kia found sleep elusive. Shirley had agreed to watch Joshua.

''That was the easy part,'' she said of finding a babysitter. ''The hard part is the going out.''

What would they talk about? What would they do? Not only did she have no idea, she didn't have the first clue as to what to wear.

At twenty-five, Kia had never been on a date. It wasn't that she hadn't been asked. Her focus had always been on Josh. The ''almost boyfriend'' she'd had in high school moved away right before things got serious between them. Then Kimberly died and left her a toddler to raise. There had been no time for dates, no money, either. It had taken all these years to get where she was today.

Kia walked to her closet and surveyed her wardrobe. An hour later, she still hadn't decided what to wear. But she was too tired to stare or care anymore. When she finally fell into an exhausted sleep, she dreamt of strong hands creating a masterpiece. When the wood turned and bronzed light cast upon it, Kia saw a family in the carved image: a woman who looked a lot like Kia, a child who could have been Joshua's twin, and a man. Try as she might, Kia couldn't get a clear image of the man's face; it wouldn't come in focus. She strained to see the father's features, but they slipped from her view like mist on a foggy night. In her sleep Kia kicked off the covers on her bed, not realizing she called Franklin's name aloud.

Chapter Five

"**I** have a confession to make," Kia said.

"Sounds interesting," Franklin replied. "Tell me more."

They strolled along Pittsburgh's Fifth Avenue looking in decorated store windows. The weather forecasters predicted snow accumulation over the weekend. Franklin could have been a catalog model the way everything fit him, from the corduroy slacks to the Cosby-esque sweater.

She, on the other hand, fretted most of the day Saturday over what she should wear. In the end, Shirley pulled several coordinating pieces from Kia's closet and handed them to her. Kia was glad she'd dressed warmly.

"I almost didn't come tonight."

As a light snow began to fall around them, Franklin waited for the explanation. Kia stopped walking and stared at winter sprites frolicking in a snow wonderland scene. The animated decorations in the window brought a smile to her face.

"I was afraid."

"Afraid of what?"

Kia glanced up at him. He looked so at home in this environment, as if he knew exactly what to say and do on a first date.

"Having a good time."

Franklin's chuckle came from deep within. The sound of it brought a smile to Kia's face. She liked hearing him laugh. They'd done a lot of that first over dinner and then through a new Christmas comedy at the movie theater.

"Well, if that's the case, I hope you've been miserable all night."

It was Kia's turn to smile. "You know I haven't. This has been perfect. Thank you."

For a moment, they simply stared at each other, oblivious of the snow falling and the people moving around them. Then, Franklin reached for her gloved hands. "No. Thank *you*, Kia Simmons."

Her smile blossomed. Kia slipped her arm through Franklin's and they resumed their window-gazing.

"Oh, look," Kia said, pointing to a window decorated with a choir of golden angels. "Isn't that beautiful."

"Yes," Franklin answered. "You're very beautiful."

Kia turned and opened her mouth to respond, but something in his eyes stayed her words. She watched as he leaned forward. Her eyes drifted closed and she leaned into him, waiting for the kiss she knew was coming.

The only thing she felt, though, was snow falling. She opened her eyes and stared into Franklin's.

"What?"

He slipped a glove off and caressed her cheek. "A man's word is his bond. And I'm a man of my word."

Confused, Kia shook her head. "And?"

"And I promised Joshua no kissing on the first date."

Kia's mouth fell open. A second later, she snapped it shut and stood erect.

"What does Joshua have to do with this?"

But she already knew the answer. Josh had everything to do with every aspect of her life. She'd put her life and her dreams on hold because she was all he had. She shouldn't have even stayed out this late.

"Never mind," she told Franklin before he could answer. "I shouldn't have expected . . . Uh, never mind."

Kia felt her face flame, and she looked away, embarrassed, ashamed. She shouldn't have expected to get intimate with him. But she'd wanted that kiss, had anticipated it more than anything else since the moment outside her apartment when Franklin leaned toward her to unlock the passenger door of his pickup.

When she tried to walk away, Franklin called her name.

In two steps he covered the short distance that separated them. "Kia, I've enjoyed your company tonight, enjoyed it immensely. I'd like to see you again."

"I don't think that's a good idea."

"Because of your son?"

She shook her head. "Because of me."

"I see."

They fell into step as they headed toward the garage where Franklin had parked the truck. When Franklin opened the door for her, Kia climbed in and reached for her seat belt, but he paused her hand.

"You can't run away forever, Kia."

"You have no right to lecture me. You don't even know me."

"Exactly," he said. "I want to get to know you. But if you shut me out, I can't."

"I need to get home to Joshua."

"He's fine and you know it. Shirley Thompkins is a school-teacher and one of your friends. He's probably having the time of his life."

"Are you saying I spend too much time with him?"

"No, I'm not," Franklin answered as he shut her door. A moment later, he sat next to her. "What I'm saying is, you are a young, beautiful woman. I know you love Joshua. He loves you, too. That's why we had a little talk."

Kia turned toward him, concern etched on her brow. "About what?"

"Man stuff."

"Stop it. Just stop it. First Josh shuts me out saying he had to talk to you man-to-man, now you're sitting there telling me the same thing. I've done the best I could. I couldn't go to college and raise him so I got the best job I could find with a high school diploma. I had to learn how to be a mom and an adult and a cook and everything else. I'm his mother and his father."

Franklin sat quietly through the storm. When tears started falling midtirade, he handed her a handkerchief.

"Thank you," Kia muttered. She removed her gloves and blew her nose and stared out the window at the station wagon parked next to them.

"You want to tell me what's wrong?" Franklin said softly.

Kia sniffled and shook her head.

Franklin put the key in the ignition and turned on both the heat and the radio, which was tuned to a Christian station playing gospel. He didn't make any effort to touch Kia or to exit the garage.

"I'm sorry," Kia eventually said. "This has been a terrific evening and I messed it up."

"You didn't mess anything up."

"Yeah, I did," she insisted. "Do you know what else I was afraid of about tonight?"

"What's that?"

"That I'd end up pushing you away." Kia sighed. "I think I just succeeded."

Franklin scooted a little closer to her. "No, you didn't. It'll take much more than that to push me away. I'm made of pretty sturdy stuff."

"Like a big redwood tree or a towering oak, huh? I've needed some stability in my own life."

"Tell me how you came to have Josh."

Kia sighed again and looked out her window.

"Tomorrow is the anniversary," she said.

When she didn't seem inclined to say anything, Franklin asked the obvious follow-up. "Anniversary of what?"

"Since the fire. I was ten when my parents were killed in a car crash. My sister Kimberly was twenty-two and had just graduated from college. I was a midlife surprise baby," she added with a small, sad smile. "Kim raised me. Then she died trying to save me and Josh."

"What happened?"

"Our house caught fire. There was some faulty wiring that had been smoldering inside the walls. By the time I woke up, flames were all over the room. Josh and I were trapped up in the attic."

"And your sister?"

"She came through the fire trying to get to us. The burns . . . She died two days later. I promised her I'd keep Josh safe, that I'd take care of him and make her proud."

Franklin nodded, understanding finally dawning on him. "So you dedicated your life to Josh." It wasn't a question.

Kia sniffled and stared out the window.

"Do you have any children?" she asked.

"No. I've always wanted them, but I've never been married. Children are gifts from God. Whenever possible, they need guidance from two parents."

"That's not always possible," Kia said. "Sometimes people are thrust into situations they can't control."

"I know. You seem to have made the best out of a situation that was thrust on you."

"You're right," she said after a moment. "About what you said earlier. There are some things I just can't teach or show Josh the way a man could. Kimberly asked me to make sure he got some religion, that's why I take him to First Baptist. He seems to enjoy it. And he gets to interact with male role models."

"What about you? I don't recall ever seeing you attend services."

Kia frowned. "That's because I don't. My parents were real big on church and God and that whole thing, but I stopped believing in God when he stopped believing in me. He took my mother and my father. Then my sister. God took everyone I've ever loved. I'm not going to let anything happen to Josh."

For a moment, Franklin didn't say anything.

"Everything happens for a reason, Kia. The Scripture tells us there's a time and a season for everything."

"Well, it's been dump-on-Kia season for a long, long time. I don't particularly care for it."

She glanced at him, saw the hurt in his eyes and felt contrite.

"It's nothing against people who do the church thing, it's just not for me."

"Then why do you take Joshua to Sunday school? Why do you hang around the church when the children practice for the Christmas pageant?"

Kia didn't have an answer for that, at least not one that she wanted to share with Franklin. Of late, she'd been wondering why her life felt so empty, so void of life. Josh always came home raving about his Sunday school class and he bugged her about letting him join the youth fellowship program. Kia hadn't agreed to that, but she had been reading his Sunday school materials.

Slowly, the lessons she'd been taught as a child came back, stories about miracles like Moses parting the Red Sea and Daniel in the lion's den. She'd even surprised herself when she realized she remembered a few Bible verses. But reciting a Bible verse or the Lord's Prayer didn't mean much, especially not to someone like Frank. Shirley had called him "strong in the Lord."

Looking at Franklin, she finally answered him.

"I don't know," she said with a shrug. "It seems like what I'm supposed to do.

"A long time ago I believed in miracles. I was baptized as a child. But then I grew up and realized that the miracles were just stories, and being baptized is . . ." She shrugged again, not at all willing to voice the doubt that would sound like blasphemy.

"I see," Franklin said.

He pulled his seat belt on and Kia did likewise. When he reached for and squeezed her hand, Kia didn't resist.

"Sometimes, Kia, the Lord whispers to you and leads you to the people He wants you to know and places He wants you to be."

"Is that why I met you?"

Franklin raised her hand to his mouth and kissed the back of her hand. "I don't know, but I'm starting to hope so. Let's pray about it."

The next morning, Kia woke up early. She made breakfast for Josh and tried to forget what day it was. By the time Josh ran into the kitchen, Kia had made up her mind.

"Wow. That's a nice dress," Josh said. "Where are you going?"

Kia put three pancakes on his plate and pulled a tub of margarine from the refrigerator. "*We* are going to Sunday school and then church."

"Really?"

"Really." She ran a hand over his hair.

Josh cringed and ducked. "Ma, not the hair. It took me a long time to brush these waves in."

Kia laughed, the sound refreshing even to her own ears.

On the drive to First Baptist, they sang Christmas carols along with the tape Kia popped into the cassette drive; Kia's voice was slightly off key, but nonetheless exuberant. She saw Josh to his classroom and then went in search of an adult Sunday school class.

Not at all like she remembered them being, Kia found herself enjoying the fellowship and the discussion the twentysomething group was having about traditional gospel music versus hip-hop gospel.

Kia's innocent question, "What's hip-hop gospel?" led to another round of spirited debate followed by someone hopping onto the piano stool and playing "Amazing Grace." Kia sang along, the words to the old hymn of the church coming to her as if she sang the song every Sunday.

"That's old school," the piano player said. "Here's the way we sing it now." With that, the man launched into a rowdy version of the hymn that, with a tambourine added and complicated-looking and-sounding clapping from the rest of the people in the class, sounded to Kia's ears more like dance club music than something that was supposed to be sung in a church.

Before she was ready for the class to end, the leader asked everyone to gather around for closing. With head bowed and eyes closed, Kia waited for someone to pray like the pastor did. But instead, the class leader asked each person to say something he or she was thankful for.

Kia's eyes flew open. By the time the person next to her spoke, Kia knew what she would say.

"Thank you Lord for getting my grandmother home from the hospital," the young woman to Kia's right said.

Then it was Kia's turn.

"I'm thankful for finding my way here this morning," she said. "And I'm thankful for new friendships and the people God puts in our lives."

Kia looked for Franklin before she and Joshua slipped into a pew for the eleven o'clock service. The sanctuary at First Baptist filled quickly. The congregation sang the morning hymn and a deacon prayed. When the worship leader stood at the pulpit to give observations, Kia figured she wouldn't see Franklin at all.

The worship leader said a special offering for the homeless would follow the morning announcements and the welcome of visitors.

"How long does this last?" Joshua whispered.

Kia shrugged and opened her bulletin.

"This is the day that the Lord has made. And we're glad you're here with us this morning."

Kia looked up. A smile split her face.

"Look, Mom. It's Mr. Frank."

"Shh."

"Would all visitors please stand," Franklin said.

Kia looked around and then toward Franklin. He nodded and she rose, along with about twenty other people scattered throughout the sanctuary.

"It gives me special pleasure to welcome you to First Baptist Church this morning. Let's give our visitors a warm welcome."

All of a sudden, Kia and Josh were surrounded by smiling faces and handshakes of welcome. A quick glance around showed that all the other visitors were being greeted in the same fashion.

Relaxing, Kia smiled, then took her seat when Franklin finished the welcome. A moment later, he slipped into the space left next to her on the aisle. She moved to make room for him. Joshua grinned.

The rest of the service passed in a blur for Kia. She felt slightly guilty that the only thing she remembered was the feel of Franklin's leg pressed against hers on the crowded pew. Then, when the minister called for altar prayer, Franklin looked at her before standing.

"Come on, Josh," she said.

Together, the three made their way with others to the front of the church. Franklin stood in the middle with Kia to his right and Joshua to his left. When they bowed their heads for the altar prayer, Franklin entwined his fingers with Kia's.

She smiled. And this time, she had no problem thinking of something to be thankful about.

Fifteen minutes later, they stood outside the church. It was cold but clear and sunny.

"Hungry?" Franklin asked.

"I am," Joshua piped up.

"Josh, please."

"How about I treat the two of you to lunch," Franklin suggested.

"Cool, man. Let's go."

Kia scowled at Josh. "That's really not necessary," she told Franklin.

"I know it's not necessary. I want to."

The simple words carried a double meaning to Kia. She looked at Franklin. In his overcoat and hat, he himself looked like a preacher.

"Please, Mom."

One look at Joshua and Kia's mind was made up. "We'll follow you so we don't have to come back for the car."

Chapter Six

They were seated in a booth in the no-smoking section at Eat 'N Park, Franklin and Kia next to each other and Joshua across the booth's wide table.

"I want spaghetti with extra meatballs," Josh announced loud enough for people three tables over to hear.

"Joshua, what has gotten into you?"

Josh shrugged and grinned broadly at Kia and Franklin. Kia could only wonder what was going through the boy's head. He'd seemed in an entirely good mood all day.

Before she had the opportunity to analyze his behavior anymore, their waitress arrived. Introducing herself as Cindi, she filled their water glasses.

"We all went to church together today," Josh told the waitress.

The woman smiled. "I'm sure you and your mom and dad had a nice time. I have to work Sundays so I usually go to Friday-night Mass."

"We're not . . ." Kia started to protest.

"What's Mass?" Josh asked.

Franklin took Kia's hand in his and gave it a small reassuring squeeze. "It's okay, honey," he told her. "Mass is the religious service for people who are Catholic, Josh. There are lots of different faiths and religions in the world."

"Do you celebrate Christmas?" Josh asked the waitress.

"Sure do."

"I'm playing Joseph in our church's Christmas pageant," he said, the pride echoing in his voice.

"Well, that's a very important role, you know."

Josh fairly beamed. "I know. He told me, too."

All of a sudden, Kia's mouth dropped. Had Franklin called her "honey?"

She glanced between her nephew and Franklin, then up at the friendly waitress. They were all in cahoots, she decided, with the single mission of embarrassing her.

She tried to tug her hand free from Franklin's. But he held on, and a moment later, Kia felt his thumb gently caressing the back of her hand. Whether the action was deliberate or unconscious Kia didn't know. What she did know was that the soothing caress stirred something in her, something she hadn't realized she didn't have until just now. Peace.

With more than a touch of wonder in her eyes, Kia shifted in her seat to study Franklin. After all this time, had the right man finally come into her life? Or was she just on a spiritual high after the rousing church service?

"Mom?"

"Kia?"

She blinked and noticed three sets of curious eyes gazing at her.

"What can I get you for lunch, ma'am?"

Embarrassed at both the direction of her thoughts and the fact she'd been caught woolgathering, Kia pointed to the first thing on the menu.

The waitress leaned forward, taking a look at Kia's selection.

"That's our early-bird breakfast special. It's only available Monday through Friday. The buffet is really good today."

Kia nodded.

"I'll be right back with your drinks."

"Can I go get my salad now?"

"May I," Kia automatically corrected.

"May I?" Josh asked again.

"Just get what you plan to eat. And save room for your spaghetti."

Seconds later, Kia and Franklin sat alone, close together in the restaurant booth.

"Penny for your thoughts."

Kia smiled as she glanced at their still-joined hands. "What about the inflation factor? Thoughts don't come cheap these days."

Franklin simply stared into her eyes.

"What?" she asked, suddenly nervous.

"This is our second date. So I'm allowed to kiss you."

Kia scooted away from him, snatching her hand from his in the process. "I, uh, I don't think that's a good idea."

Clasping her hands together, Kia licked suddenly dry lips and glanced around at everything except Franklin.

"I didn't mean right this moment," Franklin said.

"Oh."

He smiled. "You sound disappointed."

Kia sighed. "You make me confused."

"What's there to be confused about? I'm attracted to you."

"Is that allowed?" she asked.

The edges of his mouth quirked up. "It better be."

Then, in one smooth movement, he exited the booth. "Salad bar?"

Kia stared up at him. The dark-blue suit was conservative but well made. He looked just as comfortable in church clothes as he looked in his lumberjack outfit of jeans and plaid shirts.

Being honest with her errant thoughts, Kia silently conceded that the man was sexy no matter what he happened to be wearing. She, however, was another story. She'd been worse than Josh dressing for little Shelby Wright. In the end, she'd chosen a black sheath with a strand of faux pearls. Black was always a safe bet.

He held out his hand to her and Kia brought her thoughts back to the present.

Franklin wanted to kiss her?

Chapter Seven

The three lingered over dinner talking about Christmases past. Franklin regaled them with stories about previous pageants at First Baptist, the time they used live animals and the night during the dress rehearsal when a candle set the entire manger scene on fire.

Kia gasped, and Joshua's eyes widened in fear.

"What's wrong?" Franklin asked, concerned about both of their responses. "What did I say?"

Kia reached for her glass of ice water and took a sip. After a few shaky moments, she managed to tell him. "Fire is, well, it's something we don't like to talk about," she said by way of explanation.

Franklin studied Kia's face for a moment. When she wouldn't meet his gaze, he turned toward Joshua hoping the boy might shed a little light on whatever had upset Kia. But the boy sat there, twisting a paper napkin and blinking back what looked like tears.

"Hey, guys. I'm sorry," Franklin apologized as he reached a hand out toward Josh and the other to Kia.

She sniffed. "It's okay. It's been a long time. You'd think we'd have traveled a little further on the emotional road."

Franklin wanted to know what she was talking about, but he didn't ask. Whatever secrets the two shared would be told in their own time.

"We don't like fire because that's how my Mom died," Joshua eventually said. "I don't really remember her, but I remember the fire."

Kia's mouth trembled a bit. Franklin wondered if it was because of memories about the fire or because Josh didn't remember his mother. Franklin squeezed her hand, comforting her in the best way he could given their surroundings and the circumstances.

"You don't have to tell me," he said.

Kia shook her head. "It's okay. I just . . ." She paused and glanced at Josh. When he nodded his okay, she took a deep breath, then told Franklin about the fire that left them alone in the world. She told him about seeing Kim covered in flames as she frantically tried to reach her son and sister. She told him about Kim's injuries and her funeral. She also told him about the days and weeks after the fire, about how difficult it had been to convince people who didn't have faith in her that she could, indeed, raise her nephew.

"It's been just the two of us ever since."

When Kia finished, silence fell over the table for a moment, each person lost in quiet reflection.

"Thank you for telling me," Franklin said.

Kia nodded.

"I have a picture of my other mom in my room," Josh said. "I'll show it to you when we get home."

Home. Franklin liked the sound of that. And he liked the idea of keeping them safe from harm. As he paid their lunch bill and they bundled up to face the cold outside, Franklin wondered what it might take to make this special woman his wife and Joshua his son.

* * *

He saw Josh and Kia safely into her Camry, made sure they had seat belts on, then admonished Kia to drive safely.

"Mom, can we go look at the lights? It's almost dark."

Kia glanced at Josh, then to Franklin, who stood outside next to her door. "Every year we drive through neighborhoods to see all the Christmas displays," she told Franklin.

"It's lots of fun," Josh added. "And best of all, it's free."

At Kia's blush, Franklin smiled. "I have an idea," he said. "I'll follow you two home, then we can all go in one vehicle. How's that?"

Kia glanced at Josh, who was all grins. "Sounds like a plan," she told Franklin.

About twenty minutes later, Franklin pulled his truck next to the curb behind Kia's car. Before he turned off the engine, Josh was at the passenger door.

Seeing that the decision about who would drive had been made, Kia closed and locked the doors on her car, then made her way through the slush on the street to stand near Josh.

"I want to sit by the window," he announced.

By that time, Franklin had the door open for him and overheard Josh's request. Franklin's eyes met Kia's. Before he could shield it, a dawn of something intense flashed in his eyes.

Kia's heart pounded as she stared at him. If they rode three abreast in the cab and Josh got the window, that meant she'd be next to . . .

Franklin smiled, and Kia got the distinct impression that he knew exactly what she'd been thinking, and liked the idea of them sitting thigh to thigh.

"Hold on," Franklin said. "I'll come help you up."

Moments later, the three sat in the roomy cab of Franklin's big Ford pickup.

"I've never been in a truck before," Josh said. "This is cool. We get a great view."

Kia clasped her hands over her purse and sat primly between

the two males. She tried not to touch Franklin while at the same time giving Josh enough room to wiggle around as he was prone to do while looking at Christmas-light displays.

"Comfortable?" Franklin asked.

"Yes, thank you."

Kia knew she sounded like a prudish schoolgirl, but she couldn't help it, especially not when all she could think about was cuddling close to Franklin. He started the engine, put his left signal on, and pulled into the street.

"Where to, Josh?"

"Let's start over by the school. They always have lots of lights there."

"Tubman or Bethune?" Franklin asked.

"Both!"

Franklin and Kia chuckled at the boy's enthusiasm.

"Josh, if you'll open the glove compartment, there's a Christmas tape we can play. It's gospel, but I think you'll like it."

With gospel versions of Christmas music playing in the background, they drove up and down neighborhood streets "oohing" and "ahhing" at the expressions of Christmas spirit.

"Goodness, I'd hate to see their electric bills," Kia observed at a house that had every inch of brick structure and snow-covered lawn strewn with reindeer, Santas, elves, snowflakes, and a miniature train village circling the whole of it.

"Wow!"

Franklin glanced over at Josh. "I know where there's an even awesomer display."

"Where?" Josh asked.

"I'll just head in that direction. I think you'll see it."

In a few minutes, Josh yelled and pointed out the front window. Every house on two streets was decked out in holiday splendor. Franklin dimmed the lights to parking ones and joined the line of vehicles slowly and orderly parading through.

They pointed, smiled, and laughed at the various holiday scenes played out in elaborate designs and tableaux.

More than an hour later, Franklin drove them home.

"That was really cool," Josh said for the third or fourth time as they entered the apartment. "Thanks, Mr. Franklin. Today was really cool."

"I enjoyed it, too, Josh. Thanks for the company."

Josh shrugged out of his coat, scarf, and gloves, hung them on a rack and ran toward the bathroom.

"Would you like to come in for some coffee or cocoa?" Kia invited as she tugged off her gloves.

Franklin held the storm door open and shook his head. "I'd better not."

A bit of the joy Kia had been feeling faded. Her disappointment must have shown on her face. Franklin removed his own gloves and took her hands in his.

"I'd better not," he said again, "because temptation can be a terrible thing."

"What do you mean?"

Franklin pulled the door to a bit as they stood facing each other. Then, staring into her eyes, he lowered his head. He paused a breath away from her lips, giving her plenty of time to retreat. But that was the last thing Kia had in mind. She lifted a hand to his face and drew him closer.

The kiss they shared spoke more of passion than innocence. Kia had been anticipating this kiss all day, ever since Franklin's comment at the restaurant. When his lips covered hers, she realized that all of her life she'd waited for this moment and this man.

Kia thrilled at the sensations coursing through her. She'd never felt like this before—as if she walked on clouds with a chorus of angels rhapsodizing all around. Franklin deepened the embrace and Kia moaned. His kiss grew urgent and exploratory as he traced the contours of her mouth. She shivered as an intense sweetness built inside her.

"Kia," he said against her lips. "I need to go."

"Okay," she murmured as she pulled him closer.

He rained small kisses along her temple, her jaw, then closed his mouth over hers again.

A moment later, Franklin wrenched himself away from her. "Good night, Kia."

Her pleading eyes and her kiss-swollen mouth begged him to stay. Franklin shook his head. "I, we . . . We shouldn't."

Kia didn't say anything. She didn't have the words. She brought a hand to her lips and gently touched them. Then, leaning forward, she pressed her fingers to his mouth.

A sound that could have been a groan or a moan escaped from him. Kia's smile was shy as she slipped inside the apartment.

Long after she'd closed and locked her door, Franklin stood in the cold night taking deep breaths of the bracing winter air.

"Lord, give me strength," he prayed, the short entreaty all that he could manage given the physical circumstances he struggled with.

Chapter Eight

A nd that's the way it went. Over the next two weeks, Kia and Franklin saw each other at church, during pageant rehearsals, and at the eleven o'clock service Sunday morning. A couple of afternoons during the week, Kia dropped Josh off at Franklin's shop so he could work on his Christmas present for Shelby.

Josh wouldn't let her see what he was making, though. "It's a surprise," he'd say.

Kia let those moments go, even though they hurt a bit. Josh had never had secrets. When she asked the eight-year-old what he and Franklin talked about while they did their woodwork, Josh would shrug and say, "Nothing special."

Glad that he had someone to talk to and that he was learning the benefits of sacrificing his time, Kia tried not to feel like something of a third wheel. It was hard, though, particularly when Josh and Franklin seemed to have developed a close bond in a few short weeks. Kia didn't want to admit it to herself, but in her heart of hearts, she knew that Franklin was just the influence Josh needed in his life.

"And what about your life?" she asked herself.

Not willing to consider the answer to that question, Kia completed her shopping. She'd borrowed a little money from Shirley to get Josh's bike out of layaway.

The three of them had Sunday dinner together again, and with Shirley babysitting Josh, Franklin and Kia went on a date or two. Sometimes the three of them played Monopoly or Clue until it was time for Josh to go to bed. Then Kia and Franklin would sit in her living room watching a movie on video or quietly talking.

That's where they were Friday night when Kia gathered her courage to ask the question she'd been wondering about for a couple of days.

"Franklin, remember the night when we saw the neighborhood lights?"

He nodded as he crossed his leg and tucked her into the groove between his arm and chest. "That's a night I'll remember for a long, long time. Our first kiss."

She smiled. "I'll remember it, too," she said. "But I was, uh, wondering about something."

"What's that?"

Kia grimaced, not quite sure how to bring up something like this. She leaned forward, reaching for the remote control. Then, shaking her head as she clicked the television set on, she told him never mind. "It's not that important."

But it was important.

She really wanted to know why he hadn't made any other moves toward intimacy of some kind since that night. They sat together in church and held hands sometimes, but that was as far as it went. Ever since that steamy kiss at her door, when Franklin kissed her good night it was a chaste kiss on the cheek. She wanted more of what they shared that special night, or at least the reassurance that she hadn't suddenly developed bad breath or something.

Franklin sat up. "Kia, if there's something you're worried about, it is important. What's up?"

She bit her lower lip, then opened her mouth and chickened out.

Just because she found him attractive didn't mean the feeling was mutual. She enjoyed looking at him, being with him. But maybe to Franklin she was just a way to pass the time leading to the holidays.

Instead of getting into territory she didn't know how to navigate, she decided to ask a different question, one that had been bothering her just as much as the kissing issue. This, too, was a difficult line of thought, but it was easier to deal with than her personal wish for another kiss.

"Well," she ventured. "You and Josh have been spending a lot of time together lately."

Franklin nodded. "He's a good kid."

"He's seemed withdrawn lately," she said. "Even a bit moody. And that's not at all like Josh."

"Well, he's a little worried about the pageant. It's just two days away and he's gotten a sense of how important his role is."

Kia frowned. "He's worried about it? He hasn't said anything to me."

"He knows all his lines. He's ready. They're going to be great. You'll see."

Franklin reached for the *TV Guide* on the coffee table. "Anything decent on tonight?"

Concealing her sigh, Kia reached for the half-filled bowl of popcorn they'd been munching from earlier. Franklin clicked the television on and went straight to the Christian station. A televangelist preached from a pulpit framed with lush green plants. Kia looked at the TV preacher, then looked at Franklin. Maybe that was it, she thought. Maybe his religion kept him from doing anything more than being a perfect gentleman on their dates and get-togethers.

"Why haven't you kissed me the way you did that night?"

The question came out of nowhere. Kia couldn't believe she'd actually just blurted it out like that.

"And lusts of the flesh shall be the deciding factor that separates the sinner from the . . ." the TV preacher boomed.

Kia looked mortified. Franklin muted the sound.

"What was that?" he asked.

Kia hopped up. "Nothing," she said as she grabbed the popcorn bowl and headed, in a rush, toward the kitchen. She didn't realize that Franklin had followed her until she turned and bumped into him.

"Kia? Did you ask me why I haven't kissed you?"

She lowered her head and stared at the floor for a moment. Then, gathering her courage yet again, she faced him. "Franklin, I don't know anything about flirting and dating and that sort of thing. I've never had the opportunity to date. I have a responsibility to Josh, and that's always come first in my life. I was beginning to think that maybe we, you and I, were, well . . ." Her voice trailed off.

Franklin reached a hand out and cupped her chin. The mere touch of his hand sent a warming shiver through Kia. Her skin tingled and she suddenly wondered if she'd waded into too deep waters.

"Do you feel that?" he asked.

"What?" The question a breathless sigh.

"The electricity between us. It's intense. Do you feel it?"

She nodded and leaned forward when his hands skimmed her arms, sliding down to her hands. Their hands entwined and the driving need she felt surprised her, made her wonder what was missing. Involuntarily, she leaned into him. Her eyes widened when she felt the evidence of his attraction to her.

"If you must know the truth," Franklin said, "it's that I don't trust myself around you."

"What does that mean?"

"It means whenever I'm near you, I want to do things that are, well, that Christians shouldn't do." He stepped back a bit, putting a few inches of distance between their bodies.

"Oh," Kia said, the word sounding like both a question and a disappointment. "Christians aren't allowed to kiss?"

Franklin chuckled, then pulled her close for a quick hug. "It's not the kissing that's the problem, Kia. It's what it can lead to."

For a moment, they stood together, their bodies as close as they could be while fully dressed. Kia writhed against him and Franklin groaned. Then slowly, reluctantly, he pulled away from her. They were both breathing deeply.

"Oh, my," Kia said. This time her "oh" signaled a dawn of understanding. She took a breath, trying to calm her racing heart and other parts. "So, I don't have like BO or something?"

Franklin burst into laughter, a deep, hearty laugh that made Kia smile.

"Hardly."

"Well, that makes me feel better," she said. "I thought maybe you'd, you know, changed your mind about even wanting to . . ."

He took her hands in his and kissed them. "I haven't changed my mind about anything. As a matter of fact, I'm more sure than ever that what we have is special, one of a kind. But we have to wait."

As Franklin gathered his coat, Kia wondered just what they had to wait for.

Saturday, the night before the pageant, Joshua asked to be excused from the dinner table. Concerned, Kia leaned forward.

"You feel all right, honey?"

Josh frowned and tossed his napkin onto his plate. "I'm not a baby, Mom. Stop acting like I am."

With that he scraped his chair back and ran from the room.

Openmouthed, Kia stared at the empty chair, then looked up at Franklin. "What in the world . . . ?"

A moment later, Josh's bedroom door slammed. Kia rose to go check on him.

"Leave him be," Franklin said.

Startled, Kia turned toward Franklin, a quizzical look on her face. "I beg your pardon?"

For just a moment, his voice sounded like the commanding one she remembered, though vaguely, of her father's. He'd been a sergeant in the Army and ran his household like a platoon of troops.

"He'll be okay. Have a seat," Franklin said, indicating her chair. "Finish your meal."

"Franklin, what he just did and said was rude, not to mention uncalled for. I swear, I don't know what's gotten into him lately. He's been acting odd all week. With Christmas coming, you'd think he'd be on his best behavior."

"He's a boy, Kia. He has things on his mind."

Uncertain, Kia glanced from Franklin to the hall where Josh had retreated. She stood as if poised for flight, obviously torn between wanting to check on Josh and trying not to overreact to every little thing.

"And what do you know about children? You don't have any."

A shadow crossed his face, and Kia instantly regretted the words. She reached toward him. "I'm sorry, Franklin. I didn't mean that the way it came out."

He nodded, then wiped his mouth with his own napkin. "I'll go talk to him."

One hand rose to Kia's hip. "What makes you think *you* should talk to him? He's my responsibility."

Franklin got up and went to Kia's side. "You use the word 'responsibility' as if it's a chain around your ankle. Eventually, Kia, you've got to cut the shackles off. It's not an easy process, but the ankle can't grow and develop properly if it's constantly restricted."

"What are you saying? Are you trying to tell me you think I treat Joshua like a slave?"

"No, Kia," Franklin said. He traced a large finger along the now-trembling edge of her mouth. "You're a terrific mother to him. But sometimes there are things that a boy growing into a young man just can't talk to his mother about.''

With that, Franklin turned his back on Kia and headed down the hall to Joshua's room.

Kia heard the rap as Franklin knocked on the bedroom door, announced himself, then asked if he could come in. When Franklin turned the knob and entered, Kia's heart lurched.

''He doesn't need me anymore.'' The whispered words an anguish she never thought she'd ever face.

Staring blankly, she sank into the chair at the table. First Franklin, now Joshua shutting her out. She'd been rejected by both of them. *She* was all Joshua needed. At some level she'd always known that he would eventually grow up, that he'd find his own place and way in the world. But that wasn't supposed to come until he was eighteen or twenty-one.

''Not at eight. He's still a little boy.''

She'd loved him, nurtured him, and guided him all these years, years without Franklin Williams's help. Now, all of a sudden, she'd been declared unnecessary. Kia knew she was overreacting, but she couldn't help it.

First one translucent tear fell. Then another, and another.

She swiped at her eyes, a valiant attempt to stem the flow before it became a rushing broken dam. Blinking several times, Kia looked around the table. Joshua hadn't eaten much. He'd mostly played with his food, smashing and twirling it around to look as if he'd actually been eating.

Maybe he was sick!

The thought rushed through her head and her breath caught.

A moment later, she sat back. His appetite had been just fine earlier in the day. Kia sniffled. With another glance toward the bedroom where the man and boy closeted themselves, Kia stood up and cleared the table. With the stiff motions of an android following orders, she put the leftovers away, washed the dishes, left them in the strainer to dry, then looked around the otherwise immaculate kitchen.

A glance at the clock on the stove told her they'd been in there for more than half an hour now. Kia wiped her already dry hands on a cotton kitchen towel, then tiptoed down the hall. She felt like a thief in her own home, but quelled the guilty thoughts as she leaned an ear close to Joshua's door.

For the first time, the relative thinness of the walls didn't serve any good purpose. A murmur of voices told her they still talked. Unfortunately, Kia couldn't make out a single word.

Giving in to the pain of being found unwanted, sort of like a defective toy or last year's video game, she bit her lower lip. In all the years she and Josh had been together, Kia never imagined that he'd reject her counsel or throw back her concern for him. They'd had their share of disputes, but he'd never acted out like he had tonight.

With a heavy heart, Kia straightened, stared at the door for a long tense moment, then turned and slowly walked to her own bedroom.

"You owe your mother an apology," Franklin told Joshua.

"I know."

"And you've probably hurt her feelings."

Joshua sighed. "Why do women have to be so concerned about feelings? Who cares about that stuff?"

Franklin wanted to smile but he knew Josh wouldn't appreciate it. "They care. That means we need to care, too. Do you have Shelby's gift wrapped?"

Joshua nodded, then went to his dresser. Pulling open the bottom drawer, he reached all the way to the back and retrieved the package.

"Do you really think she's going to like it?"

Franklin knew that Josh's nerves were stretched thin. The boy feared he might be rejected by Shelby. But Franklin had seen the way Shelby reacted around Joshua.

"She'll love it," he said. "You took the time to make this

for her. It's a piece she'll have for lots of years. It shows her you care.''

Joshua didn't look at all convinced.

The pageant went off without a hitch. Not only did Joshua remember and project all of his lines, he helped two of the younger kids with lines they'd forgotten.

Kia and Franklin were known to be something of an item at the church. With the exception of an evil look shot her way by the flirty teenager Charmaine, everyone seemed happy for them. They sat together during the fellowship service after the pageant. Presents were exchanged.

With interest Kia watched Joshua present his Christmas gift to Shelby. The little girl, who'd changed from her Mary costume into a pretty red velvet dress, smiled shyly, kissed Joshua on the cheek and handed him a gaily wrapped package. They stood there smiling and blushing at each other.

Kia smiled. Her little boy was, indeed, growing up.

Kia had racked her brain trying to figure out what to get or make for Franklin. She eventually settled on a bottle of cologne and a scarf she managed to knit in her few spare hours.

The rest of the week leading to Christmas was spent in the usual way. Kia baked cookies, and with Franklin's help, they put up the tree.

On Friday night, Christmas Eve, Franklin called and said he had a surprise if Kia and Josh wanted to go for a late drive.

''Can we look at the Christmas lights again?'' Josh asked as Kia handed the keys to her car to Franklin.

''Where are we going?'' she asked.

''You'll know when you see it,'' Franklin said mysteriously. After driving for miles, at least forty, Franklin took a parkway exit.

From his position at the window, Joshua pointed into the distant sky. "Look at that star, Mom! It's huge."

The glow from a star off in the distance got her attention, too.

Franklin smiled. "In biblical times, the shepherds and the three wise men followed a star to the place where baby Jesus lay."

"In the manger, like for the pageant," Josh said.

"Exactly."

"Is there a manger up there?" the boy asked. Kia, too, looked to Franklin for an answer.

All Franklin would do was smile. "You'll see."

As they got closer, the traffic grew heavier. Franklin found a spot at the far end of the huge lot and pulled the car into a parking space. "We'll walk the rest of the way."

Kia didn't comment when, while walking three abreast, Franklin slipped his gloved hand into hers. As they approached the church, the star above seemed to shine even brighter. Lots of people gathered around the live manger scene being played out on the church lawn.

Josh's eyes widened and he broke free of Kia as he scrambled closer. "They're real animals!"

A sheep bleated as if confirming Josh's observation. He turned back and grinned at Kia and Franklin, then crept closer.

The life-size manger scene was being portrayed by people dressed as Mary, Joseph, wise men, shepherds, and inn guests. Bales of hay in a horseshoe shape around the crèche scene served as seats for onlookers who'd arrived early. Several sheep, a dog or two, and even a cow completed the barnlike scene. A baby cried, and the woman leaned into the wooden manger to lift him out.

The crowd "Ooohed" as if they were watching the actual baby Jesus being comforted by his mother, Mary.

Kia kept an eye on Joshua as he pressed closer to the front to see. A moment later, she felt an arm around her shoulder. When she glanced up, Franklin smiled down at her. It seemed the most natural thing in the world for her to put an arm around his waist and lean her head into his chest.

When the infant quieted, the woman portraying Mary gently placed him back in the manger with a small bottle, and a man in long robes stepped forward. He opened a large black Bible and began to read.

" 'And she brought forth her firstborn son, and wrapped him in swaddling clothes, and laid him in a manger; because there was no room for them in the inn. And there were in the same country shepherds abiding in the field, keeping watch over their flock by night.' "

The minister continued reading the famous passage from the second chapter of Luke. When he concluded, saying "Glory to God in the highest, and on earth peace, good will toward men," a choir of white-and-gold robed men, women, and children sang the hymn "Away in a Manger."

Then, another man in a shepherd's outfit asked everyone to bow their heads for prayer. At the conclusion, he told the crowd to join the choir in singing "Silent Night." That solemn hymn was followed by "Hark! The Herald Angels Sing" as all of the onlookers gathered a bit closer. When that song ended, the choirmaster motioned for two people, a man and a woman, from the choir to come forward. He lifted his hands for quiet, and then, in a rich contralto, the woman began to sing.

" 'The first Noel, the angels did say, was to certain poor shepherds in fields where they lay.' "

Her voice rang out over the entranced audience. Kia didn't realize that she and Franklin were so close until they began to sway with the music.

"This is beautiful," she whispered to him. Franklin's answering smile made Kia settle even closer. Everything seemed right in the world.

As the male soloist, a tenor, began to sing the second verse of the beloved Christmas carol, Kia glanced up at the star that shone above the church.

Right then and there, she opened her heart to the Lord,

thanking Him for leading her back to his grace. She thanked God for Joshua and for bringing Franklin into her life.

In that moment, she also realized that what seemed to be developing with Franklin was right and meant to be. Glancing up at him, Kia smiled, then looked at the bright star again.

"Thank you," she whispered.

As the two soloists alternated singing the remaining verses of the carol, Kia realized that this—being together with family and with friends while sharing the real meaning of the holiday— was what made Christmas a time of joy.

For so long, she'd associated the Christmas season with shopping, cooking, and grieving the loss of her sister. But the spirit of Christmas, the spirit of Noel, was more, so much more than presents and baked goods. When Kia smiled, her smile radiated as much light and joy as the star shining above.

Franklin leaned down toward her. Kia closed her eyes and let the moment happen.

When his lips touched hers, her lashes flew up for a moment, then drifted closed. The kiss was everything a kiss should be: tender, gentle, exploratory, and oh, so sweet. Before it became more, they broke apart. Kia smiled at Franklin and he slipped his arm around her again.

The outdoor congregation sang another Christmas carol together, then the choirmaster began singing "Joy to the World." The smiles all around as people sang from their hearts, sent a spirit of joy through the cold night. After the song, the crowd slowly dispersed as greetings of "Have a Merry Christmas" were exchanged.

Franklin waited until most of the people cleared the area, then he led Kia and Josh to one of the now-abandoned hay bales. Kia took a seat and gazed first at the crèche then up toward the bright star.

"Thank you," she whispered again. "And happy birthday."

"Josh," Franklin said.

The boy grinned up at him and nodded.

Kia's smile was indulgent as she looked at the two people

who meant the most in the world to her. "What are you two up to now?"

Franklin sat next to Kia and faced her. Josh stood just over his shoulder.

"Christmas is tomorrow, but I want to give this gift to you right now. It's a two-parter."

Kia glanced from Franklin to Josh. "A two-parter? What does that mean?"

"It means you get to open this part now, but you have to wait until tomorrow morning to open the other part," Franklin said.

"It's under the tree," Josh explained.

"Okay," Kia said. "What is it?"

"Close your eyes and unbutton your coat."

Kia's look, dubious at best, told him she had no intention of freezing to death.

"It'll just be for a moment," Franklin promised.

With another look in Josh's direction, Kia unwrapped her scarf and unbuttoned her coat. From a pocket somewhere in his coat, Franklin pulled out a flat brown box flecked with gold swirls and handed it to Kia.

"Merry Christmas," he said.

"It's maple burl," Josh said. "I picked out the wood and helped make it."

Kia traced her fingers over the smooth hard wood. "It's beautiful, guys. Thank you."

"Open it," Franklin said.

With yet another look at this man she'd fallen in love with in just a short time, Kia lifted the top from the box.

"Oh!"

Franklin lifted the diamond star necklace from its secure place in the box.

"Do you like it, Mom?"

"It's beautiful," Kia whispered.

Franklin lifted the delicate gold chain and dangled the star in front of Kia for a moment before he placed the necklace around her neck.

"You guys are terrific. This is a wonderful surprise," Kia said. "Thank you."

She glanced up at the large star in the sky, then smiled at Franklin.

"Merry Christmas to you both."

Epilogue

Kia promised Joshua that she wouldn't open her gift from Franklin until he arrived for breakfast at ten o'clock Saturday. Kia made French toast, bacon and eggs, and fresh-squeezed orange juice from the oranges she'd gotten at school.

When they finally got to open the presents, the guys made Kia go last. Dying of anticipation, Kia waited her turn, then opened the long bag from Josh. He'd made a hood-based organizer for her to hang her handbags or scarves.

Franklin's gift, in a huge box, intrigued her most. Kia ripped the paper off only to find a small box inside. And so it went, box after box of gaily wrapped, but empty boxes . . . until . . .

The small velvet box could only mean one thing. Kia smiled, already knowing exactly what her answer to the question would be if the little box in her hand held what she thought it did.

"I love you, Kia Simmons. Will you marry me and allow me to be father to Josh, husband and lover to you?"

Franklin opened the box and presented it to Kia. The diamond ring matched the necklace at her throat.

"It's beautiful," she said, leaning forward to kiss Franklin.

"Mom, you have to answer the question first," Josh said.

"What question?" Kia asked, genuinely confused for just a moment.

"Marry me?" Franklin said.

"I want him to be my dad," Josh said.

"Well, I guess that settles it then," Kia said, smiling as Franklin slipped the ring on her finger. "And I want to walk by your side all the days of my life."

Josh grinned.

This time when Kia and Franklin kissed, it was a joining of two hearts who'd found each other for Christmas and for always.

Kwanzaa Kupendi

BY

MARGIE WALKER

Dear Readers,

Asante Sana for your support and warm reception of my previous novels. I was excited by the invitation to participate in *Something To Celebrate* and sincerely hope you enjoyed my offering of "Kwanzaa Kupendi."

While suicide is not generally a subject found in romances, it is especially real during the holidays. If you know of someone who is desperately seeking a reason to live, please convince them to seek professional help.

I love hearing from you, so please keep writing me at the address below, or e-mail me at Malaikar@aol.com.

Until the next time, love and peace,
Margie Walker

Margie Walker
2400 Augusta
Suite 251
Houston, TX 77057

Prologue

T he candlelight cast its tiny glow over the corner where she sat huddled on the floor. Still, Michelle was shrouded in darkness.

The stingy illumination revealed her ravaged expression and the small revolver in her hands as she rocked back and forth. There was an offbeat rhythm to her rocking, often jerky movements, the fluidity broken by flashes of bright insight.

Suicide was not an option, she told herself, even as she considered it. She had tried reasoning with the silent cynic whose message lay on the verge of overpowering her will. It called on her to act, to end her misery.

She knew it was cowardly. As inhumane as murder. Sinful.

But so were the feelings inside her. It hurt so bad, her soul. With tears welling inside her, she felt wounded beyond repair.

Michelle swayed. She stilled. She gripped the pearl handle of the small-caliber gun. The pull to end it all was stronger than her rationale, wearing down her fight to live. She gulped and slid her right index finger onto the trigger.

The gun felt good in her grip. Comfortable, smooth, unsullied by anguish. No emotions at all. Neutral. The hand holding the gun trembled, and it lifted the gun as if guided by a resolve all its own.

"Don't do it."

"Do it. End it. This is the only way."

A remote clangor broke into Michelle's concentration, and she looked up expectantly. She strained to hear: Her curiosity was a subconscious welcome.

Slowly, she rose, sauntered across the room to the door, then into the hallway and down the flight of stairs.

With each step she took forward, the intrusion became clearer. When she reached the front door, the foreign noise became less so. A chorus of demanding voices screamed atop the consistent, staccato peel of the doorbell.

"Michelle! Michelle, we know you're in there . . . . If you don't open this door, we're going to call the police . . . . Michelle! You know how you hate a spectacle. You're going to be one if you don't open this damn door right now!"

Michelle distinguished the voices of her friends Loretta, Clarissa, and Reba. She exhaled. She felt released. She was free . . . for the moment.

Chapter One

Simon walked around his bedroom, making organized stacks of dirty laundry while he talked over the speaker phone. "You know I don't do that anymore," he replied.

"Simon, you're a psychiatrist. Licensed and certified."

Clutching a bunch of shirts to his chest, he stood directly over the speaker phone to reply parenthetically, "Licensed and certified as a sports psychologist now. I stopped practicing psychiatry—" Wincing, he fell momentarily silent. "Well, you know when I stopped practicing. I can't believe what you're asking me to do. Warning bells go off in my head just thinking about it. Do you think I haven't learned my lesson?" His voice rose incredulously. Shaking his head with vehemence, he affirmed, "I only work with male athletes now."

Resuming his work, Simon walked away from the bedside table to check for more dirty shirts in his closet. The silvery female voice of Loretta Fields-Cunningham droned on in a calm, coaxing tone of reason.

"I'm not asking you to do anything more than just talk to her . . . reason with her . . . see if you can convince her to get help."

Simon didn't care that Loretta could not see his reaction. He shook his head in rejection with each justifying request she made.

His answering machine had been full of messages from Loretta when he'd gotten back into town last night. He had known her years before he had needed her legal help. Had it not been for their close association, he would not have returned her calls, knowing what she wanted.

"Come on, Simon. You use pretty much the same training." Loretta was still making her argument. "The only difference is that you don't prescribe medication."

Leave it up to Loretta to know the difference, Simon thought with a smile. "Exactly," he said, recalling that her wit and dogged determination were exactly why he'd hired her four years ago. It was thanks to Loretta that he had a life at all. "Your friend sounds as if she needs treatment that includes medication, and I'm not the one who can help her."

Coming off a long, grueling road trip, he was exhausted. But his bank account was healthy, so he could stand being tired, he mused, pleased. Besides, he had the rest of the month to recuperate, barring any crises from his clients.

He dropped the shirts on the floor just outside the bedroom door. "I will help you find someone who is qualified," he offered.

"She won't go."

Simon sighed in disgust. "Well, check her into the hospital," he shouted to be heard, as he strode to the open suitcase on his oversize custom bed. He did not want to get involved. "Trust me, it's probably the best place for her," he said, pulling a bundle of underwear, T-shirts, and socks from the suitcase.

"She won't sign her life over to me."

Loretta's pouty, frustrated response meant she had not convinced her friend to sign over power-of-attorney to her, Simon realized with amusement. If she had, he was sure her friend would be getting the proper treatment now.

"What's the matter, Loretta? You slipping?" Returning to the door, he dropped the bundle next to the stack of shirts.

"No. It's just an indication of how bad off she is and doesn't know it," she quipped. "We took a gun from her a week ago."

"Damn it, Loretta!" Simon exclaimed. Even though he didn't know this woman personally, he was alarmed by this bit of news. He hurried to the phone, snatched up the receiver, and spoke urgently into the mouthpiece. "You should have taken her straight to the hospital. She needs to be on a round-the-clock watch. Where is she now?"

"We've had our own watch going," Loretta replied. "She's been staying with us."

Simon frowned, demanding, "Us who?"

"Ed and I."

Ed was Edmund Cunningham, Loretta's husband and law partner, Simon recalled. He exhaled an exhausted sigh; it was not one of relief.

"If she's at your house now, who's watching her? Aren't you calling me from the office?" He looked down at the speaker phone on the bedside table and depressed the bar on the caller ID. The number showing confirmed she was calling from her office. His frown intensified.

"She's at work right now," Loretta said as if he should have guessed. "Clarissa dropped her off this morning, and Reba will pick her up this evening."

While Loretta sounded pretty pleased with herself for the watch she and her friends organized, Simon knew there was no surefire plan against a suicidal mind. Loretta's plan was tenuous at best, he brooded, rubbing his chin.

"Loretta, I beg you," he beseeched her, talking with the hand not gripping the receiver. "Please get this friend of yours some professional help. Right now. Today. I've already volunteered to help you find—"

She cut him off. "With all the media reports and legal battles charging psychiatrists with creating false memories in their clients' minds, there's no one you could recommend that even

I would not be wary of. Even if we could get an appointment this time of year," she added with emphasis.

He dropped to the side of the bed and looked out onto his balcony, where a mild, wintry wind shimmied the leaves of his dying yellow-leafed plant. His gaze rose absently over the rooftops of the homes on the next street. Higher up, a blur of sun and its companion white clouds shifting in the sky seemed undecided about staying.

Simon wondered if Loretta really understood what she was dealing with. Her friend could snap at any moment; some little incident at work could do it. The demons would seize control and Loretta's friend could become history in the blink of an eye.

"I know you, Simon," Loretta said, breaking into his quiet reflection. "I trust you."

Simon bit off a curse. Leave it up to Loretta to go straight for his Achilles' heel. He felt himself capitulating, but he had to try one more time to reason with her.

"Loretta," he said, "please understand the seriousness of your friend's illness. You may not understand the reasons behind it, but it's a certainty that if she decides to kill herself, there's nothing you or anybody else can do to stop her. It is *extremely important* to get her some professional help *as soon as possible.*" He couldn't stress it enough, he thought.

"What is it about *she won't go* that you don't understand?" Loretta retorted sarcastically.

"Damn it, Loretta," he snapped back. "If you haven't been able to get her to check herself into a hospital, or even think about going to a doctor, the media hype notwithstanding, then what makes you so sure she'll talk to me?"

"I've thought of that, too."

I should have known, Simon sighed, shaking his head. He dropped to the side of the bed, crossed his legs, and waited.

"What do you know about Kwanzaa?" Loretta asked.

* * *

Michelle Craig moved through the gray fog of her existence, confident that her front was in place. No one would have ever guessed she wished they would all disappear and leave her alone. It explained why, when she got out of the cab at the back of the downtown Houston office building, she ducked into the service entrance, avoiding the festive atmosphere and Christmas decorations exhibited in the front lobby.

It was almost four in the afternoon. She had done the unusual and taken a three-hour lunch. In another hour and a half, Reba would be picking her up from work.

She passed the parking attendant sitting in a glass booth and headed for the stair entrance to begin the climb up to the sixth floor. Low-wattage bulbs lit the hard cement stairwell that seemed like a refrigerator set at sixty degrees. She was alone, and that was all that mattered to Michelle.

But she wasn't truly alone. The phantom of despair walked with her, exploding flashes of memories with bad feelings she couldn't stop from coming.

She had visited Joanna today—something she hadn't done in twenty years. She had not even thought about her mother in a long time. At least, she had not been consciously aware of doing so. Apparently, the sense of her mother had been there nevertheless, in the back of her mind, growing inside her, stealing the oxygen that flowed through her blood until she was imprisoned by lethargy.

She had gone to the cemetery in search of answers, understanding, and even release from her strained emotions. But only silence had risen from the ground beneath the weathered headstone. The same non-sound echoed from the adjacent graves holding Nora and Walter, her grandparents, in the area belonging to the Craig family plot.

She knew her grandparents had never expected to precede their child in death. Like them, she believed she would go to her grave wondering why, too. She left the cemetery feeling more empty than when she had arrived.

The climb up the steps of the office building pulled at her, but she was no more tired and strained than her normal listless disposition of late. Reaching the sixth floor as indicated by the number over the door, she pushed it open and stepped onto the dark gray carpet lining the corridor. The hallway was empty; workers were sequestered in their offices, watching the clock for the end of the workday. Michelle headed for her office on the other side of the double glass doors to do the same.

From the distance, she spotted Bob Matthew, VP of Marketing and Development, to whom she reported directly as the Director of Research. He was standing outside his office door, talking to the receptionist, who was sitting behind the center desk wearing a headphone. She pushed through the doors, entering the tastefully decorated lobby.

"There you are," Bob said.

"Yes," Michelle replied. She noted he appeared agitated. In her indifferent mind, she shrugged unconcernedly.

"Ms. Craig," the secretary intervened, "Ms. Rebecca Hawkins called several times for you. And the nurse from Dr. Clarissa Davis's office called, as did your attorney. They all want you to call them as soon as possible."

Michelle simply nodded.

"May I see you in my office, Michelle?" Bob asked.

"Sure, Bob." She noted the slight quirk of his brow. In the two-and-a half years she'd worked under him, she had never called him anything but Mr. Matthew. She was not surprised that he seemed to be. Nor did she care as she preceded him into the spacious room in browns and blues, with a view of downtown Houston. A gray mass of clouds brewed over the city skies. She felt related to them.

Removing her pale violet, all-weather coat, she thought about her strictly business relationship with Bob. She knew he was forty-four and divorced, with teenage twin girls. He hailed from

Virginia and had marketing and business degrees from Colorado State University. She doubted he knew that much about her.

"Please have a seat," Bob invited, indicating the plush, soft leather chair with armrests adjacent to the couch and coffee table.

Although navy in color, it was typically the hot seat. She had seen him chew out many of his underlings upon directing them to this chair. Draping her coat across her lap, she sat undaunted, uncaring.

"Michelle ..." Running his fingers through his graying dark hair, Bob stopped as if hesitant about continuing. Abruptly, he crossed to his massive cedar desk to get something, then returned to her, clutching a sheet of paper in his pale fist. He held it out, asking, "Michelle, what's the meaning of this?"

Before she could think to reply, he dropped onto the end of the couch closest to her and proceeded to grill her, with confusion and concern alight in his sharp blue eyes.

"Has something happened to make you unhappy here? Has the workload become unbearable? Do you need more staff in your division? What is it? Why are you quitting?"

Although she didn't show it, Michelle was surprised that her resignation had generated this level of concern. She never believed she would be called upon to answer more than she had stated in the letter. She swallowed.

"I need to ... uh ..." she stammered in reply nervously. Unable to return his intense gaze, she lowered her eyes. She felt put on the spot. Bob was forcing her to respond to more than his simple question, but to consider why she had written a notice and to defend her action.

Fashioning her reply, Michelle drew a deep breath. "I need to make some changes in my life, Bob," she said with deliberate calm. She was uncertain about the exact changes she would make, and that was a little scary. "I need time to do that. With the German expansion in the works, you need someone else to do the research. Right now, I'm just not able to do it," she said, mindful that she had not been able to concentrate on work. Additionally, she thought, she no longer even cared about it.

"Is there a problem at home?"

Besides a greeting or "How are you today?"—to which an honest answer was not expected anyway—Bob had never asked her anything of a personal nature. Michelle didn't know what to say to him.

"Look," he said as she sat in silent contemplation about her feelings. "I've checked with personnel. We owe you three weeks of vacation, and you've never taken a sick day. Why don't you take that time and get done whatever you need to. You've already made the reassignments to your staff. We've gotten the bulk of the work done. I don't expect we'll be able to do much more before next year anyway. Hell, take whatever time you need to do what you have to, and we'll see you back here come January. And I'll simply tear this up," he added, crushing her letter of resignation in his hand.

Feeling a spasmodic tremble cut across her chest, Michelle was clearly taken aback by his action. Even more unsettling was that she had thought every capacity to feel was no longer in her.

He knew diddly-squat about Kwanzaa, Simon thought, several hours after talking with Loretta. What he knew about suicide scared him senseless for Michelle Craig's life.

He was sitting in the brown swivel chair in his state-of-the-art home communications office. He was a slow, but thorough, typist who transferred his handwritten notes onto the profile form on his computer screen.

His knowledge about people suffering from what he called over-the-edge symptoms was not unusual. Observing behavior was a major part of his job. As a sports psychologist, he largely helped athletes enhance their performance through psychological principles. In that capacity, he'd seen athletes exhibit behavior that would shock some of their fans. Although he didn't currently have anyone who was suicidal, he'd witnessed a number of black male athletes who were slowly killing themselves in other ways.

While black women had the lowest rate of suicides in America, it was not uncommon for them to take their lives. And for every one that was successful, it was certain that another sister tried to, or at least thought about, committing suicide.

He recalled the sensational suicides of three very successful black women: singer Phyllis Hyman, writer Terri Jewell, and journalist Leanita McClain. He remembered feeling personally affected by Phyllis Hyman's death. He had seen her perform on several occasions, and she was one of his favorite female artists.

None of their deaths made sense. Not even to those who knew them. But that was the nature of the beast, Simon thought resignedly. Depression was a disorder that ruined lives, and if the individual suffering this illness didn't get treatment, the damage would never stop.

His attention wholly on the screen, his fingers on the keyboard, he now knew that Michelle only drank socially, which was a plus in her favor. Alcohol was a factor in thirty percent of all suicides.

However, he was still bothered by the fact that she had gone out and purchased a gun. Firearms had become the fastest-growing method of suicide. In fact, guns were used more in suicides than homicides these days. Even though Loretta and her friends had confiscated the gun, it spoke to the depths of Michelle's desperation.

She didn't have a drug addiction, nor was she suffering from some terminal disease. He was also able to cross off emotional trauma brought on from an assault or rape, aging, divorce, and financial problems—all of which were causes of depression.

As for duration, Michelle had definitely been depressed for a week that Loretta knew of. "She's been tired and stressed out, but who isn't these days?" he recalled Loretta saying.

Exhaustion and burnout were symptoms, but he suspected Michelle had been suffering more symptoms and for far longer than her friends knew. It was highly possible that she had been feeling depressed and didn't even know it.

Loretta didn't know whether Michelle had ever been diagnosed as clinically depressed, he recalled. But Michelle had ballooned up to a hundred thirty pounds two years ago. ''Now she looks like a waif,'' Loretta had said.

Even though they'd been friends for about three years now, Loretta was not aware of whether there was a history of suicide in Michelle's family. As incredible as it seemed, depression can come from no obviously discernible place, or it can be inherited. The closest family Michelle had was an uncle who lived outside of Austin, Texas. The uncle, a three-time divorcé, was her mother's oldest brother, but they weren't close.

Simon sat back in his chair, staring at the screen, wondering how her mother had died. Other than knowing that Michelle's mother had been dead for quite some time, Loretta didn't know the answer to that either. His fingers returning to the keys to type, he put a question mark under the heading of family problems.

''What about man troubles?'' he had inquired. The response led him to insert ''no significant other'' onto the form. According to Loretta, Michelle had not brought a man to any of their functions in over two years.

Not necessarily uncommon, but Simon wondered why. He chuckled, recalling Loretta's reply—''She has more than a pleasing personality''—as if he might have reneged on her plan.

With his mind in double-think, Simon knew the holidays posed a particularly hard time for those struggling with private demons. Maybe for this holiday, the tables could be turned for this woman.

Mulling Loretta's idea that he join them to help plan their Kwanzaa celebration wasn't a wholly insane plan. Besides, he reminded himself, he was not going to counsel Michelle about her problem in particular, but rather, try to convince her to seek psychological help.

His elbows on the desk and his hands steepled under his chin, he knew he would have to figure out the best way to approach Michelle when they met tonight at Loretta's.

But first, Simon thought, clapping his hands together, he had to bone up on Kwanzaa.

Chapter Two

The day's clouds never fulfilled their threat of rain, and since daylight saving time was not in effect, it was dark before six. With so many eager-to-get-home drivers on the road, headlights stretched forever on the freeway in bumper-to-bumper evening traffic. Michelle was stuck in it with Reba at the wheel.

Reba, short for Rebecca, was the shortest of the friends at five foot one inch, with a compact build to carry her bundle of energy. From a family of educators, she had a doctorate in the field, but it was stuck in a philosophy book on her bookshelf. A genius with graphic design, and self-taught on the computer, she was the proud owner of Creative Arts Ink. Her business account was average, but her reputation for producing sterling work was growing.

"I want to go home," Michelle said in a low, determined voice.

She had thought of little else since talking with Bob, whose generosity she still hadn't managed to get over. He had reached out to her, and she wondered if she had missed other such opportunities to develop a more amiable working relationship.

She never felt she owed her employer anything more than a quality performance, but it had left her void of potential allies or enemies. In the end, she only knew that her work ceased to be satisfying.

"No way," Reba replied. "Not after the scare you gave us today."

Yes, Michelle mused wearily, recalling Reba's troublesome calls every forty minutes. Clarissa and Loretta had made annoyances of themselves as well. If that were not enough, Michelle had put up with Loretta's gentle morning knocks on the door of her guest bedroom all week long.

While she had tried to be grateful that someone cared whether she lived or not, Michelle thought, it took an energy she didn't have. She knew she couldn't go on this way. Nor could she return to Loretta's home to be watched.

Reba shot the Explorer around a truck that was moving too slow for her and darted back into the lane ahead of three other vehicles only to have to slam on the brakes.

"Loretta would kill me if I took you home and you did something stupid. Oops!" she covered her mouth with her hand. "Sorry."

"Don't be," Michelle replied. "It doesn't matter," she said, holding back the tears stinging her eyes. But it did, and in part, it was another reason why she wanted to be alone.

With growing frequency, she had become supersensitive, thereby increasing her fear of making a complete and utter fool of herself by bursting into tears over the slightest little remark one of her friends might make. How could she explain that it hurt being with them, listening to them talk, since the entire time she felt that she didn't belong? She just knew she could never make them understand.

Traffic inched forward, and Reba gassed up so close behind the car ahead of them that they were practically backseat passengers in a white Honda. It could have been a rear-end accident, but Michelle didn't flinch, for she was still mulling why.

For as long as she could remember, she had been assaulted

by a blue funk that came around Thanksgiving. Normally, she was able to shake it off within a few days by immersing herself in activities or the company of others. None of those tricks had worked this time. She didn't have the energy or inclination to do anything or be around anyone, and the morbid feelings persisted.

It was never anything in particular that sent her spirits crashing, but rather a series of annoying little things that grew until they became one endogenous mess. She found fault with everything, from world affairs to the potholes in the streets.

In an attempt to fight back, she had counted all of her good fortune—a roof over her head, an excellent-paying job, and good health—she had to be grateful for. Each was discarded as handily as she rejected taking pills, poison, or jumping off the ledge to end her emotional and spiritual malady. As a result, the gratitude she had tried to force on her so-called blessings wouldn't come. Instead, dissatisfaction with her life grew.

Michelle made sure her throat was clear, her voice devoid of emotion, before she asked, "What if I promise not to do something stupid?"

"Hmm," Reba replied, pondering.

In the silence of Reba's thoughts, Michelle recalled overhearing her grandmother say, *"Joanna did a very stupid and selfish thing."* The whole family was mad at her mother, and she had sided with them. Now, she wished she could take it all back— her anger and disappointment. There was only one way to apologize to her mother now, she reflected.

"Let me see your hands."

Surely she hadn't heard correctly, Michelle thought. She turned a quizzical stare at Reba's profile. "What?"

"Your hands. Let me see them," Reba insisted, glancing across the seat at her. "I want to make sure your fingers aren't crossed."

Michelle couldn't help herself. She burst out laughing. "Do you realize how utterly foolish you sound?"

"Do you?" Reba shot back, taking advantage of a break in traffic.

Michelle only heard the sound of laughter ringing in her ears. It seemed strange and unfamiliar. But it was her voice. *Maybe,* she thought speculatively, swallowing.

"Hands."

Reba's command snapped Michelle from finishing the thought, but she recalled it later in the bedroom of her home. She paused in the middle of taking off her clothes to shake her head, amazed with the memory.

It had seemed ages since she laughed—even in derision or mockery—or expressed any sort of happy emotions. It had felt good, she thought, a wee smile breaking through the perpetual melancholy that marred her face. Maybe it was the start of getting over whatever had been troubling her.

She sighed, thinking it just wasn't long enough, as she pulled the gold ribbed-neck sweater over her head. Particularly as it became clear that Reba's retort was directed at her dejected attitude. She knew her friends found her behavior reprehensible. They wanted reasons, causes wrapped in a neat little package with a bow on top to account for actions.

Even if she could explain it, they wouldn't understand, she thought, letting her pleated gray skirt fall.

In the end, she had to *cross her heart and hope to die if she did anything stupid* before Reba would deliver her home, she recalled, feeling the onslaught of another wave of sadness. And even then, her request was not granted until after Reba had a conference call on the car phone with Loretta and Clarissa.

Recalling she had become an object and not a participant in the conversation, Michelle wanted to forget the rest as she stripped down to her undergarments. The memory persisted regardless her wish on the matter as she hung up her clothes in the closet.

Before the call ended, she was notified that the meeting that was to have occurred December eighteenth was rescheduled for tonight. Though no one had to remind her why that meeting had not been held then, she felt censured.

There had been a change as well. The meeting would now be held at her house. She didn't buy Loretta's reason about sudden plumbing problems. The toilets had worked fine the past several days.

She could have refused, but the opportunity to come home would have been denied her, she reminded herself while rifling through her bureau for something to wear. Even though she had found no refuge in sleeping at night and waking had become a chore in the mornings, she looked forward to trying either one in her own home.

Still, she felt tricked into accepting the change. If the truth be known, she was no longer interested in celebrating Kwanzaa with her girlfriends. Although each had participated in one of the Kwanzaa ceremonies held throughout the Houston community in the past, this year would be the first they celebrated together.

But it was too late to back out now. She had less than an hour to prepare.

Michelle snatched a pair of old jeans and an even older sweatshirt, then headed to the bathroom to dress. There, she looked at herself in the mirror, studying her reflection as if for the first time.

She had been told she possessed a face of fine distinction. Her dark brown coloring spread evenly over her high forehead, and she had a small nose and a pointed chin. The only distinction now showed a ragged soul in lifeless eyes, a sad clown's look in the haggard lines around her mouth.

Discouraged, Michelle blew out her cheeks. She realized that if she looked like this her friends would really have something to worry about. They would be all over her with their concern, and she would never get any peace from them.

* * *

"Well, Rudolph, what do you think?"

Rudolph was the name Simon had given his anthropomorphic lamp that stood precariously in the narrow entryway of his home. With arms and legs of flexible aluminum, a square head like a flash attachment on a camera, and reflector bulbs for hands, it was so named because at the foot of an upturned leg was a red, cone-shaped bulb that looked like a nose.

Rudolph was a year-old resident in his recently remodeled duplex in the heart of the Third Ward, not far from where his late mother had raised three sons in the Cuney Homes Projects. He'd hired an interior decorator whose good taste, it turned out, showed only in the dark hardwood floors that ran throughout his home. He was grateful to have returned from a trip in time to stop the installation of a wall of galvanized metal in his foyer, he recalled. He had kept the green marble lamp table though; it was a nice, functional touch against the soft-white textured walls.

The mirror reflected strains to a handsome champagne brown face, a robust nature. As Simon sighed at length, his broad shoulders rose and fell under a worsted wool gray sports coat. Allegedly, he'd stopped to double-check his appearance.

In reality, Simon knew he was stalling.

Loretta had called back to inform him of the meeting time: 7:30. A slight flick of the silver-chained Rolex on his wrist showed it was 7:12. He patted his chest above his heart to make sure he had the address inside his coat pocket.

Unfortunately, he mused, Loretta had more to say. It was what had brought about his present discomfort, mixed with a tad of irritation. If he were going to go through with her plan, he told himself, he'd better straighten out his attitude and lose the long face.

"*Please* don't tell her what you do." Loretta's begging plea rang in his ears.

He had agreed to try to talk Michelle into counseling, but Loretta wanted more. He didn't appreciate being put on the spot, although he understood why she felt the need for deceit.

They'd debated the difference between lying and withholding the truth for a worthless fifteen minutes.

In the name of Kwanzaa, he'd agreed to show up and pretend to be a blind date. Although he was hard-pressed to see a relationship between any of the seven principles he'd read about to what he consented to do, Simon practiced his smiles in the mirror.

Of course, he would be the first to agree that smiling was the easy part. Suppressing his purpose was going to be difficult for sure, but not as much as pretending to be interested in Michelle Craig. It had nothing to do with her.

He had lived a celibate life for so long that he was out of practice. None of his former friends would believe it, for when he played football, from high school through a year of pro ball, he had chased women as if they would all disappear tomorrow.

Penelope Franklin had changed all that for him. She had destroyed his then new career as a psychiatrist three years ago, depleting his savings in the process of defending himself against her false allegation.

Since he'd been legally and professionally exonerated, he had relearned to respect women because of the example that had been set by his mother. But he didn't want a woman in his life since he had proven to himself he could do without one.

Maybe, he thought with a shrug of his shoulders, sometime in the future, he would reconsider and find a steady companion. But now was not the time. He was busy regaining lost income and building up his freelance practice. The next step on his five-year plan was to secure a college teaching position, thereby increasing his credibility.

With a toothpaste smile on his face, Simon squared his shoulders grittily. And no woman, particularly a suicidal one, he thought, was going to get in the way of his plans.

Chapter Three

Hands patted cheeks in the reflection that revealed the potential, if not the full measure, of a formerly feisty-natured woman. Standing in the foyer of her home, Michelle surveyed herself in the wall mirror.

A quick facial, eye drops, and lipstick, after all, were not miracles for a tattered spirit. But they helped, she concluded.

She had passed through a cool shower, hoping the chill bumps would add a healthy sheen to her skin. A dab of perfume here and there finalized her dress, which included an old outfit, with emphasis on the fit.

Michelle was tired from the effort of preparing for a pretense. She hoped she had the endurance to pull it off.

If she didn't give them a reason to watch her like a hawk, she reminded herself, then they would leave her alone, granting her wish. Even though Loretta, Reba, and Clarissa were like family to her, she didn't feel close to them, the way she once had.

Lately, she admitted to her reflection, which knew the truth, she hadn't felt a strong affinity for anything. Even now, she had to shake off the invisible cloud of melancholy hovering around her.

There had been no time to do anything more than vacuum the dining room, dust the table, and pop a variety of frozen snacks in the oven. By the time her friends arrived, since they were always late for the meetings, the snacks would be ready to serve.

The phone rang. Michelle wondered which of them was calling with an excuse as she turned to reach for the portable white phone on the hall table adjacent to the darkened living room. She wished she could close that room off because she knew they would notice she didn't have a tree. Kwanzaa didn't preclude celebrating Christmas, as it was not an alternative, nor ever intended to be. She had simply decided it was useless to buy a tree when she had no intention of being here.

Just as she pressed the button to speak, the doorbell rang. "Hello," Michelle said into the mouthpiece, her other hand unlocking the door. "Why aren't you here?" she asked, pulling open the door.

Her mouth was already opened with the question to Loretta on the phone, but it dropped a little more seeing the Samsonian standing on her porch. Her mouth closed on a gulp as she stared upward of six feet and across the breadth of a fifty-inch chest. The mammoth figure was dressed in a long black wool overcoat that fell midway down his legs. She couldn't help but notice that his feet were enormous!

On a quiet gulp, she slid her eyes up to look at a charming smile on a handsome face. Michelle felt a jolt to her equilibrium, and a tremble coursed through her. *It must be nerves,* she decided.

Standing on the porch, Simon blinked. He had an instant's fond memory of his youth when his mama had always seemed able to tell when he was lying because he would blink rapidly. But there was no lie going on in his head now as his eyes shuttered open and shut in quicksilver movement, recording the angelic vision standing inside the doorway.

He felt a momentous pull of attraction, lulling him into a bovine stupor as he took in her exquisite, feminine appeal. Her chestnut hair was shoulder length, with short bangs just above long, finely arched brows. She had the complexion of lightly creamed coffee, with startling almond-shaped eyes, the color of copper, and full lips that were the hue of lightly colored persimmon.

Loretta had been right: Michelle Craig was a little thing. He wouldn't go so far as to call her a waif, even though she was slender and delicate looking in a cream-colored silk jumpsuit that showed off firm, high-perched breasts, tiny waistline, and wide, slim hips.

The night's cool air trapped in his senses the fragrant vanilla scent she wore, and awareness streaked through him like a shooting star. He hadn't even received her invitation to enter and already Simon was reminding himself why he was really here.

He had probably been called Red as a child, was Michelle's very next thought, her heart pounding as she stared wordlessly at him. He had a fair complexion with a crop of short reddish-brown hair. She'd just bet he was always into something by the touch of humor around his generous mouth and warm hazel eyes that were full of life. All that aside, she couldn't get over the enormity of him, a master of the universe.

With Loretta's chatter piercing her ear, Michelle remembered she was on the phone. "What?" she demanded, never once taking her eyes off the stranger, a massive, self-confident presence.

"He's here now," she replied. *And in a big way,* she thought. She could feel the power of his gaze. She was stunned by the intensity of warmth he gave off and disconcerted by the sweet tingle that flowed through her. "Okay," she said, ending the call.

"Michelle Craig, I presume. Hi. I'm Simon Stevenson."

He had a soothing voice, impressive, resonating with patience, which she had just about run out of, Michelle fumed silently. Her friends had gone too far, she thought, wondering which of them had found this giant of a man to entice her with.

"Yes," she replied, but couldn't remember what she was responding to. "Mr. Stevenson?"

"It's Simon."

"Okay," she said, licking her suddenly dry lips. "Simon." A thought was flickering in her brain, like the intermittent blinking of Christmas lights on a cord she couldn't seem to untangle.

"Don't tell me Loretta forgot to tell you I was coming," he said, his mouth awry in a crooked smile, revealing pearly-white teeth.

Charmed, Michelle thought, feeling it. Mentally shaking off the sensation, she clasped onto her ire. "Oh, no, she didn't forget." The cold temperature outside penetrated her clothes and alerted her witless brain. "Come in. Please." The polite addition was an afterthought.

Simon stepped across the threshold, and Michelle closed out the wind and night. After locking the door, she turned to accept his overcoat, which carried the woodsy scent of his cologne. She held it draped over her arm, feeling a strange sense of comfort by the feel and smell it carried as she walked to the hall closet.

"It sounds quiet," Simon noticed. "Is it safe to assume that I'm the first one to arrive?"

"Yes," Michelle replied. Instantaneously, her heart fluttered, thinking, *What if no one else shows up?* She shook the thought from her head, wondering what was wrong with her as she hung up the coat and closed the door to face him. *My goodness!* Her heart thudded and her wits scattered again as her eyes roved over the expanse of him, seeing just how much space he commanded. Imperceptibly, she stepped back.

"Looks like we're going to have the perfect kind of weather for the holidays, instead of a picnic," he said conversationally, brushing his hands together.

Standing fine and firm, he reminded her of the genie in Aladdin's lamp. Michelle shook her head, disconcerted. It didn't matter that Simon Stevenson was easy on the eyes, no doubt well employed, and obviously endowed with class. Her friends had again attempted to impose their wishes onto her. Well, she was having no part of it.

"What I'd like to know is why," Michelle said brusquely.

Simon arched long, thick brows quizzically. "I beg your pardon?"

"Why are you here?" she asked with an edge to her voice.

"I thought you just said Loretta told you that I was coming," Simon replied, gesturing toward the phone in her hand.

"She did, but that doesn't explain why," Michelle countered, miffed, the phone clamped in her hand like a weapon. "Is she trying to fix us up? Let me warn you, Mr. Stevenson, that I'm not interested."

"That's too bad, because based on what I've seen so far, I definitely am. And it's Simon."

He smiled, and the magnitude of it pervaded her miserable soul. Michelle shivered inwardly, spun sharply on her heels, and stormed off disgusted, leaving him to follow or not.

Simon blew the air out of his cheeks slowly. He considered, with a rather dubious expression, that maybe he had come on too strong. He'd gotten his share of second and third looks from women, so he knew he wasn't without some appeal.

Enough of that! He was not here to have his ego massaged or his desire stroked, although Michelle had definitely done that, Simon chided himself. For a moment, he carefully thought about pursuing the enticing Ms. Craig, but decided it wasn't prudent just yet. They both needed time to cool off.

Until then, he decided to spend his time taking in his surroundings. He knew seeing how she lived would reveal a little more about Michelle Craig, whom he was to view as a patient, but not treat like one.

Simon shook his head at the convoluted logic. His feelings were not so easily shaken off. With his mind salivating over her luscious hips and expressing curiosity about her legs, he couldn't get over the thought that he wouldn't have to pretend too hard to be attracted to Ms. Craig.

He peeked into the living room, which, even darkened, looked uncomfortable, with its archaic taste and dark wood Colonial furniture. He believed the outside of her home was far more inviting with its columns and promise of open, airy spaces than it was inside. He also noticed there was no tree and wondered if his observation was significant.

By the process of elimination and placement, the room across the hallway was likely a study. The door was closed. After a quick debate, he moved on. An open staircase leading to the second level of the house was beyond the study and hall closet. He wouldn't let himself think about sneaking upstairs, but instead, traipsed down the hallway, hoping he was going in the right direction.

"Wherever that may be," he mumbled softly. He was referring to both the predicament he'd put himself in and Michelle's destination.

A flower-print rug with big faded red roses and green leaves lay atop a tightly woven, well-worn beige carpet. Dingy squares along the green walls revealed photographs had been removed, creating a distinctive absence. He was curious, wondering what pictures had been taken down and why.

He came upon another door that was slightly ajar. He looked in and felt along the wall for a light switch. The room was a bathroom with an independent face bowl, toilet, and shower behind a sliding door. Done in green and white, it was clean and organized, with fresh hand towels and soap. Uninspiring.

What he'd seen so far seemed a contradiction to the spicy temperament he'd sensed just beneath the surface of the home owner's chilly facade. He wondered why Loretta had not introduced him to Michelle before now. *Quite possibly because you weren't ready for an intimate relationship,* he answered.

With a soft, raspy sound in his throat, Simon reminded himself that he still wasn't. And it wouldn't have mattered even if he were: Michelle had let her disinterest be known quite succinctly.

While he could forgo the challenge to his male pride, the question about his professional ethics to participate in such a duplicitous scheme again reared its ugly head.

With the indirect reminder of his role, he thought it was too soon to start drawing conclusions. He needed to see more of who Michelle was. If she let him get that close.

As he sighed skeptically, another intriguing thought seized him. If he hadn't been so enchanted by her loveliness, he would have realized it sooner. People who were extremely despondent usually didn't give a damn about how they looked. While Michelle certainly wasn't overdressed, he reflected, the fact that she had dressed with care for her appearance was a contradiction. He wondered what to make of it.

Flipping off the light, he backed from the room.

"Did you get lost?"

Startled, Simon froze for a fraction of a second. When he faced Michelle, or rather looked down into her annoyed expression, her eyes narrowed and her brows knitted in a frown, his toothpaste smile was in place. And thank goodness, he thought, for the woman aroused a distress of a different nature inside him.

"In a manner of speaking," he replied, staring into her remarkable eyes, "yes."

* * *

"Well, that wasn't a very bright thing to do. Why would you throw out everything only to have to start all over again?"

"Because Kwanzaa is a celebration of rebirth. There should be something different and unique every year we celebrate it."

"That's exactly my point about the expo. It's different!"

What was supposed to have been a meeting about their personal celebration of Kwanzaa had evolved into a heated discussion on the commercialization of a unique holiday that focused on the traditional African values of family, community, commerce, and self-improvement. They had been at it for nearly an hour. Michelle had long since lost the will to participate. Her energy was waning. All she wanted them to do now was go home.

After Simon's arrival, they came two by two until all of her friends and their mates were accounted for. Except for her and Simon, who were opposite each other, the rest sat around the rectangular table. They looked like the loving couples they weren't with one exception, Michelle thought sarcastically. She knew she wasn't being fair, but the sentiment was proof of her ebbing tolerance for their presence.

When she tried to pretend interest in the proceedings, her attention inevitably gravitated to Simon. He was an impossible presence to miss! Not only because he dwarfed everyone else, but rather because of the natural virility he exuded. It seemed a tangible thing that slid across the table, over the now empty platters of finger foods and cookies to land on her. She had already squirmed so much, she'd tired herself out, trying to ignore him.

And if she didn't know better, she would swear he'd been gobbling her with his eyes when she wasn't looking. She didn't want to be turned on by him, for it merely created an emotion that added to her fatigue.

First to arrive had been Clarissa Davis and her husband Vince, whom she didn't much care for, Michelle thought, directing her gaze to the couple. A telephone company executive, Vince was a whiner. Tonight, he seemed more friendly than he'd ever been before. She wondered what Clarissa had said about her to him.

Sure enough, Reba brought Alan Houston, whom she'd been dating since September. While some women complained of finding a man, berry-brown complected Reba didn't seem to have that problem. Alan was an accountant, and he looked as if matters of business occupied his mind all the time.

Then there was Loretta. She sat next to her husband Edmund, occupying the whole opposite side of the table together. The shrewd, quirky lawyers proved that a business and personal relationship could work. Ed, ten years older than his wife, was licensed to practice in federal courts, as well as in several other states. Loretta held their criminal law practice fort down in Houston.

She had met Loretta, who'd introduced her to Clarissa, five years ago while working on a Save The Children task force at Shape Community Center. Reba joined a year later, volunteering to design and oversee the printing for the group. That association evolved into a friendship in which they felt a responsibility for each other.

Their sense of responsibility had become meddlesome, she thought. Particularly each time she glanced across the table to eye Simon. She seemed to have no power to control the warm blush that streaked through her every time her gaze met his. She would have been better off if they'd brought her a puppy, for nothing could drive a woman over the edge quicker than a man. Joanne had learned that the hard way. She'd better remember it.

"I think we should join in with the National Kwanzaa Holiday Expo. I've been reading about the success it's enjoyed. More than fifty thousand people participated last year," Alan said.

The friends had bets on how long he would last after the holidays. He was a divorcé, with an eight-year-old, and she suspected Alan would just barely make it to New Year's.

"It would be great to have that kind of attendance, but this particular expo allows major white corporations to promote their products," Clarissa said.

Clarissa, a pediatrician, was the tallest of the foursome and the most tactful. She stood five five, with a light-skinned complexion, a straight figure, and long, dark hair worn in a French braid down her back. An only child, she wanted a houseful of children. That her husband Vince wasn't ready had become a source of contention in their home.

"What's wrong with that?" Vince wanted to know.

Reba shot back, "Kwanzaa should not be for sale."

"Somebody has to make some money. This is a capitalist society. What do you expect?" Vince grumbled.

"I don't expect the company that makes Kool-Aid to tell me how to mix a so-called Kwanzaa punch."

That was Loretta, a born lawyer. She enjoyed a good fight that didn't require physical exertion beyond outthinking and outtalking her opponent. A half inch separated Loretta and Michelle in height: It had been the cause of many playful arguments, as well as the start of their friendship when volunteers for a children's organization stood for pictures. Loretta was five foot three, while the status of being half an inch taller belonged to her. Loretta and her husband of six years, Edmund, wanted children, but so far, it hadn't happened.

"You don't see the Jewish people selling out Hanukkah. They don't care if mainstream America doesn't celebrate their holiday. They just want people to respect their culture."

"But Kwanzaa is not a religious holiday, and Hanukkah is," Alan quipped.

"No, it's not," Loretta replied. "But Kwanzaa was designed to reaffirm us, our ancestors, and our culture. We don't need to have it legitimized by white people. Now if we don't preserve the sanctity and integrity for which Kwanzaa was founded, then we're at fault."

"Corporate participation does not mean we're seeking legitimization," Ed chimed in reasonably. "But you must admit, it

does spur the interest for more African-Americans to participate. I know a lot of people who don't celebrate Kwanzaa
because they fear it's some kind of radical militant movement
or some strange religious cult.''

Michelle's spirits were sinking just thinking about her
friends. Unlike her, she thought, they had mates or companions
and lives beyond the sphere of their group. Feeling self-pity
slipping into her mind, she clasped her hands together under
the table in her lap so no one would see just how hard she was
struggling to hang on.

Before the meeting got into full swing, Michelle hadn't sat
still for a minute, Simon recalled curiously. It was as if she
was looking for excuses to leave the room. Though some of
the reasons were legitimate, she had eschewed offers of help
to do unnecessary minor tasks. But now that the platter of
snacks was empty and their drinks watery, she made no move
to replenish them.

He had been watching her slowly deteriorate emotionally
over the last forty-five minutes. She lent nothing to the table
but her physical presence. Which was more than enough if
this curious surge of sensation tugging at his innards was any
indication.

His mind back on task, he reflected on Michelle's behavior.
It was as if having prepared the agenda, her role was over.
There was a neutral look on her smooth brown face; she sat
primly in her seat, her hands in her lap under the table.

There was a gentle beauty about her, a character of strength
even in her placid facade, although the picture was at odds
with what he knew about her inner turmoil. He wondered what
she was thinking, whether she was really with them.

If only he could get her to look at him again, give him
another chance to read her, Simon thought. He saw the one or
two indications of life in the jewel of her eyes, but he had been
agonizing over his unprofessional feelings; hence he'd missed

her messages. Now she seemed determined to ignore him as steadfastly as her disinterest in the discussion.

"We've been carrying on and forgot all about our guest," Loretta said, a wee smile of embarrassment on her face. "Simon, we haven't heard your thoughts. What do you think?"

All eyes turned to Simon, even Michelle's. Albeit unaware of staring, she watched as Simon contemplated his reply. His expression serious, his amber eyes shone with brilliant intelligence. A thistle of excitement poked through her emotional retreat, and her pulse perked up.

"Since I've never celebrated Kwanzaa before," Simon said, "I believe I would prefer a small, intimate celebration among friends."

Though he addressed the group, Michelle felt as if he'd singled her out with his gaze. It was as if he were trying to draw a response from her. She felt stunned and light-headed, and inexplicably, a flicker of apprehension coursed through her. With her dark eyebrows slanted in a frown, she felt too exhausted to wage battle with her warring emotions. Her whole body seemed to sag in the chair.

Simon knew these people took their Kwanzaa seriously, but not to the extent of the philosophical debate they had embarked upon. While there was merit in the discussion, what he witnessed had been orchestrated by Loretta and Ed from start to finish. He suspected they banked on the others taking the positions they had in order to achieve a goal. What he couldn't figure was whether they had also counted on getting Michelle involved in their provocative exchange.

All but Vince and Alan seemed to consider his preference, he recalled. He had mistakenly believed he would have gotten unanimous support. Regardless, Michelle looked as if she didn't care. About anything.

"I just think Simon would get a better reference, but I'll go along with a small affair," Vince conceded finally.

Alan shrugged. "Make it a full-house vote. Now that we got that out of the way, what's the plan?"

The question provoked another round of discussion into the specifics. Through it all, Michelle remained stoic, Simon noticed, his lips folded in contemplation. He was desperately trying to think of a way to draw Michelle into the conversation. Loretta beat him to it.

"Hey, look," she said, speaking loud to be heard over the melee of the other voices. "Since we can't agree, I have a suggestion."

All eyes gravitated to Loretta, except Michelle's, Simon noted from a sidelong look. He suspected he had his answer about her presence, and it shored up what he had initially failed to consider: The jovial disposition she exhibited earlier, although tart tainted toward him, had been a pretense.

"Let's just appoint Michelle to plan the whole thing."

Simon observed the group's thoughtful expressions, followed by nods, then the planned verbal consents. Michelle, however, looked as if she hadn't heard her name spoken or her energies volunteered to plan the entire seven-day celebration. He felt the sting of defeat and his concern grew.

"Michelle," Simon said. "Michelle?" He had to call her again before she gave him her attention. "Michelle, how do you feel about that?"

"Feel about what?"

There wasn't even a specter of curiosity on her face, Simon noted, wondering what it was going to take to bring her around.

"Girlfriend," Reba said, folding her arms on the table, "where have you been?"

A hint of disgust darted across Michelle's face. It was so transitory, he would have missed it, Simon thought, for she quickly adopted a well-controlled, placid facade again. She seemed to have perfected that look, he thought, with anxiety writhing in his stomach.

"We've decided to let you handle Kwanzaa," Clarissa said gently.

Simon approved of her tone and her tact, but he held his breath. Not even he could predict Michelle's reaction.

"I believe we all trust your judgment to make our first-time celebration together a memorable one," Ed chimed in.

Vince added hastily, "And since we're turning it over to you, don't worry about money. We'll take care of that."

As if suddenly aware or interested in the conversation, Michelle said suspiciously, "You're turning what over to me?"

"Kwanzaa," Alan said. "Plan all seven days."

An extreme quiet settled momentarily around the table. They sat tensely, waiting.

"Okay," Michelle replied, shrugging indifferently.

Simon heard warning bells go off inside his head. While he wasn't sure what to make of her easy acceptance, he feared it wasn't good. "I volunteer to help you. When would you like to get started?"

Michelle seemed to think a moment before she spoke. "Why don't we start fresh, first thing Monday morning? I need to clean house this weekend."

Simon didn't like it. With uneasiness tightening his stomach, he calculated that Monday was three days away. He believed Michelle had no intention of planning anything—other than her suicide.

"Now that that's settled," Michelle said with a gaiety she hadn't expressed all night, "why don't you all say good night? I'm exhausted. It's been a long day."

Simon tried to send a message to Loretta behind the pleasant look hurting his face. She wouldn't look his way. He had to do something.

"Kicking us out?" he asked after an agony of indecision. "I don't believe it," he said, his voice rising in surprise. "Those cheese snacks were nice, but I'm starving." Looking at his watch, he said, "It's only eight fifty-two. Why don't we run out to get a bite to eat?"

"That's a good idea," Loretta said, catching on. To Michelle, she added, "I bet you forgot to eat a good meal today. Go grab your coat, and we'll all run out for dinner."

Michelle stood abruptly. She stared crossly from Loretta to Simon, where her gaze fastened, smoldering with defiance. "I'm not hungry." She spoke in the tone of a mechanical doll. "Why don't you all go out and get something? I'll be fine."

Her teeth were gritted as she declared herself fit enough to be alone before bolting from the room.

That's doubtful, Simon thought, but kept the impulsive diagnosis to himself.

Nervous uneasiness was tangible around the table. Simon felt it keenly in the gazes trained on him. Six pairs of eyes begged him to do something.

Chapter Four

Compelled to act, Simon got to his feet wordlessly. His expression was locked in a contemplative frown, but he didn't have a plan. On this, he would have to trust his instincts, he told himself. As he walked out, he heard a soft collective sigh of relief echo around the table.

She knew Reba didn't mean anything by it, Michelle told herself, standing over the sink in her kitchen. But as soon as the reproachful tone struck her conscious, she felt the swelling sensation that signaled the start of tears. As she sobbed softly into her hands, the tears trickled down her cheeks unchecked.

Simon assumed she had headed for the kitchen and followed that path. Long before he saw her, he heard Michelle losing a battle with muffling her cries. He now knew for certain she had been pretending all evening, and the energy that had taken her had simply run out.

That harmless rejoinder had brought a rush of bitter remembrance. She heard her grandmother's voice in Reba's tone. Joanne could do no right, and although grandmother had wished upon her, "I hope you don't turn out like your mama," she was very much like Joanne, Michelle thought.

"Michelle."

Everything moved quickly inside her and out upon hearing Simon call her name. She shuddered, wiped away the evidence of her misery with her hands, and wondered what he wanted now.

Like the aggressive defensive end he used to be, Simon wanted to run to her, console her, hold her in his arms. Instead of charging forward, he stepped back to delay his entrance, knowing she would not appreciate him seeing her cry. He knew he had to get his aggression under control, and he just wasn't thinking about the sense of protection she awakened in him.

Starting over, he measured his pace to a crawl as he headed for the kitchen. "Michelle?"

She couldn't answer. The tears had formed a lump that clogged her throat, so she quickly got a glass from the cabinet and began to fill it under the faucet. No sooner had she drunk her first sip than she felt his presence in the room. He seemed bigger than he actually was, exuding a heat hotter than a July sun. A dulcet warmth curled alongside the cold blood coursing through her veins.

The atmosphere was thick with sorrow. Simon could feel it, see it in the profile of her morose musings. An aura of vulnerability weighted her delicate shoulders, pulling her down. His compassion rose and joined the stream of longing he couldn't stop from flowing ever since he'd laid eyes on her.

"I need a paper towel. I spilled my drink on the table," he explained.

"They're right there," she said with a nod of her head toward the towel rack attached to the wall at the end of the counter nearest him. She poured the water from the glass into the sink just to have something to do; then she set the glass top down on the counter.

Giving him her back, she wished he would leave. She knew he was still there, sensed he hadn't moved. If he said anything to her, she knew she would burst into tears. God! She wished he would leave and take the others with him.

Simon wished with all his heart that he could lift the crater of despair from her heart. He would like to be the one to fill that empty spot he suspected was there. Where the hell was that star? He took an awkwardly controlled step and realized afterward his direction.

Michelle sensed him coming toward her. She feared what would happen if he touched her, yet inexplicably, yearned for, wanted the contact.

"Please," she said, gripping the edge of the sink.

"Let me help you." Every muscle inside him was racing toward Michelle as he watched helplessly. It seemed she remained in an attitude of frozen stillness forever before a lachrymose sigh escaped her lips. She gulped, struggling to contain her composure. "Michelle, let me—"

"If you want to help," she said tightly, in a near whisper, "leave and take them with you." She flashed him a sidelong look. "I told you I was tired."

The slight tremble of her full lips before she folded them into her mouth and the glassy intensity of the tears in her bright copper eyes turned Simon inside out. His hands closed and opened in fists at his sides to restrain himself.

"You're more than tired, Michelle." No longer able to obey her command or his own, Simon touched her smooth, trembling lips with one finger.

Michelle jerked her head from him and held herself rigidly. "Don't . . . don't start," she said, twisting her head from side to side. "I have enough people after me. Just go. Please."

Dropping his hand to his side, Simon weighed her request for a second. From now until Monday seemed like an eternity, and he didn't believe Michelle would last that long. With a decisive expression on his face, Simon left.

Michelle felt something inside her call him back as she watched him go through her blurry gaze. Regret seemed to heighten her despondency, and she caved in to the tears that had been brawling to come out.

"What's wrong with me?" she cried. "Why do I feel like this?"

Clutching her stomach, she crumbled to the yellow-and-white tiled floor in a knot of anguish. She felt unwanted, unloved, and unworthy of either.

That was how Simon found Michelle when he returned. He was carrying two overcoats. Spotting her huddled on the floor next to a cabinet, he dropped both of them and went to her.

Michelle wasn't aware of Simon until he kneeled next to her. She held up a hand to stop him from coming any closer and scooted as far into the wood cabinet as she could go.

"No way."

Simon didn't realize he'd spoken aloud as he pulled her into his arms.

Michelle tried to fight him, but she didn't have the ability or the strength. She acquiesced to his precious power as he held her next to his chest.

"You need a hug, lady," he said, rubbing her back with long, gentle strokes. "We all need a hug every once in a while."

Michelle couldn't even think, she was crying so hard. She barely understood what Simon was saying—something about needing hugs. Something about the feel of his arms around her made it feel true.

Soon, whatever he was saying ceased to matter; she became content just to listen to the sound of his hypnotic voice lulling her into solace. Soothing words, nothing heavy with advice, nor anything she could take personally. With the quilt of gloom lifting, she realized he was telling her a tale. Like a bedtime story she'd longed to hear as a little girl.

"One night I went to the all-night pharmacy to pick up a prescription for a bottle of cough syrup. I was just standing around talking to the pharmacist about nothing when this dancer showed up. She asked the pharmacist what she could take for the rash on her tongue. She even opened her mouth and showed it to him. Ugh!" he said with an exaggerated shudder. "I was thinking to myself, 'You need to take your tongue to a doctor.'"

He noticed Michelle's cries had subsided to sniffles. She was listening to him, so he continued.

"Anyway, the pharmacist asked if she was allergic to anything. And out of the blue, she offered, 'Well, no, not really, and I don't think it's oral sex either. I haven't had it in a long time.'"

"Oh, my goodness," Michelle chortled, amused. She lifted her head to look headlong into his mirth-filled expression. A sudden shyness seized her as she realized how close she was to him and became aware of the gentle fire now growing inside her that took the place of her distress. "You made that up, didn't you?"

"I swear it's the truth," he replied, his eyes lively with the sound of humor in his voice. "Some people just have no shame."

Michelle lowered her gaze. She should have been utterly humiliated; instead, she feared he would see just how comfortable she was in his nearness. "Like me, huh?" She didn't want to move.

"Hey! Hey!" he said, scoffing at her attitude. "It wasn't meant to be personal. Now that you're feeling better, can we get up? I'm getting a cramp in my leg." *The cramp didn't exist in his leg, but it was damn close and rising.* "You're heavy for such a little thing."

"Ha-ha," she said mockingly as she got to her feet.

Simon extended his hand to her. "Help me up," he commanded.

Even though Simon did most of the work getting up, Michelle pulled, unprepared for the contact that sent an electric current shooting up her arm. It joined the fire already in her and flared into a gushing warmth. She wrapped her arms around her as if she were cold.

"You could probably throw me across the room with your baby finger," she said nervously.

"My baby finger knows better than that," he replied, picking up the coats with one hand. "Besides, it's too weak from starvation to do any more than just hang there." He wiggled his baby finger lamely. "Look at it. Doesn't it look hungry to you?"

"You're a nut."

"If I had one of those, I'd eat it. Come on. Let's go to dinner. We can go to Copeland's," he said, his voice rising eagerly. "I want two big bowls of gumbo, a platter of fried catfish, and a saucer of their homemade biscuits."

His attitude was infectious, and Michelle had to smile, even as she rejected his offer. "No, you go on," she said, with regret. "I can tell you're really hungry. You've been talking about food all evening."

"But I don't want to eat by myself." He held out her coat for her to get in.

Despite the awful clamoring inside her to go, Michelle tightened her arms across her chest and shook her head. "I'll be poor company."

"I promise you won't have to make conversation for me tonight," he said humorously. "Talking is not what I have in mind. At least, my stomach doesn't. I intend to stuff my face. Come on," he cajoled.

"A friend of mine told me about this place, and I've been eager to try it out," Simon said an hour later.

"This is my first time, too," Michelle replied, reaching for her glass of water.

They were seated in a cozy corner in the restaurant, which was doing brisk business, serving hungry patrons with Zydeco music playing softly in the background. Simon was polishing off his catfish dinner.

"The food's great. I'm glad we came."

"I agree, but I don't dare eat another bite. I'm stuffed,"

Michelle exclaimed. She slumped back against her bench seat. Even as she eyed the plates, saucers, bowls, and glasses on the table between them, she couldn't believe she'd eaten as much as she had. It was evident, as Simon had promised, she hadn't had to make much conversation.

With his fork hoisted in the air over her plate, he asked, "Then do you mind if I have those?" He was referring to the fried shrimp she'd left untouched.

"Be my guest," she replied.

Simon transferred them to his plate, then forked one into his mouth. He made a sound of delight in the back of his throat, chewing with the same gusto with which she'd seen him eat his own meal.

Confident he was too preoccupied to notice, Michelle studied him while he ate. He wasn't the most attractive man she'd ever seen, but he was cute. He had a kind of durably boyish face with proportionally man-size features. High cheekbones accentuated his big, round hazel eyes under sweeping lashes; his full lips blended into a strong chin.

Ironically, she liked looking at him. She especially liked his eyes. Despite the glint of humor they held, kindness lived there, too.

"I'm really looking forward to celebrating Kwanzaa," he said around the food in his mouth.

I'll bet, she thought, not revealing her disbelief. "Great."

She knew Loretta didn't tolerate just anyone in her circle of friends, unless she was certain that person was like-minded. She didn't buy that Simon had never celebrated Kwanzaa before, but it was a good cover, befitting Loretta's strategy-plotting mind to secure her a holiday date.

Still, she had to admit it was possible that Simon was telling the truth. If he knew anything about her, which would have been because Loretta told him, he hadn't let on. Nor had he mentioned the humiliating behavior she displayed at her house. For that, she was grateful.

"Are you sure you don't want anything else?"

"Maybe a stretcher to carry me out of here," she replied, chuckling lightly with amusement.

Simon laughed along, declaring, "You won't need one. I'm sure I can carry your weight now."

Michelle knew he was joking, but the gleam in his eyes— a faintly eager look of affection—unnerved her. Just like that, she began to believe he could carry any weight, his majestic size aside. Staring at the expanse of his shoulders, her own burdensome thoughts stole into her conscience. She stiffened, determined to keep them at bay, denying them permission to intrude.

Her struggle must have been visible, for Simon asked, "Are you okay?"

Michelle forced a smile and weakly nodded her head. "Oh, I'm fine."

"Dessert?" a waitress stole up to the table to ask, her expression hopeful.

Simon didn't let her down. "What do you have to tempt a man with?" he asked.

The waitress rattled off the choices by rote. Michelle shook her head, amazed as Simon finally decided on the coconut-pecan pie with ice cream on top. "What about you?" he asked her.

"No way," Michelle declined. Simon certainly did have a healthy appetite, she thought with amusement and, strangely, approval. Granted, he was a lot of man to feed, she thought, feeling a peculiar and almost imperceptible tremor.

The waitress cleared the table and left to fill his order for dessert.

"You must have skipped eating today," she commented, wondering how much food he consumed in a normal sitting. Ironically, it wasn't his food consumption that intrigued her most, and she chided herself for the thought.

"I have to keep up my strength," he replied, his eyes twinkling again as he looked at her.

With an odd sensation spiraling through her, Michelle realized she was really beginning to like this big bear of a man. He had made her laugh. He even made her tingle all over. And she really didn't want to.

Did she?

Chapter Five

S he had been too weak to fight last night.

Every time Michelle thought about how easily Simon had manipulated her to abide by his wishes, she could have screamed. She was close to doing just that now, she seethed silently.

"What if somebody has some disease we don't know about?" Simon posed with a look of dread on his face. "I don't want to drink behind them and get their germs."

Absently massaging her temples, Michelle wondered how she could have ever believed Simon was a mature, responsible individual when he was turning out to be as inquisitive and combative as a precocious child making an issue out of everything! "You won't get any germs," she grounded out.

It was not quite noon, and they'd debated about the solid wood *kinara* versus the brass one. She'd given in to the solid wood. Then they'd argued over which design to use for the *mkeka*: a fine white silk fabric embroidered in gold or the colorful black, red, and green straw one. That had been her win after she'd explained that the straw mat was preferable.

Now, he was suggesting that each of them drink from separate cups.

"I remember when I was a kid," Simon continued, "my mama used to always tell me and my brothers not to drink behind anybody. She didn't even like us drinking behind each other. It's not healthy. You run the risk of catching something you don't want. And it could kill you."

Michelle sighed with exasperation as she glared down at Simon. He was sitting on the floor in the middle of the opened boxes and the things he'd withdrawn from them. Surrounded by Christmas tree paraphernalia, he looked like a big kid. The top buttons of his red-and-gold flannel shirt, worn over chocolate corduroys, were open, revealing the fine hairs dotting his chest, an expansive tawny wall of taut skin and muscle.

No, strike kid, she corrected herself, for his physique, every vibrant, firm inch of him said *All Man.* She shivered as an unexpected tremor of pure desire flashed through her.

They were in her family room, the nicest room in the house next to her bedroom. Though it didn't look that way now since they'd raided the closets and deposited boxes containing items from previous Kwanzaa celebrations. Simon had lugged more than she'd instructed—proving he was hardheaded as well— so now her den looked as if they were preparing for a garage sale.

"Since you have seven candles, I don't see why we can't have seven cups," Simon persisted contrarily.

Michelle stopped flitting around like the butterflies in her stomach to answer. As she met his brilliant hazel-eyed gaze, the butterflies responded with a full flutter flap of movement inside her. She nearly forgot what she intended to say.

"If you want to be mathematical about it," she quipped, "you figure one cup for each of us in the group equals eight. Now, tell me how you plan to rectify that." She hadn't intended to start Kwanzaa preparation until Monday anyway, she recalled in defiance of the dance of life he'd awakened inside her.

"Well . . ." Simon pondered aloud.

He was looking at her with a sheepish little grin, his handsome face smooth, clean shaven, and oval, with strong features that when exaggerated with emotions revealed his rascality. She wondered if he had been having fun at her expense. Regardless, he looked so lovable, her heart rolled over in her bosom. And she had admitted perplexedly, it was not the first time her heart had performed gymnastics since he'd arrived.

"I guess you've got a point," he conceded. Rubbing his chin, he added, "Let me think about this a little more."

Muttering a sound of disgust, Michelle turned saucily from him to resume her search in the boxes. She felt more baffled by the conflicting feelings he created in her than by his stubbornness.

Tackling the boxes, she realized she had more Christmas decorations, light bulbs, and whatnots while only two small boxes contained items related to Kwanzaa. Still, she recalled, Simon had seemed surprised that she had anything at all. She wondered fleetingly why he had believed that.

"Since the cup is basically a symbolic gesture—" Simon resumed.

Michelle cut him off. "Not symbolic. Functional," she corrected as she carefully crossed over his legs to look into a box.

Still, thinking about his intensely probing nature forced her to consider the kind of man she enjoyed being with. She was somewhat rattled when he was the only example that came to mind, reminding her of just how long it had been.

"Well, I can toast unity and all the other principles just as well drinking my *own* libation from my *own* cup," he insisted.

Michelle rolled her eyes. She wondered if there was a serious side to Simon. But more important was that she wasn't as annoyed with him as she pretended. With confusion as her counsel, she picked up the wooden cup from one of the boxes. It was chipped, so it would have to be replaced. "The purpose of the *kikombe cha umoja*—"

"The what?" he interrupted, looking up at her dumbfounded.

"The communal unity cup," she enunciated slowly.

"You don't have to talk like that. I'm not retarded," he chided with a chuckle. "Maybe you need some more sleep," he suggested, frowning as if in pain.

"If somebody," she emphasized with her hands on her hips and amazement in her expression, "hadn't come ringing the doorbell at nine in the morning, *maybe* somebody else would have gotten more sleep after going to bed at six because somebody felt like working off his dinner by driving fifty miles, all the way to Galveston to park on the beach."

The memory was immeasurably sweet, and Michelle felt the sensation anew. By the time she finished ranting, she had a look on her face that was akin to the warming smile on Simon's.

"It was nice, wasn't it?" Simon said, his voice and expression mirroring serene contentment. "Seeing the sunrise, watching the waves crash against the seawall, feeling the ocean spray." He inhaled deeply, smiling at the reminiscence.

Michelle concurred with an unconscious nod of her head. She recalled feeling so soothed by Simon's manner that she had fallen into bed like a lead weight after he'd brought her home at six this morning. She had slept more soundly than she had in months. Waking had been a treat, despite the scant amount of sleep she'd gotten and the ungodly hour of Simon's arrival.

"We ought to do that again," Simon said, staring up at her intensely.

Michelle was startled by the flame she saw in his eyes, yet his proposal sent her spirits soaring, and the sensation brought a warm tingle to her depths. She was just so glad to feel something other than despair that these unusual emotions weren't that bad in comparison, she rationalized.

"Will you put those Christmas lights back in the box? And let's stay focused," she admonished. "We still have to go to the grocery store. Several of them,'' she added, speaking to herself. Checking items in the box, she added, ''I don't know how we're going to get everything done within the next seven days before Kwanzaa. Particularly since we have to compete with last-minute Christmas shoppers.''

''Why does Kwanzaa have to last seven days?'' Simon asked. He was on his knees, replacing the items as she had requested. ''I mean, there's nothing wrong with it, but it reminds me of the seven deadly sins.''

''I bet you were a handful as a child,'' Michelle replied. She didn't doubt he was even more of a handful now.

''You'd better believe it. Caught a beating just about every day,'' he said unabashed.

''That's probably why you associate the number seven with sins,'' Michelle retorted with mirth in her voice, which died when she recalled that lust was one of those sins. ''The seven cardinal virtues are stressed in Kwanzaa,'' she explained patiently, pulling candle nubs from the box. She laid them on the floor, reciting, ''Truth. Justice. Propriety. Harmony. Balance. Reciprocity. Order.''

''But those virtues are not the seven principles of Kwanzaa.''

''No,'' she replied. ''I was just giving you background information. We aspire to those virtues because they result in good character, which all cultures emphasize. So people of different religions shouldn't have a philosophical problem with celebrating Kwanzaa.''

''I guess the founder thought of everything. What's his name again?''

''Dr. Maulana Karenga,'' she said, feeling on solid ground. She could talk about Kwanzaa in her sleep. ''He created Kwanzaa during the Black Liberation movement of the sixties, while he was a member of the Us organization. The members wanted something to celebrate their newfound sense of identity and their acceptance of Africa as their homeland.''

The doorbell rang, ending the lecture Simon spurred on with his questions.

"Simon, will you get that please?"

"Simon, cook breakfast. Simon, get the vacuum cleaner. Simon, get the door," he grumbled good-naturedly, getting to his feet. "I don't know what makes you think I'm here to be your gofer. And don't make any decisions until I get back."

"That's what you get for showing up so early," Michelle called after him, chuckling.

"I fully intend to look at everything you've written down over lunch," he yelled back.

The man was preoccupied with food, Michelle thought, with a pleasant sigh respiring through her. His preoccupation was no doubt healthier than hers over him, she told herself, thinking of the inexplicable feelings that resulted from it.

Just when she felt ready to scream, he made her laugh. In the next instant, desire assaulted her senses. Even though it was great to feel good, she thought, returning to work, she mustn't let herself get carried away by the sensations Simon seemed to provoke in her. Or believe they were any more serious than he was.

But a tiny crevice in her thoughts suggested she was already tenuously linked to Simon.

Being around Michelle like this, he could easily forget his purpose. Seeing her smile and hearing her delightful throaty laughter, he could let himself forget the cries of help she'd sent out to her friends, who wouldn't let themselves believe she was capable of committing suicide until it was almost too late.

I really could, Simon thought in silent assurance, a wistful murmur in his throat.

As he sauntered up the hallway toward the front door, he considered he was holding up pretty well, too, for a man on the verge of a breakdown himself. Enduring her nearness highlighted what he'd been missing by washing his hands of women, and it had been pure hell to stay comfortable in his pants. Every so often, he caught himself wanting to act on the affection he felt coming from her when she thought he wasn't paying attention. The only trouble was that nothing about her escaped him.

Simon sighed deeply, surprised by the energy he'd had to exert to restrain himself.

Michelle was a serious-minded woman, not easy to approach. But it was easy to see she could be as playful as a girl or as composed as the intelligent, well-read woman that she was. Her emotional upheaval aside, she possessed a strength and stamina at odds with the slenderness of her body.

He more than liked being with her. She was an extremely desirable woman, and when he added her other qualities, he realized she was worth amending his five-year plan for. His wish to help her overcome her demons caused a quake inside him. The reason was not wholly altruistic. And that, too, was a problem. For if she ever discovered he was more than a "blind date" for the holidays . . .

"Well . . ." He shuddered thinking about her reaction.

Even though he was pleased about her present animated mood, he knew this was no time to congratulate himself. They—he and her friends—had to be more cautious than ever, for the severely depressed who showed signs of improvement were in greater danger of committing suicide. No longer paralyzed by misery, Michelle could use her intelligence to logically rationalize killing herself.

In the foyer, he noted the door that had been closed last night was still closed. He looked over his shoulder behind him. Alone, he turned the knob. Locked. Simon released it, then opened the front door to the delivery man in a brown uniform.

"I've got a package for Ms. Michelle Craig. Will you sign for it?"

After signing for the package and wishing the delivery man a happy holiday, Simon headed back, carrying a medium-sized box wrapped in brown packing paper. He couldn't help noticing the Austin, Texas, address. Recalling when he'd first learned about Michelle from Loretta, he guessed the package was from her uncle.

This should make her happy.

As he stood quietly on the edge of the family room, Simon stared mesmerized at Michelle. She was sitting on the floor, with her back to him and her legs folded as she wrote on her clipboard. The sleeves of her burgundy pullover were pushed up her slim arms. The old jeans caressed the delectable shape of her hips. He nearly swore, but did wipe the beads of perspiration from his forehead, thinking a set of gorgeous thighs and some fine legs were hidden from his sight.

He commanded himself to relax, riding through the sensual assault to his body, and forced his attention to the room. It was by far the most unique, imaginative specter of decoration and was probably more representative of Michelle than any other he'd seen in this house. He recalled thinking that when he had first entered.

With a sliver of a view into the kitchen, the room included a full bar with a brown marble top, while gold-rimmed crystal glasses and whatnots hung overhead. It fronted a waist-high wall mirror along the west wall, then cut off to form a nook with a card table and chairs under a modern chandelier. The fourth glass wall gave a view of the spacious backyard. Crispy gold and orange leaves littered the wooden patio deck and plastic flower-print furniture.

A few feet from where he stood and three steps down was a socially inviting enclave of wood, leather, and glass. He overlooked the litter of boxes to note the various rugs from the Continent interspersed atop a plush persimmon carpet, whose color matched the velvet wallpaper. A wide, circular, glass-topped coffee table on a wooden base provided a conversation piece at one end of the green leather sectional, whose pieces were set in and around the spiral-grain-patterned birch-wood backings. Four-foot-high birch-based standing lamps, checkered-colored leather bean bags, and throw pillows completed the friendly ensemble.

But three pictures were missing from the east wall above the waist-high, built-in bookshelves. As he had last night, Simon wondered what pictures had been taken down and why.

Michelle looked up over her shoulder and their gazes met. Staring into her copper eyes, which were even brighter with satisfaction in them, Simon felt that damnably unwelcome surge of excitement she provoked in him again. He quickly summoned one of his many practiced smiles, announcing, "Package for Ms. Craig."

"Oh?" Michelle replied. She unfolded her body from the floor and started toward him. He met her halfway, on the top landing, and lowered the package for her to see the address. Her expression quickly changed from pleasant to distasteful. "Oh," she muttered dryly. With a sharp turn, she walked off.

Simon noticed a slight change come over Michelle, but he was more befuddled by the jangle he felt, as if chains were connecting inside him. He could almost hear them locking in place. "Where do you want me to put it?"

I'm not going to let it get to me. Michelle was digging in a box. "Anywhere," she replied absently.

"Aren't you going to open it?" Simon asked, watching her flit from box to box, looking for something. He frowned, puzzled by her reaction.

"No," she replied succinctly, her head twisting and turning as she looked for something. *Michelle already knew what was in the box. Every year since her grandmother had died in 1996, Uncle David had sent the same instructions and some little impersonal gift.*

Michelle snapped her fingers as if suddenly remembering something; then she walked to the coffee table, where she picked up the wooden cup. She shook her head, put it down, then looked around the floor for something else.

"You mean you're not the least bit curious?" Simon asked, somewhat incredulous.

"It's from my uncle in Austin," she replied, unimpressed. *I'm not going to let it get to me.* "It's probably some expensive trinket that he had his secretary buy that I won't like anyway.'' She picked up her clipboard, folded herself onto the floor, and began looking over what she'd written.

The words were a blur, for she was filled with remembering. The first time, it had been a detailed letter explaining that the tax notices—county, city, and school—came this time of year. Did she have enough money to pay them? If not, let him know. If it was a cold season, had she remembered to wrap the pipes? If it was warm, when was the last time she checked the freon in the air-conditioner unit?

Simon would have liked to believe that Michelle's sudden distant disposition and antsy behavior were signs of creative tension, he thought with his lips pressed together. But he knew better. His eyes narrowed as he thought back to just a few minutes ago when he'd questioned her about Kwanzaa. It wasn't just for his clarification, but an attempt to tap into her subconscious sense of pride, which she obviously possessed and displayed through her knowledge of Kwanzaa. He'd hoped it would be a guide to help steer her out of the pit of her emotions. Instead, her replies were rote, he recalled. She didn't need to think about what she already knew, which meant he was going to have to ask more thought-provoking questions. This package was a good place to start.

''Hmm,'' Simon muttered. For a second, he feared Michelle wouldn't respond.

Finally, she looked over her shoulder at him, asking, ''Hmm, what?''

''Sounds like a sore spot.''

She turned away from him. *Uncle David had accepted an invitation to spend Christmas with her once. It had been a disaster. After a meaningless exchange about each other's welfare, they had little or nothing to say to one another. The turkey was too dry, the piecrusts too hard, the gravy not thick enough. Nothing she'd done was as good as his mother's work.* ''I don't want to talk about it.''

"Why not?" he said, stepping down into the area. "It's the season for clearing old wounds, good cheer, peace on earth, goodwill toward men, and all of that."

She could only recall one time when he'd asked sincere, probing questions. That had been on her twenty-seventh birthday. Her grandmother was still alive then, and the two of them had watched her like twin buzzards. She knew what they had been thinking. Joanne had died when she was twenty-seven, and they were looking for any signs that she might duplicate her mother's self-destruction.

"Will you just put that box away and help me finish this?" she said brusquely.

Simon knew her tone wasn't directed at him. Still, he felt uncharacteristically offended. "You don't have to get so mad about it," he said with gentle scolding. Nevertheless, he was rather curious about his internal reaction, wondering why he allowed himself to be affected by her tone.

Michelle's shoulders heaved with the exhausted sigh she emitted. *She had to admit, however, she was just as relieved when she'd turned twenty-eight.* "I'm not mad, Simon. I just prefer to forget."

Simon kneeled in front of her. "Can you?" he asked, his expression concerned, his tone gentle. "Besides, you know it's going to haunt you all day long." He suspected she had been running from whatever had brought on her depression, and he didn't want her to run away anymore. "Why don't you just open this box and get it out of the way?"

"I bet your mama had to hide your Christmas presents every year." *The forced smile on her face was small and it hurt, but she was trying, Michelle thought, determined not to let this innocent box get to her.*

"Yeah, and it didn't do her any good. My brothers and I were awesome treasure hunters," he boasted proudly. He was keenly attuned to her inner struggle.

Simon was trying, too. Bless his soul, she thought with silent admiration. "All right," Michelle acquiesced. "I'll open it now," she said, setting the clipboard aside.

"Great," he replied, setting the box on the floor in front of her.

"You mentioned brothers last night," she said, fiddling with a strand of her hair. She stared down at the box, and an anxious frown line formed across the ridges of her brow. "How many do you have?" she asked, her voice distant.

What was it about her uncle that caused this sudden anxiety? Simon wondered. He almost wished he'd left it alone. "Two," he replied, watching her closely. "Joshua, my older brother, is a defensive football coach. My baby brother, Carl Wayne, plays pro basketball."

"Are you going to get to see them for the holidays?"

"They hope not," he chuckled.

Clearly puzzled, she asked, "Why not?"

"Because it means their teams are winning and they get to play another day. I don't have a problem with the arrangement," he shrugged matter-of-factly. "We spent a couple of days together during the Thanksgiving holiday, and we're going to meet up at the Super Bowl."

"Are you close to them?"

Simon had to strain to hear, for her voice was barely lifted above a whisper, her copper eyes brimming with a somber, wistful look. "Definitely," he replied, forcing amusement to his voice. "My mama would rise from the dead and beat our butts if it were any other way."

"That must be nice," she said wistfully, returning her somber gaze to the box.

"I take it you and your uncle aren't close."

Michelle shook her head, then licked her lips. "No."

"Why is that?"

Michelle stared at him, wordless for a moment, her eyes shining like liquid. Their depths held guilt, shame, and such sadness that it nearly brought tears to his own eyes.

"He blames me for my mother's death," she replied at last.

Simon didn't let on about the jolt he felt. He cleared his throat before casually replying, "Oh? How did your mother die?"

"She shot herself."

Chapter Six

Pondering what she owed Simon, Michelle ambled circuitously about the room. Although he had not asked for details, she had seen expectancy dart across his expression.

What did she know about this man, Simon Stevenson? He was a stranger after all, she told herself, feeling his eyes track her every movement.

She sat at the table adjacent to the bar and stared into her own thoughts.

There, she saw herself struggling against a dense cloud of darkness, trying to reach the promise of light that loomed in the distance. She wanted to reach that light, the sun, with its power to bathe her in warmth. She knew instinctively who had brought the daystar to her.

She felt Simon move, then saw him slide onto the chair across from her. His expression was calm, but his thoughts were impossible to read. Yet the aura he exuded into the air, a tender stillness, a bright strength, called to her. Before she knew it, she said, "My mother wasn't the coward I am. She put the gun in her mouth and had the guts to pull the trigger."

Simon went all quiet inside upon hearing the connection

*she'd made between her mother and herself. Not to mention
the fact that she didn't admit how far she had been driven to
the point of nearly taking her own life. He doubted the omission
was an oversight; the memory of it remained in her subconscious. Feeling a tight ball of anxiety in his chest, he knew for
certain the memory was not gone—it was still there, ready to
rise again.*

Michelle was looking at Simon's big feet through the table's
glass top. Even though they sat facing each other, she couldn't
bear to look him squarely in the eyes. There was still that
measure of fear that he would consider her a limited, pathetic
woman who had not learned to *get over it*.

Wetting her lips nervously, she said, ''My mother liked to
go fishing. She never caught anything, and if she did, she never
brought it home.''

*To ask her about the omission would surely eliminate every
inroad he had made, which had been a giant step considering
the length of time they had known each other, Simon was
thinking. But because he wasn't sure enough about her emotional stability to handle the whole truth from either of them,
he decided not to risk probing in that regard. At least, she was
talking.*

''Before she left home that morning, she told her husband
she was going fishing at the dike in Texas City. Nobody thought
anything of it,'' she said, anguish seeping into her eyes. ''Except
me.''

Michelle felt herself reeling under the memory of that spring
day. She balled her hands into tight fists.

*Simon took Michelle's delicate hands into his: They were
as cold as ice. Still, a warming shiver coursed through him.
His heart thudded anxious beats as he studied her reaction,
fearing she felt what he felt.*

*A nodding look of gratitude softened the lines of sadness
from her face. But Simon wasn't sure what to think when
Michelle slipped her hands from his to cross her arms over
her bosom.*

"It was the night of the school play, and I was in it," Michelle resumed, her voice girlish and barely audible. "A local playwright, Thomas Meloncon, wrote it for our school. I didn't have a major role. I was just ten, in the fifth grade. Sixth graders had the leading roles. I remember . . . I remember looking for her, peeking out from backstage every few minutes before I had to go on."

She never showed up."

As Michelle fell utterly quiet, immersed in her childhood recollections, Simon felt empathy roar through him like a wounded lion. She was staring into space, a dazed, catatonic look on her face.

She had been angry and deeply disappointed with Joanne for not showing up, Michelle recalled. For the rest of the night she had agreed with every unkind word her grandmother had said about her irresponsible mother. That was before she learned the reason why.

"Michelle . . . ?" Simon called to her gently.

Simon was curious, eager even, to know how her relatives handled this tormenting loss to a ten-year-old child.

Slowly, the lost-in-memory look on Michelle's face metamorphosed into recognition and, subsequently, a self-deprecating expression that tried to form a smile. It was a grim attempt that caused Simon to nearly lose his composure. He clasped his hands together in his lap under the table.

Michelle rose and pushed away from the table in one fluid motion to walk to the center of the room. She realized, astonished, that she'd never told anyone this story before. The hurt, the shame, the misery, and the guilt had all remained frozen inside her all these years—ultimately stealing away her will to live.

Feeling Simon's eyes on her, Michelle risked a look at him. There was nothing like censure or scorn on his handsome face. She wondered fleetingly when she'd elevated Simon up from cute. He looked every bit like a tower of strength, and she couldn't help the fanciful notion that her life would have been different if he had been there for her. She was reminded that he was here now. Feeling fascination in her expression, she inhaled deeply, then continued.

"The police who regularly patrolled the dike found her van parked on the side of the road the next morning."

Michelle ambled about as she spoke, never once losing sight of Simon. As he angled his body in the chair to follow her movements, she noted his pectoral muscles were in perfect unison with the movement of his arms.

"Some fishermen who had been out since the previous evening knocked on the back doors to borrow a net." Her breath skipped and she swallowed, determined to finish what she'd started. "They saw her lying there ... like she had fallen asleep." Shaking her head, her face frowning and her voice pathetic, she said, "But she wouldn't wake up when they banged on the doors."

Michelle drew another deep breath. "I didn't know what it meant at first. I mean, I knew what the word *suicide* meant, but for some reason, in relationship to my mama, I couldn't figure it out. Grandma finally told me to stop asking all my questions 'cause nobody knew the answers. 'All you need to know is she is not coming back anymore,' she said."

Simon opened his hands, and splayed his fingers on the tabletop. He had to force his body to remain relaxed, his hands open and fingers loose, when all he wanted to do was pound something with his fists.

Michelle didn't realize how tense she had been until all the muscles in her body seemed to relax and the cold inside her to thaw. She felt a strange sense of freedom. Talking about the history that had haunted her for so many years made her feel better than she'd ever believed possible, she thought, gazing at the box on the floor where she'd left it. Simon was easy to talk to, she thought. And that helped.

She picked up the box and carried it to the table.

Simon was looking up at her, and Michelle simply stared back at him. She felt pleased with herself, with him. His light brown eyes glowed, and she wondered if his look of enthrallment was mirrored in her own face.

"I guess it's time to open this."

"You look like you could use some sleep."

"You're the only one who has noticed," Simon replied laughingly.

If he were big, then Ham was colossal. Nicknamed for his favorite food, Ham was Dr. Hannibal Sertima. It was not the name his Haitian parents gave him, but the only one anyone knew. Still, like everyone else, Simon called him Ham. Except today, when he needed counseling.

"Have a seat and tell the doctor your troubles. But be quick about it," his big voice boomed amusingly. "I have to pick up my wife's Christmas present before five."

Dr. Sertima's office fit his size and his warm personality. In his mid-fifties, he had been mentor, advisor, and friend when Simon was in medical school. After Simon had earned his degree, Ham had invited him to join his adolescent psychiatry practice in the Almeda Medical Building.

Like Simon, he preferred big furniture in earth tones. There was no view to speak of behind Ham's head, but the soothing blue walls were decorated with colorful renditions of tribal masks from ancient cultures.

Simon took a chair in front of Dr. Sertima's massive black walnut desk. Even though Simon tried to suppress it, he was uncharacteristically nervous.

"Come on, Simon. Don't make me pull teeth. I'm not a dentist. Why are you wearing such a long face? You thinking about coming back and don't know how to ask? Well, you should know you don't have to ask."

Simon inhaled deeply. "No, that's not it. I wish it were that simple." A prearranged schedule made with Loretta had allowed him to leave Michelle in her and the others' care. He'd already explained they had to be more vigilant than ever, even though Michelle had been trying mercilessly to withdraw from them. The truth was she needed their support, whether she accepted it or not. They could help ward off her feelings of loneliness, guilt, worthlessness, and sometimes even rage. Especially since the arrival of her uncle's package.

"Okay," Simon said, ready to talk, "here's the deal."

Starting at the beginning, Simon relayed to Dr. Sertima how he'd become involved in a scheme to convince a woman who was suicidal to seek psychological help. "Her name is Michelle Craig, and her mother committed suicide twenty years ago."

Simon sensed a barely perceptible movement in Dr. Sertima, a tensing as he muttered, "Hmm. How old is Ms. Craig now?"

"Thirty," Simon replied. "Her mother's death occurred in April, but her purgatory begins around Thanksgiving."

Nodding his head thoughtfully, Dr. Sertima talked out loud to himself. "A traditional holiday when all the family is present. The mother's absence would be keenly felt." To Simon, he commanded, "Go on."

Simon hesitated a fraction before starting his recollection from Michelle's sketchy memory of her mother's suicide. He remembered feeling acutely flawed for recognizing her sensuality despite her vulnerable demeanor.

"Simon . . . Simon . . ." Dr. Sertima had to call him twice to get his attention.

"Sorry."

Simon continued, highlighting the story with his observations and interpretations based on things Michelle had said and what she hadn't said. Her story was one of a child born out of wedlock to a young woman who herself wasn't ready to be a mother, but who'd sought love futilely from the wrong person.

The more comfortable he became in that chair, the deeper he was drawn into the treasure chest of his mind, a memorable collection of senses and images that housed Michelle in his thoughts. Like a lingering emotional resonance, it even stored the warm sensations he'd felt in her presence.

The offspring of Nora and Walter Craig—Michelle's uncle,

David, and her mother, Joanne—were encouraged to become a lawyer and a doctor, respectively. Any interest or hobby perceived to be outside the scope of those fields was met by scorn, largely by Nora, for her husband, a railroad engineer, was often away on long trips.

Suffice it to say, Nora Craig attempted to live her dreams through her children's lives. She controlled them, and resistance to her wishes was met with punishment. She didn't physically abuse them; she simply withheld her affection—emotional abuse.

The uncle, David Craig, went to law school, so he hadn't suffered as Joanne had, but he was a prisoner to Nora as well. When Joanne declared a business major, all funds for her college support were cut off. Still, she showed Nora that other professions could be just as financially rewarding. She created her own business, which she called *Joanna's Jewels,* "because it had a nice ring to it."

But it wasn't enough for Nora, so Joanne sought attention and love from other sources.

"Michelle's grandmother never approved of them either," Simon said, repeating what Michelle had said. However, he couldn't mimic her speaking in her grandmother's tone: " 'You thought you were in love with Michelle's father. And he only hung around as long as it took him to help make her.' "

Simon went on to tell Dr. Sertima that the count of Joanne's misplaced love included one near marriage and a short, disastrous one. Michelle never got to know her stepfather, for her mother capitulated to her grandmother's wishes not to "uproot this child from her home until you can make a certain one for her."

She had spoken to her uncle today. Frozen midstep, with her head tilted, Michelle realized incredulously that it was only the second time this year that she had actually heard his voice.

With a shake of her head, she walked into her bedroom and

An important message from the ARABESQUE Editor

Dear Arabesque Reader,

Because you've chosen to read one of our Arabesque romance novels, we'd like to say "thank you"! And, as a special way to thank you, we've selected four more of the books you love so well to send you for FREE!

Please enjoy them with our compliments, and thank you for continuing to enjoy Arabesque...the soul of romance.

Karen Thomas
Senior Editor,
Arabesque Romance Novels

Check out our website at
www.arabesquebooks.com

SPECIAL OFFER!
4 FREE BOOKS

ARABESQUE ®

A PRODUCT OF

BET BOOKS™

3 QUICK STEPS
TO RECEIVE YOUR "THANK YOU" GIFT
FROM THE EDITOR

Send this card back and you'll receive 4 FREE Arabesque novels! The introductory shipment of 4 Arabesque novels – a $23.96 value – is yours absolutely FREE!

There's no catch. You're under no obligation to buy anything. You'll receive your introductory shipment of 4 Arabesque novels absolutely FREE (plus $1.50 to offset the costs of shipping & handling). And you don't have to make any minimum number of purchases—not even one!

We hope that after receiving your books you'll want to remain an Arabesque subscriber. But the choice is yours to continue or cancel, anytime at all! So why not take us up on our invitation to receive 4 Arabesque Romance Novels, with no risk of any kind. You'll be glad you did!

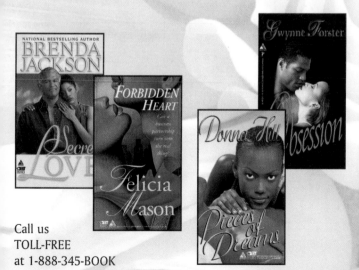

Call us
TOLL-FREE
at 1-888-345-BOOK

THE EDITOR'S "THANK YOU" GIFT INCLUDES:

- 4 books absolutely FREE (plus $1.50 for shipping and handling)
- A FREE newsletter, *Arabesque Romance News*, filled with author interviews, book previews, special offers, and more!
- No risks or obligations. You're free to cancel whenever you wish... with no questions asked.

BOOK CERTIFICATE

Yes! Please send me 4 FREE Arabesque novels (plus $1.50 for shipping & handling). I understand I am under no obligation to purchase any books, as explained on the back of this card.

Name _____

Address _____ Apt. _____

City _____ State _____ Zip _____

Telephone ( ) _____

Signature _____

Offer limited to one per household and not valid to current subscribers. All orders subject to approval. Terms, offer, & price subject to change. Offer valid only in the U.S.

Thank you!

ANOH0A

Accepting the four introductory books for FREE (plus $1.50 to offset the cost of shipping & handling) places you under no obligation to buy anything. You may keep the books and return the shipping statement marked "cancelled". If you do not cancel, about a month later we will send 4 additional Arabesque novels, and you will be billed the preferred subscriber's price of just $4.00 per title. That's $16.00 for all 4 books for a savings of 33% off the cover price. You may cancel at any time, but if you choose to continue, every month we'll send you 4 more books, which you may either purchase at the preferred discount price. . . or return to us and cancel your subscription.

THE ARABESQUE ROMANCE CLUB: HERE'S HOW IT WORKS

ARABESQUE ROMANCE BOOK CLUB

P.O. Box 5214

Clifton NJ 07015-5214

went straight to the bookcase nestled in the far corner of the room. Perusing the shelves for a particular book, she wondered why Simon had been so insistent that she call her uncle, even though she was glad she had. Uncle David had seemed genuinely happy to hear from her.

He'd been gabby even, she realized and chuckled. But not once during the entire time they spent on the phone had he asked about anything as impersonal as house maintenance. He even apologized for not calling himself, but hoped it was okay with her if he came for a visit the day after Christmas.

There was someone he wanted her to meet. A woman. Her name was Amelia Lofton. They loved each other and were going to get married in February.

He'd said all that in one mushy breath, Michelle recalled, amazed. Simon's image intruded into her thoughts, and she caught herself smiling, feeling all giddy inside, like the sound of euphoria she'd heard in her uncle's voice.

Who knows? she thought. Maybe she would have some good news of her own to share with Uncle David by then.

"Girl, you're being foolish," she chided herself, plucking a book from the bottom shelf.

She headed from her room in search of Reba, who was supposed to have come up to get this book, she clucked. Walking into the hallway, she wondered where her friend had gone. She took several steps into the hallway and saw that the attic door was open. Her shoulders sagged, and annoyance sullied her expression.

That door had always been closed, Michelle mused, staring at it. The past was locked behind it—where she wanted it to remain. Or where she had tried to keep it, she told herself.

Still, she was used to it being closed. She was not pleased seeing it any other way.

Even though she had told Simon—in so many words—that she would unlock her repressed ill thoughts and feelings, she guessed she still wasn't quite ready to go all the way yet. Now, as she stared at the door, mere inches away, the distance seemed insurmountable.

An hour later, Simon sat pondering silently. With Michelle keenly in his thoughts, he felt a deep abiding appreciation for his own family, particularly his mother. Even though they'd spent a number of years on welfare, their mother had never held him or his brothers responsible for the decisions she made. It seemed that Nora Craig had not been happy with her choices and had made her family suffer for them.

"What was in the box?" Dr. Sertima asked.

"A brief, apologetic note for not having shared with Michelle the things in the box before now," Simon replied. In the back of his mind, he still saw Michelle. Watching the strain in her face as she opened the package with trembling hands, then withdrew the letter—which she'd placed aside to read later—followed by a series of items. Each item evoked awe from her, restoring color to her lovely face and life to her expression.

"They were things her mother had made for her uncle that he now wanted Michelle to have." He, too, had been impressed by Joanne's talent and it was reflected in his voice as he elaborated. "There was a *mkeka* measuring twenty-four by forty-two knitted in red, black, and green straw; a *kinara* of mahogany with the seven principles etched in black just beneath each gold-lined holder; a matching cup with an engraved map of Africa; and last, but not least, a quilt bearing the colors of African nations surrounding a flag of red, black, and green in the center."

Simon fell silent, recalling that Michelle was weeping by the time she'd inspected each item, which had been tagged *Joanna's Jewels*.

"I see," Dr. Sertima replied noncommittally.

"There was also a document transferring ownership of the

house over to Michelle,'' Simon added. "I had her call her uncle as soon as I saw the letter."

"Because he was giving away his possessions, you suspected his action was a suicidal gesture," Dr. Sertima said.

Simon nodded affirmatively, a small sheepish look on his face. "It turned out to be more of a gesture of closure, however. Her uncle claimed to have found his soul mate. He's in love. Michelle told me he'd already been married three times, and each marriage ended in divorce."

"Well," Dr. Sertima said, clasping his beefy hands together on the desk, "since it's too late for you to get out, I'd advise you to tell her who you really are."

Before he could even think, Simon blurted, "You really think that's what I should do?" He was amazed by and uncomfortable with the advice.

"Hell, you didn't need me to tell you that. You're already a little bit in love with this woman."

"That's preposterous! How can anyone be a little bit in love?" Simon rasped sarcastically. "Besides, I only met her twenty-four hours ago."

"All right," Dr. Sertima said, spreading his hands open. "I'll concede that you're in love with her."

Simon's mouth fell open, emitting a gasp of profound disbelief.

"Hey, you asked for advice. Don't throw daggers at the doctor just because you don't like what he says. I've listened to your tale, and I can hear things in your voice that I know you were trained to keep to yourself. I hear a judgmental tone against her grandmother. I hear censure for her mother. I hear utter distaste for the men her mother chose to love. I hear disgust for the uncle, who, for whatever reasons, hasn't been able to face her after all these years."

Stunned, Simon squirmed in the chair, gripping the armrests, his heart alternately slamming into his ribs and skipping beats

in his chest. He could feel the giveaway heat steal into his face.
Realizing his mouth was still hanging open, he closed it.

"Girl, why don't you do something with this room?"

It was the first thing out of Reba's mouth the moment
Michelle appeared. She started to ask Reba what she was doing
up here. Instead, she said in a slightly peeved tone, "I found
the book you were looking for." She held up the book, which
proved her point that the *zawadi* were gifts to encourage
achievement and reward accomplishment, not meaningless
items to exchange whimsically as Reba had implied. "It was
exactly where I told you it was in my bedroom."

They were standing just inside the largest bedroom in the
house, a half level above the second floor. The room had been
claimed by years of dust and disuse. Neither, however, marred
the image planted in her mind.

Michelle couldn't believe she had never ventured up to this
room in all these years. But for so long, she recalled, she had
been forbidden to enter. It was no wonder that she'd forgotten
it existed.

"Clarissa and Loretta are waiting for us downstairs,"
Michelle said, hoping her words were enough to encourage
Reba to leave.

All three had arrived within five to ten minutes of Simon's
departure, she recalled as Reba walked deeper into the room.
He had some last minute shopping to do, which he promised
would only take a couple of hours. She missed him already,
and he'd only been gone an hour, she thought, surprised by
her eagerness for his return. Just one more hour to endure her
friends' visit, she told herself, sighing heartily.

"Looking at this room from the outside," Reba said, "I
thought this was the attic."

Michelle didn't reply, for she knew an answer would launch
a conversation she didn't want to have. She acknowledged
silently that Reba was partially right. The rectangular suite was

part attic and part add-on, which her grandfather had done when Joanne was pregnant with her.

She had spent her last night in this room—the night they buried her mother, with whom she'd shared the room for the first ten years of her life. Her grandmother had come in the very next day and cleaned everything out, promising to put Michelle in the room that used to be her uncle's. It was now her current bedroom.

Melancholy and memories poured over Michelle in waves as she looked about the room. The moss green carpet had become striped from the hard wood floor that held a thin layer of dust. A set of tall windows faced the street below; they had deep ledges wide enough to sit and huddle. The yellow paint had faded on the walls, but she could still envision the flower-print curtains that had covered them. The curtains matched the spread that had covered her twin bed, while Joanne's had been a solid yellow. They had had matching white lacquered furniture on each side of the room, with Joanne's near the street, and hers closer to the back wall, next to the bathroom.

With her gaze returning to the front windows, Michelle could almost see the girl she had been sitting on the sill many an afternoon waiting for her mama to come visit. That had been after she married Charles Baker, whom her grandmother hadn't trusted.

She didn't remember him much, but her mama had never let her down, Michelle recalled. Sometimes they would knit, or she would help Joanne arrange flower baskets, or they would read and watch television. She relished every moment of those precious afternoons.

Her grandmother would inevitably put an end to them. How many times had she cried herself to sleep after her mother had left? She couldn't recapture the happy times they had spent together.

Anger bubbled inside her as she remembered those lonely nights and the unpleasant disruptions that had preceded them. During those times when Grandmother Nora chided Joanne, she had wanted to defend her mother. She had wanted to make Nora Craig shut up and leave Joanne alone and just love her for who she was!

Then her mother would have loved her, because she would have had an example.

Michelle's heart cried with that thought and it rushed through her mind like a tidal wave. She felt dizzy accepting the terrible knowledge of her childhood fear. It was even more daunting to realize that it had grown up with her, like a dreadful blueprint from which she lived.

"I see all kinds of things you can do with this room," Reba said. "Clean the walls and repaper it in your favorite color and rag paint the walls to divide the areas. I would leave this," she said, kneeling to knock on the floor.

Michelle listened to Reba with a vague sense of reality. She was still reeling and reflecting. Things—images, memories, feelings—that had been hazy were becoming clear to her. She realized she was afraid to live. She had always been, she mused ruefully.

Walking toward the back of the room, Reba opened the bathroom door and looked in. "Just what I thought," she said, facing Michelle, her expression excited with the prospects on her mind.

With her microscopic insights unraveling in her mind, Michelle massaged her forehead. She was astonished to realize all the unresolved garbage she had been carrying inside her all these years.

"You can divide this room into three areas. Knock out this bathroom wall and install a Jacuzzi here."

Despite her heart pounding in her bosom, a strange calm seemed to fall over her. Much the way she felt when Simon was near, she thought, smiling unconsciously.

Reba was measuring off three feet. "And make this area your bedroom," she proposed, spreading her arms wide to demonstrate. "You can even have a half-moon platform built in front of this wall to extend about here," Reba added, again walking off the distance. Pivoting to face the front of the room, she said, "And this area can become the sitting room."

Catching Reba's enthusiasm, Michelle had to admit that not only did she like Reba's suggestions, but she was also envisioning a few ideas of her own. Thinking about them excited her, but her eyes widened as she considered the cost of such changes. Not to mention what her uncle would think. Shaking her head, she said unconsciously, "Uncle David wouldn't go for it."

Reba uttered a sound of disgust as her hands flew to her hips. "Didn't he give you this house?"

Michelle smiled, embarrassed. "I guess I haven't gotten used to the idea," she said in a small voice. Still, she was not impulsive. Looking around the room, imagining the changes, she muttered, "An arm and a leg. And maybe a foot, too."

"Hey, where are you guys?"

Reba walked to the door and replied, "We're up here." She faced Michelle with her hands on her hips. "What are you mumbling about now?" she asked querulously.

"I said it would cost a fortune."

"Aw, girl, come on," Reba chided. "Sell some of those stocks you've been purchasing all these years. Splurge on yourself. Live a little."

"I don't know," Michelle said indecisively.

"What's not to know? What have you worked so hard for if not to provide yourself a little comfort and satisfaction? Hell, you can't take it with you." Realizing her faux pas, Reba clamped her hands over her mouth.

Hot quick anger charged through Michelle, then died like the thud of a misspent bullet, replaced by a ricochet of humor. She could hear Simon saying the same thing, she thought, laughing silently at herself.

"What are you doing up here, debarking a tree to make paper?" Loretta asked with chiding as she entered the room with Clarissa right behind her.

Both noticed the stilted atmosphere and looked back and

forth from Michelle's peevish expression to Reba's frozen, wide-eyed, chagrined look.

Michelle shook a finger at Reba, declaring, "If you say, 'Oops,' I'll hit you with something."

"What's going on?" Clarissa asked.

Winking at Michelle, Reba replied, "Just trying to convince our sister to live a little—that's all."

Chapter Seven

Simon was reluctant to face Michelle just yet with Dr. Sertima's diagnosis on his mind. He'd yet to answer to his own
satisfaction whether Ham had read the situation right, for his
lusty longings blocked sound analysis. And they showed no
signs of abating since all rational thought fled the moment she
let him in.

"Hi again." Michelle greeted him with a lovely smile, an
eagerness in her eyes.

"Hi back," Simon replied. He thought she looked ready for
something, but he doubted it coincided with what was in the
back of his mind.

"We're in the kitchen," she announced. Leading the way,
she asked, "Did you finish your shopping?"

"Uh, yeah," Simon stammered in reply, grateful her back
was to him. His gaze had zeroed in on her soft, round behind,
outlined deliciously in those jeans. It seemed his senses were
trailing after her like some horny beast.

"Good," she declared. "As soon as I get rid of these folks,
we can head out for the grocery store."

"Great," he replied, his voice lacking enthusiasm. He felt as if he needed *couch* counseling.

Michelle turned her head to laugh at him over her shoulder just as they reached the kitchen. The "girls" were standing around the counters. He thought they all looked giddy with guilt as they chorused, "Hi, Simon," with innuendo in their voices.

He reckoned he'd been the topic of conversation. "Hi," he said back, a knowing twinkle in his eyes. Bags from a popular sandwich shop littered the counter. He picked up one. "Where's mine?" he asked of no one in particular.

Clucking, Michelle rolled her eyes and Clarissa clasped her hands over her face, appalled.

"I'm sorry, Simon," Clarissa said sincerely. "I didn't think you would be here, so I only got four."

"Clarissa, I was only joking," Simon replied.

"Why don't you polish off the rest of Michelle's?" Reba suggested. "She only took two bites out of it."

Loretta's hands shot to her hips. "You are just too damn tacky," she chided Reba.

"What?" Reba replied guilelessly. "What did I say that was so tacky? Huh? Tell me."

Simon noticed Michelle as she ducked quietly from the room. He breathed restoratively, realizing it must have been the first breath he'd drawn into his lungs since she'd opened the door to him.

"How's it going?" Loretta asked in a whisper, keeping an eye out for Michelle's return.

Noting their eager gazes in inquisitive expressions, Simon replied, "How's what going?" Yeah, he played dumb. He refused to get into a conversation about Michelle here. He'd already demonstrated he wasn't too bright by participating in this cockamamie scheme in the first place. He was certainly not going to run the risk of getting caught in her home. That surely smacked of bad timing, he thought, although he didn't think there was ever a good time to dispense bad news.

He was rescued from further query, and the girls' dumb-founded expressions vanished, when Michelle returned. She was loaded with overcoats, which she distributed to each of her girlfriends.

"This is yours. This is yours. And this is yours. Thanks for dropping in with lunch." Clasping her hands together in front of her, she concluded sweetly, "It was really nice of you. Have a good day, and I'll talk to you later."

"Damn!" Reba swore laughingly as she slipped into her coat. "Looks like you're trying to kick us out. I wonder why."

"Probably because you have the tact of a tick," Loretta quipped as she pulled the hood of her coat over her head.

"I still don't know what the big deal is," Reba retorted with a huff.

"Don't forget Christmas Eve dinner at my place," Clarissa said.

With Michelle pushing them toward the front door, Clarissa lead the parade from the kitchen. Out of view, she yelled back, "Seven-thirty. And it's formal."

Knowing the message was for his benefit, Simon loudly replied, "We'll be there, decked to the nines and on time!"

He didn't know what love for a woman was supposed to feel like, he thought, peeking into the sandwich bags. Hell, if he could answer that, he'd have charged his clients a mint instead of a hundred bucks an hour to counsel them when the subject had come up. Athletes were little different from anyone else, with or without money.

They wanted to know how to tell whether the women they were dating wanted them for their humanity and not just for what their money could provide. Everybody wanted the answer key to love. And he was no different, Simon sighed.

He located the bag that had been Michelle's, and sure enough, her sandwich had hardly been touched. After getting a bottled water from the refrigerator, he stood at the counter and began polishing off Michelle's leftovers.

In his dreams, he imagined the love-at-first-sight scenario

was a thunderbolt descending from the heavens to strike a man in the chest hard enough to knock him to the ground. He conceded he'd been thrown for a loop upon first meeting Michelle, but he'd thought the sensation was lust.

Confident that he could control that physical manifestation known as desire, Simon guessed, nodding his head, that he hadn't given it much more thought. When it came, he simply relished it, reveled in the feeling. He never believed it could hurt him.

Chewing, he thought he had been so well insulated after his experience with Penelope Franklin, who had nearly destroyed his career, that even if it *did* happen, he would have recognized the symptoms right off.

How arrogant he was, he chided himself. It was his own misreading of the signs of a delusional mind that had gotten him into trouble in the first place. But even then—he recalled, biting viciously into the sandwich—he was dating the woman, not counseling her or her son, who she had accused him of making sexual advances toward.

The sandwich finished, Simon drained the bottle of water. Still gripping the empty plastic container, he pondered whether it was too late.

He could extricate himself from making another major mistake right now, Simon told himself. All he had to do was tell Michelle what he did for a living.

Regret bolted from his gut in a belch. He knew he would never see her again, for she would surely give him the boot. Confession was not an acceptable preference, Simon thought with a vehement shake of his head.

He further feared her reaction in her present mental state as his diagnosis was still incomplete: He didn't know whether suicide was still an option in her mind.

Michelle returned shivering and blowing into her cupped hands. "Ooo, it's cold outside," she said, her body trembling.

Setting the bottle on the counter, Simon said, "Here, let me see if I can help."

The moment he took her cold hands in his, a quick hot jolt of desire, like a low electrical current, shot up his arms. With the memory of his previous attempt to comfort her in mind, he counseled himself to breathe. Slowly, the sparks subsided, settled easily into his veins as he briskly rubbed his hands over hers.

"You're a regular boy scout," Michelle said.

There was a little nervousness to her laughter; she seemed winded as if she had been running. Simon wondered about the small sound that came from her throat: a sigh of pleasure. Whether from the warmth restored to her hands or something else, he didn't know. He wanted to believe he was the cause.

"I aim to please," he replied. *You should aim to tell her the truth,* an internal cynic taunted him. "Why don't we light up the fireplace in the living room?" That would be the perfect opportunity, he thought. All toasty and warm, she might not get so mad when he told her, he rationalized.

Michelle eased her hands from his, her gaze averted elsewhere. "We don't have time. The grocery stores are going to be packed as it is. We'd better get going."

Simon nodded his agreement. *He had tried to tell her,* he thought in an attempt to absolve himself.

Try harder next time! his conscience screamed at him.

The next several days flew by like a whirlwind. Michelle didn't know who was doing what to whom. She had believed she was teaching Simon about Kwanzaa, while it seemed he was teaching her quite a different ritual altogether.

In fact, she couldn't remember the word *Kwanzaa* passing between them, she thought, lying in the comfort of her bed one night. It shored her suspicion that the celebration wasn't new to Simon at all. Tingling with delight, she decided she didn't care anymore.

The phone rang, intruding into Michelle's mellowed senses and pleasing muse.

With a curious frown on her face, she sat up and flipped the switch of the lamp on her bedside table. Answering the phone on the table, she said somewhat suspiciously, "Hello?"

"What's up?"

"What's up?" she echoed, astonished. Identifying the caller's voice, she chided, "Loretta, do you know what time it is?"

She had only been home long enough to change into her gown and climb into bed, Michelle recalled. She had eschewed taking a shower until tomorrow because she was so tired, albeit pleasantly so. Glancing at the clock on the table, she answered before her friend could speak, "It's two fifty-three in the morning."

"Yeah, we know."

" 'We?' " Michelle replied.

"Hi, Michelle," Clarissa and Reba sang.

Michelle sagged a little, thinking she had been looking forward to a good night's rest. Simon had insisted upon it, she recalled, informing her he wanted to get an early start at the grocery stores. The number of people shopping them tonight had overwhelmed them both, so they had gone to a movie instead.

"Don't y'all have something better to do than wake people up in the middle of the night? Some of us like to sleep, you know," Michelle said sternly, keeping her amusement from her voice. She remembered that since Simon couldn't sleep on an empty stomach, dinner had followed.

"Then one of us should have gotten home to bed before the rooster crowed," Reba retorted.

"What do you want this time of morning?" she asked, trying to keep the smile from her voice, having already discerned that the call had not been made because of an emergency.

"Where have you been all evening?" Reba asked.

"Yeah," Clarissa chimed. "I've been trying to reach you since about six."

Loretta added, "You forgot to turn on your answering machine."

"Did any of you want anything important?"

"Yeah," Reba shot back. "What kind of kisser is Simon?"

Michelle covered the mouthpiece and held the receiver away so they wouldn't hear the chortle of laughter that burst from her.

"Re-ba," Clarissa scolded.

"Hell, if she hasn't even kissed him yet, she's moving too slow," Reba declared undaunted. "He's a lot of man to explore."

So much for sleeping. Once they started, it was nearly time to wake up before they bid her good night and Michelle could dream of kissing Simon.

Only the night's sleep didn't end with a kiss. But it was just a dream.

Michelle wondered if Simon was as fascinated by her as she was by him. She wondered how she compared to his other women. And she wondered what kind of kisser he really was.

She could satisfy her curiosity in her dreams. She had done a lot of exploring in her sleep. But as she walked alongside him, she didn't feel the satisfaction of her guesses since a knot of need had lingered in her groin ever since the suggestion had been planted in her mind.

The very next afternoon, they were strolling through Mac-Gregor Park, selecting pinecones and twigs that would be used to enhance the Kwanzaa projects they would make each night.

It was a cold, brisk afternoon. A white sun sat fixed high in the blue skies, but it gave off very little heat. Dressed for the weather in jeans, boots, leather jackets, and scarves, each was carrying a bag to hold her finds.

"Michelle . . ."

"What is it, Simon?" she asked, wondering what was causing his knitted brows. An extra beat of silence passed before he spoke again.

"I was thinking about the *Nguzo Saba*. Did I say that right?"

He had butchered the Swahili name for "seven principles," but Michelle had a feeling it wasn't what he'd meant to say in the first place. She corrected him kindly. "It's *n-goo-zo sa-ba.*"

They spoke loud to cover the distance between them and be heard over the traffic that zoomed by on MLK Boulevard, which ran along the east end of the well-used, ten-acre park.

"Anyway," he resumed, "I know there are seven principles to celebrate on the seven days, but nobody has told me what the principles are."

So Loretta had not lied to her in order to play Cupid on the sly, Michelle thought, mildly surprised. "Well, I guess we'd better correct that right now," she said, smiling to herself as she began her lesson. "The days, in the order that they are celebrated are," she said, enumerating, "*Umoja,* which means unity."

Michelle paused for a fraction of a minute, thinking about her selfish behavior toward her friends, the closest people to a real family she had. She felt bad about it and vowed to change as she continued.

"*Kujichagulia* means self-determination. Collective work and responsibility are *Ujima,* while *Ujamaa* means cooperative economics. *Nia* is purpose." She paused again, thinking she had fallen way short of practicing that principle as well, for she had come to feel that there was no purpose in her life. With a rueful sigh, she pressed on, "*Kuumba* is creativity, and the last one is *Imani,* which means faith.

"Why don't you try saying them?" she suggested.

While Simon was attempting to repeat the seven principles, Michelle's mind drifted. It was apparent that she had not been off to a good start celebrating Kwanzaa, she mused. The principles that she had long ago committed to memory should have been intrinsic to her daily life, not something she dragged from the closet on December twenty-six to practice through the first of the new year, she scolded herself.

"Did I get them all right?" Simon asked.

Masking the guilt of hypocrisy she felt, Michelle pasted a smile on her face. "Yeah, you did fine," she said softly. "Now back to work."

Simon nodded and obediently resumed picking pinecones. Michelle was still mulling the lapses in her practice of Kwanzaa. Inevitably, she wondered what Simon stood for as she stole stealthy glances at him, while absently and indiscriminately making her cone selections.

Soon, Simon replaced Kwanzaa completely in her thoughts. She felt her heart skip upon seeing him bent from the waist as he examined several cones that were on the ground. Her gaze roved the length of him, noting appreciatively the way the jeans clung to his cute butt, his powerfully muscled thighs.

So thoroughly was she enjoying the view, she froze like a deer caught in headlights when he suddenly stood and looked directly at her. He had a broad grin on his face, as if proud to have scrounged up three healthy pinecones, which he held up for her to see.

Michelle hoped his eyesight was less than twenty-twenty, for surely he would have noticed the blush that crept through her like a thief.

Dropping the cones in his bag, Simon said, "I know the general meaning of those words, but how are they related to Kwanzaa?"

Each time he saw Michelle, Simon thought, feeling the bovine grin on his face again, he wondered how she could be more beautiful to him than she had been the day before. Watching her grow stronger, like a flower in bloom, before his very eyes filled him with an exclamation of delight.

"Unity is the foundation principle, as well as a practice," she said, walking toward him. We must do it in order to have it. Among other things, unity refers to a oneness that gives us an identity as a people of African descent."

"I see," Simon said. There was a healthful sheen to her

complexion, and her hair was a rich and glowing auburn. She laughed more, and her smiles invaded her eyes. He mumbled his soft approval of the glovelike fit of the jeans caressing her hips. He thought she seemed to be picking up a little weight—no doubt from all the meals he'd insisted she consume with him. "Let me take a stab at the next one."

"Okay. Self-determination," she prompted with a nod.

"If we define ourselves as one people, African-Americans," Simon said, collecting his thoughts for the right words, "then we should make decisions that are in our best interest."

"That's fantastic," Michelle said, impressed.

She looked so pleased with him, Simon thought, that he wouldn't tell her he'd hit the books on Kwanzaa. He began to wonder if there was a difference between guilt and regret.

"Why don't you take the next one, too?" she suggested.

"Oh that one's easy," he replied confidently. "Collective work and responsibility refers to our combined efforts to do those things we've defined as being in our best interest."

And so it went, with Simon putting his spin on the remaining principles, allowing Michelle the time to reflect on them, which meant their bags were not as full as they'd intended.

"There's one thing you have to remember though," Michelle said, examining a twig.

Michelle fell silent while watching him with an intense look on her face. Simon didn't believe she actually saw him, but his pulse pounded hard in his body nevertheless. He felt as if the time he'd been waiting for had arrived. He swallowed the lump lodged in his throat; it was an obstacle to the confession on his tongue. He had known such an attraction would be perilous, he cursed.

"We must always give thanks to our ancestors for their contributions and make a commitment to continue their work for the betterment of our lives," Michelle said at last.

He noticed her voice was lowered to a barely audible tone and her expression was marred in thought. He believed deliberation about her mother or grandmother or both had caused her sudden somberness. Though they had to be like twin ghosts haunting her, he didn't want despair to attach itself to her soul, he thought, watching her duck out of view behind a tree.

Simon didn't know what he was going to do as he sneaked up on Michelle. She was leaning against a tree and her head was bowed. As quietly as possible, he held his bag of leaves over her head, then released it.

Sputtering, Michelle spun to look at him, flailing leaves off of her. "I'll get you for this," she threatened, giggling like a schoolgirl.

"I'd like to see you try," he replied, replenishing his bag with more leaves.

The park leaves had never been used so merrily as they were in Michelle and Simon's game of chase and retreat. The initial purpose of going there was temporarily suspended to play.

On a pass, Michelle just missed Simon, who was surprisingly quick and nimble for a man his size. She needed a way to make up for it, she thought, stuffing her bag again while he ran off to do the same.

Michelle couldn't believe the thought that came to her. She couldn't believe she could stoop so low as she began her pursuit. Simon saw her from the distance and readied himself.

Deliberately, Michelle cautiously fell to the ground, moaning and clutching her ankle with one hand; the other was behind her back with her bagged leaves. Simon was kneeling at her side in a jiffy, as she'd anticipated.

"Let me see," he said, setting his bag aside to take her foot. He placed it on his thigh, pushed up her pant leg to slide her ankle boot off.

Michelle moaned, but it wasn't pain she felt when he peeled the colorful striped sock from her foot. He was so gentle as he examined it. A flash of hunger worked its way up her leg. Her heart was thumping erratically in her bosom. She pressed her lips together to suppress the wanting cry in her throat.

Simon lifted his head, asking, "How does this feel?" He applied a little pressure to one side of her foot.

She couldn't speak. She averted her head so as not to reveal the want reflected in her expression. She grunted instead.

"And this?" he asked, his finger sliding back and forth across the bottom of her foot.

Michelle couldn't decide what to say—yes, it hurt; or no, it didn't hurt. She forgot to squirm or show any signs of discomfort. His touch felt so good, she groaned, and it was her undoing.

She just knew guilt loomed in her expression when she looked up at him. His expression held a look of entreaty, with a crooked little grin on his mouth, and his eyes glimmering shades of desire.

"Want me to kiss it and make it better?" he asked, all the while tending her limb with his big, gentle hands.

Michelle could do no more than bob her head up and down. "Uh-huh," she heard her voice croon.

Simon lifted her ankle slightly and simultaneously lowered his head to plant a feather-light kiss on her ankle. Michelle forgot all about the bag of leaves behind her.

Chapter Eight

Simon felt as if he were in a perpetual sweat. He knew his days were numbered and wondered why he kept punishing himself. As much as he wanted to feel Michelle's softness against his bare flesh, he knew he didn't dare get as close to her again as he had in the park. Not until he disclosed the truth.

Tell her the truth and erase the specter of violating your professional ethics, he counseled himself, as he looked into her sweet, trusting face, her sparkling copper eyes. There was no way to tell that another twenty-four hours had passed between them, for his wants had not lessened one bit.

She was sitting across the table from him, as enticing as ever in her magnolia sweater ensemble. It hugged her fine body to distraction and blended beautifully with her brown complexion and the gentle touch of makeup on her face.

What was killing him even more, Simon thought, was that he knew she wanted him, too.

"I didn't realize you'd played football," Michelle said. "I guess I should have," she added, "but I never was much of a sports fan. How long did you play?"

They were at another restaurant, not Simon's favorite, but

one that served his purpose. It was a chain establishment with a family ambiance, and it seemed quite a few with children had decided to dine out. Consequently, the conversational din was loud.

"It seemed I was playing football before I started walking," Simon replied on a chuckle. "I loved the game, but in high school it got a little more serious."

They were nursing frothy cappuccinos. Dinner was over, but their table held platters of various dishes they had eaten. Ironically, Simon had had to pretend to be ravenous and force himself to eat. The burden of his lie was so heavy that it had filled his stomach, while his sexual hunger played havoc with another part of his anatomy.

"How is that?"

If she didn't stop casting those riveting dulcet gazes at him, Simon thought, he would jump across the table and soothe the beast growling in his loins. "It was more than just a game of healthy, competitive fun. It was a ticket to college . . . if you were good enough."

"That sounds like a job," she said. "One little mistake or accident and your career is over."

Michelle tweaked her nose with displeasure. It was just another of her charming traits, Simon groaned inwardly. "Not if you really enjoy playing the game," he replied. "I played all through high school and college without one major injury. Then after one year of playing with the Saints, my football-playing days were over."

The waitress who'd taken their order returned to the table. "Would you like me to clear the table now?" she asked, smiling weakly, trying not to look dead on her feet.

"Yes, please," he replied.

The waitress loaded their empty dishes onto a circular tray. Simon took the opportunity to draw a couple of deep breaths and gather the strength to proceed. His football story was the lead-in to telling Michelle what he did for a living. From there, he hoped the cookie didn't crumble irreparably, he thought, watching the waitress juggling the tray as she left them.

Michelle resumed the conversation. "What happened?"

Simon cleared his throat. "The second season had just started," he said, absently brushing his hands together. He wished she was sitting next to him, where he could hold her hand or at least feel her response. "The first game as a matter of fact. I was chasing down the Rams' QB on a blitz when a rookie lineman came crashing into me. It wasn't an illegal block or anything." He could tell the story matter-of-factly, without the pain of remembering, for he'd told it countless times while promoting the value of getting an education to high school and college athletes. "And I'd certainly been hit a lot harder.

"But this time," he added, folding his hands on the table before him, "I couldn't get up. My heart was racing, I could barely breathe because of this horrible stinging pain in my chest." He tapped himself with a fist over the breast pocket of his blazer. "It just got tighter and tighter. It felt like Superman was wringing my insides like a rag. It was my first ride on a stretcher. I passed out before I got to the hospital." He leaned back against the booth with a chuckle on his lips. "When I woke up, a day had passed. The doctors said I'd suffered a mild stroke."

"Oh, no!" Michelle exclaimed.

Her hands flew to her face, which was contorted with concern for him. She hadn't even known him then, Simon thought, squirming uncomfortably with that all too familiar ache and nervousness. Over the past several days, he had come to realize that what he felt for Michelle was deeper than desire for physical intimacy. It touched every nerve inside him. He knew for certain he wanted this woman for more than the holidays. The truth was inescapable. He hoped whoever said that the truth will set you free knew what the hell he was talking about.

Simon stretched an arm across the back of the booth, his

imagination wandering. It was all he could do to keep from jumping up and moving to her side of the table.

"Oh, yeah." He bobbed his head. He imagined her body sidled alongside his. "So I had a choice to make." Imagined her sizzling hot with desire. "Take a chance and keep playing, hoping the medication worked." Imagined him inside her and the look that would come over her expression because of his loving. He was working himself into a fervid frenzy, his body rock hard under the table. He took a much needed drink of water, adding, "Or find something not so stressful."

"Obviously you quit," she said. She folded her hands on the table. "You know, it just dawned on me I don't know what you do for a living."

The moment had arrived. Like a bucket of ice cold water, it cooled the temperature of his tumescent nature. Simon sat a little straighter, a little stiffer in his seat, staring into her face, with its adorably engrossed look. He sucked in a deep breath as normally as he could manage. The truth would break her heart, he thought, squirming uneasily, feeling trapped.

"A little of this, a little of that," he replied at last. "Don't worry. I can pay the bill," he joked as guilt rumbled violently inside him. "I understand you're a researcher of some kind. What's that about?"

"I don't want to talk about it."

" 'Santa Claus, go straight to the ghetto. Santa Claus . . .' "

A black blues band performed a lively, upbeat version of the old tune for the patrons inside and outside of Bayou Blues, a supper club located in Bayou Place.

Bayou Place was a recent development adjacent to the city's downtown theater district. Men and women bedecked in fine jewels, minks, and designer evening attire joined the heavy foot traffic on the surrounding sidewalks. All were assured safety by the patrolmen on horseback, who worked in conjunction with the blue and whites that frequently cruised the area.

Houston was lit up . . . well, lit up like a Texas Christmas tree. Simon had brought her here where it was not only festive and loud, but cold and crowded, even though it was barely seven-thirty at night. Soul food, hickory-smoked wood, barbecue, and Italian fare created a unique harmony of smells in the dark night air. There was even a sake lounge with a Japanese menu.

Simon had carved out a place for them on one of the wide cement porches that surrounded the club. She sat between his legs, with his arms around her. While he shielded her from the season's chill with his magnificent broad body, he couldn't protect her from her thoughts.

"Why did you bring me here?" she had asked upon their arrival a half hour ago. Leaving the restaurant, she had requested to be taken home.

"Because I can tell you need to work some things out, and I don't want you to be alone. You don't have to tell me what they are, and—"

He had fallen silent. "And what?" she had prompted.

"I want to be with you regardless," he had replied.

That simple admission had sealed it for Michelle. She no longer wanted to leave to be left alone with her thoughts. So here they sat, enjoying the blues and sipping hot apple cider with bourbon from tall porcelain mugs.

It was homey and comfortable, a sort of safety net for her thoughts, which were in shambles. Made worse by the rambunctious sensations festering inside her. It was Simon's fault, she thought, smiling into her mug. But it was a commendable culpability.

She had been interested in what he had to say, for sure, she thought, her eyes twinkling with her secret. Having spent the entire day shopping with her girlfriends and listening to their advice, she'd wanted Simon so badly all during dinner that she couldn't think about anything but the feel of him. He would have been shocked if he'd guessed her thoughts, she chuckled into her cup. She had shocked herself.

She knew she had sent out enough signals to him. She also knew any other man would have obliged her wishes in a second. But not Simon. It made her wonder fleetingly whether she had made a mistake by sharing the despair of her life with him. But if he had acted any differently not knowing about her past, she thought, she wouldn't have responded to him the way her senses did react every time he was near.

Content with her realizations regarding Simon, Michelle turned her thoughts back to what had nearly caused the end of a very pleasant evening.

The mention of work had killed the contented atmosphere at the table where they had dined. She had felt it instantly, Michelle recalled. She knew it derived from her, but she was helpless to make things right again. Simon had tried to engage her in a discussion about work, but she'd refused. Finally, he gave up and steered the conversation away from work, but it was too late. It was locked in her mind, leading her straight to even more twisted thoughts to ponder.

While work had once been a panacea that sustained her self-esteem, she had begun to feel incompetent on the job. Although she'd caught several mistakes before anyone learned of them, she didn't believe her luck would hold out. She feared the next mistake would blow up in her face. That was partly why she had resigned, for she had lost the strength to keep her personal feelings from intruding on her ability to do her job. In a way, Bob Matthew, her boss, had saved her professional life, but had unintentionally imposed a commitment she was still uncertain about.

She was good at her job normally, but it wasn't what she wanted to do for the rest of her life. It dawned on her that she had been governed by the ghost of her grandmother's wishes to get a *real job*.

She hadn't let herself think about it until Simon appeared in her life. He seemed to give her all kinds of feelings she'd never had before. It was as if he gave her a fantasy to live. There was no other way to explain it, except to say that when she was around him, she felt as if on the precipice of something wonderful about to happen.

She wondered if that was how her mother had felt, if that was what had driven her to do something that her own mother would never approve of. If only she could venture a guess as to why it had not been enough to satisfy some mysterious craving Joanne had had, Michelle pondered.

The question inevitably led her to the topic of men, male companionship. Her mother had not been so lucky in that department, always fooling herself into believing she had found Mr. Right. Not even the man she married had been able to give her what she was looking for, what she apparently needed so badly that not even her own daughter could provide.

Michelle wished she could put all of the blame on her grandmother for Joanne's inner turmoil. But in a way, she had failed her mother, too.

No, she amended, with a sense of disquiet. They had failed each other, and there was no way to make it up. Not as long as she was alive anyway. She shivered as a creeping uneasiness arose from the bottom of her heart.

"Cold?" Simon asked, his warm breath fanning her ear, his arms tightening around her.

"No," she shook her head gently, lifting the mug to drink her spiced cider. The disquieting sense subsided, along with her defenses, replaced by a mellow sweetness that spiraled through her.

It was Christmas Eve. Last-minute shoppers were everywhere, with a dozen or so in the Black Heritage Gallery on Almeda, where Michelle and Simon had come to get a set of candles for the *kinara*.

Michelle was a regular. She knew the owner and recognized many of the customers, who also seemed to know each other here. Conversations hinted that the gallery was a meeting place where even strangers, comfortable in the friendly atmosphere, chatted like old friends. She was standing in an unofficial line at the counter, awaiting her turn to be served. Simon was wandering around like an excited kid, looking at the paintings and artworks in one of the other large rooms. His attitude had lifted significantly since their arrival, she recalled.

When he'd picked her up this morning, he had seemed nervous and antsy. He further surprised her by declining breakfast. It had caused her an anxious moment, opening the door to doubt. She wondered if she had been wrong about him.

It was possible he'd just lost interest, or maybe she wasn't as important to him as she had thought. Maybe this was all a game and she was nothing more than another conquest to him, as her mother had been time and time again.

Still, it was too late to deny her strong feelings for him. She could only hope she wasn't deceiving herself . . . that the sensations she felt were not just arousal that bespoke lust. Unlike her mother, and perhaps, because of Joanne's pursuits, she hadn't gone through a string of lovers. Not that she hadn't considered it, particularly when her grandmother had been alive. She had known then it would have been solely out of pure spite. But truthfully, with two exceptions, she'd met no man who had elicited notions of commitment from her or aroused her enough to sleep with him.

Michelle shuddered imperceptibly, intrigued by the idea of sleeping with Simon.

Huge colorful masks of animal heads, standing African wood carvings, and framed limited edition prints by some of the masters of African-American art made up the work in the front room of the gallery. But they were not what held Simon's attention, nor caused the tight grimace on his face or the rhythmic clenching of his fists. It was what he saw from the room when he looked outside the picture window.

His old office was right across the street. He was surprised to learn that the gallery was here even when he had been a member of Dr. Sertima's clinic.

While slightly embarrassed he had not patronized the gallery, he was glad he hadn't, for surely he would have known the owner or her staff, and she or they him. He hadn't considered seriously enough the possibility of running into someone he knew, but coming here today had certainly pointed out an oversight. It had a sobering effect on him.

He couldn't postpone it any longer, he told himself. He'd already let too many opportunities pass. He had to find the strength to tell Michelle the truth. Soon, he vowed, knowing he couldn't let another twenty-four hours pass.

The woman in front of her took her package, and Michelle stepped up to be waited on. With a sidelong glance, she saw Simon return to the area nearby. She seemed to have a sixth sense about him, she thought, sliding her purchase across the counter to be rung up.

"Girl, what ocean did you snag him from?"

The softly voiced question was accompanied by an admiring gaze; it came from Robbie, the gallery's owner. Michelle's gaze followed hers to stare at Simon, who was admiring yet another painting. She had to admit that he looked absolutely delicious dressed in navy from top to bottom. She didn't need a mirror to know her face reflected the sensual thoughts she entertained.

"His name is Simon Stevenson," she replied shyly, but there was nothing timid about the rhythm of her heartbeat. It had been steadily growing stronger since she'd met him.

"Simon Stevenson?" Robbie said, her face scrunched up. "I know that name from somewhere. Well, it'll come to me. Is he a keeper?" she pressed, her voice a conspiratorial whisper.

"I don't know yet," Michelle replied, but her dreamy-eyed expression belied the uncertainty of her words. "We'll see," she added, knowing it was her own futile attempt at protecting her heart from hurt.

"Consider this one sold," Simon said, directing his voice to Robbie.

Michelle led the way to see the picture he referred to, with the owner close behind her. Delightful amazement filled her gaze, and she voiced it, murmuring a sound of awe.

Simon had selected the painting of a mythical character whose robe bore stitches of the minute detail inherent in a cross hatch pattern for which the artist Charles Bibbs was widely known.

"There are a couple of other pieces I'd like to get too."

Robbie stuck a "sold" sticker on the picture. "Lead the way," she said to Simon. Behind his back, she winked at Michelle, mouthing, "Keep this one."

The stars were out this cold Christmas Eve, but they couldn't hold a candle to the light of approval beaming in Simon's eyes. Michelle felt a dumb smile on her face. Her mouth had gone dry, even though she was tempted to suggest that they pass on Clarissa's dinner party as she returned his approving stare.

Simon stood just outside her front door, magnificently attired, with adoration of her in his expression. She studied his formal elegance. He was decked out in a classic black tuxedo and kente vest over a white shirt.

He tugged at the bow tie at his neck. She took a shallow breath.

Michelle noticed Simon didn't take his eyes off her the entire time he sauntered inside, closed the door behind him, and took her hands with his surprisingly warm fingers. His reaction let her know the dress was worth every red cent she'd paid for it. An ankle-length silk poplin gown in purple, it curved low in the front, with a circular opening at the back. Small diamond-studded earrings and black patent leather slingbacks completed her ensemble. She silently thanked her girlfriends for talking her into spending some of her well-earned money.

"As you can see," Simon said at last, his voice a husky whisper, "I'm speechless."

"Probably a first," Michelle teased, with a nervous imitation of laughter in her voice. She could no more tear her eyes off him than she could stop breathing or smelling the pleasant masculine cologne he wore.

His mouth curled into a lopsided smile and his brows rose over bright eyes, creating an innocent, wolfish look. "You look absolutely stunning."

"So do you," she said shyly. Her heart was beating up a storm. When he looked over her shoulder behind her, she frowned curiously, then heard his sharp intake of breath. "What's wrong?"

"Just checking to see if there's a back. And there isn't." His eyebrows arched, then knitted into a thoughtful frown. "How many people does Clarissa normally have at her dinner parties?"

Michelle wondered where he was headed with his question. "There will be twenty of us."

"Hmm," Simon pondered aloud, looking at her intensely. "I hope I don't have to stay chained to you tonight."

"Why would you do that?" she asked, but found the idea of his nearness sublimely amenable, feeling a ripple of desire.

"To make sure every able, red-blooded male animal knows that you have been taken off the market," Simon replied indulgently.

Michelle tingled, thrilled by the underlying sensuality of his words. "And have I been taken off the market?" she asked, looking up at him coyly.

Simon exhaled a dramatic sigh. "You have to ask?" he replied, his voice deepening into a caress as he dipped his head to hers.

His cool lips pressed against hers, Michelle felt as though a single drop of hot liquid was oozing down her spine. She shivered, and Simon wrapped his arms around her, pulling her closer to him.

As she nestled within his solid embrace, the kiss intensified. His mouth was firmly on hers. Then his tongue thrust inside her mouth for a tantalizing exploration. She slipped her hands inside his coat, holding him around the waist for dear life, lest she sink into the sweet wanting well building in her loins.

Slowly, he withdrew his mouth from hers and stared into her eyes with unmasked desire and a deep soulful look. He breathed a long drawn out breath.

"We'd better get going," he said.

Michelle forced a blink, hoping to hide her disappointment. Then she cleared her throat and yielded to his suggestion, reluctantly. "Just let me get my coat."

The kiss was like none she had experienced before, drugging in its sweetness, packed with power. As she withdrew her coat from the hall closet, Michelle knew she wouldn't be able to concentrate on anything else all night.

Chapter Nine

S ilently, Simon exhaled, exhausted.

    Another day had passed, and it was almost over. If he didn't make a way now, he told himself, he'd burst with the secrets burning deep inside him. He didn't know how his personal confession would go over. Maybe he was fooling himself about her reaction, but he never felt more right about his feelings: He was in love with Michelle.

Crazy, huh?

"I didn't get you anything," Michelle exclaimed with regret tempered by delight.

"You accepted my invitation to spend Christmas with me," Simon replied. "That's gift enough for me."

Horrid weather on Christmas made for a delightful prelude to a lazy, laid-back day indoors. Jingle-bell jazzy tunes played softly throughout Simon's home. But the room sang its own carol, as age-old as the first song, strumming chords of sensuality.

Simon had made her wait until after dinner to open her gift, which she now held in her lap, carefully tearing the colorful foil wrapping. They were sitting on the plush white carpeting in his sparsely decorated and softly lit living room.

No expense had been spared decorating his tree, which Simon struggled to make his focal point. But it was no competition for Michelle, who looked as desirable as when she arrived this morning, still glowing from a perpetual state of joy.

"Simon, you shouldn't have. But I'm glad you did," she said gleefully. Her throaty laughter filled the shadows in the room.

The prohibition of touching her was driving him crazy. Simon felt as if he was taking a test to see how much longer he could hold out. Knowing he was still in possession of the truth, he was determined to win.

He'd told enough lies—hollow vows that died in his throat each time he tried to tell her what he did for a living. He hoped that by knowing *who* he was would lessen her anger about *what* he was.

"Oh, you didn't! You didn't!" Michelle beamed happily. With her arms expanded to hold up a painting, she admired it with a dreamy-eyed stare.

Entitled "African Goddess," it was the second painting by Charles Bibbs that he'd purchased at the Black Heritage Gallery. It matched the style of "The Mystic," which Simon intended to hang in his bedroom. Even though Michelle had been present when he had bought them, it didn't lessen her surprise, and he was all the more pleased by her reaction.

"I can't believe it. It's absolutely gorgeous. I love it," she gushed in phrases typical of one experiencing something wonderful.

Michelle set the painting on the couch and leaned across the distance between them. "Thank you," she said plainly. Her eyes, sparkling like polished jewels, caressed him with an intense look. Then her lips were on his for a light kiss that sent a shudder through him. He closed his eyes and inhaled deeply, sealing her taste in his mind.

More. More, his thoughts pleaded, his eyes still closed.

* * *

Michelle decided that Simon had been a gentleman for far too long. When she moved to kiss him in appreciation of his gift, she stayed on the floor, kneeling in front of him.

Now, she smiled into the hint of a grimace on his face. His eyes were still closed, but his expression was akin to restraint. She could smell his excitement. The sensation was as thick as a rope inside her, too. She intended to free them both of long, pent-up desires.

The thought had played havoc with her senses from the time he kissed her chastely on the cheek after taking her home from Clarissa's. She had already been simmering from his previous kiss and she hadn't been able to sleep soundly for the all-pervasive yearning in her body.

Ever so slowly, Simon opened his eyes, a curious frown on his face. When he saw her expression—a wide-open display of her wants—his nostrils flared as he inhaled deeply and darts of concern came into his eyes.

"Don't worry," Michelle said softly, her mouth a breath away from his. "I know what I'm doing."

Her lips touched one side of his mouth, then the other. Michelle took her time sampling his lips. She felt him tremble seconds before her hands splayed across his chest.

Neither the ladylike correctness her grandmother would have cautioned nor shyness stood a chance in the face of her longings. Desire tugged at her innards, applying pressure to every nerve and cell in her body, clamoring to break free.

She liked the smell of Simon, the feel of him weakening to her. A shudder racked his body as she moved in closer to him and his power, straddling his firm thighs.

He was really shaking now, and she smiled, pleased by her power. Lifting her head slightly, she noticed the beads of perspiration sprouting across his forehead, his top lip. He didn't know what to do with his hands, so he kept making fists in the air.

"Michelle." His voice trembled as he looked at her anxiously.

His eyes were glazed in amorous amber need, and it was the look Michelle held in her thoughts as she again pressed her mouth to his. His lips were responsive, but she could still feel the control he exerted over his want. The thought of it only made her more determined, increased her excitement, emboldened her.

Her hands began to knead his shoulders while her lips tantalized his flesh in feathery kisses about his face: left cheek . . . right cheek . . . chin . . . neck. She felt the tension rippling through his body.

"Touch me, Simon," she commanded, her voice a whisper, her tongue dipping into his ear. As hardheaded as she knew he could be, she was confident he would obey.

Grunting in obedience, he wrapped his arms around her waist, pulling her closer to him, and smothered her mouth in a kiss rife with passion and need.

He tasted good, and she was starving for him. She couldn't get enough, and neither could he. His tongue ravaged the inner recesses of her mouth. Their hands crossed, his seemed everywhere at once; hers roamed his head, his shoulders, and his sides, where she grabbed the bottom of his sweater to pull over his head.

She breathed in the magnificence of his wide, thick chest. He was as fine without clothes as he had been with them, and she could hardly wait to get the rest of them off him. Her grandmother would have been mortified by her behavior, the anticipation that caused her body to shudder, ache, and burn.

"Simon."

His name was an affirmation to her decision, to the sense of rightness she felt, to the question of certainty in his desire-laden eyes.

Michelle couldn't even remember what she'd worn now as

she basked under the fiery hunger in Simon's eyes, sitting before him in nothing but her black silk teddy and socks.

His mouth captured hers in a possessive kiss. His hands gentled, exploring the tender places on her body—the inside of her breasts, the back of her knees, the inner sides of her thighs. She begged for him in whimpering sighs until he inserted a finger into the hot center of her, and it took her breath away.

The phone rang. It was like a time-out to breathe for both of them. Their foreheads together, they listened as the phone rang again.

"I forgot to turn on the answering machine," Simon said on a ragged breath.

Damn it, he didn't want to move. And even as he silently cursed the blasted phone, Simon knew he'd been saved by the bell. He should have never let this get started in the first place, he upbraided himself, as his breathing returned to normal.

Reluctantly, he let Michelle go when she climbed off his thighs. Then he slowly got to his feet. She leaned across the couch, her arms crossed over her bosom. He swallowed and looked down at her with sheepish regret. He shuddered anew, thinking she had felt so good in his arms; her body had fit perfectly next to his.

The phone rang again.

"Maybe it's important," Michelle said, her mouth crooked in a sympathetic smile.

Simon nodded absently. "I'll be right back," he said, silently cursing and chiding himself. "Make yourself at home. I should have a cover or something upstairs in the hall closet."

"That'll give me a chance to . . ." Michelle started, then stopped. "Where's your bathroom?"

"Right on the other side of the hallway," Simon replied at the door before vanishing. "Watch out for Peeping Tom," he yelled back.

* * *

Michelle frowned, wondering what Simon was talking about as she followed the path he indicated. The living room door was right off the entryway. The logical direction from here was left. She almost passed the closed door to her right.

Opening it, she found the light switch on the wall and flipped it on. She looked around and jumped, startled. As her breathing settled back to normal, she laughed and shook her head, now understanding Simon's warning.

A window had been painted onto the wall and a man was peeping through it. She should have expected something silly like that from Simon, having met Mr. Rudolph.

How so characteristically Simon, she thought with a chuckle. Damn! How she liked that man, she beamed, taking care of her business. It was a good thing the phone rang, she told herself.

Even though the interruption cooled her ardor, there was no doubt in her mind about how this evening would end. She and Simon had been tiptoeing around each other for the past several days. Like two kids entertaining thoughts of getting their feet wet. Well, that was not the best analogy for what they had in mind, she corrected herself resolutely, but it was close enough.

Nothing like this had ever happened to her before. The feelings were new, and the depths of them shocking and surprising. She was looking forward to more of those wonderful sensations.

She had known there was something special about Simon from the very beginning. She didn't see any reason to halt or prolong the inevitable. Time would tell, but for now she loved Simon Stevenson. Or she was in love with him. Arguing over the difference didn't matter, she told herself, washing her hands in the sink.

She knew she wanted him—warts and all—in a relationship for all time. Just the way the principles of Kwanzaa had been designed.

Drying her hands, Michelle left the bathroom and returned to the living room. Simon had not returned, and she was getting chilly.

She ventured upstairs in search of that hall closet for something to cover herself with.

At the top of the landing were doors on either side. The one to her left was empty. She recalled Simon telling her that he had been in no rush to decorate all the rooms. She checked the room to her right and saw it was his bedroom. An oversize bed dominated the room done in earth tones with splashes of gold. Though he had the standard bedroom furnishings, her attention always strayed back to that bed. She thought about her gift for him, and she could hardly wait for him to finish his call.

With a quivering shudder of craving, she ducked into the room she thought would be the bathroom. Unfortunately, there was nothing but clean towels, so she left.

Across the hall from his bedroom was another one that was filled with exercise equipment. A few steps away, she found the hall closet. It was a door away from where she could hear Simon's voice. She grabbed a big towel and wrapped it around herself, then started to return downstairs. Curiosity got the better of her and she headed for that room instead.

Simon was on the phone. His back was to her when she stood outside the door, looking into what was obviously his home study. She tiptoed in and began to look around.

Not only did she notice the uncluttered decor, but the walls where his certificates of appreciation and college degrees hung. She advanced stealthily so as not to disturb him. Her eyes fell and remained as if stuck on the one from Louisiana State University College of Medicine adjacent to his license to practice psychiatry in Texas.

A feeling akin to shock ran through her as she realized what that meant. Her rage and anger built up slowly. Mortification joined her wrath as she recalled she'd damn near raped him when she felt he was moving too slow.

Simon had been more than a setup as a blind date, she

thought furiously. She should have known he was too good to be true. She had been a case study to him, and no doubt, her friends had been in on it. Not just in on it—they had probably planned it, she thought, tears building in the corners of her eyes.

It all came back to her. Breathing hard as if she couldn't get enough air into her lungs, she remembered she had never been allowed to be alone. The times she wasn't with Simon, she recalled, her friends had taken his place to baby-sit her. That could only mean he knew everything about her, not just her misery and scarred soul, but her failed attempt to end her life.

Hence, everything about his presence in her life since that time had all been planned. She had never been so humiliated in her entire miserable life.

Simon spun his chair around to see her. His expression metamorphosed into painful regret when he stared into her face and the hot angry look residing there now.

"Hold on," Simon said into the phone, then cupped it in his hands.

"Where's your couch?" Michelle demanded, her head whipping around the room. She clutched the towel around her tighter.

Simon stared, stupefied, wordless.

"I thought all shrinks used couches," she said nastily. She cursed the tears that fell from her eyes, but wouldn't release the towel to wipe them away.

"Michelle," he said, gulping, "let me explain."

"How much do you charge?"

"Huh?"

"What is your professional service going to cost me, Dr. Stevenson?" she fired off at him, stepping out of his reach.

"Michelle, you're way off base."

"Am I? You can't convince me that the three busybodies fixed me up with you solely because of your good looks," she said snidely.

"So you admit I'm attractive?"

She ignored his playful attempt. "Are they paying you for your services?"

"You know what I've done with you, and I resent the implication that I'm a whore."

"Are they paying you?" She spat out the words.

"Why can't you just accept that we're attracted to each other and that is the only reason neither of us has walked away by now. Heaven knows you're not the easiest woman in the world to get along with," he said, trying to cajole her.

Michelle would not be amused. "You've had plenty of opportunity to move on," she snapped. She felt a wretchedness that was beyond pain; it was nothing like the depressing emotions she had suffered before he had come into her life. "Why didn't you?"

"I already told you why, but you weren't listening," Simon said, looking at her with a plea for friendship and understanding in his eyes. "I'm attracted to you, woman," he ground out fiercely over her. "And damn it, I want you to live. More importantly, I want you to want to live. And I damn sure want you to want me as much as I want you."

Michelle refused to let herself believe him, though her innards betrayed her. All the pieces of her shattered soul seemed to gel back together in acceptance of that thought, her very private desire. She had to get away now before she made an even bigger fool of herself.

"Go to hell," she screamed, running from the room.

"I'm there now," he muttered.

But Michelle didn't hear him, nor see the look of dejection that marred his expression. She raced down the stairs to the living room to retrieve her clothes—a soft peach pullover and gray stirrup pants. She dressed hurriedly. Her boots were in his closet, where she raced to get them.

"Michelle!" Simon called from the top of the stairs.

Michelle left the carryall she'd brought. It contained sweet-smelling toiletries and the sexy nightgown she had hoped Simon would appreciate, she recalled, slipping her boots on. How stupid of her!

"Michelle, come back here," she heard Simon yell as she tried to shrug into her coat. She managed to get her shoes on, but not her coat as she fiddled with the lock at the front door. The alarm went off when she opened the door and it continued to scream its warning as she skipped down the three steps of the front porch.

Hadn't her mother given her enough examples of foolish pursuits? How many bricks did she have to be hit with before she realized she was no better than her mother, who had gone to her grave unfulfilled and unhappy?

Oblivious to the stinging cold temperature, Michelle didn't know where she was going as she raced across the small front yard. The street was lined with cars and homes boasting Christmas decorations, but no one seemed to have ventured outside.

"Michelle, come on. Let's talk," Simon called from the doorway.

Michelle ran, trying to put on her coat at the same time. Simon was coming after her. She had to hurry.

"I'll take you home if you still want me to," he yelled from the porch, struggling to get into his coat. "But we are going to talk about this."

"You don't have anything to say I want to hear," she yelled. She got the gate open. Wiping away the tears from her eyes, she bolted, carelessly, mindlessly, out into the street. More tears fell to blind her path.

She could barely see where she was going, and she definitely didn't see the driver of the big black Lincoln until—*thump*—she slammed into the front of the car, rolled over the hood, and bounced off onto the hard, cold pavement, unconscious.

Chapter Ten

Michelle didn't know where she was when consciousness returned. It wasn't a typical room, but a space nonetheless, translucent white and infinite. Threatened by the strangeness of her surroundings, she felt a nervous fluttering pricking her chest

She pivoted slowly, circuitously, then saw them. Her eyes blinked repeatedly, focusing on the line of people that stretched as far as she could see. They seemed a distance away from her, yet so close.

"Where am I?"

"Just outside the Great Halls of Maati."

Michelle twisted quickly, this way and that, looking up and about warily, to see who had spoken. But there was no one. She appeared to be alone. Her heart pounded as panic rose increasingly in her.

"I am here, Ms. Craig."

An explosive murmur of surprise was all Michelle got out before the apparition appeared. Was she dreaming? she wondered.

"No."

It answered her thought, leaving her utterly speechless, with wide-eyed curiosity that rivaled her fear. She stared, but couldn't discern for certain if *It* was real: a huge translucent image attired in layers of a chalky white robe.

"Who . . . who are you?" she stammered to the figure, which seemed more myth than man. "Who are those people? What are they doing?"

"I am simply your Guardian. They are awaiting their turns for the weighing of the heart ceremony."

Her insides quaking, Michelle sucked in a deep breath. He or *It* was referring to the Judgment Hall, the place of accounting, where the life of the deceased's heart was weighed against the feather of truth. She knew that through her readings of Dr. Karenga's extended book, in which he elaborated on the philosophy out of which Kwanzaa had been created. She also realized what that meant for her. Her whole body tightened, and then she took a breath.

"Am I . . . am I dead?" Michelle asked, her hand over her rapidly beating heart.

"We shall see."

"What do you mean by that?" she asked impatiently. "Either I am or I'm not."

The Guardian gave her a look such as one would give an impertinent child. "We met before when you were in such a hurry to get here. But you still may not be ready."

Michelle frowned, straining to remember, but mostly to understand.

"Oh, yes. It was me. Only I came in forms you would not recognize. Look at them now. See how your absence has affected them."

Michelle, albeit still somewhat skeptical, looked to where he pointed. Within seconds of taking in the scene, an astonished gasp escaped her. There, where they often met for "girlfriend" chats, in the room right off Loretta's bedroom, were her friends, each huddled within herself in agony.

Clarissa sat on the edge of the window, rocking back and

forth, her arms wrapped around herself as silent tears poured from her eyes. She stilled and swallowed as if she hadn't been breathing at all. Her shoulders trembled from the control she tried to exert over her sorrow.

The wailing dirge singeing the air largely came from Reba. She couldn't, nor did she seem to want to, control the sobs racking her body. She collapsed on the beige carpet near the navy velvet armchair and dropped her head on the cushioned seat.

Pacing aimlessly, looking lost, Loretta ran her fingers through her braids, twisting them about on her head. She dropped her hands helplessly to her sides and stared at nothing. What Michelle knew about Loretta, who liked to believe that her shoulders were big enough to carry any weight, was never more evident than in her ravaged expression. Dried tears stained her face, leaving a trail that went from her eyes, then down her soft cheeks.

"*It was my fault,*" *Loretta said woefully.* "*I should have known better. Simon tried to warn me that nobody could stop someone who wanted to commit suicide from doing so.*" *Beating the side of her head, she exclaimed,* "*I should have listened.*"

"*I could kill her for doing this,*" *Reba stammered out through her tears.* "*She promised she wouldn't do anything stupid.*"

"*But she couldn't help it.*" *Clarissa came to her defense.*

"*Right,*" *Loretta snapped sarcastically.* "*She missed seeing that big old Lincoln and ran right into it.*"

Through their mournful expressions, they exchanged a subtle look of acceptance. Michelle realized they believed she had committed suicide, that she had killed herself on purpose.

"It was an accident," Michelle protested. But they couldn't hear her. Each was locked in her solitary space as they grieved over Michelle's absence from the group. It was as if her death had created a distance between them in life, for they didn't go to each other to give comfort for their collective loss.

If she had believed that death didn't hurt, she'd been mistaken by her ignorance, she thought. The pain she felt seeing this picture of grief before her was more wretched than she ever would have imagined.

"How do you like being dead now?" *He* asked.

Michelle couldn't answer for the tears clogging her throat, the thoughts swarming through her mind.

She wondered if Simon believed she had deliberately taken her life, as well. She couldn't blame him, recalling how badly she had behaved upon learning what he did for a living. She'd allowed sophist reasons to overshadow her honest feelings, faithful emotions that touched her soul. She realized now she had been afraid to believe herself worthy of them and, consequently, denied herself an opportunity to be loved and admit her love for him.

Michelle turned her gaze on the Guardian, but could barely make him out for the tears blurring her vision. All she could think was that *it hurt like hell,* but she wasn't referring to death.

"I guess you would think it's overrated, huh? Well, there's more to see."

The scene changed with a whoosh of sensation. Michelle saw herself lying in a casket. She was going to be buried in a new dress, the color of persimmon, which her friends had once agreed looked great on her. The casket was the finest mahogany, with silver handles and blue velvet bedding.

Watching the eulogy service, Michelle detected disbelief among the mourners. There was also scorn in some of the faces of former coworkers and neighbors who attended her funeral. Bob Matthew, however, had tears in his eyes. He shook his head sadly every so often as if he blamed himself.

Michelle read his lips as he muttered to himself, *"I should have recognized the signs."*

Her friends were the last to leave the cemetery. One by one, they and their men placed lilies on her casket. It hurt her to see Simon there, too, and a breath skipped in her bosom. Her gaze was riveted on him; he looked as handsome as ever dressed in black.

But the light was gone from his hazel eyes, which were now dull and dry. His mouth was pinched, and those lips, which could contort in the most mischievous of grins, were turned down.

He kissed a lily, then placed it on the casket. His hand lingered there a moment; he gulped hard as if swallowing down tears, then walked off hurriedly.

Michelle felt terrible regrets collide with a tremor of pure desire inside her. It was more painful to realize that even in death she was still affected by him and there was nothing she could do about it.

They all stood by the limousine, the driver waiting for them to get in. *"Are we still going to try to celebrate Kwanzaa? I don't know about you, but I don't feel like celebrating."*

"Even though Michelle is not here to celebrate with us in person, her spirit is here," Simon said with that reasonable, patient manner of his. *"She put a lot of work into planning it. I think going through with her plans is the best way to honor her. If we don't, we'll never forgive ourselves."*

"Speak for yourself," Reba said scornfully.

Her three friends got in the limousine, leaving Simon standing alone as the car drove off. Michelle screamed defiantly at their action, but none paid her any attention.

"Thank you, Simon," Michelle murmured in a tone of defeated resignation in appreciation that he had stood up for her. To her Guardian, she said in a small, forlorn voice, "Well, that's that. At least everybody came."

"No. Not everybody."

The scene melted into another. Back in the living room of her home, a man sat in one of the old chairs. His head was bowed and tears streamed silently down his face. Gripping a glass filled with dark liquid, he was mumbling to himself. It was her Uncle David, but he wasn't alone. Michelle wondered who he was talking to.

She didn't have far to look, for a woman walked into her small-screen view. The woman took the glass from her uncle's hand and set it on the coffee table. Michelle strained to hear what was being said, but couldn't.

"See," her Guardian said.

"I can't hear anything."

"Oh. Sorry about that."

It was as if he suddenly turned on the volume.

"I've been so busy nursing my own hard feelings that I never thought about how Michelle was feeling," David was saying. *"It never occurred to me that she would be even more affected than I was. I guess I just assumed that children always got over things so quickly."*

"She could have just as easily come to you, David," the woman replied.

"No," he replied, shaking his head in harsh musing. *"She couldn't. I never permitted it. Nor would I have known what to do about it."*

"Give yourself a little more credit than that," the woman said, kneeling at his knees, taking his hands in hers. *"Don't bear all the guilt. You have to move on with your life. To do otherwise would only continue the cycle of ill feelings."*

"I know you're right. But . . ." He fell silent. Michelle saw his Adam's apple throb in his throat, and he couldn't complete his thoughts.

"Who is that woman with my uncle?" she asked.

"That's his soul mate. Amelia Lofton."

"Oh, yeah," Michelle replied with awareness, recalling her uncle had said he'd found the love of his life at last. She was very different from his other wives who all were tall, model-thin, cold-looking women he'd believed sophisticated. From her manner, Amelia appeared affectionate. Matronly looking, with warm, friendly brown eyes. Michelle felt good about her presence in her uncle's life.

"I'm glad he has someone," she said.

"Yes. If he doesn't allow your death to ruin it."

Michelle flashed him a wry look. She didn't like the responsibility held over her head like that.

"Hey," the Guardian said cavalierly, "it happens."

"Simon!" Michelle exclaimed anxiously. "What's going to happen to Simon?"

"Ah, yes, the man who captured your heart," her Guardian said with a kind of fatal melancholy. "Well, let's see."

Her handsome Simon looked utterly despondent. His broad shoulders were anchored with anguish. His steps no longer spry, his movement clumsy and uncoordinated. How she longed to see his crooked smile, the laughter in his eyes, the zest for life that emanated from him.

Her friends hadn't changed their minds, leaving Simon to celebrate Kwanzaa all by himself. Michelle bit back the cry in her throat as she watched him set up the Kwanzaa paraphernalia he'd bought at the Black Heritage Gallery.

The seven candles in the wood *kinara* sat atop a piece of red, black, and green *mkeka* mat of *kinte* cloth. Several ears of corn, *vibunzi,* were laid out right next to his *mazao,* assorted fruits and nuts in a handwoven basket. His unity cup sat empty next to a crystal pitcher of clear liquid.

He fiddled in his pockets, then withdrew a small packet of matches. His hands were shaking so badly it took three tries before he was finally able to light the black candle in the center. Michelle saw the tears well up in his eyes and begin to stream down his face. She clasped her hands to her heart and bit down on her lip.

"Tonight is supposed to be the night that unity is celebrated," Simon said, his voice wavery with tears. *"Umoja. Well, there's only me, Michelle. But you already know that since it's my fault that neither you nor the group we started out with is here."*

"No, Simon, it's not your fault," Michelle screamed.

"I don't know the words to the libation statement that Dr. Karenga wrote. We were counting on you for that," he said.

"*At least, I was. So instead, to you, your life, and all that you gave me in such a short time . . .*"

"No, it's not supposed to be for me," Michelle cried. "It's for the brave men and women who came before us, who lived, loved, struggled, and built a home for us in this country. We pay respect to those who gave so much—their love, strength, and blood so that we can continue to sow our seeds, build, and grow in unity and strength. . . ."

Simon filled his cup and held it high in a toast. "*For you, Michelle, beautiful woman that you were. You'll always be beautiful to me.*" *He held the cup to his lips with tears falling silently down his face.* "*I'm going to miss you. I'm going to miss you for a very long time.*"

Simon set the cup on the table, blew out the candle, turned off the light, and left the room.

"I guess that proves something," the Guardian said. "The little mountains you people build from anthills," he added with a *tut-tut,* shaking his head.

Michelle, with nothing but time to think about what her Guardian had said, did. She had blown Simon's efforts out of proportion. What he had done—withholding his identity from her—wasn't any different from what her friends had done, and that was to care for her. The form their concern took may not have been what she would have chosen, but they believed they were acting in her best interests, as did Simon.

He had given her the feelings she had never been able to define or ascribe for herself. He'd opened the door she had kept shut to living and invited her into and guided her through a new world. If only she could . . . She shook her head. It was useless thinking about second chances now.

"Wouldn't you like to see more?"

Without awaiting her reply, her Guardian simply spread his hands, palms up, and she watched the second night unfold. Again, Simon was left to celebrate *Kujichagulia* alone. This time, at the ceremony's end, he was able to actually drink a sip of the libation drink of white grape juice in a toast to self-determination.

Her Guardian didn't stop there, punishing her more by bringing one image after another for her to view.

On the third night of *Ujima,* collective work and responsibility, Simon was joined by Loretta and Ed. The atmosphere in which they celebrated lacked the festive nature of Kwanzaa, but at least Simon wasn't alone. Afterward, Loretta turned to Simon.

"I'm sorry we blamed you. I know it wasn't your fault," she said contritely. *"You warned me, but I ..."* The tears dangling from her lashes fell, her voice faltered, and she couldn't go on.

"Come on, babe," Ed said, pulling her into his embrace. *"It's going to be all right."* He reached out and took Simon's hand in his for a firm shake. *"It's going to be all right."*

The atmosphere improved a little, as more of her friends joined in Simon's celebration. Clarissa lit the candles of the preceding three nights to finally pay homage to the fourth night's principle of cooperative economics.

"Tonight and all nights of the year, we celebrate the spirits of those who have gone before who represented the spirit of Ujamaa," she said, *"and the spirits of others who work in our communities to create and nurture economic organizations that enable all of us to prosper ...."*

This night, the celebration lasted longer than before as they all sat down to dinner, albeit a somber one.

"Habari Gani?"

"Nia," *they replied in unison.*

Reba arrived without Alan to lead the fifth night's celebration of purpose.

Vince accompanied Clarissa on the sixth night to open the celebration of creativity. Also the night of the *karamu,* Simon rearranged and decorated the room with the help of the others. A red, black, and green color scheme dominated the room, with the *mkeka* placed in the center of the floor and food placed creatively around it. Six of the candles burned brightly.

"Habari gani?"

"Kuumba," *came the reply.*

"For our people everywhere then," he said. He called out the names of leaders dating back to the first heroes in African-American history while Kwanzaa music played subtly in the background. "And for our dear friend Michelle. And for future generations who will live because we struggle. . . ."

After dinner, they did the project Michelle had recommended. Using the colored paper and the pinecones and twigs, they designed a memory book. Simon took pictures with his Polaroid, and they inserted them into the book. The evening's ending activity, however, only served to sadden them again, for Michelle's picture was noticeably absent from their collective effort.

There was nothing Michelle could do but watch. She'd never felt more helpless—not even when she had been alive. At least then she had had people around her who cared and who managed to stimulate her enough to want to live, despite the fight she had put up.

She had watched as Reba, displaying more tact than any thought her capable of, convinced her uncle David and his woman Amelia to attend the last night's celebration of faith.

"This is the seventh and final night of Kwanzaa in which we celebrate Imani, faith . . . something I'm sad to admit has been lacking in the Craig family," David said. Amelia touched his arm affectionately, and he gave her a sad smile. "On this night, we dedicate ourselves to uphold the values of the principle Imani, and all the seven principles, in the year that has just come. We will have faith in our future, in our people, ourselves, that we may work to create a better world. . . ."

Afterward, he wiped the tears from his eyes and cleared his throat. "I'd like to break from the traditional celebration now and give you something," he said to the group. "I know Michelle wanted you to have these things." He ducked from the room to return carrying three large pictures. "She had these locked in the study with your names on them," he said, giving one picture each to Loretta, Clarissa, and Reba. The pictures, titled The Arc of Life, *had been painted by Dr. John Biggers. They brought tears to her friends' eyes.*

"They shouldn't be separated," Loretta said. She exchanged a meaningful look with her friends, who nodded in response. One by one, they handed their pictures to Simon. "We know she would have wanted you to have these."

Michelle missed them all, but Simon, she missed the most. Her throat ached with regret, the torment of her incomplete knowledge beat at her thoughts.

Chapter Eleven

Groggy and disoriented, Michelle awakened slowly. She blinked her eyes several times, trying to figure out where she was and why. Lying still, she listened to the continuous plop of water hitting metal.

Michelle was lying on a narrow bed within the confines of a small space congested with gadgets. Feeling pressure around her head, she lifted her hand and felt a tug on her arm. Looking at it, she saw the blood pressure wrap that was attached to a small machine slightly on the other side of where she lay, monitoring her pulse. A bandage was wrapped around her head.

She lifted her head cautiously to look around her. Determining that another of the gadgets was a portable life support system, she confirmed that she was in the back of an ambulance.

As she rose to her haunches, she wondered how long had she been here? It couldn't have been for long, she thought, frowning, but it seemed like forever. In fact, it seemed as if she had seen sketches of her life pass before her eyes.

A whisper of terror shot through her and her hand flew to her heart. It was pounding fast and furious. She believed it was due to her unknown fear. Other than that, she felt fine, albeit astonished.

She was alive! She was alive! The refrain echoed silently in her head.

The din of voices raised in contention seized her attention, and her gaze followed the noise. Standing outside by the open doors an attendant talked to someone whose voice she recognized the instant he spoke.

Michelle sat up slowly and instinctively called out, "Simon."

Instantly, three heads peered into the ambulance, each wearing a version of amazed surprise on its face. As if suddenly aware of their gaping silence, they began talking at the same time.

"I was just insisting that they take you to Ben Taub Hospital."

"We've been trying to tell him that Riverside Hospital is closer."

"Ben Taub is full anyway."

Michelle ignored the argumentative chatter and swung her feet gingerly to the floor of the ambulance. She had no time to waste now, she thought, feeling the blood streaming spiritedly through her, compelling her to live.

Simon was staring at her with relief on his face, wonder lighting his eyes as he extended a hand inside the ambulance to help her climb out. As soon as her feet touched the ground, he draped a protective arm around her shoulders.

"What's going on here? Uh, Miss . . ." said the blue-uniformed police officer who appeared from the side of the ambulance.

"Everything is all right," Michelle said. "Simon will take care of me."

"You bet he will," Simon vowed, sweeping her up into his arms. "I'll do better this time," he promised with a broad smile plastered across his face.

"Wait! I've got to get some information from you!"

* * *

"Oh, God! I thought I'd lost you. Are you sure you're okay? Let me check," Simon said a short time later.

There was a sense of anxious urgency in his voice. His hands trembled ever so lightly as they examined her body. Michelle knew that just the feel of her was more assuring for him than any words she could say.

"Wait right here. I'll be right back," he said, dashing from the room.

Michelle knew it was useless to call a halt to whatever action Simon had decided to take. Lying in his bed, she was still reeling from the incident.

It wasn't the car accident she thought about. She knew that part had been real, but with the passage of time, she again wondered if she had dreamed the rest.

Had she actually been given twenty-four hours to live by a man or a ghost claiming to be her Guardian? Or had she simply been given a dose of shock to prove a point? Regardless, the point had been made and the insights she had gained felt true.

She remembered Simon's remark about the seven cardinal sins, to which she in her arrogant wisdom had replied something about the cardinal virtues inherent in Kwanzaa. She should have paid more attention to the sins, for she had committed several of them.

Denial and pride had prevented her from seeking help when she had been emotionally overwrought and then made her turn away from support when it was offered. She had nearly lost her capacity to experience emotions, as well as her physical being.

Michelle exhaled deeply, then drew a fresh round of air into her lungs. She had a thought that it would clear her mind, allowing her to be true to herself. For a change, she thought.

When Simon returned, clutching his black medical bag at his side, he pulled up inches from the foot of the bed, staring at her. It was as if what he saw on her face froze him in place.

Despite the concern marring his expression, he was absolutely gorgeous.

It was Michelle's last thought, and then she began to speak from her heart.

"I didn't mean to run in front of that car and damn near get myself killed," she said plainly. "I don't want to die. At least, not before my time . . . and not by my own hands."

She noticed Simon inhale and exhale as if breathing had been suspended in him. Her expression gave him permission to sit on the side of the bed. Close enough for comfort, quiet strength, but nothing else. He placed his bag on the floor.

"There was a time when I wanted to, though." Michelle resumed her confession, then paused momentarily. "I went out and bought a gun. I was going to kill myself the same way my mother killed herself. It seemed I didn't know her from me or vice versa." Her lids closed for the second it took another breath to respire from her. "I had my will drawn up. All of my money is going to the educational fund at the center where I met Loretta, Clarissa, and Reba. They were going to get all of my pictures. I intended to give the photographs of me and Joanne together to Uncle David.

"I thought I had it all worked out. I was afraid, but I didn't know what else to do. I didn't believe there were any other options.

"I hurt so bad. It wasn't a physical hurt, but rather a torment that I couldn't touch. Then . . .

"Then my guardian angel showed up." A smile broke out on Michelle's face, but it didn't replace the pensive look still there in her eyes. "Loretta, Reba, and Clarissa." A chuckle of fond remembrance burst from her throat. Tears began to slip from her eyes and slide down her face. She didn't realize she was crying until Simon seemed to blur slightly in her gaze.

Michelle didn't bother to wipe her tears away as she looked at him with love brimming through her joyful tears. "And they brought me you, and you brought me life."

Simon stared gawking with reverence in his gaze. His

Adam's apple twitched in his throat. "I don't know what to say," he admitted humbly.

"I don't want you to say or do anything. Just . . . just love me."

Michelle reached out a hand to Simon.

"That would be hard not to do," he replied, accepting her invitation, holding both her hands next to his heart.

She was used to it now, Michelle thought pleasantly, feeling the jump-start sensation that jolted her heart and pulsed through her veins every time Simon was near. She relished its tender tingling and reveled in the fact that she could feel. She had never been more confident about anything in her life than she was of her love for this wonderful man.

"I love you, Simon Stevenson. And don't believe for one second," she added laughingly, "that what I feel for you is some misplaced sense of gratitude, Dr. Stevenson." She returned his stare, caressing his face with her eyes, smiling in response to the look of victory on his face.

Simon embraced her tenderly. "Michelle . . ." he said, his voice affected, his body trembling next to hers. He lifted his head to stare headlong into her face, his expression telegraphing his love, his want, and his need of her.

Michelle felt a zealous reverence. The sensation streaming through her sizzled with a feeling that exceeded physical desire. She would have died a thousand times over again to feel what she felt, she thought, shivering with delight.

"I've said it to myself so many times," Simon said, "that I feel as if I'm repeating myself. I love you, Michelle Craig. I love you."

They surrendered to the crush of feelings that drew them together in an embrace of unbound love for all time. Michelle felt certain she would take this love to the grave with her.

Epilogue

"*Hari gani?*"
    "*Umoja.*"

Sunday, December 26, 1999—Michelle considered it the first day of her rebirth. It could also be her last. But since that was beyond her control at this point, it was not a concern she worried over, for she'd made her vow. It started with loving herself and learning to accept and appreciate who she was.

That alone seemed to expand the capacity of her heart and her mind, for she felt her love heighten for Simon, her friends, Uncle David, and the woman who was soon to be Aunt Amelia. She was surrounded by them today, and that was all that mattered.

"Tonight is the night we celebrate the spirit of *Umoja*—Unity," Michelle said.

With Simon at her left side, she lit the black candle in the center of the *kinara*. All were gathered around the long table that held the items of Kwanzaa. The atmosphere was serious, yet it pulsed with joyful celebration. A sense of gratitude for family, friends, and life permeated the living room of her home.

She would never know for sure why her mother had taken

her own life. She more than believed, however, that if Joanne had been surrounded by the kind of supportive friends she had around her, she would be alive today. If Joanne would have been found by her own Simon, then maybe she would have found the strength to see value in her own life.

"Tonight and all nights of the year, we celebrate the spirit of those who have gone before who represented the values of *Umoja*."

She couldn't change the past, Michelle mused, but she could live—even if for twenty-four hours—a life that positively affected the future by what she did today, in the twenty-four hours she did have.

Simon had invited Dr. Hannibal Sertima and his wife Niobe. Michelle had caught Ham, as he'd been introduced to her, watching her pleasantly all evening, with a kind of musing, conspiratorial expression. If she hadn't known better, she would have sworn he was her Guardian.

"We celebrate the spirits of all who have gone before who understood the need to maintain unity in our family, our communities, our nations, and our race."

That said, Michelle filled the unity cup with grape juice and drank a sip before passing the cup to Simon. His smiling eyes met hers over the rim of the cup with a look that illuminated his warm affections for her. She accepted the look quietly, locking it in her heart for keeps as he passed the cup to the next person.

A new face among them was that of Bob Matthew, her boss. Celebrating Kwanzaa didn't preclude participation by white people. Bob's acceptance hinted at a possible meaningful relationship. He didn't hesitate when the cup reached him. Taking a sip, he passed the cup on to Alan, who had come as well. His presence signaled an attempt to make a commitment to Reba.

"We celebrate the spirits of all of those who understood that all children of Mother Africa around the world have a common heritage and a common destiny,'' Michelle said as Reba passed the cup to Loretta, then to Edmund.

''Tonight and all nights,'' Michelle said as Loretta passed the cup on to Vince, ''we celebrate the spirits of all of those who are here with us.''

The cup reached the beginning, and Michelle held it next to her bosom.

''Tonight and all nights, we celebrate the spirits of those who are yet to come.''

Happy Kwanzaa!

Truly
Everlasting

BY

BRENDA JACKSON

To my husband, Gerald Jackson Sr.
Thank you for always believing that I could do it.
You are still the one after all these years.

The Lord's blessing is our greatest wealth. And he adds no sorrow with it.

—Proverbs 10:22
(Taken from the Living Bible)

Dear Readers,

Christmas is a special time for me. I love the time spent with family and friends, the hectic chore of shopping for those special gifts, and the sights and sounds of the holidays. But most importantly I enjoy the holidays as a time to give a part of yourself to others.

In writing *Truly Everlasting,* I hope I've done just that. I hope this story gives you a part of me. It's the part that believes not only in the power of true love, but also in the power of the heavenly Father for which Christmas is celebrated. Believing in both makes a person's life complete. Trask Maxwell and Felicia Madaris were truly meant for each other. They just didn't know it. I hope you enjoy reading how they come to realize that fact and how their lives become complete for the New Year.

I would like to thank my many readers for their continued support and love for my stories. I will continue to make every effort to create stories that will bring a smile to your face and earn a special place in your heart.

Keep those letters coming. I enjoy hearing from you. For those who have never written to me, please do so. I promise to write back if you include a business-size self-addressed, stamped envelope with your letter. Send to me at the following address:

Brenda Jackson
P. O. Box 28267
Jacksonville, FL 32226

You can also visit my Web site: http://www.tlt.com/authors/bjackson.htm.
Many blessings to you during the holiday season and throughout the coming year. May your joy be truly everlasting.

Happy Holidays,

Brenda Jackson

Chapter One

A s expected the party was in full swing.

It seemed everyone had been invited to welcome the guest of honor back to Houston. As far as those present were concerned, Trask Maxwell had been away from home too long.

The attendees had followed Trask's football career, which had begun in high school, then later escalated during his college years at Texas Southern, where he had been the recipient of the Heisman Trophy for three consecutive years. After college he had remained in Houston to play professional football for the Houston Oilers. He had proven that, when it came to legendary football talent, Houston grew its own.

After playing for the Oilers a number of seasons, Trask had left for Florida to join the Miami Dolphins and later he had played for the Pittsburgh Steelers. It was there in Pittsburgh, nearly two years ago, at the age of thirty-four, in a grueling game against the Denver Broncos, that he had suffered a knee injury that had subsequently ended his football career. By that time, Trask Maxwell had obtained five Super Bowl rings and earned the distinction of being known as the greatest running back in the history of the NFL.

The people of Houston were proud of "The Max," the nickname the press had given Trask during his football career. And no matter what team he had played on, they always supported him because he was one of their own. He was the pride of the city. There was no doubt in anyone's mind that he was Houston's favorite son.

Across the room Trask Maxwell stood with a group of friends discussing their favorite topic—football—and his new job as sports commentator on Monday Night Football. His attention, drawn away from the conversation swirling around him, went dead center to the woman who had just arrived.

He frowned. No woman could rub him the wrong way like Felicia Laverne Madaris . . . or whatever last name she was using these days after her two failed marriages.

Trask released a heavy sigh. He shook his head, wondering how in the world Felicia had managed to snag the first husband, not to mention the second, with her wild and reckless lifestyle as well as her razor-sharp tongue. He deliberately dismissed the fact that she was a gorgeous woman. As far as he was concerned, her beauty didn't matter. Felicia was trouble with a capital T. She always had been and always would be.

Her father, Robert Madaris, had been killed during the Vietnam War, before Felicia's second birthday. The six surviving Madaris brothers had pampered their niece and unselfishly catered to Felicia's every whim. In other words, they had ultimately spoiled her rotten. So rotten in fact that she had decided that any man she married would have to continue to lavish her with all the nice and expensive things she had grown accustomed to receiving. Thus, Felicia had declared that she would only marry for money.

And she had done just that. Twice.

Trask tried to remember when the animosity between Felicia and him had actually begun. All he knew was that as far back as elementary school she had been a thorn in his side, a real pain in his rear end. Their inability to get along had gone on for so long that it was something they both accepted and never thought much about. It was a foregone conclusion that whenever they were in the same place, they somehow managed—quite nicely and without very much effort—to get on each other's nerves.

"It's not a good omen for the guest of honor to be caught frowning."

Trask's attention immediately turned to the person who had made the statement. He noticed that he and the host of the party, Clayton Madaris, were now standing alone. Trask didn't miss the glint of amusement in his best friend's eyes. "You should have considered the possibility of my frown when you and Syneda put together your guest list," he said in a deep Texas drawl. Involuntarily, his gaze strayed back across the room to Felicia. He knew that Clayton was aware of just what invited guest he was referring to.

Clayton shrugged his shoulders. "Felicia's invitation was automatic. She's family."

"That's your misfortune, Clayton. For Pete's sake, man, look at her. I don't believe the dress she has on."

Clayton's curious gaze settled on his cousin Felicia. She was wearing a clingy black dress that had a slit up the side that revealed a startling amount of thigh—nearly too much thigh. And when she raised her hand in greeting after hearing someone call out to her, it was quite obvious from the deep cut of the dress that she wasn't wearing a bra. Her being braless would not have been an issue if the top portion of her outfit hadn't been made of sheer material. A tiny scrap of cloth kept her breasts from being completely exposed, and it teased more than it covered.

Clayton shook his head at the brazenness of his cousin's dress. His wife Syneda owned a number of revealing outfits, but he couldn't recall anything of Syneda's that was *that* daring. He cleared his throat. "You know Felicia, Trask. The family used to get on her so much about not dressing femininely that now she likes using her clothes to make a statement."

Trask shook his head, remembering how Felicia had hated

wearing dresses. Growing up, she'd always preferred wearing T-shirts and jeans. "Well, if it was her intent to draw attention to herself, then she has succeeded," he said curtly as he watched Felicia cross the room to join a group of women.

A wry grin covered Clayton's mouth as he glanced around the room. "I hate to tell you this, Trask, but you seem to be the only single male here tonight who's not appreciating her outfit."

Trask snorted. "And you of all people know why. Unlike the others, I'm immune to your cousin's charm."

Clayton shook his head. Trask being immune to Felicia's charm was an understatement. The three of them—Trask, Felicia, and he—had been born the same year, with Trask being older than Clayton by three months and older than Felicia by six. As far back as Clayton could remember, Felicia had always been a tomboy who had followed him and Trask around. That had been fine with him, but their being a threesome had never fared well with Trask because of Trask's and Felicia's overcompetitive natures. They competed against each other in everything. Their long-standing rivalry and feud was something their families and friends tolerated and ignored. At least they had ignored it until Felicia's announcement in the tenth grade that, instead of going out for cheerleading, she wanted to try out for the football team. If Trask could play, then so could she. There was no doubt in her mind that she would play better.

A huge smile curved Clayton's lips at the memory. Felicia's announcement had prompted her six uncles to step in and quash her athletic plans. It had probably been the first time the six Madaris brothers had unanimously said no to their niece about anything. An angry Felicia had gone out for cheerleading instead. But even from the sidelines, where she was supposed to be cheering for her team—of which Trask was a member— she had managed to dish out a hefty amount of grief to the team's star player. She had used her position as a cheerleader to constantly rattle and annoy Trask. And it hadn't stopped in high school. When Clayton and Trask had decided to remain in town and attend Texas Southern, Felicia—to her uncles' delight, Clayton's amusement, and Trask's dismay—made the same decision. That decision had given Trask another four years of Felicia's continued hassling.

"Well, one thing is for certain," Clayton finally said after a few moments of silence between them.

"What?" Trask asked, raising a dark brow.

Clayton smiled. "There's nothing tomboyish about her anymore. She's made the transition from tomboy to sexy lady extremely well."

Felicia Madaris pretended to be absorbed in the conversation going on around her as she watched Trask out of her peripheral vision. She couldn't help but smile with a smug amount of satisfaction. He was frowning, which meant her appearance tonight had upset him.

Good. Let him steam, she thought. *He'll get over it, and if he doesn't . . . oh, well.*

Excusing herself from the group of women, she turned and headed toward the table that was loaded with refreshments. As she walked, the side slit in her dress widened with each stride she took, showing a silk-clad thigh and presenting Trask, whom she knew was still watching her, an eyeful.

Let him look since that seems to be his pleasure lately, Felicia thought. She couldn't help but remember how hard he had watched her at Trevor and Corinthians Grant's wedding reception three months ago. It was as if his gaze had been glued to her every movement. She hadn't liked it then and she didn't like it now. And just as she was doing tonight, she had completely ignored him.

He probably wouldn't like being ignored tonight of all nights, not when he expected everyone to welcome him home with loving arms. And what could be worse than for someone to have a party in his honor and then have one of the guests totally ignore his very existence?

He would soon find out.

"Gosh, just look at 'The Max'. He's too sexy for words," Felicia heard a feminine voice say not too far away.

"Oh, I'll do just about anything to get his attention," another feminine voice added.

Felicia rolled her eyes upward. She was not like some of the other women here tonight whose hearts were going pitter-pat at the thought of being in the same room with Trask and who were hoping he would send some encouraging look their way.

As Felicia picked a sweet roll drenched in blueberry topping off the table, she couldn't help but remember why she had decided to ignore Trask again tonight. It had begun five months ago with Clayton and Syneda's wedding. Both she and Trask had been asked to be a part of the wedding party. Not knowing about her and Trask's feuding past, Syneda had paired them up as a couple. Felicia had later learned that, when Trask had gotten word that she would be his partner for the wedding ceremony, he had insisted on someone else.

In all actuality, unknowingly, he had done her a favor since she hadn't wanted to be paired up with him any more than he'd wanted to be paired up with her. However, the thought that he'd had the audacity to complain about it really grated on her last nerve. As far as she was concerned, being a sports celebrity had gone to his head. And if that was the case, then she was just the person to bring him down a notch or two, and she would take great pleasure in doing so.

"So how do you like being married?" Trask asked Clayton in an attempt to draw his attention away from the refreshment table and the woman standing beside it.

"I can't imagine my life any other way now. There's never a dull moment with Syneda. She's all the woman I'll ever need," Clayton said, shaking his head. He was still in awe at the depth of his love for a woman with whom he rarely agreed on anything, but she was a woman he couldn't imagine ever being without.

"If anyone would have told me how much I'd enjoy being a married man, I would not have believed them," Clayton added.

He looked up at Trask and smiled. "Maybe you should try it."

"No, thanks. I'll pass," Trask replied in a deceptively controlled voice. "I'm still recovering from the fact that Trevor has tied the knot, too," he said, thinking of his other childhood friend, Trevor Grant, who had also gotten married recently. "I hope there's nothing wrong with the air in this city since it seems that bachelors are dropping like flies around here."

Taking Trask's ribbing in stride, Clayton sipped his wine before responding with a grin, "I don't know if there's something in the air, Trask, but I've heard there's a possibility something's in the soil. So if I were you, I wouldn't go out tumbling around in the dirt, not even to play a friendly game of football," Clayton said, chuckling. "I would hate for this thing they call love to get under your skin. And take it from a man who knows, once love gets to you, there's nothing you can do about it. So beware of Houston's dirt."

Trask was barely listening to his best friend's words. His attention was once again drawn to Felicia. A guy had approached her at the refreshment table and appeared to be coming on to her. If the man had any sense, Trask thought sympathetically, he would leave the irritating, infuriating, smart-mouth Felicia Madaris alone.

The kitchen was crowded with caterers busy at work replenishing the food supply. Felicia acknowledged them as she passed through on her way to the patio. She needed to get a breath of fresh air. The man who had approached her at the refreshment table had nearly talked her ears off. How he had managed to converse nonstop between a mouthful of food had totally amazed her.

Once she reached the patio she took a deep breath. There was nothing like good Texas air to clear your mind and get the blood circulating. It was nearing the end of November already. It was hard to believe that Thanksgiving was next week, which meant Christmas wasn't far behind. She smiled when she thought about the approaching holidays. Her four-year-old son, Austin, was eager to begin working on the Christmas list that he would be sending to Santa.

"So this is where you ran off to."

Felicia whipped around. She was surprised Trask had followed her outside. He had caught her off guard, and she hated being caught off guard by Trask Maxwell.

"So what's it to you?" she asked flippantly. He stood leaning against the patio wall with his hands crossed over his chest, eyeing her speculatively. Felicia hated it when he studied her that way, as if she were some type of bug under his microscope.

Trask shook his head. Felicia was still full of lip and as feisty as ever. Nothing had changed. "I came to make sure you're all right," he said smoothly, as he continued to look at her. "The man you were talking to a few minutes ago is Lewis Hunter and he's loaded. I know how anxious you get when it comes to rich men, so I was curious as to why you let Hunter get away. Even from across the room I could tell he was interested in you."

Felicia's gaze darkened. She was trying hard not to let Trask get on her nerves any more than usual. "The only thing Mr. Hunter was interested in was getting a closer look at my breasts. His eyes were glued to them the entire time he was talking to me."

"Hunter must have poor eyesight. With that outfit you're wearing you don't need a close-up view. I could see all I wanted to from across the room," Trask said coolly.

Felicia had to smile, although it wasn't a friendly one. "No kidding. You were able to see that much?"

When Trask nodded, she said, "In that case, you should be able to tell me my bra size."

Trask's gaze traveled downward from her face and locked in on her chest. "You don't wear bras."

Felicia wrinkled her nose at the accuracy of his response. He of all people should know since all through high school she used to complain constantly about having to wear them. She had sworn up and down that when she moved out on her own she would never wear a bra again. And she hadn't.

Trask took a step toward her, coming fully into the patio's lighting. "So am I right?"

Felicia looked up at him, suddenly wishing he'd stayed back in the dark. His chiseled features were now clearly visible. She hated admitting it but Trask Elgin Maxwell was a good-looking man. He was dark on dark in dark. Everything about him was dark, and she couldn't help wondering about the old saying "the darker the berry, the sweeter the juice."

His skin was a shade of deep, dark chocolate, and his short hair was curly black. His eyes, his most striking feature, were as dark as black ink. He was tall, way over six feet, and his shoulders were massive. His body was sculptured, well defined, and built. Unfortunately, it exuded virility and for some unknown reason Felicia felt her entire body responding to it.

"I asked if I was right," Trask repeated.

Felicia frowned, not understanding the attraction she suddenly felt and definitely did not like. She totally and outright refused to even consider any interest in Trask on a personal level. She never had had any and she never would have any. Her sudden attraction had to be the result of those sweet rolls she had eaten tonight. All that sugar was turning her brain to mush.

"If anybody ought to know it's you and Clayton. How many times did the two of you hear me complain about wearing a bra?"

"Too many. In fact I still have the first bra your mother

bought you. You couldn't wait to get to school that day to take it off. You gave it to me to get rid of.''

Felicia couldn't help but remember that day. Nor could she help smiling at the memory. ''And you didn't get rid of it?''

''No, I kept it. I figured that one day you'd ask for it back.''

She smiled sweetly up at him. ''Hardly.''

Trask came a step closer. ''In fact, Felicia, while packing to move back here, I came across something else of yours that I have.''

Felicia raised a curious brow. ''What?''

He smiled wickedly. ''I still have a pair of your panties.''

She gave him a cutting look. ''A pair of *my* panties? I don't think so.''

Trask chuckled. ''I know so.''

Felicia frowned and searched her memory for the slim chance that she had given him a pair of her undergarments at one time or another. She, Clayton, and Trask had done a lot of crazy things as teenagers growing up, but . . .

When she was convinced she had never given him a pair of her undies, she glared at him. ''How did you get them? I don't recall ever giving them to you.''

''You didn't. I acquired them during one of those famous panty raids at Texas Southern. It was during our freshman year.'' He chuckled softly. ''I didn't know girls' underwear came in so many shapes, sizes, and colors.''

''And you think you snatched a pair of mine?''

''I know I did.''

Felicia's gaze narrowed at him. ''I hate to be the one to burst your bubble after all these years, but you didn't get a pair of mine.''

''How can you be so sure of that?''

''Because just like the bra, I never got the hang of wearing panties either.''

Felicia watched as Trask's gaze shifted from her face and slowly moved downward to zero in on the middle part of her body. The heat of his gaze was so hot, she actually felt her pelvic muscles burn with its intensity. She blinked and stared at him, wondering what on earth was happening to her and why Trask was looking at her that way. Was he searching for proof of what she had just said? If that was the case, then she would oblige him. She took a full turn around slowly, to show him just how clingy and smooth the dress fit her body.

"See, Trask, no panty lines." She saw his jaw drop slightly and she smiled. The thought that she had shocked him kept her smiling.

"You're kidding about not wearing undergarments, aren't you?" Trask finally found his voice to ask. The tone of his voice was considerably low.

Felicia waited a few seconds before answering his question. If his gaze hadn't heated her up moments earlier, the huskiness of his voice sure did. She felt her heart pounding as she became aware of another side of Trask. A very desirable side.

"Maybe. Maybe not. Only my body knows for sure," Felicia said glaring. She didn't like the sexual awareness she was experiencing from being around him.

Unknown to Felicia, Trask was also experiencing a similar episode of sexual awareness. And he didn't like it any more than she did. He suddenly noticed how the patio lights danced across her features. Her smooth skin was a rich creamy shade of cocoa, and her eyes, which were a deep, dark brown, openly revealed whatever mood she was in. During his day, he had seen them go from naughty to nice ... but mostly naughty. Her hair, which for years had been hidden under her Chicago Cubs baseball cap, was a rich, glossy black; it touched her shoulders in a very chic style. His breathing wavered slightly when he noticed just how sexy her lips looked when she was angry. And the thought that there was a possibility that she didn't have a stitch of clothing on under her dress ...

"You enjoy being a tease, don't you, Felicia?" Before she could answer he added, "Just look at the way you're dressed." He spoke curtly, trying to retain control of his mind and body.

Anger flared in Felicia's eyes. Under no circumstances would she take insults from Trask. "So I like a little razzle-dazzle and flash in my wardrobe. What's it to you, Trask Maxwell?"

"It means nothing to me. What you do is your business."

"I'm glad you know that. Now if you'll excuse me, I have other, more important things to do with my time than spend it out here with you."

"Like looking around for husband number three?"

"Why? Are you interested? I know for a fact you're loaded. With all those endorsements you're doing, and with your new job as a sports commentator, you probably have megabucks rolling in. Should I add your name to my list of prospects?" she asked angrily.

Felicia saw the anger darkening his cheekbones and was giddy about it. It filled her with joy to know she had ticked Trask off yet again.

"It's women like you that I'm determined to stay away from," he said coolly.

"Smart move," Felicia responded with a deceptively sweet smile. "Now if you'll excuse me I'm going back inside."

When she made a move to walk past him he touched her arm to stop her. The contact was hot, quick, electrifying. She knew he had felt it, too, when they both jerked back at the same time. They stared at each other, astonished, amazed, and momentarily at a loss for words.

It was Trask who finally broke the silence. He tried to ignore the sizzling current that had flashed between them, although an indescribable heat had gathered in the lower part of his body. He took a closer step toward her. "Aren't you going to welcome me back home, Felicia?"

"In your dreams," she replied, recovering enough to get the words out and taking a step back. She didn't like the idea of his big body being too close to hers, especially now that the nipples of her breasts had suddenly become taut and achingly hard. She crossed her arms over her chest so that he wouldn't notice that fact.

"To be quite honest with you," she continued, trying desperately not to forget that the two of them didn't get along, "I'm not sure there's room enough in Houston for the both of us now."

"We'll make room."

"In other words, you'll stay out of my way, and I'm to stay out of yours."

His smile was slow, sexy. "That's a deal, sweetheart."

Felicia tipped her head back, looked him straight in the eyes, and tried to keep a lid on her temper. "That's fine with me."

She had no intentions of doing the customary thing and shaking hands with him to seal their agreement. The mere thought of touching Trask again heated her in too many places . . . especially one very intimate place. Knowing she had to get away from him as soon as possible, she quickly turned and went back inside, where the party was still in full swing.

Trask was left alone on the patio to ponder two questions. The first one of which was, what in the world had passed between him and Felicia tonight? And the second was, did she or did she not wear undergarments under her clothing?

Chapter Two

Felicia felt an overwhelming sense of relief when she opened the door to her home less than an hour later. She was totally disgusted with her inability to defuse the feelings of sexual desire that Trask had effortlessly ignited within her tonight.

Her mind kept replaying images of him dressed in those sexy black jeans and that black sports shirt. Again the description of dark on dark in dark came to mind. And the memory of his scent—manly, musky, and male—made tremors ripple through her. For the first time ever, Trask had unsettled her—so much in fact that, after leaving him on the patio, she had immediately left the party. It had taken the entire drive home to try to pull herself back together.

"Mrs. Evans, I didn't expect you back this early." The cheery voice of Mrs. Woods met her in the foyer. The elderly lady lived next door with her son and daughter-in-law and, on occasion, kept Austin for Felicia.

"I'm sorry. I did it again," the older woman added before Felicia could respond to her statement about returning early. "I forgot your last name isn't Evans anymore."

Felicia smiled. She had known that, when she had made the

decision to go back to using her maiden name of Madaris, it would cause some confusion. But she had not wanted to use her former husband's name any longer. Especially now, since her second husband had remarried.

"That's all right, Mrs. Woods. No harm's been done. I know it'll take some getting used to," Felicia said, coming into the living room and placing her purse down on the table. "How was Austin tonight?"

Mrs. Woods beamed. "He was fine as usual. Tyra came over and played with him for a while. As usual, the two of them had fun together."

Felicia nodded. Tyra was Mrs. Woods' six-year-old granddaughter. Although there was a two-year difference in Tyra's and Austin's ages, they were perfect playmates. Now that Tyra had started school, they didn't get to see each other as much as they used to. Felicia was glad to hear that Tyra and Austin had spent some time together tonight.

"You should be proud of yourself, Mrs. Madaris," Mrs. Woods continued. "Austin is such a special little boy. And he's so smart, too. There aren't many four-year-olds who can read and write as well as he does. Tonight, he and Tyra were busy working on his letter to Santa." Mrs. Woods chuckled. "I believe it's three pages long, too. I imagine a boy his age would want a lot of stuff."

"Yes, I imagine he would at that," Felicia said, sharing Mrs. Woods' chuckle as she walked the older lady to the door. "Thanks again for watching Austin for me tonight."

"It was my pleasure. Like I said before, he's special. Good night."

"Good night, Mrs. Woods." Felicia closed the door and leaned against it for a moment. Mrs. Woods was right. Austin was a special little boy, and she was so thankful that he was hers.

A shudder passed through Felicia when she thought of how close she had come to losing him nearly five months ago. If nothing else, that had been her wake-up call and had made her take a closer look at her priorities in life.

Moving past the living room she immediately went into her son's room. He was there in his bed, sound asleep. Although Austin had recently gotten a haircut, his hair still had distinct curls in it. Those curls had been the only things he had inherited from his father and her first husband, Steven Gardner.

Steven was the spoiled, rich son of Andrew Gardner, a businessman who owned several hotel chains along the West Coast. She had met Steven at a party while visiting a friend in California. She had been drawn to his good looks, his bad-boy image, and most importantly, his money. Within a week they had gotten married. Not once did she consider the fact that she didn't love him. All she had cared about at the time was that marrying him fit nicely with her plans to wed a man of wealth.

It didn't take long for her to discover that Steven had only married her to spite his parents. And if his sudden change in attitude toward her hadn't been a rude awakening, then meeting his parents for the first time definitely had.

Felicia had been so used to being pampered all her life by her family that, when she had encountered the elder Gardners' hostile attitude toward her, she hadn't known how to handle it. They hadn't hesitated to let her know that, as far as they were concerned, she was not good enough for their son. But the one thing she refused to do was disappear from Steven's life as his parents had suggested. Even after finding out she was pregnant, they didn't change their attitude toward her.

Steven had accused her of deliberately getting pregnant to keep him trapped in their marriage. And his attitude toward her had worsened. Two weeks after Austin was born, Steven had informed her that he wanted out of their marriage. She had returned to Texas a divorced woman when Austin was merely six weeks old.

Steven had never bothered to come visit his son, and last year she had received word from friends in California that he had gotten killed in an auto accident. He had been intoxicated and had lost control of his car while traveling at a high rate of speed. She had tried calling his parents and had eventually left messages when she hadn't been able to reach them. Like Steven, they had never come to visit Austin or acknowledge his existence. But each year at Christmas time she would send them a photo of Austin with Santa. They had never acknowledged those photos either.

Releasing a heavy sigh, Felicia walked over to the window, pushed the curtain aside, and looked out at the darkness. You would have thought that her disastrous marriage to Steven would have taught her a lesson about marrying for money instead of love, but it hadn't. By the time Austin was celebrating his second birthday, she was getting married again—this time to a prominent surgeon by the name of Charles Evans. Again she had found herself marrying for money instead of for love.

At first it seemed things were going great between her and Charles. She enjoyed her role as a doctor's wife and thoroughly appreciated how generous he was with his money. Her appreciation ended the day she discovered he was having an affair with one of his patients. She'd had the misfortune of walking in on the two of them while they were making love one afternoon in his office. A little more than a year later, she was divorced once again.

Charles's betrayal had angered her. It had made her bitter, resentful, and spiteful. And those attitudes would have continued had she not come close to losing Austin. She would never forget that day as long as she lived.

She had gone out on a date that evening and had left Austin with a baby-sitter. The sixteen-year-old girl had been highly recommended by a few people in the neighborhood. Felicia would never forget the call she had received at the restaurant, advising her that Austin had nearly drowned in their pool and was being rushed to the emergency room. The girl had left him alone for a second to go back in the house to answer the phone. Luckily she had known CPR and was able to administer first aid until the paramedics had arrived.

The next twenty-four hours had been critical, and at one time, it was doubtful that Austin would make it. It had struck her hard that she had spent all her free time pursuing wealthy men and had not seen to it that Austin received adequate swimming lessons.

That night, while facing the possibility of losing her son, she had realized something very elemental. She didn't need an extravagant lifestyle to be rich. Being rich was not always measured in terms of material possessions. That night, it had suddenly become crystal clear that for four years God had blessed her with the greatest richness of all: her son. Having Austin had made her the richest woman on earth. She had not fully understood until then that she had not obtained her wealth from any material gain, but as blessings from God.

In the hospital's chapel, she had earnestly sought forgiveness and had prayed to God for another chance to appreciate the rich life that He had already given her: a life with her son. The Lord heard her prayer and answered it. Two days later, Austin had been released from the hospital to go home, suffering no permanent damage from his near death experience.

Felicia thought about all the changes she had made in her life since that night. Positive changes. Everyone, including her family, had been surprised by those changes. And through it all, the entire Madaris clan had provided her with unwavering support. It was wonderful to have such a large close-knit family that was constantly spreading so much love and care. Her family, she belatedly realized, had always been a blessing by being there for her through the years. Their presence had been another richness she had taken for granted.

Felicia closed her eyes briefly when she remembered Trask's accusations tonight about her looking for a rich husband. If only he knew how wrong he was. But then, he saw her as the old Felicia, the one who had always made marrying a rich man a priority. His snide barbs tonight about her looking for a rich husband indicated as much. He probably would be shocked to know that she had not dated since that incident with Austin.

Felicia turned to move away from the window. Going back ver to Austin's bed, she was about to pull the covers up around im when she saw his letter to Santa beside him. It was the ne he and Tyra had worked on together. And it was three ages long, as Mrs. Woods had said.

Curious as to what all Austin wanted for Christmas, she took e letter into the kitchen. She sat down at the table and began ading.

Dear Santa,

My mommy said I've bin a good boy this year, so I hope u will give me my Christmas wish. Mor than any-thing, I want a Daddy. I had 2 daddies befor but they didn't stay. Please give me a daddy who will stay forever. I no that is a lot to ask for, so if you can't give me a Daddy who will stay forever, can u pleaze give me 1 jus for the Holidazs? If I could get him earlay, he can help us pick out our Christmas tree. I promiz to give him back to u on Neu Year Day. I want him to do guy stuff wiz me. I luv my mom, but she does not know how to do guy stuff. And my big couszin Clayton is marriz now so he doesn't come around az much. A Daddy for the Holi-dazs is all I'm asking four this year. Pleaze give me a daddy to luv me.

Austin

A knot formed in Felicia's throat after she read her son's tter to Santa. Dragging her hands down her face, she wiped e tears that flowed from her eyes and willed herself to remain alm and not fall apart.

Austin's letter made her soul ache. It also made her feel like complete failure because, after her two marriages, her son till didn't have a father he could depend on. It just wasn't fair at the one thing Austin wanted she would not be able to give him since she had vowed never to marry again except for love. And she didn't see herself falling in love anytime soon.

Tears continued to flow from Felicia's eyes. Her son would be disappointed when he didn't get the Daddy he wanted for the holidays.

Trask heard the sound of distant thunder as he entered his apartment. He had enjoyed the party that Clayton and Syneda had given for him tonight. It had been so good seeing old friends again, as well as meeting new ones.

He glanced down at the business card a woman had discreetly slipped into his hand. On the back of it, she had written the words:

> "Call me anytime, Cherie."

He smiled. She had been quite a looker. He just might give her a call. With the move back to Houston, and starting his new job, he had been too busy to get involved with a woman. He hadn't realized just how much he missed a little female companionship until tonight. He must be in a pretty bad way if he could develop a sudden case of the hots for someone like Felicia Madaris.

With a heavy sigh, Trask had to admit his case of the hots for Felicia hadn't actually been all that sudden. He didn't have to do much struggling to recall that he had been unable to keep his eyes off her at Trevor's wedding reception three months ago. The dress she had worn to the reception had been a lot less revealing than the one she had worn tonight, but it had been an eye-catcher just the same. Clayton had been right about Felicia using her clothes to make a statement. Not every woman could get away with wearing the kind of outfits he had seen Felicia parade about in. Most women didn't have the body to fit them. But he couldn't ever remember a time he had not seen

Felicia in something that had not looked as if it had been designed exclusively for her.

Like that clingy black thing she had worn tonight.

Shaking his head, he headed for the kitchen, thinking how quickly his body had responded to seeing her in it. And if that didn't beat all, during his drive home from the party, he had kept thinking about her. It still drove him crazy when he thought about what was or what was not under her clothes. His heated imagination had made the bottom part of his abdomen throb and ache. When she had done that slow turn for him out on the patio, to show him just how smoothly her dress had fit, he had wanted to use his hands to travel down the length of her. And when he had put his hand on her arm to stop her from going inside, he had been dazed by the heat that touch had aroused in him. Even now, just thinking about it was seriously interfering with his breathing.

Trask struggled to catch his breath and thought there was only one solution to his problem. He evidently needed some intimate time alone with a woman. Tomorrow, he would give this person named Cherie a call.

Chapter Three

Clayton Madaris released a deep, heavy sigh as he handed the letter he had just finished reading to his wife, Syneda. The two of them sat on the sofa facing Felicia, who was sitting in a wing-back chair. Her eyes were red and puffy. After reading Austin's letter to Santa, Clayton understood why.

He shook his head. "I should've been spending more time with—"

"No, Clayton," Felicia interrupted him, knowing exactly what he was about to say. "Don't even go there. You've spent more than enough time with Austin, and I appreciate that. But you're married now, and Austin has to understand that you can't come around as much as you used to."

Felicia gave a wry smile to the cousin she had always been close to while growing up. The two of them had always been thought of as the untamed members of the Madaris family. Even before Clayton had gotten married, when he had been regarded as Houston's most eligible bachelor, he had made time for Austin, as well as for his nieces and nephews. All the children in the Madaris family thought the world of him.

"You don't know how much it meant, knowing you were there for Austin when you really didn't have to be. I've never really thanked you for it either," Felicia said sincerely.

"You don't have to thank me. We're family, Felicia," Clayton said in earnest.

"Yes, we're family, and I never appreciated that so much until now. I never knew how blessed I was in having all of you until that day I almost lost the most precious person in my life. You were all there for me to lean on when I needed you the most."

Clayton nodded. He knew exactly what day Felicia was referring to. He and Syneda had returned from their honeymoon in St. Thomas to discover Austin had been rushed to the hospital. The entire Madaris family had gathered in prayer for the little boy, who was fighting for his life.

Since then, the family had noticed the changes that had taken place in Felicia. Nearly losing her son had opened her eyes to a number of things. Clayton was proud of how she had turned her life around by getting her priorities straight.

"What do you need us to do?" Syneda asked in a near choked voice after reading the letter. "Tell us, Felicia, and if it's possible you know we'll do it."

Felicia nodded. She really liked the woman Clayton had married. They were both attorneys, and the really neat thing was that even before Clayton and Syneda had declared their love for each other, the Madaris family had considered Syneda as a part of their family. And Syneda's best friend, Lorren, was married to Clayton's oldest brother Justin. Justin and Lorren lived in a small town near Dallas.

"After reading Austin's letter, I think he wants someone to do all those guy things with him that I can't do," Felicia said.

"You *can* do them," Clayton said with a chuckle as he remembered just how well she had competed against him and Trask in any sport.

Felicia couldn't help but grin at Clayton's comment. "Okay, maybe I can, but I doubt that, even if Austin knew I used to be an ace at doing guy stuff, it would make a difference to him. In his mind, I'm still a girl. He thinks he needs a man to do certain things with."

Felicia took a deep breath before continuing. "The reason I came by is to get information on the Big Brothers Program, which is an organization that I know you're involved with, Clayton. I want to know how I can go about signing up Austin. Although it's probably too late for him to be matched with a mentor before the holidays, at least he'll have something to look forward to next year."

Clayton shook his head somberly. "The Big Brothers organization is a great one, but unfortunately, Austin's too young to be accepted in the program. The minimum age requirement is six years, so it will be another two years before he's eligible. And I can't think of any other mentoring programs around town that don't have an extensive waiting list. There are more young boys needing mentors than there are men who're willing to give up some of their time to spend with them."

Felicia nodded. Her features were filled with grim acceptance of what Clayton had just told her.

"But don't worry. Once I let Dex know what's going on, I'm sure that, like I plan on doing, he'll want to spend more time with Austin over the holidays, too."

Felicia released a heavy sigh. Dex was Clayton's second older brother, who also lived in Houston. "But Dex has a family of his own. I can't ask him to give up his family time for Austin. That wouldn't be fair. This is something I'll have to work out myself."

"Where's Austin now?"

"He's spending the day with Mom."

The doorbell sounded and Syneda excused herself to answer it. Clayton checked his watch. "That's probably Trask. We're watching the game on the tube today. The Steelers are playing the Cowboys."

Emotions began swirling inside Felicia at the mention of Trask's name. She didn't want to question the heated sensation she suddenly felt in the lower part of her body. "Then I'd better leave. Just last night Trask and I agreed to stay out of each other's way," she said, standing and shrugging into her jacket.

"You don't have to leave, Felicia."

"Yes, I do, Clayton. The approaching holidays are a time of peace. And peace is a word Trask and I don't know the meaning of when we're together."

"That's an understatement, Felicia Laverne," a deep, heavy voice said from behind her.

Felicia went completely still before forcing herself to turn around. Trask stood leaning against the doorjamb with his arms folded across his chest. And he was glaring at her. But his glare wasn't all that she saw. For some reason, her gaze zeroed in on his masculine physique. The shirt he wore was tucked neatly into the waistband of a pair of Dockers and it fit snugly across his broad chest. Despite the unfortunate timing of his arrival, a part of her—the part that was now on some sort of an adrenaline high—was glad to see him. She shook her head. If she actually believed that she was glad to see Trask Maxwell, then she had truly gone and lost it. That thought didn't sit too well with her, and she returned his glare.

"Trust me, big boy, had I known you were going to show up, I would have left long ago. On second thought, maybe I should go ahead and make my day by hanging around and ruining yours," Felicia said crossly. She just couldn't help getting on Trask's nerves any more than he could help getting on hers. The two of them had no hope of ever getting along.

She took a deep breath when Trask straightened to his full, imposing height and walked into the room. She tilted her head back to look up at him when he came to stand before her.

"Has anyone, other than me, ever told you that you have a smart mouth?" Trask asked, frowning. He lifted a dark brow upon noticing her puffy red eyes. His frown was immediately replaced with concern. He grabbed her arm. "Hey, what's wrong with you?"

Just like the night before when they had touched, a hot, quick sensation ripped through the both of them. But this time Trask didn't release her.

He didn't have to. Felicia jerked her arm out of his grip. "There's nothing wrong with me, Trask, so back off."

Across the room, the attorney in Clayton knew it was time to intervene, or he would be faced with the possibility of defending one of them against murder charges. He looked at his best friend. "Trask, I have those papers ready for you to sign." He then turned his attention to his cousin. "And, Felicia, you're welcome to stay. In fact, you can keep Syneda out of trouble while Trask and I watch the game."

Syneda threw a surprised, questioning glance at her husband. "I was going to fix dinner. What kind of trouble can I get into in the kitchen?"

Clayton smiled at his wife. "Plenty. You haven't mastered the art of cooking quite yet."

Trask began signing the papers Clayton had given him. All of them pertained to the Foundation. He liked sharing a part of himself with the city he loved. That was one of the reasons he had established the Trask Maxwell Foundation at the beginning of his professional football career. It was a way to give back to Houston's youth the same opportunities he had been given. Through his Foundation, countless youth programs had been established to provide disadvantaged youths a chance to succeed in both academics and sports. His foundation also went further by aiding single mothers and senior citizens and by supporting various food drives.

When Trask pushed aside the last of the papers he had signed, a movement outside on the patio caught his attention. Felicia had agreed to stay a while to help Syneda with the cooking. Evidently the two women had decided to move out of the kitchen and throw something on the grill instead.

He watched Felicia, fascinated by her jeans. The tight-fitting denim seemed to mold itself to every curve in her body. He had to remind himself to breathe when he saw her bend over to pick up something, presenting her nicely rounded backside to him. It occurred to Trask that he didn't see any panty lines. He nearly groaned at the thought of what that possibly meant. His gaze drifted with interest over the rest of her. She had the type of body that could make a man forget almost anything.

With concentrated effort, Trask forced his gaze from the view on the patio to Clayton, who was stuffing the papers into his briefcase. "Okay, Clayton. What's wrong with Felicia?"

Clayton stopped what he was doing, tilted his head to one side, and considered answering Trask's question, then thought better of it. "It's personal."

Trask shrugged. "So? What's that's supposed to mean, man? Everything with Felicia is personal. I guess she's upset because she lucked out last night and didn't find some rich fool to become husband number three."

Clayton didn't respond immediately. He stood, picked up the television remote control off the desk, and walked over to the sofa and sat down. "Felicia isn't looking for a husband, rich or otherwise."

"Since when?"

"Since she's gotten her priorities straight. She's changed, Trask."

"Oh, no. You'll never convince me of that," Trask said, coming to join Clayton on the sofa. "I got sliced with her razor-sharp tongue last night."

Clayton sighed. "I doubt that will ever change. The two of you have been at it since kindergarten. There are some who even claim the two of you used to throw baby bottles at each other from your cribs while in day care. For some reason you and Felicia seem to enjoy antagonizing each other." He frowned at Trask. "Don't you think it's time to give it a rest?"

"She always starts it," Trask mumbled as he took the remote out of Clayton's hand.

Clayton rolled his eyes upward as he took the remote back.

"For crying out loud, Trask. Will you just listen to yourself? You sound just like you did in kindergarten, even worse because now you're a thirty-six-year-old man. Don't you think it's time for you and Felicia to act your ages?"

Trask opened his mouth to say something, then closed it when he thought about what might happen if they did act their ages. Somehow he would find a way to assuage this hunger he had developed for her. After all, he was a man with strong needs, and Felicia was definitely one hot number. "Trust me, Clayton. You don't want that to happen," he finally said.

Clayton raised a brow. "Why not?"

"Let's skip it. But I still want to know why she was crying. Either you tell me or I'll call the uncles to get the scoop." Trask knew that threatening to call the uncles would start Clayton talking. The last thing anyone needed was for Felicia's six uncles to get worked up at the thought that something was wrong with their precious, darling niece.

"Why are you so interested in what's wrong with Felicia, Trask? Why do you even care?"

Trask sighed. He had asked himself that same question a number of times since seeing Felicia's puffy red eyes. His reply, when it finally came, was surprisingly gentle and totally out of character for him. "Let's just say that I care for old times' sake. Felicia and I go back a long way. And although she's the most exasperating woman I know, I do care."

Clayton blinked and shook his head as he convinced himself he was wrong. Surely he had not heard a bit of tenderness in Trask's voice. Or had he?

He stood, deliberated for a few moments, then walked over to his desk to retrieve the letter. Returning to Trask, he handed it to him. "This is Austin's letter to Santa."

Trask raised a brow. "Austin?"

"Yes, Felicia's four-year-old son. He was the ring bearer in my wedding, remember?"

Trask nodded as he unfolded the letter and began reading. When he had finished, he lifted his head and looked up at

Clayton. His best friend, he noticed, was eyeing him speculatively, as if he was contemplating something. He had been friends with Clayton too long not to know how his mind operated.

Trask crossed his arms over his huge chest and narrowed his gaze at Clayton before saying in a voice edged with steel, "If you love your life, don't even think it."

Clayton shrugged as an innocent smile curved his lips. "It was just a thought."

Trask stood. "Squash it. There's no way I'll consider being a holiday dad to Felicia's kid. No way."

Chapter Four

Trask had never been so anxious for an evening to end as he had tonight. Cherie had been nice ... too nice. She had yessed him to death practically the entire evening. Her plastered smile had become so tiresome that it had downright exhausted him. Never before had he met a woman so agreeable, so easy to get along with, and so outright boring. Even the fact that she was a real head turner hadn't helped her case.

He shook his head as he opened the door to his condo. He must be getting old and set in his ways. What other excuse could he come up with for being so nit-picky about a woman? The first thing that had turned him off was the fact that, when he had arrived to pick her up for dinner, she had answered the door with a couple of cats lurking around her heels. He didn't like cats.

The second thing had been the fact that although she had looked absolutely sensational in her outfit—a minidress that had shown off her trim waist, shapely legs, and rounded hips—when she had leaned down to pick up one of her kitties, he had seen ... panty lines.

That had been another turnoff.

Trask shook his head. A lot of women wore lacy lingerie under their clothes. In the past, one of the things that used to heat his blood was the idea of something black, silky, and soft underneath a woman's clothing. Now it was the thought of a woman wearing nothing at all underneath her clothes that not only heated his blood but had his pulses leaping with fire. That thought, coupled with the vision of a pair of unrestricted, unconfined, firm, and uptilted breasts, really pushed him over the deep end and got him all hot and bothered. And lately when he got hot and bothered, only one name readily came to his mind.

Felicia Laverne Madaris.

"But why?" he asked himself as he went into the kitchen to get a cold can of beer out of the refrigerator. Why did the thought of Felicia do that to him? If he didn't know better, he would swear the woman had cast some sort of spell on him.

After taking a huge swallow from the icy-cold can, he wiped his lips with the back of his hand before flopping down in a chair at the table. He thought it was completely hilarious that he could have constant thoughts about a woman he didn't particularly get along with.

He sighed as he remembered what had happened Sunday when he had shown up at Clayton's house to watch the game. That had been the day his troubles had begun—right after reading Felicia's son's letter to Santa.

After the game he had gone out on the patio to discover Felicia had decided not to stick around after all. She had left after helping Syneda put the ribs on the grill. It was just as well that she had left. The Steelers had lost to the Cowboys, and his mood hadn't been the best. And knowing Felicia, she would have deliberately worsened it.

His next streak of bad luck occurred when his brother Alex had shown up late Monday morning to take him to the airport. Alex, who normally was as timely as any clock, had overslept. Alex's lateness had made Trask miss his flight, and he had to spend an additional two hours stuck at the Houston airport. He had arrived in San Diego on a flight that had been more rugged than any game he'd ever played in.

And things had only gone downhill from there.

Some irate fan who hadn't liked one of the calls against his favorite team by a referee had forced his way into the sports room to give his opinion on national television. The network had immediately gone to a commercial break, but not before well over a million television viewers had gotten a blistering earful of just what the discontented fan thought of the referee and the referee's mother.

Returning to Houston yesterday, Trask had looked forward to his date with Cherie. All day the thought of naked bodies and silken sheets had kept him on the edge of anticipation. Sitting home alone and sipping a can of beer before ten o'clock was a sorrowful anticlimax.

Suddenly feeling hot, he loosened a button on his shirt when his thoughts again drifted to Felicia. He had to admit that she had a problem on her hands. He of all people understood her son's needs. His own father had walked out on his mother not long after Alex had been born. Trask had been ten years old at the time. His mother, who had worked long and hard hours as a nurse to make ends meet, could not fill the void created by not having a father in his life. All of his friends had fathers who were always there at their games, and he'd had no one. He had tried not to let that matter to him.

Trask took a sip of his beer when he thought of one particular time when it *had* mattered.

When he was fourteen, and in junior high school, he had played a number of sports. Someone had come up with the idea of having a father-son banquet to end the season. Unfortunately for Trask, he had been the only member of the team who didn't have a father. At first he had thought about not attending and had even mentioned such to Felicia and Clayton. Clayton, who'd also been scheduled to attend, had convinced him to go and had even volunteered to share his own dad for the occasion.

That night, Trask had learned the true meaning of caring. During the ceremony, when the person presiding had asked him and his father to stand, Trask thought he would be standing alone—until he had looked around and seen six other men stand with him. The six Madaris brothers had come to stand in his father's place. Although he was sure they had come because Felicia had asked them to, the thought that they had taken the time to be there with him had touched him deeply.

He'd had Felicia to thank for that night, and now her own son was going through a similar turmoil in his life.

Trask shook his head. The thought of being a holiday dad for Felicia's son was ludicrous. First of all, he didn't know the first thing about being a father. His brother Alex was still single, so he didn't have any nieces or nephews. The closest he had ever gotten to small children was whenever he came into contact with some of his former teammates' families.

Besides, he thought, it wasn't as if he had a lot of free time on his hands. He traveled three days a week. And it was nearing the end of the football season, which meant playoffs. He loved football, and although he didn't play the game professionally any longer, he still enjoyed watching it. His idea of having a good time was sitting in front of the television watching football. It didn't matter who was playing: high schools, colleges, or the pros. To him words like *offense, defense,* and *Bud Light* were sweet music to his ears. What in the world could he do with a four-year-old who was probably too young to know the difference between a football and a basketball?

Trask swore softly. He blamed Clayton for even showing him the letter in the first place. He blamed Felicia for having married two rich, but irresponsible men. And he blamed himself for caring.

His thoughts shifted back to Felicia's ex-husbands. What real man would turn his back on his own son and not be there for him? According to what Clayton had told him, even before his death, Steven Gardner had not once come to see his child. And although her second husband had not been Austin's natural father, his marriage to Felicia had made him the little boy's stepfather. Didn't that relationship count for something?

Trask crushed his empty beer can in his hand, thinking about his own sorry excuse for a father. After not seeing him since the age of ten, the man had had the nerve to show up at the hotel on the night before Trask's first Super Bowl game, requesting free tickets for him, his new wife, and his pimple-faced stepdaughter.

Trask stood and went over to the counter to grab a bag of chips. His thoughts again returned to Felicia and her son. Who'd ever heard of a dad for the holidays anyway? In the letter Austin had written to Santa, the kid claimed he would return his holiday dad on New Year's Day. What if the kid changed his mind and became attached? How far would he go to have his way?

Trask had once been a witness to a kid in the shopping mall having a temper tantrum. That scene had reminded him of a rabid animal being shot. The little boy had all but foamed at the mouth. Evidently the intended performance had worked since the kid's mother had practically bought out the entire toy department to shut him up and to get him from rolling all over the floor.

Trask frowned. And knowing Felicia, her child was probably a spoiled brat just as she had been. He tried to recall how the kid had acted at Clayton's wedding. Since everything had gone smoothly, he guessed the little boy had been on his best behavior that day.

He shook his head in disbelief that he was even having these thoughts. He must be crazy to think twice about doing anything to help Felicia out. The two of them would argue constantly, which wouldn't make a good impression on the kid. But then, maybe, just maybe, Clayton was right. Maybe it was about time for him and Felicia to began acting their ages. And he had to admit that acting their ages did have some merit. Especially if it would relieve this constant, nagging ache in the lower part of his body.

He had blown it with Cherie tonight, which meant he was still hard up, literally, for female companionship. Trask again thought of Felicia and gave a thoughtful purse of his lips as he considered the depth of just what he might be getting himself into. The idea that what he might be getting himself into was Felicia's curvaceous body made his blood sizzle. The thought of his body moving deep inside hers made an outpouring of sweat form on his forehead. Desire, the likes of which he'd never experienced before, tore through him. He was shocked how fast his heart was thundering in his chest.

Standing and moving quickly, he headed for the bathroom. He needed a cold shower—and fast. Then later, he would think some more about how he could make Felicia's little boy a happy kid for the holidays—and make himself a satisfied, sated man.

He smiled. As for how he would handle Felicia, he had every intention of doing something about that smart mouth of hers—like kissing it till it ached, while moans of ecstasy slipped through her ripened lips.

Maybe it was about time he put Felicia in her place. And at the moment, he couldn't think of a better place than his bed.

A week later

The infuriating woman had the nerve to open the door with her face completely covered with night cream. And if that didn't beat all, Trask thought, Felicia's head was fully covered with some ugly looking scarf. But her perfume, an alluring and enticing scent, was her redeeming asset. The fragrance stirred to life the heat within him.

He had been reluctant to drop by unexpectedly on the off chance she was entertaining male company. He now felt safe in dismissing that possibility since she definitely didn't resemble a woman trying to impress anyone with her looks tonight.

The eyes that stared at Trask through all the mud on her

face narrowed, first in surprise, then in annoyance. "What are you doing here?" Felicia asked testily.

Trask couldn't help but smile. He had to hand it to her. She could make the most unwelcome person feel . . . most unwelcome. "May I come in, Felicia?"

"Why would you want to come in? Besides, it's late."

Trask frowned. He didn't need her to tell him it was late. He had been driving around town for the past couple of hours, trying to talk himself out of the decision he had made that afternoon. Two weeks had passed and he hadn't been able to get her son's letter to Santa out of his mind. Nor had he been able to get her out of his mind. He had finally come up with a plan on how to kill two birds with one stone.

"I know it's late, but we need to talk so let me in—unless you're afraid."

One thing Trask knew about Felicia, in addition to having a razor-sharp tongue, she was competitive by nature and enjoyed challenges. And he had deliberately just thrown her one.

"What do you mean we have to talk? And what do you mean unless I'm afraid? Just who or what am I supposed to be afraid of, Trask Maxwell? Definitely not you."

"I believe otherwise."

Evidently she thought something was funny, Trask thought, watching her throw her head back and burst into a fit of laughter.

"You're cute, Trask, real cute," she said when her laughter had subsided. "And this conversation is utterly ridiculous. I refuse to participate in it any longer."

"Even if it means making your son happy for the holidays?"

As he knew it would, that statement got her attention. It also made him the recipient of a look that suddenly went from slightly amused to dangerously chilling.

"What are you talking about, Trask?"

"Clayton let me read your son's letter to Santa."

"So you read it," she snapped. "Big deal." Inwardly, Felicia suddenly considered it a big deal. She didn't like the idea of

Clayton sharing that letter with Trask. He would seize any opportunity to ridicule her.

"I'm offering my help."

Felicia raised a brow. "Your help? And just how do you think you can help?"

Trask doubted she would want him to go into the details on her doorstep at eleven o'clock at night. "I think we need to discuss this inside."

Trask knew he had aroused her curiosity, which was another weakness of hers. Curiosity had gotten her into trouble a number of times while they were growing up. He remembered how her curiosity about kissing had driven her to want to experiment with him. She had expected him to sit still, like a statue, while she discovered just what kissing was all about. At the age of sixteen, on a rainy afternoon, when they should have been in her bedroom studying, they had called a truce long enough to explore the art of kissing.

"Trask, I'm talking to you."

Trask realized that, while his thoughts had been in the past, she had been talking to him. "Sorry. What were you saying?"

Felicia frowned at him. "I said come in." She stepped aside to let him enter. After closing the door, she led him into a huge, nicely furnished living room.

"Stay," she ordered before turning and leaving him alone.

Trask's gaze traveled the full length of her long, lithe body which was clad in a slinky, silk robe, until she disappeared from sight. It was only then that he remembered the order she had snapped at him.

Stay? Did she think she was giving orders to some mutt by the name of Rover or Rin-Tin-Tin? He had no intentions of following her orders and staying put. Defiantly, he left the living room and decided to conduct a personal tour of Felicia's home.

Although the house was large and tastefully decorated and in a very nice area of town, he had expected a lot more for a woman who'd made a career out of marrying for money. There were no maids or butlers scurrying about. Evidently husbands one and two had shoved prenuptial agreements down her throat. He immediately dismissed the idea. Knowing Felicia, she would have shoved them right back and would have told them just where they could put those agreements. That meant there must be another reason why she wasn't living off her ex-husbands' wealth. According to Clayton, she had opened some sort of dress store last year. He wondered if that was her primary source of income right now.

Trask shrugged. Her money or her lack of it wasn't his business, he thought as he made his way into the kitchen. After a thorough glance around, he decided her kitchen was too big. He couldn't see her spending much time in it, and he seriously doubted that she ever took the time to prepare her son a home cooked meal. Fast foods were probably her specialty. He wouldn't be surprised to discover that she was on a first-name basis with the people at Burger King.

"I thought I told you to stay put, Trask."

Trask turned around. Felicia had washed the gook off her face, removed the dorky-looking scarf from her head, and changed into a tank top and a pair of stretch pants. He wondered if all her clothes were clingy or skintight. His body tightened just looking at her. He also wondered if there was anything between her skin and the snug-fitting pants she had on. He doubted it since his keen vision didn't see any panty lines.

"I asked what you're doing in my kitchen when I told you explicitly to stay put in the living room."

Trask's mouth quirked into a smooth smile. "With the tone you used, I assumed you were talking to some invisible dog you have wandering around here. You definitely weren't talking to me."

Felicia sighed. Maybe the tone of her voice had been a bit waspish, but what did he expect. He was the last person she had expected to appear on her doorstep. Especially since she had been thinking about him constantly over the past two weeks. She had thought he would drop by Clayton's parents' home for Thanksgiving dinner. And when he hadn't, she had been disappointed for some unknown reason. Later she had convinced herself that the only reason she had wanted to see him was because she'd been in the mood to argue with someone, and he would have been a good candidate. And now seeing him standing in the middle of her kitchen wearing a tan sports jacket with a blue T-shirt, a pair of brand-name running shoes, and a pair of sexy blue jeans made her think her large kitchen suddenly seemed small.

"So how do you think you can help?" Felicia asked.

Trask studied her thoughtfully before saying. "By offering to be Austin's holiday dad."

For a moment Felicia just stared at him, letting his words sink in. He was willing to be the temporary dad Austin had asked Santa for? Why? Why was he making the offer? There had to be more to it.

"What's the catch?" she asked suspiciously. There was something about the way he was looking at her that set her entire body on edge. Her already jittery nerves were playing havoc with her overactive hormones. They were hormones that had never misbehaved until Trask was around.

Trask took a step toward her, closing the distance between them. He reached up and gently brushed his hand lightly against her cheek. "It seems, Felicia, that I have this little problem that you can help me with, while I'm helping you out of your tight spot. So I'm more than willing to be your son's holiday dad in exchange for something."

The mere touch of his hand upset Felicia's balance as explosive currents raced through her. A hot ache grew in her throat, and she forced out her words. "In exchange for what?" The sound of her voice was like a silken whisper.

The look in Trask's eyes was dark, seductive, and sensuous. The sound of his voice when he responded was deep, husky, and magnetic.

"In exchange, I want you to be my holiday lover."

Chapter Five

Felicia's mouth gaped open in shock. Surely she had not heard Trask correctly. There was no way he could have said he would volunteer to be Austin's holiday dad if she would be his holiday lover. But after one look at the quirk on his face that slightly resembled a smile, she knew she had indeed heard him correctly.

And that was when she began seeing red.

"Are you crazy?" she demanded.

The smile that tugged at Trask's lips widened. He thought Felicia looked totally delectable when angered. "No, I'm not crazy," he said soothingly. "But I am somewhat in need right now."

Felicia lifted a brow. She had an idea just what type of need he was referring to. "That sounds like a personal problem," she snapped.

"It is, and one I hope you can help me solve. You help me out with my problem and I'll help you out with yours."

Felicia was livid. "Do you think for one minute I'll let you use my son in exchange for sexual favors?"

Trask leaned against the counter. "Use your son? I don't

see it that way. We will be making him happy for the holidays, and in turn we'll be making ourselves happy. There's no way you can deny that you don't want me as much as I want you.''

''I hate deflating your oversized ego but you're wrong, Trask. I don't want you.''

''You're lying to yourself, Felicia, and you know it. Don't you think I've picked up on this sudden attraction between us? Hell, I don't understand it, but I've stopped trying to figure it out. All I know is that we have this itch for each other that desperately needs scratching. Admit it. You want to make love to me as much as I want to make love to you.''

''In your dreams.''

''Yeah, there, too,'' Trask chuckled slightly. ''I've made love to you a number of times these past two weeks in my dreams. Now I'd prefer the real thing. There's nothing wrong with a man dreaming about a desirable woman. The problem starts when he thinks about her while he's awake. And you, Felicia, have crept into my daily thoughts, and I see no other way to get you out of them.''

He took a few steps toward her, stopping barely a few inches away. ''What are you afraid of? I've never known you to be afraid of anything before in your life, and definitely not of me.''

''I'm not afraid of you.''

''Then prove it and prove me wrong. Prove that you don't have the hots for me like I have them for you. Prove that what I feel is one-sided and that you have no desire to get into my clothes like I want to get into yours.''

He leaned slightly forward, his lips mere inches from hers. ''Prove it, Felicia, by letting me kiss you,'' he said, his voice a breathless whisper. ''And if I don't get the response I want from you, I'll leave. But I'll still be Austin's dad for the holidays regardless of the outcome of our kiss. Agreed?''

''I don't . . .'' Her voice trailed off when Trask moved his mouth closer.

''Agree, Felicia,'' Trask admonished in a low, husky voice.

"What do you have to lose? Especially since you claim you don't want me as much as I want you. Unless you think you will lose."

His words, as he had known they would, tossed a challenge she couldn't or wouldn't ignore. Her eyes, he noted, were filled with defiance and desire. He was hoping that desire would win out.

Felicia frowned. "Okay, I agree, but I won't lose, Trask. You will."

She reached up and ever so casually pushed the jacket off his shoulders before placing her arms around his neck. She decided to be the aggressor, and the tip of her tongue darted out and touched his lips before sliding inside his mouth.

Trying hard to ignore the feeling of blood rushing fast and furious through her veins, she closed her eyes and deepened the kiss as their lips fused together in a lingering, heated and delicious moment.

And that was where she made her mistake.

With a skill that undoubtedly came from years of experience, Trask masterfully, unhurriedly, and purposefully took control. He moved his mouth hungrily over hers, devouring its softness and capturing her sweetness. He methodically drugged her with a sensation Felicia didn't know could exist. She was shocked at the response coming from her, and she was shocked even further when she realized she was helpless to do anything about it. The need he was arousing in her was too strong. But her stubbornness refused to let her surrender. Even when the kiss began sending her stomach into a wild swirl, she would not admit defeat. A part of her was determined to make Trask as crazy with desire as he was making her.

Their tongues dueled relentlessly as they reveled in the heat of each other's mouths. The feel of Trask's muscular arms around Felicia, as he crushed her to him, made her moan.

When Trask finally raised his head, it was only for a few seconds, to breathe in much needed air before lowering his head again, showering kisses around her lips and along her jaw.

"Competition over," he rasped near her ear in a deep, husky tone. "Now for pleasure."

Felicia felt his hands tighten around her as he lifted her and set her on the table to straddle his thighs. In the split second that her mind rationalized what his definition of pleasure might be, he again smothered her lips with demanding mastery. Shivers raced through her and another small moan escaped her throat when she felt his hand move underneath her top.

Leaving her mouth burning with fire, he lifted her top. She arched her back when his tongue began a slow journey from her collarbone down to her bare breasts. His mouth tantalized the throbbing tips, which had swollen to their fullest.

Months of celibacy began taking their toll on Felicia, and she felt her body instinctively sliding forward, seeking out the hard part of Trask. She wanted to rub her body against the huge straining bulge she saw beneath the fly of his jeans.

Trask saw just where Felicia's passionate gaze was centered. His hand pressed at the small of her back as he urged her closer toward the heat of him. When her body found its mark, the teasing friction of her clothes rubbing against his hardness made them both gasp.

He tightened his arms around her and deepened their kiss when his body stroked against her. With her tightly straddling him, their bodies meshed together from thigh to chest. When Trask's body became even harder, and when Felicia felt his hand lightly caress her thighs, passion, the like of which she had never known before, inched through her veins, and her breath came in long, deep moans. She reached out and her fingers began toying with Trask's zipper.

"You want more, Felicia? You want the real thing?" Trask growled out the questions, but did not wait for her answers. He picked her up off the table and into his arms. When her hands inched underneath his shirt, he clenched his teeth against rising need. His abdominal muscles contracted, and his entire body became inflamed in passion—red-hot passion. He no longer thought of victory or which one of them had come out the winner. All he could think about was that never before had he felt a need to bury himself inside a woman. Deep.

He wanted her now. This minute. This second. The hard urgency of his body demanded that he take her, here ... on the table, on the counter, on the floor, wherever.

But another part of him knew they would find more pleasure in a bed. He began walking down the hall toward her bedroom with her in his arms. Then he stopped. Her little boy, who was wiping sleep from his eyes, was coming out of his bedroom. The unexpected sight of Felicia's son helped rein in Trask's control.

"We got company, sweetheart," Trask whispered to Felicia as he reluctantly slid her down his body and out of his arms.

Felicia's overdriven passion vanished the moment she saw her son. She hurried to him and crouched in front of him. "Austin? Baby, what's the matter? Do you need to go to the bathroom?"

He didn't say anything for a few seconds as he continued to wipe the sleep from his eyes. When he did focus his gaze, it went beyond her to Trask, who was standing a few feet away from them.

It seemed to Trask that for the longest time the little boy stared at him. Then his sleepy little face broke into a huge, happy smile. He ran past Felicia and launched himself against Trask, grabbing hold of his leg.

"He did it, Mommy! He did it! Santa gave me a daddy for the holidays!" The little boy looked up at Trask with soft, pleading eyes. "And you will love me, won't you?"

The unexpected question was asked so innocently and so desperately that it hit Trask full force in the chest and in his heart. He thought the look on the kid's face was priceless; it touched him deeply. Suddenly, immediately, Trask's emotions opened as something stirred deep within him.

Reaching down, he effortlessly picked Felicia's son up into

his arms. And for a fleeting moment, he felt a sense of purpose as he cuddled him close. He turned his head toward Felicia when he answered the question her son had asked.

"Yes, I will love you."

"Promise?" The little boy asked shyly, but pleadingly.

Trask could hardly answer because of the lump that formed in his throat. "Yes, I promise."

Felicia turned her back to them, but not before Trask saw the tears glistening in her eyes.

Chapter Six

Felicia had only to look across the room at Trask and Austin sitting close together on the sofa to know that the entire idea of Trask being the boy's holiday dad was a mistake. Oh, it wasn't that he and Austin weren't getting along, because they were. In fact, in her opinion, they were getting along too nicely. It seemed they had totally forgotten her very existence. What really bothered her was the fact that the man she rarely got along with was getting along perfectly fine with her son.

As she sat on the love seat watching as Austin eagerly told Trask about all the things he wanted them to do together for the holidays, her heart went out to her son. She hadn't realized just how starved he had been for male companionship and a father figure in his life.

She shook her head as she studied Trask. He seemed to be hanging on to Austin's every word. She didn't like admitting it, but he was a natural at handling her son. If she didn't know better, she would suspect he had a kid or two stashed away someplace and just wasn't saying so. But she knew that wasn't the case. If Trask had fathered a child, he would be the type of man to acknowledge it. He would not abandon his child like Steven had abandoned his.

Felicia's thoughts then drifted to what had happened earlier in her kitchen and what probably would be happening this very minute in her bedroom if Austin hadn't awakened. She couldn't believe she'd actually lost control like that. She would never be able to look at her kitchen table again without remembering how she had unraveled in Trask's arms.

There was no doubt in her mind that he thought he had gotten the best of her, but she had news for him. As far as she was concerned, he hadn't played fair. How was she to know that his kissing abilities had changed that much since they were sixteen? And how was she to know that he was now a man with masterful hands? Those big, strong hands of his—the same ones that had held numerous footballs while he raced down the field to score touchdowns—had had her so aroused, she probably would have let him have his way with her right there on the kitchen table. All she had wanted was to be released from the sexual torment he'd been putting her through.

She frowned. And that wasn't good. The last thing she wanted or needed was anything from Trask Maxwell, especially sexual release. But then, all it took was one glance at him sitting on her sofa, looking big, sexy, and irresistible, and she could feel her muscles tense in a very private place.

Felicia quickly reined in her unexplainably fiery and passionate attraction for Trask as she glanced at the clock on the wall. It was past time for Austin to go back to bed and for Trask to leave. And after he left, she would go about making sure her head was screwed back on straight. Kissing Trask, tasting him, and rubbing her body against his had literally knocked it off.

"All right, Austin Gardner, it's time for you to go back to bed now, so tell Mr. Maxwell good night."

"But, Mommy, I want to stay with Daddy a little while longer."

Daddy! Felicia's mouth dropped open, and her and Trask's gazes snapped locked for a moment. After getting over her initial shock at hearing Austin call Trask daddy, she was about to say something to correct him, to let him know that Trask was *not* his daddy, but she didn't say anything when Trask shook his head, silently advising her not to.

However, she was never good at taking orders, especially when they came from Trask, and a few moments later, she began speaking anyway. "Austin, sweetheart, I think—"

"Your mother thinks if you don't go to bed now, you'll be too tired to go with me to pick out that Christmas tree tomorrow," Trask interrupted.

A huge smile covered Austin's face as he nodded. "Will you be here in the morning when I wake up?"

"No, he won't be here," Felicia answered, not giving Trask a chance to. "Mr. Maxwell is leaving. Now tell him good night."

"But, Mommy, why can't Daddy stay here with us? He can sleep with you in your big bed."

"Yeah, why can't I?" Trask asked teasingly as a devilish smile curved his lips.

Felicia narrowed her eyes at Trask, suppressing an urge to give him a good, hard slap. Instead, she gave Austin her full attention. It was time to set matters straight once and for all.

"Because, sweetheart, although you may have asked Santa for a daddy, Mr. Maxwell will only be around to spend some time with you for the holidays. He won't be here forever, so you shouldn't think he will. He goes back on New Year's Day. You remember him from the wedding don't you? He's your cousin Clayton's friend. You may even run into him every once in a while after New Year's now that he's moved back to town. But, Austin, Santa kept his part of the deal and you need to be ready to keep yours, sweetheart. Mr. Maxwell won't have any reason to come around here to this house after New Year's Day. Understood?"

"But, Mommy, I—"

"No, Austin, there aren't any buts. Understood?"

Austin held his head down and stared at the floor. "Yes, ma'am."

Felicia nodded. She then decided to take another approach in correcting the other issue—Austin calling Trask daddy. "Now tell *Mr. Maxwell* good night."

"Good night, Daddy."

"Good night, Austin."

Felicia raised her eyes to the ceiling when her tactic didn't work.

"Daddy, will you tuck me back in bed?"

Trask glanced over at Felicia for her consent.

Felicia released a heavy sigh. Some days it didn't pay to get out of bed. "It's okay," she said dryly.

Taking Austin's smaller hand into his large one, Trask turned, and he and Austin walked out of the room leaving Felicia alone.

Felicia turned away from gazing out of the window when she heard Trask return. The fifteen or so minutes that he had been gone had given her time to think—really think. And the more she thought, the angrier she got.

Trask took one look at her face and her hands, which were balled up into fists at her sides, and immediately knew something was wrong. "What's the matter with you?"

"You have really done it this time, Trask. I never thought you would stoop so low. I just figured out why you're doing this."

Trask crossed his arms over his chest and returned Felicia's belligerent glare. Her pouty lips, he thought, were made for kissing, and not for spouting off words that didn't make any sense to him. A shudder passed through him when he remembered how the feel and taste of her lips on his had generated heat throughout his body. He forced his attention from her lips and met her eyes. Unfortunately, he didn't get any help there. He couldn't help but recall how those same eyes, which were now dark with fury, had been dark with passion less than an hour ago.

"And what exactly am I supposed to be doing?" he asked. *Other than thinking of a way to get you back in the kitchen and onto that table again,* he thought.

"I can think of no reason for your wanting to spend time with Austin other than to get back at me for harassing you all these years. I can't believe you would go this far. Having a father figure around for the holidays means everything to Austin, and I won't let you fill him with hope, dreams, and meaningless words of love, then break his heart. He's calling you daddy for heaven's sake! And to make matters worse, he's made all these plans he thinks the two of you will do together."

Tears of anger misted Felicia's eyes. "How could you do that to him? If you want revenge, then go ahead, Trask, go after me. But I won't let you hurt my son."

A taut, tense moment of silence passed between them, and Felicia watched as utter rage covered Trask's face. She didn't think she had ever seen him that mad before and it surprised her. And with that surprise came the common sense to take a few steps back when he began advancing toward her. His eyes, she noted, flashed fire. And for the first time in all her dealings with Trask, she had a feeling she had gone too far.

"Other than my mother, brother, and Clayton, you should know me better than anyone, Felicia. You of all people know my history," he said in a voice filled with fury.

"My father turned his back on me and Alex, the same way Austin's father turned his back on him. You know how hard that was for me as a child growing up. In addition to the holidays, I had those sports events to deal with. Unlike others on the team, I couldn't look up in the stands and know I had a father there rooting for me. I didn't have a father giving me that special smile or a thumbs up to let me know how proud he was of me," Trask said, not even trying to control the anger in his voice.

"The reason I'm doing this for Austin is because I've been

where he's at now. I know exactly how it feels to want a father figure around for the holidays. Do you know how much I appreciate your uncles for what they did for me during those times? There was never a game that I played in while in high school, college, or the pros that I didn't know for certain that one, some, or all of your uncles were somewhere up there in the stands cheering for me. I think I did my best because of them. They proved they were proud of me, regardless of whether I was winning or losing."

Felicia's hands untightened and the anger she had felt earlier suddenly left her. Trask was right—she knew his history. She had always been a part of it. Although she and Trask had bickered relentlessly as kids, she and Clayton were the ones he had shared his innermost thoughts and feelings with.

"Trask, I—"

"No, Felicia, for once you will shut up and listen," he snapped. "Unlike what you think, one of the reasons that I've decided to spend time with Austin is because he's a Madaris. And I owe a lot to your family, for being there when no one else was. It's the least I can do. It's something that I want to do."

He didn't add that, for some unknown reason, he also felt close to her son mainly because Austin belonged to her. "And as far as him calling me daddy, I don't have a problem with it and neither should you. A daddy and everything he's supposed to represent is a part of Austin's holiday fantasy, so it comes natural to him to call me that because to him that's who I'll be for the next four weeks."

Trask hesitated before continuing. "And what I'm doing for Austin has nothing to do with this feud between us. We've been at each other's throats for years. It's more out of habit than anything else. What happened earlier tonight, in your kitchen, proves that we can get along. In fact I think it's a pretty enjoyable experience when we do."

"I wish you wouldn't bring that up."

Trask stared at her lips for a moment, before blinking and

refocusing on her face. "Yes, I'm sure you wish I wouldn't," was his reply.

Felicia's face turned a darker brown before she cleared her throat. "Look, Trask. Maybe I did draw the wrong conclusions about your reasons for wanting to spend time with Austin for the holidays, and I apologize. But when it comes to Austin I can't help but want to protect him."

"Of course you can't and you shouldn't. He's your son."

Felicia nodded. "And although you have the best intentions for wanting to help, it may cause more harm than good. Austin has already gotten attached to you. He's never called anyone daddy before."

Trask frowned. He knew the situation with her first husband, but didn't know much about the second one, other than that he had screwed around on her. "He didn't call your second husband daddy?"

"No. Charles preferred that Austin call him by his first name."

Trask opened his mouth to say something, then closed it. He could give her an earful about what he thought about that tidbit.

He didn't have to say anything. Felicia clearly read the emotions that had crossed his face, but like him, she decided to leave it alone. "Anyway, Austin really believes you're the daddy he's asked for."

"And for a while I will be."

"But we'll have to continue to make sure that Austin understands this is a temporary arrangement."

Trask nodded and released a deep sigh. "I don't get it. I could have been any other man who dropped by tonight. Why did he take one look at me and think I was the one Santa delivered?"

Felicia frowned. "Because for your information, Trask Maxwell, I don't have men dropping by. Since I moved here nearly six months ago, there has never been a man who's come to this house other than one of my family members." She didn't want to go into details about why she had moved out of her other home to this one and why she had not dated since then. "To Austin, it's a rare occurrence to see a man here that he's not related to. So naturally, he assumed you were sent by Santa."

Trask raised a brow. "What do you mean you don't have men dropping by? You date, don't you?"

"No."

Trask looked at her as if she had gone foolish. "What do you mean by no?"

"I mean just what I said. I don't date and haven't dated in nearly six months."

"Why?"

"That's none of your business."

"What if I said that I'm making it my business." He took a step that brought him closer to her. "And the main reason is that tonight I got just the response I wanted to get out of you, so now you're it."

"Your plaything for the holidays?" Felicia sneered.

"No, my lover for the holidays, and I don't like sharing. So whether or not you're dating *is* my business."

Felicia opened her mouth to tell him just where he could put his business, but never got a chance to do so. Trask's mouth swooped down on hers, effectively absorbing any sound she was about to make. His kiss was strong, sure, and sensuous as his tongue stroked, sucked, and soothed. Felicia's legs didn't feel quite so steady and her heart began beating three times its normal rate. Again, she felt powerless to do anything but return Trask's kiss.

Trask broke off the kiss. The look on his face at first was tender, then arrogant when he said, "Yes, it's a very enjoyable experience when we do something other than bicker back and forth. You did agree to be my holiday lover, and I've never known you to go back on your word, Felicia."

He smiled at her glare. "Cheer up, sweetheart. This is the

season to be jolly. Joy to the world, deck the halls, and all that good stuff.''

Trask knew that, if given the chance, she would do more than deck the halls right now. No doubt she would deck him good. The look of anger on her face indicated as much. Remembering that she could throw a good right punch, he thought it was best to leave before she decided to do so.

"Good night, Felicia. I hope your dreams are as pleasant as mine will be." He then turned and walked out of her house.

He couldn't help but chuckle when he heard the sound of her door slamming shut behind him.

Chapter Seven

The first two weeks of being Austin's holiday dad turned out better than Trask had thought possible. For some reason he had expected trouble from Felicia, but she hadn't done anything to cause any problems.

As Trask stepped from the shower and grabbed a towel to dry off his body, a picture flashed in his mind. He kept seeing the look on Austin's face when they had gone to pick out a Christmas tree. Seeing the happiness shine in the little boy's features had only reinforced his belief that he had done the right thing by agreeing to be his holiday dad. And he knew that Felicia had seen it too. Maybe that was the reason she had decided to lie low and not interfere. She had tried getting out of going with them to pick out the tree, but Austin would not hear of it. The kid had declared that getting a tree was a family affair, something a daddy, mommy, and child were to do together. So she had relented and gone with them.

After they had returned to her house with what Austin claimed to be the perfect Christmas tree, Felicia had announced she was fixing dinner and that Trask was welcome to stay if he wanted to. At first he had hesitated. He of all people knew that Felicia wasn't a wiz in the kitchen, but out of curiosity, and because he knew that deep down she really hadn't wanted him to stay, he had accepted her invitation.

It turned out that the surprise had been on him. The meal she had prepared—baked fish with crab-meat dressing, green beans, potato salad, and squash casserole—had been one of the best home-cooked meals he had eaten in a long time. And every meal he had shared with her and Austin after that had been just as delectable. Now that his mother had remarried and moved to Waco, he didn't get as many home-cooked meals as before. And although he knew he would always be welcomed at Clayton's parents' home, he didn't want to wear out his welcome. So, on occasion, he and Alex would meet at one restaurant or another for dinner. And when Alex, who was a private investigator, was out of town, he would grab something at a restaurant and take it home and dine in.

Another thing that had surprised him was the relationship Felicia had with her son. She was fiercely loyal and protective, and no matter what she did, she always put Austin first. He knew the reason she was not dating had something to do with Austin, but he wasn't sure why, and she wasn't saying.

Trask smiled when he thought of the little boy whom he had spent so much time with over the past two weeks. He was a swell kid and a pretty smart one at four years old. He also had good manners and was respectful of others. And to Trask's surprise, for a four-year-old, Austin knew a lot about football and completely understood the game. When Trask had questioned Felicia about it, she had rolled her eyes at him before asking what he had expected with the majority of her family being football fanatics.

Trask couldn't help but chuckle as he slipped into a pair of faded jeans. He had already checked the list Austin had given him to see what was in store for the coming week, which was the week leading up to Christmas. When he returned to Houston on Wednesday, he was to drive Austin around town so the two of them could check out the homes decorated with Christmas lights. On Thursday evening, he had agreed to attend the Christmas program at church because Austin had a part in the play. Then on Friday, Christmas Eve, he would have dinner with Austin and Felicia. Then after Austin went to bed he would step into the role of Santa and help Felicia put together any toys that needed assembling.

Trask had to admit he was looking forward to doing all of those things as much as Austin was, and that in itself was surprising. When he had first begun spending time with Austin, he had intended to do so only a couple times a week. But now he saw him practically every day that he was in town. He never would have thought that spending time with a four-year-old would be so enjoyable. But it was. Austin was fast becoming a special part of his life each day.

After slipping his feet into his slippers, he moved out of his bedroom and headed toward the kitchen. When the doorbell rang, he frowned, wondering who his visitor could be as he walked toward the door.

''Who is it?''

''It's Felicia.''

Trask's frown deepened. He wondered why Felicia was paying him a visit. As soon as he opened the door and took one look at her, he had his answer. Felicia was known to be a sore loser. It was evident from the way she was dressed, she intended to get back at him . . . big time. She stood in his doorway, the epitome of temptation and desire.

Trask crossed his arms over his chest and scanned her outfit, if you really cared to call it that. Her blouse already had the top button undone, showing a glimpse of the creamy skin above her breast. The skirt was so short that calling it a mini would have been too mild a term to use. For some reason it looked even shorter with the three-inch heels she had on. And to make matters worse, it was tight. Way too tight. Her outfit was a knock-'em-off-his-feet number, and already he felt himself losing his balance. He knew he had to get a grip.

''What are you doing here, Felicia?''

She smiled up at him. But Trask knew that smile. For two weeks Felicia Laverne had patiently waited for what she considered the right time and now she was out for revenge. Evidently, she hadn't gotten over losing to him that night in her kitchen.

He graciously moved aside when she didn't respond but boldly sauntered into his condo without an invitation. His gaze immediately followed her as she went straight to his sofa and sat down, as if she had every right to be there, and as if it were an everyday occurrence for her to show up at his place dressed to seduce.

"I came to make a delivery," she finally said, crossing her bare legs one over the other and deliberately baring shapely thighs.

Trask was so busy keeping his gaze glued to Felicia's legs and thighs that he didn't notice the paper bag she had placed on his coffee table.

"Gramma Madaris sent you some of her bread pudding. She cooked a special batch for the holidays and knows just how much you enjoy it."

Trask watched as she then tugged at the hem of her tight miniskirt with the pretense of trying to pull it down. Her effort only raised the skirt a little higher. He drew in a long, deep breath as he continued to watch her. He had a feeling that things were about to get even more brazen. She tilted her head coyly, sweetly, and suggestively, and her smile widened when she looked up at him.

"But I don't think you'd enjoy her hot bread pudding as much as you would enjoy hot sex. Would you, Trask?"

He hadn't actually been listening to anything she had said since his mind and gaze were on something else. However, she had immediately grabbed his attention when she said something about . . . hot sex.

He cleared his throat. "Excuse me? What were you saying, Felicia?"

She uncrossed her legs and sat up straight on the sofa, giving him another luscious view of her thighs and making a dizzy sensation flow through him. "You aren't paying attention, Trask. I said that Gramma Madaris asked me to drop this off for you tonight," she said, pointing to the brown paper bag that was sitting in the middle of his coffee table. "She made a batch of her bread pudding for the holidays and wanted to make sure you got some."

She leaned back in her seat and crossed her legs again. Her lips curved and her lashes lowered when she asked coyly. "And you do want *some* . . . don't you, Trask?"

That question caused every muscle in Trask's body to become consumed with sharp currents of desire. *Oh, he wanted some all right,* he thought, knowing just where she was coming from— and more importantly, just where he wanted to go. His fingers itched to caress every part of her body, especially those curvaceous thighs she evidently enjoyed exposing to him. He would enjoy nothing better than to caress her legs, then slowly and deliberately move his hands higher as they traced a sensuous path toward . . .

Felicia stood. "Well, I have to go."

Trask frowned. He was having one hell of a time trying to keep up with Felicia's conversation. He was desperately struggling to keep pace with her, but he felt his pulse jump when she stood. The shapely beauty of her in a tight miniskirt made his body harden even more. "Where do you think you're going?"

A hot stab of uncertainty touched Felicia. When she had arrived moments earlier, she had hoped that Trask would take the bait. And from the look of him, she thought, as her gaze strayed slowly downward to the zipper of his jeans, he had taken it in a big way. But now, she had this gut feeling that she had bitten off more than she could chew.

Her plan had been a simple one. She was going to get back at Trask for making her resolve weaken that night by doing the same to him. She had wanted to leave his condo tonight with the satisfaction that she had made him beg for her. The same way she had almost begged for him two weeks ago in her kitchen. But now the only thing she wanted to do was get out of here. Unfortunately, he stood between her and the door.

She should have known she was headed for trouble when he had opened the door wearing just a pair of jeans. And when her gaze had followed the curly hair on his bare chest downward, past his navel until it dipped into his jeans, she had almost lost her train of thought. Her body's reaction to his chest had spurts of hungry desire spiraling through her veins. Her senses were inflamed by the scent of his freshly showered body. Some parts of his hairy chest were still wet. And the thought of rubbing her bare breasts against his damp chest sent a strong passionate flame through the soft core of her body. Any thought of being in control of any situation involving Trask would be just an illusion. He had too much sex appeal.

"I asked where you think you're going, Felicia?"

His words, low and husky, reclaimed Felicia's attention.

"I'm going home. I just dropped by to make that delivery for my grandmother." Felicia swallowed hard when Trask slowly walked over to stand before her. The look in his eyes was dark and completely sexual. The impact of his gaze was devastatingly strong.

"No, I don't think that's why you *just* dropped by," he said in a low, deep voice. "I think you dropped by for something else, too."

Felicia turned a darker shade of brown. "Something else like what?"

He reached up and his finger touched the top button of her blouse, which was already undone. He watched her gaze follow the movement of his finger as it left that top button and moved to the second. With a flick of his fingers, he undid that button.

"I think your main reason for coming over here was to try to use your feminine wiles on me. For some reason you thought that you could seduce your way out of our agreement."

Felicia drew in a deep breath when Trask's fingers lightly touched her skin when they moved to the next button and undid that one too. "And you don't think I can?"

He looked up at her. His gaze darkened even more. "I don't think you can what?"

She licked her lips to moisten them. "Seduce my way out of our agreement."

He shrugged as he became enraptured with her scent. The enticing smell of her perfume surrounded him, pulled at him, and teased him. The buttons he had undone exposed a nice section of her creamy soft skin above her breasts. He wanted to taste her skin and leave damp kisses over the top of her body before moving lower.

"You can try. But I may as well warn you, Felicia, it will be rather difficult. I've dreamed of you even more this week, and my need and want for you is still at an all-time high."

Leaning down he kissed the side of her neck. "If you're here to play games with me, then don't, because I won't let you. Not tonight at least, because I want you too much."

The feel of Trask's tongue against her skin caused every pore in Felicia's body to surge with passion. The feeling also made her head spin. "I wanted to be the one in control. I wanted to hear you beg," she confessed silkily and desperately, as she leaned closer toward Trask. Against her will, her heart pounded as desire began consuming her.

"Then you're not listening very well, sweetheart," Trask said in a low, intimate whisper. "Because I am begging." Pulling her into his arms, he said. "Pay attention because my body is begging hard for you. And you *are* in control, Felicia, because I've never felt so out of control in my life."

Trask's lips captured Felicia's at the same time his hands splayed wide across her backside, bringing the lower parts of their bodies closer. He wanted her to feel just how hard his body was begging for her. He didn't want any doubt in her mind about just how much he wanted her. A part of him wondered why on this level, this very intimate level, they were on the same accord, and they had the same wants and desires. There was no time for cross words or animosity. There was only time for satisfaction.

Trask's body throbbed in heat when he continued to kiss Felicia with a fire that blazed out of control. Suddenly, he picked her up in his arms. "This time there won't be any interruptions, sweetheart."

No sooner had the words left his mouth than his doorbell rang.

"Who is it?" Trask yelled out at the top of his voice, annoyed at the unexpected and unwanted interruption. If his visitor was Alex, he would literally kill his brother for his bad sense of timing.

"Trask, it's me, Cherie. I apologize for not calling first, but I brought you a present," a soft female voice said on the other side of the door. "If you're busy, I can come back later."

"Cherie! Who's Cherie?" Felicia hissed as she scrambled out of Trask's arms. "You had the nerve to tell me you don't like sharing, but you expect me to?" she asked, stomping to the door and snatching it open before Trask could stop her.

A surprised Cherie stood on the other side of the doorway and faced a fuming Felicia. "No, he isn't busy, Cherie. He's all yours." She then walked past the woman.

"Felicia, come back here!"

Ignoring Trask when he called out to her, Felicia kept on walking.

Chapter Eight

"**M**an, I have a serious problem."

Clayton's features did not show any surprise at Trask's statement when he looked up from the television set and met his best friend's gaze. "I figured as much when the Steelers made that third touchdown, and it didn't get any sort of reaction from you."

Familiar with Trask's sometimes closemouthed personality, Clayton leaned back in his seat and waited for him to start talking. He just hoped whatever he had to say wouldn't run past the commercial break.

"It's Felicia," Trask finally said.

Clayton frowned. "Felicia? What about her? What have the two of you gotten yourselves into now? Your decision to be Austin's holiday dad has been the talk of the family. The uncles are taking bets as to how long you'll last."

Trask shrugged. "I don't see why. Austin's a good kid."

"It's not how long you'll last with Austin that they're taking bets on. It's how long you'll last with Felicia. You two are premeditated murder just waiting to happen."

"That's not all we are just waiting to happen," Trask commented bitterly.

It suddenly occurred to Clayton, after he looked at the taut expression on Trask's face, that quite possibly he did have a serious problem. "Okay, what's going on with you and Felicia?"

"If I told you, you wouldn't believe it."

"Try me."

Trask released a deep sigh. "I have a bad case of the hots for her, man."

Clayton gave him a look that clearly said he didn't believe it. "For Felicia?"

"Yeah."

"Felicia Laverne Madaris?"

"Yeah, can you believe that?"

"No." Clayton shook his head as he tried to clear his brain. "You can't have a case of the hots for Felicia."

Trask raised a dark brow. "And why can't I?"

Clayton shrugged. "Because you just can't. You've known Felicia all your life. You more than anyone have seen her at her worst. The two of you can't be in the same room with each other for ten seconds without going at it about something." Clayton shook his head again. "Your interest in Felicia isn't normal."

"Fine. Great. Then tell that to my body," Trask muttered angrily.

A smile curved Clayton's lips. He was torn between amusement and utter disbelief. He couldn't help but remember that not too long ago he'd found himself in a similar situation of being attracted to a woman whom he didn't get along with. He had ended up falling in love and marrying her. But at least he and Syneda had gotten along most of the time. Trask and Felicia didn't get along the majority of the time. "You do have a serious problem, don't you? Just when did this problem begin?"

Trask leaned back against the sofa, feeling tired and frustrated. "I picked up on something when I flew home for Mom's wedding in April. It was a real weird feeling, man. I couldn't take my eyes off Felicia. It was like I was seeing her for the first time. I mean really seeing her, and I actually liked what I saw. I'd never had such a reaction to a woman before, and the thought that the woman was Felicia almost blew me away."

He shook his head, remembering. "That's why I decided not to pair up with her for your wedding in June. But that didn't help matters much since I couldn't take my eyes off her then either. But things really got bad at Trevor's wedding reception. She noticed me looking at her and deliberately tried making matters worse by ignoring me and then by being the flirt of the century with the other guys that were there."

Trask took a long, deep breath before continuing. "Things have really been heating up since I've moved back here."

Clayton nodded, clearly fascinated. "Is this case of the hots one-sided?"

"No."

"Then what's the problem?"

Trask wondered just how much he should tell Clayton. After all, Felicia was his cousin. But then, Clayton was also his best friend, and if he couldn't confide in his best friend, then who could he confide in.

"Felicia dropped by last night to deliver a package from your grandmother. Gramma Madaris sent me some of her bread pudding. Well, things kind of got a little hot and heavy between me and Felicia, and then I had an unexpected visitor."

"Who?"

"Some woman I met at your party name Cherie. I had taken her out a few weeks ago, and she took it upon herself to pay me a surprise visit."

"I take it Felicia didn't take too kindly to that, huh?"

"That's putting it mildly."

Clayton grinned, placed the television remote on the table and stood. "Well, I hate to tell you, man, but you do have a serious problem. After her second husband screwed around on her, Felicia is rather touchy when it comes to infidelity."

"I'm not married to her, Clayton," Trask said defensively.

"No, you're not. Nor are you engaged to her, and as far as I know, neither of you has dibs on the other. All you have is a case of the hots, which can easily be remedied."

"But I don't want *just* that."

Clayton stared long and hard at Trask. "Then what exactly is it that you do want?"

Trask looked at Clayton, startled by his question mainly because he didn't have an answer. With Felicia, for years there had always been some unexplainable, unacknowledged, and unwanted emotion tugging at him. It was those same emotions that had often made him ask her family about her whenever he didn't see her for long periods of time. And those same emotions that had always tempted him to shake some sense into her one minute and want to kiss her senseless the next.

"I honestly don't know what I want."

"Then maybe it's time for you to find out, Trask. Like I told you before, Felicia has changed."

Trask nodded. He had picked up on some noticeable changes in her since spending time with Austin. Like her ability to cook decent meals for one, and her fierce loyalty and devotion to Austin for another.

"She claims she hasn't dated in nearly six months," Trask said softly.

"She hasn't."

Trask met Clayton's gaze. "Why? What happened?" All kinds of reasons flashed through Trask's mind, and he didn't like any of them. "Did something happen to her that—"

"No, nothing like that," Clayton said quickly after reading Trask's mind. "It has to do with Austin."

"What about Austin?"

Clayton hesitated, wondering just what he should tell Trask. He wasn't even sure it was his place to tell him anything. But then, he, Felicia, and Trask had never really kept secrets from each other. That was one of the things that had made their friendship so special during their adolescent years. Felicia used to talk to him and Trask about anything and everything. They'd even known just how much she hated having cramps each month.

"Clayton, I asked what about Austin? And what does he have to do with Felicia not dating?"

Clayton sat back down. He might as well forget about them ever getting back to the game. It seemed Trask had found something he considered a whole lot more important than football. And Clayton hadn't thought he would ever live to see the day that happened.

"The incident occurred the day Syneda and I returned from our honeymoon."

Trask frowned. "What incident?"

"The day Austin almost died."

Trask got out of his car, then stood leaning casually against it as he stared at the sign outside of Felicia's shop. All this time he had assumed that she owned some sort of a dress store, but instead, Felicia's Boutique was a lingerie shop.

He folded his arms over his broad chest and crossed one booted foot over the other. If that didn't beat all. The woman was making a living selling those silky, lacy underthings that she herself despised wearing.

Trask shook his head as he thought of what Clayton had shared with him a few hours ago. After hearing it, for some reason that he still didn't understand, he had wanted to go to Felicia and see her. More than anything he wished he could have been there when it had happened to give his moral support as her family had done. Knowing how much she loved her son, he could just imagine how traumatic nearly losing Austin had been for her.

A part of him was glad that at least something good had eventually come out of it. Felicia had done a complete turnaround with her life and now it appeared that she had her priorities straight.

Another part of Trask, a very selfish part, was glad about her decision not to date anyone. The thought of her with some other man bothered him. In the past, she had chosen the men in her life in much the same way she had lived her life: fast, foolishly, and recklessly. She had targeted their financial holdings instead of their goodness and integrity as the basis for husband material. And now, because of it, her son was suffering. There was no doubt in Trask's mind that Felicia realized that now.

Trask took a deep breath. He would be leaving town first thing in the morning and would not be returning until Wednesday. After the way Felicia had left his place last night, he wanted to see her and talk to her. Deep down he wanted to do a lot more than that, but seeing her and talking to her would have to suffice for now.

A few minutes later, he walked into Felicia's shop. The place was pretty crowded with female customers. Clayton had told him that normally Felicia didn't open her shop on Sundays. However, like most merchants, she had opened at noon to take advantage of the holiday shoppers.

Trask glanced around the huge, plush room, which was filled with scantily dressed mannequins wearing all types of sexy lingerie. He suddenly felt outside of his element when he stood directly in front of a mannequin wearing a sheer nightie. He felt heat rise in his face when the first thing he noticed was that the seat of the panties was missing.

"May I help you, sir?"

Trask turned toward the feminine voice and looked into the smiling eyes of an attractive young woman who was evidently a sales clerk. He cleared his throat. "I was looking for Felicia Madaris."

The young woman, who appeared to be in her early twenties, gave him a thorough once-over before answering. "Felicia is with another customer right now," she said, smiling smoothly. "Are you sure there's nothing that I can help you with?"

Trask's brows lifted at what he immediately recognized as

a blatant come-on. He had been around long enough to know when a woman was trying to flirt with him.

His mouth spread into a thin-lipped smile. "Yes, I'm sure there's nothing you can help me with. I want Felicia. She's the only one who can help me." His smile widened. "With my purchases," he added for good measure.

The young woman nodded. "I'll let Felicia know that you're here and that you'd like her special attention."

Trask didn't have to wait long for Felicia to appear. She rounded the corner with a very irritated look on her face when she saw him. He shrugged, doubting she would go off on him in front of her customers. Today she was dressed in a very chic pants suit. He thought it was a pity since he always enjoyed looking at her legs and thighs.

"Trask? What are you doing here?" she asked in a very professional but brittle tone of voice.

A smile curved his lips. "Like everyone else, I'm Christmas shopping."

She glared at him. "Fine, I'll have one of the sales ladies help—"

"No. I want you to help me."

"I'd rather not."

"And I'd rather you do."

Felicia glanced around and noticed that she and Trask were the object of a number of her customers' attention. Trask was well known in Houston and most people considered him a celebrity. His visit to her shop had a number of people curious and no doubt word of it would spread. If a superjock like "The Max" could patronize her lingerie boutique then other men might decide that doing so wasn't a feminine thing and follow his lead.

Knowing how to take advantage of a promotional opportunity when she saw one, Felicia turned a syrupy smile on Trask and said, "Why, certainly, Mr. Maxwell. I'd be more than happy to help you with your purchases."

Trask lifted a brow at the sudden change in Felicia's attitude, and after glancing around he saw the reason for it. He hadn't been born yesterday, and he of all people knew Felicia.

"I'd really appreciate that, Ms. Madaris. I want to purchase a special gift for the woman I'm presently interested in."

"Oh, you mean that size 3OA who showed up at your place last night?" she sneered in a low voice.

Trask suppressed a laugh. If he didn't know better, he would think Felicia was jealous. "No. Cherie means nothing to me. The woman I'm interested in is probably a size 36C, but I'm not too sure since I've never seen her in a bra. I have seen her breasts though. They aren't small nor are they large. In my opinion they're just the right size. They're the kind that can easily get a man aroused. Unfortunately, I don't get the chance to see them as often as I'd like."

"What a pity."

"Yeah, tell me about it."

Felicia glared up at him. "What exactly did you have in mind for this person, Mr. Maxwell?"

"I really don't know since she claims she doesn't wear underthings." He motioned to the mannequin wearing a satiny blue bra and matching panties. "So this outfit won't do. She would find something like this too confining."

"Most types of lingerie are."

"Well, I'm hoping you can show me a few things that will help me change her mind."

Felicia frowned. "Some women's minds aren't easy to change, Mr. Maxwell."

Trask's chuckle was low and sexy. "Yes, I know, and believe me, my woman will be a hard nut to crack."

He saw the quick flash of fire in her eyes. "Your woman?"

"Yes, my woman. I decided before coming here today that I would make her my woman."

Felicia's brows lifted at that bold declaration. "Really? This is all rather interesting. What exactly was she to you before you decided to make her your woman?"

Trask looked at Felicia and gave her a full-blown smile before answering. "A pain in my rear end."

Before Felicia could come up with the blistering response Trask knew she was capable of making, he rushed on and said, "I'm ready to make a purchase now, Ms. Madaris, and we can start off with this sexy number here," he said, indicating the bra and panty set on the mannequin before them. "And by the way, this is a real nice place you have here."

"It's ten minutes before the start of the pregame show, Mr. Maxwell."

Trask nodded before pushing aside the papers on his desk. He had arrived in New York early today and had managed time to tape a few endorsements for Nike. Then he had gone Christmas shopping for his mother and brother. While in Macy's, he had visited the toy department and picked out several things for Austin as well. It had been a strange feeling selecting toys for a four-year-old, but he had enjoyed doing so. A number of the things he'd purchased for Austin were games the two of them could enjoy together.

He then turned his thoughts to Austin's mother. He hoped that yesterday he had laid to rest any thoughts she might have had that he was interested in Cherie. In fact, he had made it clear that *she* was his woman. Now whether Felicia had agreed with his assessment of their relationship was another story. In fact, he wouldn't be surprised to learn that she didn't think they had a relationship at all. Oh, there was no doubt in his mind that, when the time came for her to become his holiday lover, she would. Felicia was not one to back down on any agreement that she'd made. But that didn't mean she would have to like it. To be quite honest, he expected her to come kicking and screaming all the way to the bedroom. But he wouldn't give her that opportunity. When they did make love, he intended for her to want him as much as he wanted her. And he intended to make their union special.

Trask smiled. Maybe he was losing his mind, or maybe he'd already lost it, but the thought of an affair with Felicia wasn't such a bad idea. There was definitely some explosive chemistry between them. Just thinking about her turned him on big time.

Rising from his seat, he took a deep breath to calm his overheated body. He needed to mentally prepare himself for tonight's show. The two teams that were battling it out were archrivals, and the expected television audience was well over two million. But for once, his heart and soul weren't in it. Right now, he would rather be back in Houston spending time with Austin or making out with Austin's mother. He missed the two of them already.

Straightening his tie, Trask decided that tonight he would let them know that he was thinking of them.

"Mommy! Mommy! My daddy is on TV."

Felicia smiled at Austin's excitement before closing the magazine she'd been flipping through to give a cursory glance toward the television screen. She immediately wished she hadn't.

Trask looked good, and she wished she didn't always notice that fact. She also wished that she hadn't promised Austin that he could watch the game tonight until the end of the first quarter. Since the game had started at seven, it hadn't interfered with his bedtime. But still, she didn't like the idea of Trask invading her home on the big screen. She was still upset with his insinuation yesterday that she was his woman. Well, she had news for him. She had stopped being anyone's woman after she had divorced Charles. At least one good thing had come out of Trask's visit to her shop. Today Felicia's Boutique had been jam-packed with men doing some holiday shopping for the women in their lives.

"Mommy, Daddy is talking and I want to hear."

Felicia picked up the remote and turned the volume up a

little more. As far as she was concerned, it had been up enough, but as always Austin was ready to hang on Trask's every word.

"Before we go into a commercial break," Trask was saying, "there're two special people I want to say hello to. Hi, Austin. I miss you and I can't wait to see you on Wednesday. And, Felicia, you take care."

"Mommy, Daddy said he missed me."

"Yes, sweetheart, I heard him." A part of Felicia couldn't help but soften. When it came to Austin, Trask was doing everything humanly possible to make him feel special for the holidays. She knew that being acknowledged on television meant a lot to her son because it showed how much Trask cared.

"He said hi to you, too, Mommy, didn't he?"

Felicia smiled down at her son. "Yes, sweetheart, he did."

"My daddy's super, isn't he?"

For once Felicia had to agree. "Yes, he sure is."

Chapter Nine

If asked, Felicia would have admitted that she'd had a funny feeling all day that something bad was going to happen. She had tried dismissing the thought since it was the week of Christmas and everything had been going great so far. But she knew that the period of holiday bliss was about to come to an end when she glanced up from arranging a few sale items on display and saw Steven's father walk into her shop.

The first question that came to her mind was, what was he doing in Texas? Houston was a long way from Los Angeles. Not for one minute did she think he had finally come to visit his grandson since he had never acknowledged Austin since the boy had been born.

The one and only time the Gardners had seen Austin had been when they had paid a visit to the hospital the morning after she had delivered. Even then, they were trying to convince her to get out of their son's life.

Felicia stopped what she was doing and watched the elegantly dressed older man's approach. During the ten months that Felicia had been married to Steven, she had discovered that, more than anything, Andrew Gardner loved power. Power to make people do whatever he wanted them to. That was one of the reasons Steven had constantly defied him.

"Mr. Gardner, this is a pleasant surprise." Felicia forced the words out to the man, who was glancing around her shop. And the look of disapproval on his face was evident and it spoke volumes.

"I should have known you'd be running some type of place like this, Felicia," Andrew Gardner thundered, ignoring the fact that she had a few customers in her shop.

Knowing whatever he had to say to her was better done in private, Felicia said, "Evidently there's a reason for your visit. We can talk in my office." Without saying another word, she led the way.

No sooner had her office door closed behind them than Andrew Gardner decided to get straight to the point of his surprise visit. "I want my grandson."

Felicia shook her head, certain she had misunderstood the man's words. "You want to visit with him?"

Andrew Gardner's gaze flickered over her as if she were daft. "No, I don't want to visit him. I want custody of him. Elvia hasn't been herself since Steven's death. Having the boy around will do her some good."

Complete outrage took over Felicia's body. Did they think Austin was some kind of a toy for Elvia Gardner to play with? "How dare you come here and demand my son? Neither of you have acknowledged him since he was born. Not once have you come to visit him, nor have you done something as simple as pick up a phone to call him or write him a few lines."

She went to stand before the man. "I've sent you pictures of him every year and you've never acknowledged them. Even Steven was a poor excuse for a father since he never visited or called Austin either. And now you have the nerve to come here and insinuate you want custody."

Andrew Gardner's gaze darkened, and he straightened his body to stand erect to his full six feet five inches. It was a gesture that was made to intimidate. "I'm doing more than insinuating. I'm telling you what Elvia and I plan on doing. The reason we never acknowledged your son is because we never believed he was really Steven's although Steven claimed that he was. All the members in our family have very light complexions and your son did not favor any of us."

"That's because he favored me," Felicia stormed, pointing to the cocoa coloring of her skin. She was livid at the thought that the reason they had never accepted Austin as their grandchild was because he hadn't been born *light* enough.

"I suggest you leave now, Mr. Gardner, or I won't be responsible for my actions."

"Fine. But hear this, young lady. You are not fit to be the mother of my grandchild and this place proves it. I'm going to make sure my attorneys expose you as the unfit mother that you are. We know you only married Steven for his money and that's why I made damn sure you didn't get one penny. And I know about your second husband and that you married him for money as well. You're nothing but a gold digger. If you were any sort of a decent woman, you would be married now and providing my grandson with some sense of family stability. If you want to play hard, that's fine with us. You will definitely be hearing from our lawyers."

A speechless Felicia watched as the older man walked out of her office.

Trask knew that something was bothering Felicia when he arrived at her home to take Austin on their preplanned drive around the city to see the Christmas lights. Although she consented to go along with them for the ride, she had very little to say. That was definitely not like Felicia.

Even after they returned to her home, and she had fed them another wonderful home-cooked meal, she had been unusually quiet. It was only after Austin had been put to bed that he got the chance to question her about it.

He stood in the doorway of her kitchen, watching as she put the last of the dishes away. "Would you like to tell me what's bothering you?"

"What makes you think something is bothering me?" she snapped at him. "You think you know me so well, but you don't. You don't know anything and—"

Felicia stopped talking and covered her face with her hands, unable to deal with all she had been through that day.

Trask came farther into the room. Something swept through him when he saw her composure crumbling. He walked over to her and pulled her into his arms. "Hey, what's the matter? Talk to me, Felicia. What's bothering you? You know you can tell me anything. You always have."

Felicia was intensely aware of her small body being enveloped in Trask's larger one as he held her to comfort her, and the warmth of his hand caressing her back as he tried to console her. His strength suddenly became the fortitude she desperately needed right then. His strength became hers as she tried to deal with what she was going through.

After Mr. Gardner left her shop she had refused to give in and call her family. Over the years they had always been there for her to run to and, in some cases, hide behind. But now, she was determined that this one time she would handle things on her own. She just hadn't realized doing so would be so hard. And she hadn't counted on being this scared. The Gardners were heartless, callous people who would stop at nothing to get what they wanted. And right now, they wanted Austin. There was no way she would ever let them have her son.

"Talk to me, sweetheart."

Trask's tender request made Felicia lift her head from his chest. She raised her gaze and met his and paused, startled by something she saw in his eyes. Or was it something in her eyes that was reflecting in his? At that moment, she was too stunned at the way she suddenly felt to decipher which of the two it was. Evidently so was Trask. Instead of trying to figure anything out, they leaned into each other and did something the both of them had wanted to do again since the night she had shown up at his place.

They kissed. And they kept right on kissing.

Trask's mouth relentlessly tasted Felicia's, using his tongue to explore, enthrall, and entrance. A part of him hungered for her. It wanted her in a way he had never ever wanted another woman. And he needed her in a way that he didn't think was possible for any human to need another. But he wanted more than just a form of sexual release. He wanted to discover things with this new Felicia that went beyond the bedroom. He wanted to be a constant and permanent part of her life. And he wanted to make her son his.

Trask suddenly broke off their kiss and took in a long, deep breath when it hit him hard and heavy that he was in love with Felicia and probably had been for some time. That realization got her hauled back up against him as his mouth covered hers once again. This time, unknown to her, there was a promise in his kiss. There was a solid determination there, too. Somehow, someway, Felicia would come to love him as much as he loved her. He would make sure of it. Their years of habitual squabbling were about to end. Now what he wanted to look forward to was a lifetime of loving.

Picking her up in his arms, he walked out of her kitchen and into her living room. He sat down on the sofa with her cradled tenderly in his lap.

"Okay, tell me what's wrong, Felicia."

Felicia's face quivered as she tried not to break down again. For a short while, Trask's kisses had made her forget. "They're trying to take Austin away from me," she said softly, not meeting Trask's gaze.

Trask stared down at her, confused. He reached out and placed his finger under her chin and tipped it up so their gazes could meet. "Who's trying to take Austin away from you?"

Felicia couldn't stop the single tear that fell from her eye.

"Steven's parents. Mr. Gardner came to see me today. He said I'm unfit and that they would take me to court to get Austin." Tear glazed, pleading eyes stared at Trask. "But I won't let them have him, Trask. I won't."

Trask pulled her closer into his arms and kissed her forehead. "Of course you won't." He gently rocked her in his arms before saying, "I arrived back in town around noon today. Why didn't someone call and tell me what was going on? I saw Clayton before coming over here tonight, and he didn't mention anything about this."

Felicia released a deep sigh. "He doesn't know. No one in my family knows. You're the only one I've told."

Trask stared at her, more confused than ever. "Why? You know they'll help you if they—"

"But I can't depend on them this time. I can't let my family fight my battles forever. I will fight for my son on my own, Trask. I have to do this. Austin means everything to me and I won't let them take him away from me."

Trask couldn't help but admire the courage and determination he heard in her voice. But little did she know that she would not be fighting anything alone. He would be there with her all the way. She was his woman, the woman he loved. And Austin had become the son he had always wanted.

"Even if you don't want your family's help, you should have consulted Clayton and Syneda for legal advice. I understand that Syneda is one of the best family attorneys in the business, and that her specialty is custody and domestic relations. I'm sure she'll know exactly how you should proceed with this."

Felicia shook her head. "I really didn't think about that. The only thing I could think about was that I didn't want my family to come running to my rescue."

"But they love you, Felicia, and that's what being part of a big family is all about: knowing someone will be there when you need them. And that's what love is all about, too: being there for the person you care a lot about. Remember that."

He leaned down and kissed her lips before placing her out of his lap and next to him on the sofa. "I'm going to give Clayton and Syneda a call and ask them to come over."

He reached out to pick up the phone. Before dialing he turned to Felicia. "Don't worry, sweetheart. No one is going to take Austin away from you. Trust me."

Syneda Madaris was one sharp attorney, Trask thought as he watched her in action. She knew all the questions to ask, every bit of information to probe and each hypothetical situation to consider.

And then there was Clayton, who was a prosecutor's nightmare. He was there to remind Syneda of moot points, irrelevant information, and possible objections. Together they made one dynamic team of lawyers. But what Trask really appreciated was the fact that they were straightforward and honest in letting Felicia know what she would be up against.

"I wish I could tell you the Gardners' claim is frivolous and not to worry about it, but I won't," Syneda said sadly, but truthfully. "Custody battles aren't cut and dry like they used to be. The mother doesn't always win anymore."

"But I love Austin and I'm a good mother. I've always put him first," Felicia said in a small, quiet voice.

Syneda nodded, knowing firsthand that was true. Even when Felicia had lived a self-indulgent lifestyle, she had always put her son first. "That may be the case, but there are some who won't see it that way," Syneda responded honestly. "It really will depend on where the petition is filed. California is more liberal than most states, and your past lifestyle won't be such a factor there. The main focus will be the present. But if it's filed here in Texas, that's another story. Most Texans are found to be conservative and moralistic. Your past history will matter, so you may as well prepare yourself for that."

"So what are our options?" Trask asked when the room became despondently quiet. Just by looking at Felicia he knew she was clinging harder than heck to her self-control. He could tell that hearing what Syneda was saying was taking a toll on her.

"Well, if it came to that, we could pull in a bunch of character witnesses who can attest that Felicia is a good mother, but then . . ."

Trask noted Syneda's hesitation. "But then what?"

Syneda released a deep, heavy sigh. "But then, that's hoping the opposing side doesn't find out about Austin's near drowning incident. Although it was by no means Felicia's fault, I can see them using it as the sole basis for their complaint."

Trask turned and watched Felicia's reaction to Syneda's statement. Tears suddenly appeared in her eyes. "It wasn't your fault, Felicia, and you can't continue to blame yourself for it," he said to her.

"But I should have been with him. I should never have gone out on a date that night and left him with a sitter."

"Parents leave kids with baby-sitters all the time, Felicia," Clayton added. "No court will fault you for that. All Syneda is saying is that evidently the Gardners are people who are used to others being intimidated by their wealth and power. They will try to use anything and everything against you. They won't play fair, and you just need to be prepared for it. I know this may sound archaic, but it would probably help your case tremendously if you were married now. It would show a sense of commitment and an embracing of family values on your part."

Felicia didn't say anything for the longest time. Her eyes were downcast and her hands were tightly clasped in her lap. When she did lift her gaze to them and began speaking, her voice was filled with all the dismay that shone in her face. "I'm frightened. Austin is all that I have. I can't lose him. I can't."

Trask stood and walked over to her and knelt before her. He took her hands in his. "And you won't. If it takes every penny I have, I'm going to help you fight this thing. You won't be alone in this, sweetheart.''

He pulled her down to him, and when her body sagged defeatedly against his, he held her tight to calm her trembling. Pulling her closer, he kissed her hair. "You are a good mother to *my* son. Don't ever think otherwise. We'll do whatever we have to do. Even if it means getting married immediately. And considering the circumstances, that may not be such a bad idea.''

Felicia pulled back out of Trask's arms to look at him, stunned by the words he'd spoken and the offer he had made. Surely he wasn't serious. But one look in his eyes told her that he was. In the three weeks that he had spent with Austin, he had come to care deeply for him. Just as Austin considered Trask his daddy, Trask had begun thinking of Austin as his son. That was something neither Steven nor Charles had ever really done. And at that moment, she knew he was right. She would not be alone in her fight against the Gardners. Trask would be there with her because he felt he had a personal stake in the outcome as well. He would do anything, even alter his lifestyle for her child. He had already done that by volunteering to be Austin's holiday dad.

Tears glistened in Felicia's eyes as she continued to look at Trask—really look at him. And what she saw went deeper than his handsome outside features. She saw a man who genuinely cared. She couldn't think of the words to say to tell him just how much claiming Austin as his had meant, or how touched she was at his offer of marriage to help win her case. Cupping his face in her hands, she leaned down and kissed him.

Across the room Clayton and Syneda watched the tender scene unfolding before them, doubting very seriously that Trask and Felicia remembered their presence. Clayton held open his arms to his wife and she walked into them.

"I think it's time we left. We've done all that we can for tonight,'' Syneda whispered to her husband.

"Yeah," Clayton said, shaking his head at the couple, who were still kissing. When it didn't appear they were going to come up for air anytime soon, he decided to clear his throat to get their attention. Both pairs of eyes swung to him and Syneda when the couple remembered they were not alone. But neither Trask nor Felicia had the decency to look embarrassed, just annoyed at the interruption.

A slow smile curved Clayton's lips. "Seems like you've been playing in Houston's dirt, Trask."

At the bemused looks on Felicia's and Syneda's faces, Clayton's smile widened as he explained, "It's a private joke."

Trask let himself into his condo feeling tired and strained. He had left Felicia's house not long after Clayton and Syneda. Although he had read the invitation to stay longer in her eyes, he had placed her needs before his. It was apparent that she needed to rest. Today had definitely been a bear for her. Here it was two days before Christmas and she had to deal with the possibility of losing her son.

He had kissed her thoroughly before leaving. The flavor of her mouth, the distinctive fragrance of her perfume, and the way her body had fit close to his rammed his memory, making him take a slow, deep breath. Walking away and leaving her tonight had been the hardest thing he'd ever had to do.

Trask checked his watch before picking up the telephone to make a call. He then dialed the number.

"Yeah?"

"Alex, it's Trask. I need your expertise."

"For what?"

"I want you to do a little investigative work into the background of a man from California by the name of Andrew Gardner."

He could hear his brother's sleepy yawn before he asked, "What exactly are you looking for, Trask?"

Trask thought about Alex's question. It was time to show

Andrew Gardner that he wasn't the only one who could make power plays. He smiled as a word Clayton had used tonight suddenly came to his mind. "Dirt. I want dirt and plenty of it."

Chapter Ten

Felicia woke up bright and early Christmas morning, thinking that this would be a day Austin remembered for a long time. Although he had a number of presents under the tree, she knew he considered his best gift of all to be the one he had received early: a daddy for the holidays.

She released a long, deep sigh as she got out of bed. She had made a decision to push Andrew Gardner's visit to the back of her mind and not let the man ruin her holidays. She simply refused to let him take away her joy for the season. Worrying about his threat would be a waste of energy, and she needed all of her energy for a little boy who would wake up in an hour or so, excited and happy.

As Felicia went into the bathroom she thought about Trask—a man whom she had always considered nothing more than a thorn in her side . . . until recently. In the last two days, he had become her mountain of strength, someone she could lean on.

A warm, contented feeling swelled inside her when she thought about the tall, broad-shouldered, powerfully built man who had shown nothing but gentle kindness to her son. A man who two nights ago had offered himself to her in a way no other man had ever done—honorably and unselfishly—when he'd suggested they marry. She considered it amazing how their relationship had changed. Even her uncles had noticed the harmony between them at Austin's play the other night.

All of them had watched her and Trask with curious and cautious eyes, as if they were seeing it, but not believing it. Everyone was so used to them constantly sniping at each other. Her uncle Lee had informed her that everyone was assuming she and Trask had called a truce for the holidays because of Austin. They just hoped and prayed that none of them were around when the truce ended and things with her and Trask got back to what they considered normal.

Liquid heat gathered low in Felicia's abdomen when she thought of the kisses they'd been sharing recently. In her opinion, the kisses were no longer enough. It seemed that each and every time they kissed things got hotter and heavier, and their passions flared fast and furious.

Like last night.

After he had put the last training wheel on Austin's bicycle, he had placed his tools aside, stood, and turned to her. She had been standing against the doorframe of the living room, watching him and, all the while, appreciating the look of his big, muscular body.

"Come here."

Without any regard for the slight command in his voice, she had walked into his arms for the kiss she knew awaited her there. His taste had been dark. It had been alluring. It had been seductive. No man had ever made her feel the way Trask made her feel, both physically and mentally.

Realization suddenly gripped Felicia, almost staggered her when it dawned on her just why she felt that way. She had fallen in love with Trask. She struggled to catch her breath and knew it would be useless to go into cardiac arrest about it. She should have been smart enough to read the handwriting on the wall weeks ago when he had become a nightly invader of her dreams.

And if she were real smart, she would admit she had probably loved him for quite some time. What other reason could there be for sniping at him all those years unless it had been to hide her true feelings. She had been the one to start a scrapbook on him when he'd first begun getting media recognition in high school, and she had kept it updated since. She had been the one who had cried a river of tears on Trask's mother's shoulder the night he had gotten injured in that game against the Broncos. And she had been the one to bully and harass him into enduring the many months of physical therapy that had followed.

All because deep down she had loved him.

She leaned against the bathroom sink as she tried to get her bearings. Now that she knew she loved Trask, what was she going to do about it?

Felicia took a deep breath when she heard the soft knock at the door. Trask had said he would be coming over early. He wanted to be there when Austin got out of bed.

When she opened the door, he smiled at her and her heart became filled with an indescribable feeling of love. "Good morning, Felicia. Merry Christmas."

Her eyes locked with his for five long seconds and she wondered how on earth she could have wasted her years fighting with him when she could have been loving him. She returned his smile. "Good morning, Trask. Merry Christmas to you, too."

He stepped inside her house, closed the door behind him, and placed a huge shopping bag filled with gifts on the floor. She saw him glance around to make sure Austin hadn't gotten up yet before reaching out and pulling her into his arms to kiss her. She could feel the heat of him through the pair of jeans and pullover sweater she had put on.

A minute or two later, he pulled back slightly. "Kissing you isn't enough anymore, sweetheart," he whispered.

Felicia smiled up at him. She had thought the same thing

earlier. "I've been wondering when you were going to figure that out."

Trask shook his head, chuckling. "Are you trying to be a temptress?"

Her smile widened. "Would I ever?" she asked softly, cuddling closer to his body.

He immediately thought of the night she had unexpectedly shown up at his place, showing quite a bit of legs and thighs. "Yes, you would."

She moved her body seductively and suggestively against his. "Then I guess I am."

The movement made Trask groan deep in his throat. "You're something else—you know that?"

Just for good measure she rubbed her body against his again. "Yeah, I got it from a very reliable source that I'm a pain in your rear end."

Trask leaned down and lightly brushed her lips with his. "Yes, you used to be. Now you're a pain in my front end. I ache for you all the time, baby. Feel?"

Felicia felt his hardness pressed against her. The feel of him would have weakened her defenses if she'd had any. "Yes, I feel it." She then looked at him. She wanted to see his facial reaction with her next words. "And I want it."

Trask's eyes darkened with heat. His expression became taut with the desire. He leaned forward as his hand cupped the back of her neck to bring her mouth to meet his when the pitter-pat of little feet sounded on the hardwood floors. They stepped apart mere seconds before Austin raced into the room.

"Mommy! Daddy! Has Santa come yet?"

Trask, Felicia, and Austin spent Christmas Day together. After opening all the presents under the tree and then exchanging some others, they enjoyed a delicious Christmas breakfast. Then the visitors started arriving.

First Felicia's mother came by bearing gifts. And before

noon, all of her uncles had dropped by, except for her Uncle Jonathan, who was Clayton's father. Since she would be joining her Uncle Jonathan and his family for Christmas dinner, she had not expected a visit from him. And as was tradition, Austin would be spending the night with Uncle Jonathan and Aunt Marilyn. All of their grandkids would be spending Christmas night under their roof, and Austin had always been included in that number. It gave all the younger cousins a chance to spend some time together. Felicia wondered how Uncle Jonathan and Aunt Marilyn handled all of them. Justin, their oldest son, had three kids; their second son, Dex, had two; and their daughters Traci and Kattie had one each. Adding Austin to the mix meant a total of eight kids.

Putting the last of the wrapping paper that had gotten thrown over the floor in the trash, Felicia walked out of her living room and headed for Austin's bedroom. He and Trask had been in there for an hour or so building something with the Lego blocks that Trask had given him for Christmas.

She slowed her steps when she reached Austin's bedroom door. She was about to open it when she heard her son's question.

"Daddy, you'll stay until New Year's, won't you? You won't be leaving me before then, will you?"

Felicia heard the worried tone in her son's voice. Cocking her head, she listened for Trask's response. "No, I won't be leaving before then."

"I wished you were a forever daddy; then you wouldn't have to go. I love you."

She could hear the tightness in Trask's throat when he replied, "And I love you, too, Austin."

Backing up, Felicia returned to the living room. She'd almost forgotten that Trask was only supposed to be a part of their lives until New Year's Day. And that was only a week away. She wondered how her son would handle it when his holiday fantasy ended. She wondered how she would.

Her son wanted a forever daddy, and now she found herself wanting a forever lover.

It was almost ten o'clock that night when they returned to Felicia's home from having dinner with her uncle and aunt. More nervous than she could ever remember being around Trask, Felicia opened the door and let them inside her house. She had left all the lights off except for the one in the kitchen.

"I'll get the lights," she said, moving toward the table lamp not far from the door.

After the room was bathed in brightness, Trask's footsteps echoed softly on the hardwood floor when he came up behind her. "And I'll get this," he said, turning her into his arms.

Felicia knew she was lost the moment their lips touched. She also knew that a few steaming-hot kisses would not satisfy either of their hungers tonight. And from the way he was kissing her, she could tell he knew that as well. She also knew he intended on doing something about it.

And she thought it was about time.

She returned his kiss with as much passion as he was putting into it. It was a kiss that sent the pit of her stomach into a wild swirl and demanded a response from her.

So she gave him one. Then several.

The feel of Trask's muscular arms around her, holding her firm against him, sent a burning desire and an aching need throughout every part of her body. She instinctively moved against him, eliciting a moan from deep within his throat. He pulled back and looked down at her.

"Felicia."

The breathlessness in his voice stimulated the full length of her spine. The look on his face sent her pulse racing. There was a raw, sensual look of need in the dark depths of his eyes. She lifted her arms to circle his neck and brought his mouth back down to hers to feed more greedily off the hot, sensuous taste of him. She had never been more aware of the full height of her desires until now.

"I want to get inside you," he growled raspily as he placed a series of slow, shivery kisses along the side of her neck.

A delicious shudder tore through Felicia's body. He kissed her again, and the wanting displayed in the kiss she returned was just as hungry, urgent, and desperate. The low, primal moan from deep within her throat pushed him over the edge.

He wanted her. He wanted to get wrapped up in those legs and thighs she often used to tempt him with.

Trask tugged at Felicia's sweater, pulling it over her head, then tossing it aside. Exposing her breasts to his view made him hotter, hungrier. The need to taste them became elemental. So he did just that.

The feel of Trask's mouth on her sent heat flowing straight to the very core of Felicia. His teeth nipped, scraped, and branded her. She surrendered, gasping for air when a multitude of sensations raced through her body. She was vaguely aware of him pulling her down on the huge Oriental rug on the floor.

His hand then moved lower to the top of her jeans. He slid the zipper down as far as he could, then inserted his fingers inside the opening, determined to discover what she did or did not wear under her clothes. He released a deep, tormented groan when he touched her intimately; and at the same time a flood of heat slashed through Felicia's entire body with his touch.

Felicia saw the hot tide of desire rise in Trask's features. His breathing quickened when he withdrew his hand and quickly began removing her shoes and socks. He then tugged impatiently at her jeans as if it were of grave importance to take them off her.

She felt his urgency, and she shared his white-hot greed. Easing up, she let him pull her jeans down, then off her. Then he peeled off the very skimpy, very sexy, and very provocative pair of silk g-string panties.

Almost frantic with a need that matched Trask's, Felicia got on her knees and reached up to remove his shirt, nearly tearing it off him. Then she began placing hot, torrid kisses all over his chest while her impatient fingers frantically worked at his belt buckle. Easing his zipper down, she eased her hand inside his jeans, as he'd done with her earlier, and felt the hardness of him. She desperately needed to feel that part of him inside of her.

Felicia's touched electrified every nerve in Trask's body. Never had he been so totally consumed by uncontrolled passion. When she freed that part of him from the confines of his jeans, he barely restrained himself before pushing her back, straddling her, cupping her hips in his hands, and thrusting inside her. Settling hard and deep in the very core of her, his mouth absorbed her moan, as well as his own.

With an urgency that had blood pounding in his head, sweat popping off his brow and breath ripping from his lungs, he moved inside of her. Her hips shot upward to cradle him when the tempo of his strokes increased. And when she locked her legs around him, to hold him tight, he groaned out his release at the same time that he heard her groan out hers. Their sounds echoed in the room as they were thrown into a wave of turbulent completeness.

Even after that shattering release, Trask couldn't stop his strokes from coming fast and furious at an increased pace. He threw his head back and held her hips in place with his big hands as he continued to thrust deeper and deeper. Being inside her was making him crazed. It was as if his body couldn't get enough of her hot, feminine flesh. He continued to thrust into her, stronger and harder. And when he felt her convulse beneath him as pleasure once again rammed into her body, he screamed out her name when a second climax overtook them. He pressed himself deeper inside of her when they were both rocked hard into oblivion.

Trask mumbled something she couldn't hear. And for a while Felicia was too drained to ask him to repeat himself. In fact, she didn't think she could move and was just beginning to breathe again.

She felt Trask lift himself off her. Then he slid free of her. "Let's go to bed," he suggested. His voice was a guttural whisper as he picked her up into his strong arms and carried her to the bedroom. He kissed her before putting her on the bed and then began removing the rest of his clothes.

"That was the first time that I've ever made love to a woman and not given any thought to using these," Trask said, getting the foil packet out of his wallet.

"That's okay. I'm on the pill, remember?" Felicia said.

Trask nodded, placing the condoms aside. He did remember. During their senior year in high school, a doctor had placed Felicia on the pill to help alleviate her bout with painful cramps each month. He shook his head, thinking just how much personal information they had shared with each other during that time.

Coming back to the bed he joined her there, gathering her into his arms. His hands began touching her again, everywhere, and she felt the heat in her flare up once more.

"Now we'll take it slow and easy," he whispered huskily, before devouring her mouth. And once again the two of them gave in to their desires.

The only sounds in the room were Trask and Felicia's attempts to breathe normally again. He lay on top of her. Her arms were wrapped tightly around his neck, and her temptingly delicious legs and thighs were tangled with his. Their bodies were still joined and neither of them was ready to break the intimate connection.

Trask raised his head and looked down at Felicia before placing a gentle kiss on her lips. "Marry me."

She traced her finger along his smooth jaw and cheek. "Because of Andrew Gardner's threat?"

His large hand covered her fingers and held them in place

on his face. "No. Because I love you, and I want to be with you always. I want to spend the rest of my life loving you, making up for all the time we've lost when we were constantly fussing and fighting with each other."

Tears shimmered in Felicia's eyes. "Oh, Trask. I love you, too. I think I always have. That's probably why I harassed you all these years: to get noticed."

He leaned down and placed another kiss on her lips, finding joy in the fact that she loved him, too. "Trust me. You were noticed. I've been fighting my own attraction to you for some time. That's the reason I asked Syneda to swap you as my partner at the wedding. Being around you would have driven me insane. I was trying hard to fight my feelings for you and my attraction to you."

He tucked a loose tendril of hair behind her ear. "I also want to marry you because I love your son, and I want to make him mine. He already has my heart, and I want to give him my name. I want to be more than a holiday dad to Austin. I want to be that forever daddy—the one who'll be there for him when the going gets rough as well as during the smooth times. I want to be the father to him that I never had."

He looked deep into her eyes. "No matter what happens with the Gardners, I won't be marrying you because of that. I want to marry you because you've always been a part of my life, and I've discovered recently just how much I like having you there. I want to start this New Year off right with you, Austin, and me as a family. Let's get married on New Year's Day."

New Year's Day? That's only a week away, Felicia thought. "Are you absolutely sure?"

"Yes. I've never been surer of anything in my life."

Felicia grinned. "The family won't believe it. They'll all go bonkers."

Trask chuckled. "Yeah, I know, but it won't be anything

new. The two of us have always managed to stir up anxiety in our families anyway. So what about it? Will you marry me on New Year's Day?''

With love and joy shining in her eyes, Felicia smiled up at him. "Yes."

Chapter Eleven

Felicia scowled furiously at the document she had just received. More than anything she wanted to crush the petition of custody in her hand and destroy it, but she knew what her next step had to be. Picking up the phone she dialed Syneda's number. She forced herself to remain calm. No matter what, there was no way the Gardners would get their hands on Austin.

She pressed her lips together in frustration as she waited for Syneda to answer the phone. It was two days after Christmas and most businesses had reopened. However, Clayton and Syneda had decided to keep their law office closed until after New Year's.

"Hello."

The breathless sound of Syneda's voice made Felicia wonder if she had interrupted something.

"Syneda, did I catch you at a bad time?"

There was a pause, then another breathless response. "No, of course not, Felicia. You didn't catch me at a bad time."

"Yes, you did!" Felicia could hear Clayton hollering out those words in the background, close to the phone.

"I'm sorry," Felicia said. "I shouldn't have called. You two were—"

"Not doing anything we can't continue later," Syneda cut in after hearing the shaky sound of Felicia's voice. "Don't mind Clayton. Is something wrong?"

Felicia closed her eyes. Everything was wrong and Trask was in Miami to host one of the playoff games tonight. "Yes. I got the petition of custody from the Gardners' attorney today and I—"

"Hold everything. I'm coming right over. Are you at home or at the shop?"

"The shop. It was delivered soon after I arrived."

"Have you called Trask?"

"No."

"Why not?"

"He's in Miami and won't be back until Wednesday. I can't expect him to drop everything and rush home."

"But he told you to—"

"I know what he told me, but I can't do that. I have to try to take care of this myself."

Felicia began chewing at her bottom lip. Before Trask had left, he had made her promise that she would call him if anything came up while he was away. They had announced to her family yesterday, after the church service, that they would be getting married New Year's Day. Her mother and her uncles were still in shock. And after they'd placed a long-distance call to Trask's mother in Waco, she, too, had found their news hard to believe. The only person who had not been surprised by the news had been her grandmother. She claimed she had known all along that they were meant for each other and that it was about time they stopped acting foolish and figured it out before someone got hurt. Felicia and Trask had decided to keep the news from Austin to surprise him.

"Look. I have an idea that I want to run by you," Felicia said to Syneda. "How soon can you get here?"

"I'm on my way."

*   *   *

Syneda frowned. "Are you sure you want to do that?"

Felicia sighed miserably before answering, "I have to try to appeal to Mrs. Gardner's decent side."

"Are you sure she has one? I doubt it. From everything you've told me about her, appealing to her decent side would be a waste of time."

In the space of a few torturing seconds, crippling fear raced through Felicia's mind and made her think that going to California and talking to Elvia Gardner would be a waste of time, but she had to try.

She looked at Syneda. The two of them sat opposite each other at a table by the window in Felicia's office. "I'm willing to try anything at this point, even believe Elvia Gardner has a heart."

Syneda regarded her steadily. "As your attorney, I probably should advise you against it. I think we have a pretty strong case, especially since you and Trask are getting married. The petition was filed here in Texas and your marriage will help things a lot. And having it filed here may be another plus for us. Your Uncle Jake Madaris's name carries a lot of weight in this state, something the Gardners evidently don't know."

Felicia stood and looked at Syneda. Her expression was as uncertain as her mind was determined. What Syneda had said about her Uncle Jake was true. He was her father's youngest brother and he was only nine years older than she. Jake Madaris was well known and well thought of in Texas. But still . . .

"I have to do anything and everything to avoid a nasty court battle with them, for Austin's sake," she finally said to Syneda. "They are his grandparents."

"Yeah, right. They are grandparents who didn't want him because his color wasn't light enough. I have a big problem with that," Syneda said rather sharply. "Any grandparents who can turn their back on their grandchild for any reason, especially because of race, creed, or color aren't fit to be grandparents."

Felicia nodded as she suddenly realized just how close to home Austin's situation was for Syneda. Her grandfather had turned his back on her and not accepted her either as a child. He had also kept her existence a secret from his son, who had been Syneda's biological father.

Felicia clasped her hands behind her back and took a long deep breath. "I agree but I want to do the right thing, even if they didn't."

"And what if your little chat with Mrs. Gardner doesn't work?"

Felicia didn't want to think of that possibility. She was hoping that things would work. "Then I'll come back here and get prepared for the fight of my life."

"Hi, gorgeous. Where's that husband of yours?"

"Trask! What are you doing here? You weren't expected back until late tomorrow." Syneda nervously stepped aside to let him enter the house.

Trask lifted a brow slightly when Syneda finished her sentence. If he didn't know better he would think she wasn't glad to see him for some reason. "I finished up early."

"Felicia wasn't expecting you back."

Trask looked at Syneda curiously. "No, she wasn't. I talked to her last night. I thought I'd surprise her today."

You're definitely going to surprise her, all right, Syneda thought as she lifted a hand to her forehead, feeling a headache coming on. She had tried to convince Felicia to let Trask know what she was doing and where she was going, but she had refused. "Clayton's out back. I'll let him know that you're—"

"Syneda?"

"What?"

He came to stand in front of her. "Would you like to tell me what's going on?"

Syneda stared up at Trask. He was looking at her in the

exact same way that Clayton looked at her when he knew she was up to something. "Nothing is going on. You're imagining things. It's just that you weren't due back until late tomorrow."

Trask heard the chagrin that lurked behind Syneda's words. "We've already established that fact." He crossed his arms over his chest. "Was there anyone hoping that I wouldn't come back early?"

Too quickly Syneda said, "Of course not."

Trask stared at Syneda for a minute. She was definitely nervous about something. He decided to play a hunch. "May I use your phone? I want to call Felicia's shop to let her know that I'm back. Maybe the two of us can do lunch."

"She's not at the shop," Syneda blurted out unintentionally. Her palm immediately flew to her mouth.

Trask looked thoughtful as he pulled her hand back down. "Oh. Then I'll try calling her at home."

Syneda sighed deeply before saying, "She's not at home either."

He frowned. "Where exactly is she?"

Syneda hesitated for a few moments before answering, "She left for California this morning."

Trask's frown deepened. "California? There had better be a good reason why Felicia went to California without telling me about it."

Syneda shrugged and smiled sheepishly. "I can give you her reason. It's up to you to decide if it's a good one."

Felicia stood in the entry hall and waited for the maid to announce her. When she thought she had been forgotten, she heard the footsteps of the older woman returning.

"Mrs. Gardner will see you now."

Felicia followed the older woman into a large living room. As she looked around at the expensively decorated room, she couldn't help but remember the first time Steven had brought her here, nearly five years ago. She thought the same thing now as she had thought then. This was a house and not a home. There was no love flowing through these walls, only greed. Felicia shook her head. How could she have ever thought that wealth was more important than love?

"Mrs. Gardner will be down in a minute."

When the woman left her alone, Felicia crossed the room to study a number of paintings on the wall. Originals, all of them.

"Felicia? What are you doing here?"

Felicia turned. Elvia Gardner stood in the doorway between the living room and dining room. Nothing about her had changed. Although she was a beautiful, older woman, the expression she wore was just as hard as the diamonds around her neck.

"Felicia, I asked what you're doing here. If you've come to see Andrew, he's—"

"No, I didn't come to see Mr. Gardner. I came to see you."

Elvia Gardner paused a moment before saying, "If you're here about the custody suit, then you shouldn't be talking to me, but with my attorney."

"I'm hoping the two of us can settle this out of court."

"Are you willing to give me full custody of my grandson?"

Felicia shook her head. "No."

"Then we have nothing to say. I'll have Mariah show you out."

Felicia took a deep breath to break the anger that had begun settling in her chest. "Why do you want, Austin? You've never cared for him one way or the other before. He's your grandson and you've never been to see him, and now you want custody of him. That doesn't make sense."

An amused grin tugged at Elvia Gardner's lips. "It would make sense if you knew all the facts. It seems, my dear, that my grandson is now a very wealthy little boy. We recently found out that Andrew's father had left Steven a hefty amount of shares of stock in a very productive diamond mine in South Africa. With Steven's death, those shares passed on to his son, the Gardner heir. Although Andrew and I still aren't absolutely convinced your little boy is truly Steven's son, the fact remains that Steven believed he was and claimed him as such. And in this case, that's all that matters.''

Felicia's eyes widened in shock—not at the news that Austin had shares of stock in some diamond mine, but at the realization that wealth and power were the reasons the Gardners wanted to take Austin away from her.

Anger suddenly replaced the shock in Felicia's eyes. She placed her hands on her hips. ''I can't believe this. You'll try to take my son away from me to gain more wealth?''

''Humph,'' Elvia Gardner snorted. ''We're doing more than try. Our attorney feels confident we'll succeed. Now if you don't mind, I'm on my way out. Next time, I'd prefer you not come here. If you have some sort of grievance, contact my attorney. Otherwise, I'll see you in court.''

Felicia stared at the woman for a moment. She had come all this way to make peace for Austin's sake. But Syneda had been right. Mrs. Gardner didn't have a decent side. ''No, I don't think so.''

The woman cocked her head and looked at her quizzically. ''You don't think so what?''

Felicia pulled her composure together and met Mrs. Gardner's cool gaze. ''I don't think you want to see me in court.''

''And why wouldn't I?''

Felicia glanced down at the floor to control her anger, then regained eye contact with the older woman. ''Because if we go to court, I'm going to make sure Mr. Gardner knows the truth. Although Austin is Steven's son, he is not a Gardner heir.''

She saw the look of unease in Mrs. Gardner's eyes. ''I have no idea what you're talking about.''

''Then by all means, let me spell it out to you. If you dare take me to court for my son, then I'm going to make sure Mr. Gardner knows that Steven was not his son. I'm sure you breathed a sigh of relief when he was born light enough to pass off as Mr. Gardner's so he wouldn't be suspicious of anything."

Mrs. Gardner nervously shifted her weight from one foot to the other. "Where on earth did you get something so ridiculous?"

"From Steven. He found out the truth while we were married. He had proof, and if I have to, I'll prove it as well."

"You won't and can't do anything. Steven's dead." There was a sharp edge in Elvia Gardner's voice. There was a tinge of uncertainty and wariness there, too.

"Yes, but I doubt his blood type matched your husband's. Modern technology can prove or disprove anything. I'll do just about anything to keep my son away from you. I'll never let him live here and be raised in this type of environment where money is everything and integrity means nothing."

Felicia took a step closer to the older woman, who had suddenly gone speechless. "If I have to, I'll expose information about your short but productive affair with one of Mr. Gardner's business associates some years ago. How Steven got hold of the information or how he intended to use it one day is no concern of mine. All I know is that I won't hesitate to use it."

Felicia tightened her purse straps on her shoulder. "If you try to take my son away, I'll make sure everyone knows that Austin is truly not a Gardner heir. If I were you, I'd think of some way to halt this custody suit. Think about it."

Without having anything else to say, Felicia walked past the woman and out the door.

Felicia's plane arrived back in Houston close to nine o'clock that night. She had had every intention of returning before dark, but due to bad weather conditions in Los Angeles, her plane had been delayed. She had called her mother before leaving California and asked if Austin could spend the night since she would be arriving back in town after his bedtime.

Felicia turned into her driveway and came to an abrupt halt.

Trask's Lexus was parked there, and the lights were on inside her house. Since she had never given him a key to her home, she could only assume he had gotten the spare one from her mother.

Felicia hesitated a moment before opening the door. She was not sure exactly what she would say to Trask. She had not called him when she had received the petition of custody as she had promised him she would. Taking in a deep breath, she closed the door behind her.

"I was wondering when you'd be getting home."

The deep tone of Trask's voice made Felicia jump. She glanced across the room and saw him leaning against the doorway that separated the living room from the foyer. Their gazes locked for a long moment before she answered, "Have you been waiting long?"

"Long enough."

Anxiety jittered through Felicia's stomach. She had argued with Trask countless times. Why did the thought of doing so again bother her so much? Her next question was tentative. It was meant to sound casual, but somehow it didn't come out that way. "My mother gave you the key?"

"Yes. I guess she trusts me."

A stab of guilt caught Felicia up short when she saw the look of something in his eyes. "I trust you, too, Trask. Going to California had nothing to do with me trusting you. It had everything to do with me standing up for myself."

A part of Trask understood where she was coming from. Syneda had made darn sure of that when she had explained things to him earlier that day. Felicia had been spoiled and pampered so much by the men in the Madaris family that now she needed to believe she could fight this one all by herself. He had wanted to do what her uncles had done for her over the years: protect her by fighting her battles for her.

He straightened up and walked slowly over to her. When he stood before her, he reached out and ran his fingertips across her cheek and looked deep into the depths of her dark eyes. "And did you?"

For a moment, Felicia was so captivated by the look he was giving her, as well as by the feel of his hand on her skin, that she completely forgot what their earlier conversation had been about. She took a deep breath and held it for a moment, then slowly expelled it before asking, "Did I what?"

"Stand up for yourself."

Felicia noted the caring, the tenderness, and the concern in his voice. She also saw the love he had for her shining deep within his gaze. "Yes."

A bit of a smile touched Trask's lips. "Good." He reached out for her hand and brought it to his mouth and let his lips brush lightly across her skin. "And now where does that leave me?"

Felicia frowned at first, not understanding Trask's question. His touch was preventing her from thinking clearly. But a part of her felt his need to know his place in her life. He wanted reassurance. She reached up and slipped her arms around his neck.

"It leaves you just where you've always been, Trask: a very intricate part of my life and of me. To be more specific, it leaves you right dab in the middle of my heart. I love you."

She felt the tremor ripple through his body with her words. She then brought his mouth down to hers to kiss away any more doubts he might have. The kiss was everything Felicia meant it to be. She kissed him with all the love she felt within her.

She pulled back and her hands rested against his tautly muscled chest. "Make love to me, Trask." Her voice quavered with her request and with her plea. "I need you to love me."

"And I will, forever," he said, sweeping her into his arms and carrying her into the bedroom. Placing her on the bed, he slowly began removing all of her clothes. He wanted to make love to her all night. He didn't want to hear the details of her visit to California just yet. They would discuss that later. All he wanted was to make love to her, to get deep inside her and be as one with her, mind, body, and soul.

When his naked body joined her in bed, he pulled her into his arms. Her skin felt soft and her scent was arousing. "I want to try things a little different tonight," Trask suggested in a deep, husky voice before capturing her mouth with an intensity that left nothing to one's imagination.

He wanted to try things a little different tonight? Felicia didn't think either her mind or her body could handle the idea of that happening. She thought of all the things he had done to her on Christmas night and all the ways she had responded to those things. They had made love all through the night. She hadn't thought her body could handle that much lovemaking. Just when she thought that she couldn't possibly take any more of him, and that he had satisfied her to the limit, he would touch her again, letting his hands and his mouth do their magic. The mere brush of his fingers and lips on her skin would have her wanting him again.

And now, from the feel of his hand moving down her back, his fingers caressing the sensitive skin of her arms, and his mouth locked tight with hers, tasting her with his tongue, she had a feeling they were about to pull another all-nighter.

And she was looking forward to every delicious minute of it.

Trask broke off the kiss. He'd never before in his life wanted a woman the way he wanted Felicia. And as he looked down at her naked limbs entwined with his, he thought the picture was perfect, erotic, and seductive. His gaze traveled from her breasts to her stomach, then down to a very enticing part of her anatomy. It lingered there for a moment before finally moving lower to her thighs and legs. He wanted her. All of her. Every delectable inch of her.

"Felicia," he murmured, reaching down and lifting her into his arms. Shifting his body, he stretched her out atop him. Firmly holding her hips in place, he smoothly joined their bodies to a perfect fit. "Tonight, you ride," he whispered huskily.

When she felt the heat of him hard and deep inside her, she released a deep groan, marveling at the way Trask could make her feel. "Tonight, I ride," she repeated before closing her mouth over his.

And just as if she knew what he wanted, she rode him hard.

The sound of Trask's heavy sighs and quickened breathing echoed in the room. The feel of his hands touching her everywhere and the feel of his muscled body beneath her made Felicia's body hum with desire. Her pulse raced with an urgency of fulfillment. And when she thought she couldn't possibly give or take any more, she heard Trask growl out his release at the same moment her body shuddered into hers.

Afterward, when she lay over him, too exhausted to move, to think, or to breathe, she felt the fullness of him inside her getting hard again. She snapped her head up off his chest and looked into his eyes, once again amazed. She was caught by the intensity of his gaze. The man had the stamina of a stallion and the sex drive of a bull. Passionate heat seemed to be a part of him and his desire for her was absolute. They would have a long and wonderful life together if they didn't kill themselves from overindulging in lovemaking first. The thought of being stretched out over his muscled body while he was planted deep within her renewed a want and need within her.

"Ride again," he suggested sensuously in a hoarse whisper before lifting his hand to her nape to bring her mouth closer to his for another long and deep kiss.

And she did just that.

Chapter Twelve

"You have two more days before New Year's. None of us will think unkindly of you, Trask, if you want to call the whole thing off."

Trask couldn't help but grin at the serious expressions of the six men who had invited him to lunch. "Call off the wedding, you mean?"

"Yes," Milton Madaris answered. Being the oldest of the brothers, he had appointed himself their spokesman.

Trask shook his head. "You're suggesting that I skip out two days before the wedding? May I remind you that the woman I'm marrying happens to be your niece."

"And that's why we're letting you know that we won't think unkindly of you if you call it off. We love the girl dearly, but all of us recognize that Felicia is kind of headstrong, willful, and outspoken. With her past two marriages, she's proven that she may be too much for most men to handle."

Trask couldn't help laughing. Felicia being too much to handle was an understatement. He couldn't help but remember how, a couple of nights ago, she had given him the ride of his life. A very enjoyable ride at that. "I'll take my chances."

"But we're here to let you know that you don't have to. We know that the reason you asked Felicia to marry you was because of the chance she might lose Austin. But now since the Gardners have suddenly decided to drop their custody suit, you won't have to marry her."

Trask took a sip of his drink and looked at all six men. The only one who seemed slightly bored with the entire proceeding was the youngest of the brothers, Jake Madaris. Like him, Jake seemed slightly amused.

"The reason I asked Felicia to marry me is because I'm in love with her. I would have gotten around to asking her anyway. That petition really had nothing to do with it."

"Let me get this straight, son," Jonathan Madaris was saying. "You mean to tell us that you and Felicia actually love each other?" he asked in amazement. "But what about all those years the two of you spent fussing and fighting?"

Trask shrugged. "I wish I could explain it but I can't. I think it was meant for us to go through all of that and get it out of our systems. Now we can have a marriage of peace and harmony."

All six uncles looked very doubtful about that.

"Are you sure marrying Felicia is what you want?" Lee Madaris asked for clarification.

"I'm positive. Now do I have your blessings?"

Nolan Madaris snorted. "Yeah, you have our blessings. But more than that, you also have our prayers. And believe us, son, with Felicia, you're going to need them."

Syneda sat back against the sofa smiling. "I think what Trask wants to do is a wonderful idea and I'll be glad to handle that for him."

Felicia nodded. "It means so much to me that he wants to legally adopt Austin. Steven was never a father to him and the Gardners were never grandparents. Trask wants to be what Steven never was, and knowing Trask's family, his mom and

Alex will be eager to give Austin all the love the Gardners never gave to him. Trask, Austin, and I will be a family. A real family."

She sighed. "I just hope the Gardners don't try causing any more trouble."

Syneda smiled. "I doubt that they will. Mrs. Gardner did the right thing in convincing her husband to drop that custody suit. Things for them would have gotten ugly. I assume Trask mentioned the report Alex gave to him on Andrew Gardner."

"Yes." Felicia shuddered at the information that had been contained in the report. She never knew just how ruthless her father-in-law was until she had read the report. He had been involved in a number of underhanded business deals, even some payoffs to a well-known politician from California. And the thought that he'd had the nerve to question her morals made her furious.

"Trask wouldn't hesitate to use the information Alex uncovered if the Gardners start causing problems again," Syneda pointed out.

"Yes, I know. Wealth isn't everything," Felicia said. "I had to find that out the hard way. I just hope one day the Gardners realize that, too."

Syneda's smile widened. "So how are the wedding plans coming along?"

"Fine. It won't be anything extravagant, just a private ceremony with family."

"And Austin still doesn't know?"

A slow smile crossed Felicia's face. "No. But I'm going to talk to Trask tonight. We may have to go ahead and tell him. As it gets closer to New Year's Day, he's trying to prepare himself for Trask's departure. I think we should go ahead and take him out of his misery."

Syneda chuckled. "I agree. Will you and Trask be going to Trevor and Corinthians' New Year Eve's party tomorrow night?"

"Yes, but we're leaving before the strike of twelve. We

want to be together somewhere private so we can bring the new year in right. Then on New Year's morning, everyone is to meet at Mom's for the wedding at noon."

"Any honeymoon plans?"

"We're spending the night at this quaint little bed-and-breakfast on the Gulf that Trevor's sister Gina told me about. Then we're coming back to take Austin to Disney World for a few days. And later, after our trip to the Super Bowl, Trask and I will make plans for a much longer honeymoon. We're thinking about going to Hawaii."

Syneda could see all the love shining on Felicia's face and in her eyes. "I'm glad everything worked out for the three of you."

Felicia laughed. "I'm glad, too."

Trask and Felicia decided to tell Austin about their wedding plans when they put him to bed that night. They knew they had made the right decision after listening to him modify his prayers to say:

"Thank you, God, for letting Santa bring me a daddy to love me. It was my best holidays ever, and I'm going to remember it as long as I live. And when my daddy leaves me after New Year's Day, I'm going to be a big boy and try not to cry. Just don't let him forget me because I'll never forget him. And I will never stop loving him as my daddy. Amen."

After Austin had finished, the impact of his words seemed to hang in the room for a second. Felicia's gaze met Trask's and she saw him swallow tightly. He then reached down, and with big strong hands, he pulled Austin up from off his knees and into his arms. He held him tight as he gently rubbed Austin's mop of curly hair.

For the longest time Trask didn't say anything. He tried to swallow the lump that had lodged in his throat, but couldn't. All he could do was hold the child he considered his own and give thanks for the miracle that brought him into his life. He cocked his head to one side and looked at Felicia. Tears misted her eyes and he understood. It was time to tell their son that they would be a family and that he was not going to go away on New Year's Day. It was time to let Austin know that he would be his forever daddy.

Taking a deep breath he set Austin down on the bed between him and Felicia. He looked down into the child's face, which looked so much like the woman he loved. "Austin, how would you like to be my son forever?"

Austin's gaze flew from Trask to his mother, then back to Trask. "That means you won't leave me on New Year's Day?" he asked in a hopeful voice.

"Yes, that means I won't leave you on New Year's Day. Your mom and I are getting married New Year's Day. The three of us will live here for a while; then we'll build a bigger house with a bigger yard sometime later. It also means you'll get a new name. How does Austin Gardner Maxwell sound?"

Austin smiled. "Good! Will Mommy get a new name, too?"

Trask chuckled. "Most definitely."

Austin nodded happily. "She's had other names before."

Trask looked at Felicia and his smile widened. Instinctively his hand reached over for hers. "Yes, I know, but Maxwell will be the last name she'll ever have."

Austin nodded with a wide grin on his face. "And you'll be my forever daddy?"

"Only if you want me to."

Austin threw his arms around Trask and exclaimed excitedly, "I do! I do! I love you, Daddy."

Once again Trask held his son tight in his arms. "And I love you, son." He squeezed Felicia's hand. "And I love your mom, too." Leaning over with Austin still in his arms, he kissed his future wife. "We're going to be a family."

"Yes," Felicia agreed, feeling Trask's warm lips brush against hers. "We'll be a family."

Epilogue

New Year's Day

Felicia decided not to have any bridesmaids. Instead, she thought it would be more fitting in her situation to have bridesmen. And she couldn't think of anybody more perfect than her uncles. Since Uncle Milton, being her oldest uncle, was the one to give her away, her other five uncles stood as bridesmen.

Clayton, Alex, and Austin stood beside Trask as his best men. In a way, her uncles stood in as Trask's best men as well. Just as Trask had always said, the six Madaris brothers had always been there for him, and today was no exception.

"I now pronounce you man and wife. You may kiss your bride," the minister said, smiling.

"At least the child had the good sense to save the best for last. And Trask is the best. He has to be to want to take her on." Felicia felt her cheeks heat in embarrassment with her grandmother's outburst.

Trask tossed back his head and laughed. "No, I'm the one

who got the best. A wife and a son—what more can a man ask for?"

"Peace," Lee Madaris hollered out.

"Everlasting love," Trask's mother, Jolene Maxwell Thomas, piped in.

Trask caught Felicia up in his arms and swung her around. "What Felicia and I have is truly everlasting."

"What about peace?" Lee Madaris hollered out once again.

Trask's lips found Felicia's and he kissed her long and hard.

"By golly you got your answer, Lee. I think they have found peace at last," Nolan Madaris exclaimed, laughing.

Trask and Felicia were too busy kissing to stop and agree with him.

ABOUT THE AUTHORS

Virginian Felicia Mason is an award-winning novelist and has worked as a newspaper reporter, columnist, copy editor, editorial writer, and as a college journalism professor. She is active in several writers' groups and is a member of Romance Writers of America.

Margie Walker can barely remember a time when she wasn't writing. She married her college sweetheart in their final semester at Texas Southern University, where she graduated Magna Cum Laude. She holds a Secondary Teacher's Certificate and a Master's Degree in Speech Communication. While raising her sons, she worked in radio and as a journalist. In addition to writing, she is an Adjunct Professor of Communication at her alma mater. Walker lives in Houston with the three loves of her life, and a ferret.

Brenda Jackson lives in the city where she was born, Jacksonville, FL. She is a graduate of William M. Raines High School, and she has a Bachelor of Science degree in Business Administration from Jacksonville University. She has been married for twenty-seven years to her high school sweetheart, and they have two sons, aged twenty-two and nineteen. Presently, she works for a major insurance company. She is also a member of the First Coast Chapter of Romance Writers of America, and she is a founding member of the national chapter of Women Writers of Color. Her other books for Arabesque include *Tonight and Forever, Whispered Promises, Eternally Yours, One Special Moment, Fire and Desire,* and "Cupid's Bow," which is part of the *Valentine Kiss* anthology. Her next book, *Secret Love,* will be released in February 2000.

More Sizzling Romance From
Brenda Jackson

__**One Special Moment** 0-7860-0546-7   **$4.99**US/**$6.50**CAN
To help her brother's company, Virginia Wingate must convince superstar Sterling Hamilton to endorse their products. Instantly smitten with the beauty, Sterling now must prove his intentions are for real and that he will cherish and love her . . . forever.

__**Tonight and Forever** 0-7860-0172-0   **$4.99**US/**$6.50**CAN
Returning to her roots in Texas, Lorren Jacobs never expected to meet handsome widower Justin Madaris . . . or to succumb to her passion. But they both must fight through painful memories to fulfill all the promises of tomorrow . . .

__**Whispered Promises** 1-58314-097-2   **$5.99**US/**$7.99**CAN
When Dex Madaris is reunited with his ex-wife Caitlin, he not only discovers a daughter he never knew he had but also learns that no heartache, no betrayal, is so strong as to withstand the enduring power of true love.

__**Eternally Yours**   0-7860-0455-X   **$4.99**US/**$6.50**CAN
Syneda Walters and Clayton Madaris are just friends—the last two people likely to end up as lovers—but things heat up when Syneda accepts Clayton's invitation to join him for a vacation. He must get her to trust him by convincing her that she will be eternally his.

Call toll free **1-888-345-BOOK** to order by phone or use this coupon to order by mail.
Name _____
Address _____
City _____ State _____ Zip _____
Please send me the books I have checked above.
I am enclosing $_____
Plus postage and handling* $_____
Sales tax (in NY, TN, and DC) $_____
Total amount enclosed $_____
*Add $2.50 for the first book and $.50 for each additional book.
Send check or money order (no cash or CODs) to: **Arabesque Books, Dept. C.O., 850 Third Avenue, 16th Floor, New York, NY 10022**
Prices and numbers subject to change without notice.
All orders subject to availability.
Visit our website at **www.arabesquebooks.com**